THE · SEDUCTIONS
O·F
NATALIE · BACH

THE · SEDUCTIONS
O·F
NATALIE · BACH

A NOVEL BY

William Luvaas

LITTLE, BROWN AND COMPANY   BOSTON ⋄ TORONTO

FIRST EDITION

LIBRARY OF CONGRESS CATALOGING-IN-PUBLICATION DATA

Luvaas, William, 1945–
    The seductions of Natalie Bach.

    I. Title.
    PS3562.U86S4   1986   813'.54   86-91
    ISBN 0-316-53768-3
    ISBN 0-316-53769-1 (pbk.)

A different version of an excerpt from this book,
entitled "Ash Wednesday," was first published in
the Spring/Summer 1983 issue of Touchstone.

BP

Designed by Jeanne Abboud

Published simultaneously in Canada
by Little, Brown & Company (Canada) Limited

PRINTED IN THE UNITED STATES OF AMERICA

FOR CINDY

*All persons, places, and events
included herein are purely a
product of the author's
imagination. But what the author's
imagination may be a product
of is anybody's guess.*

PART ONE

1963

CHAPTER ONE

ME

ALL RIGHT, NOW AS FAR BACK AS I CAN REMEMBER —
I will always remember Mattie: shiny black cheeks that I glazed with ten thousand slobbery kisses, which she tolerated. Mattie tolerated everything. Except that time I called her a black rat. I had no idea what it meant. She locked herself in the bathroom and her sobs seemed to shake the entire building, while I leaned against the door crying with her — not sure what I had done, but knowing it was awful. Some voodoo thing that Mattie sometimes told stories about. Certain Mother would kill me for it when she got home from work; pounding on the door, *Mattie dear, please open*, cutting me with the ice blue sabers of her eyes as I cowered at her feet. Finally, Mattie did open (or maybe it was David with his clothes hanger trick), eyes boiling blood at corners,

finding a rawness in my heart. Mother coaxed it from her — she could
always manage that. "Children don't mean nothin' by it, Mizz Bach,"
Mattie said, daubing at her eyes with a Kleenex wad, as I tugged her
starched white skirt. But Mother dragged me away, Mattie protesting,
"Don't do her hard, Mizz Bach. She know she done wrong."

But Mother did. Welts that boiled over my legs and behind a peace
offering from white employer to black employee. Later we, all three,
held one another and cried. I looped a wreath of paper dolls and baseball cards around Mattie's neck and kissed all the shiny promontories of
that great round face, so love returned to her eyes. That night Mattie
didn't cook but came as guest of honor to Charles Restaurant, where
she ordered fried chicken and got chicken Kiev, over which she ex-
claimed (a bit wobbly on three vodka tonics), "If I served something
skimpy as that, I'd get leave to walk home directly," laughing her big
throaty laugh and all of us with her. Except Adam, too preoccupied
with jazz bands and pregnant girlfriends to laugh with his family;
though sometimes he smiled.

And I remember Mr. Cherry who came Friday nights and sat on a lip
of the couch, working his hat slowly around the hub of a knee, discussing politics with Dad, while Mattie took her time showering and dressing: for, as she said, "You don't never want a man to think you in too
much of a hurry to see him."

Like Dad, Mr. Cherry wore a Groucho Marx moustache, the beginnings of a deferential, almost pained smile in permanent residence
about his eyes. Each greeted the other's comments with a tentative little
chuckle — not obsequious, only a bit embarrassed at the whole huge
awkwardness of humankind. So before I knew that difference in skin
color signifies anything, I knew already that people come out of the
same molds. Dad would pour a stout glass of Johnny Walker Red for
each of them, which they nursed with a relish that raised them high
above the woes and petty enmities of the city, and I know they both
enjoyed these Friday evenings before each went off to his separate Friday night.

I was four when we moved to the big house in New Jersey — Garden
State, living proof the American dream is truly a nightmare. My first
day in school all the kids encircled me, taunting, "Christ killer, Christ
killer!" "Un-uh," I cried, "all I ever kill is bugs." Tommy O'Brien,
paunchy middle-aged eight-year-old, shoved me. "Think that's funny,
do ya? I'll show ya what's funny." He knocked me down and gave me a

shiner. Back home, Mattie fussed, Mother paced like an angry panther, mumbling that nothing had changed since her Brooklyn childhood, except good Catholic boys were slower about slugging girls — even Jews! — in those days, giving her time to work behind and get hold of their ears while they worked over her brother. "If they ask again, Nattie honey, you tell them, *I'm a human being.*" So next day I boasted, "I'm a human being," proud as Mommy. They threw hands to mouths and tittered. Tommy O'Brien bullied me around the playground. "Youse is dirty jew-bastards, that's what youse is." My tears only whetted his appetite. But everyone has a weak spot. Tommy O'Brien's scalp looked like Vermont after a blizzard. He was soon avoiding me. He could hit and hit, it didn't shut my mouth.

My friends were all "ethnics," meaning, in homogeneous Huntington Park: Swiss Heidi, Italian Maria, and spastic Eleanor. The melting pot four. Me not welcome in Maria's house on suspicion of kikeishness, Eleanor not in mine on suspicion of lice. Only my friendship with Heidi had the full benediction of parents. But Heidi moved away in third grade.

Summers were long and lonely — too far away from friends to walk, and Mother, away at work, couldn't drive me. David and Adam rode their bikes, but I was always too young. I couldn't catch up to them. I lay back on Agnes Wolfhound's soft tummy under a grandfather maple, stripping leaves of grass and spotting dreams in clouds on the horizon. The lawn stretched like a green heaven to the road, and sometimes I galloped after Adam in my Roy Rogers outfit as he mowed the grass, shooting down Indians that pursued us just beyond a cloud of clippings. David called me "tomboy," though I very properly assured him I couldn't be a boy if I was a girl. But I'm getting ahead. . . .

I couldn't have been more than five when I was awakened night after night by Mom/Dad's voices spatting like cats through the big house. Mother's rising sharply, then falling off into long silences, when — if I listened hard, sitting up in bed — I could hear her crying and became very frightened. I could make out very few words: Dad pleading, *I need you, Zoe. The business needs you* — Then Mother, *She needs me, too. She's just a baby.* Finally, he won. And I never forgave him for taking her away from me. Those first weeks I searched the house for her. Mattie said, "Your mama gone to the office, honey. You saw her leave this morning yourself." I didn't believe her. I searched everywhere, calling into the cellar, "Mommy are you hiding?" At last, lay defeated on her big bed. The books shelved up one wall began to snicker at me; they laughed out loud. I screamed and Mattie came to hold me and coo a gospel hymn. They put me in a nursery school, but I huddled shivering in a corner, or tore up other kids' projects — knowing they hadn't been sent there to get rid of them.

Though Mother gave me weekends, nothing was the same. Often she wasn't home until after I was asleep. She had flown the cocoon and become ZILLA BACH, bright-winged fashion butterfly, teasing the world with her dress designs — and the family with her affections. I remember a home movie *Bachanalia!* Mother dancing about in see-through negligée like Little Egypt, ringed by us kids, tumbling over each other for her attention. David clowning, woo-wooing his eyes up her skirt; Adam covering his face, giggling through finger cracks; and Me dancing with her, hands-a-hip, kicking up my legs in a frisky tarantella, one of Daddy's sober homburgs sunk down over my fish-bulge eyes; while Mother, clenching a white rose in her teeth, grinned back over a shoulder at the camera — and Dad, cameraman, nonpresence. When I had grabbed his hand to dance, he recoiled, almost in horror. For it was about then that what little affection my father had shown me ceased altogether. He was careful to lock the bathroom door, quick to cross his pale legs — covering knees with robe like a prissy girl when I came down for breakfast — scared to death of his little daughter with the Buster Brown haircut.

It was about then, too, I began to notice my low status in the family. My brothers always the ones bragged about to guests: Adam on his piano and David on his bicycle. I was just the baby girl, cute but not taken seriously. When I had something to say at dinner, a pained look crossed their faces and someone would say, "Not now, Nattie, David is talking — " David was always talking.

Dad drove Mattie to the station Saturday morning to catch the train to Harlem and picked her up again Sunday night. Since I couldn't imagine Mattie in the bombed-out squalor I had seen along el lines — where, according to David, giant rats and shriveled humans fought for possession of one another's babies — I imagined she went off to heaven for the weekend, in her gleaming white nurse's dress. She sang in the celestial choir and, when the spirit come to her, might catch a glimpse of God himself — that radiant, towering old gentleman in a scrollwork Mosaic beard. Crawling into her broad lap Sunday night, I asked,

"How was heaven?" She laughed and said, "Glory, Mizz Bach, this girl tickle me. I know you raising her a Jew. Yet and still, sometimes I think she be half Baptist."

Mattie wasn't happy in New Jersey. Mr. Cherry no longer came Friday nights — reluctant to ride the train in the fluorescent glare of suburban faces. Besides, David and I squabbled nonstop; so that by late afternoon Mattie collapsed in a chair, sausage arms drooped at her sides, mumbling, "Your mama too busy to be worried about nasty children when she come home." Vaguest undertone of reproof in her voice, as if she really meant: nothing rightly should come before her children.

It was some time before Mr. Booker T. Jones, giant scowling sledgehammer man, whose eyes always seemed choked with concrete dust, followed her home one day from the market. When Dad offered Mr. Jones a Scotch, he muttered in his dark growl, "I rather wait outside." Mattie entertained Mr. Jones in her sitting room off the kitchen, where they sat watching TV and he made funny gestures that set her laughing — as he raised a thumb to back-tilted lips and nodded towards the back door. Asking, wasn't it my bedtime yet? Hadn't I anything better to do than trouble Aunt Mattie when her cousin come to visit? Couldn't I go mess up my mama's makeup or somethin'? Mattie scolded, "Don't pay him no mind, honey. He just showing off, making a big fool of hisself." "Go on now, girl," he would persist, "don't be meddling in grown-folks' bizness," a fluted high note creeping into his hoarse growl. I would flare nostrils, tilt back my head like a princess, knowing full well I could do whatever I pleased until 9:30 on Friday night. And Mattie laugh: "That girl, I b'lieve one day she delight me to death."

At last Mommy came to get me, her eyes making no compunctions about Mr. Jones, who stared fixedly at television. I'd slobber kisses over Mattie, then position myself hands-a-hip before Mr. Book, squinching my lips into a frog face. That fierce dark giant of a man throwing this tiny girl a swift sidelong glance, closest he could find to a smile.

Mommy took me upstairs and tucked me into bed. She kissed me and I locked fingers around her neck. "Don't go to the office tomorrow, Mommy," I begged. She assured me that tomorrow was Saturday, rubbing a hand back through my hair until my eyes closed and I began to float, wafted on the honeyed potions with which she touched the parts of her body. She telling the story of a little boy and girl on Coney Island: the pink-sticky smell of cotton candy and the grownup smell of fried clams, singing roller-coasters and parachute jumps from which children drifted away on Technicolor balloons . . . and me on the gentle breathings of sleep, kissed with a smile. Afterwards, she stood in the hall and cried softly for the small girl with a commuter mother.

Often I shot straight up with terror in the night lamps of my eyes when she switched off the lamp. "Mommy . . . where are you going, Mommy?"

"I'll be just downstairs, honey."

"Don't leave on the turnpike, Mommy."

"No, honey."

"Mommy . . . did you kiss me?"

"Yes, honey. A million hugs and kisses."

"Did you look under the bed, Mommy?"

"I looked," she said softly, her silhouette already a dream in the doorway. "Good dybbuk Devora is sleeping on the rug." (I glanced down, though knew she was invisible.) "Now make your magic thumbs, Nattie sweet, and go to sleep." That was the cue for our bedtime ritual, an incantation chanted in unison:

> *Don't turn out the hall light*
> *Don't close the bedroom door*
> *And don't forget to tuck me in.*

"Night night, Nattie honey — "

"Night night, Mommy — "

Then, all alone, the night growled at me. Dustmice scampered under the bed and walls grew slimy. I whimpered, though knew Mommy too far away now to care. Menacing hulk of night in which nothing is taboo — any anxiety can slip from its corner into a skin. Mommy gone and Mattie's hands full with Mr. Jones. Though he a little comfort, for what evil would dare try and get me with that huge fierce man in my house? Such a contrast to Daddy. Although I knew deep down that Mommy alone could protect me.

At last dreams. A family living happily on a palm tree island, where no one went to work and we ate fruit that fell from trees, whose juice cured Daddy's emphysema and made him strong so he could dive down with my brothers into the deep blue sea and bring up fish in his teeth, and Adam wore his handsome football uniform every day.

More often nightmares. Real doozies. I would wake up with Mother stroking me, my screams still echoing from walls. Once, all of them crowding the room: Mattie and Mr. Jones — eyes flashing, looking as if he would indeed tear to pieces whatever had set this child shrieking — Daddy huffing from the stairs, David rubbing sleep from his eyes. That's when, lying on Mattie's lap, my head on Mommy's knee, I announced that I was a very lucky little girl to have two mommies. Then, when Mother was still a mommy.

David was more than a brother. He was friend, playmate, protector, confidant, and as close as I really came to a father. He told me that walls whisper naughty words while we sleep; and, after we saw *The Legend of Sleepy Hollow* on television, he chased me around the house, hoof-clicking his pink tongue, blowing out spit bubbles — a torment I both hated and loved. David said that a Headless Hallman lived in the upstairs linen closet down the hall from my bedroom and that it might come out any night, so I better listen hard and be ready to duck quick if it threw its head, his eyes growing so big as he told me that I believed him implicitly. That night I pulled the covers up just enough to cover my earlobes (every child knows that tender earlobes are a favorite tidbit of monsters), leaving a crack to peek out. I lay perfectly still, listening to the whisper-slither night. Suddenly, to my sweetest horror, I heard a liquidy clicking of hooves: clippity clop, clippity clop . . . closer and closer. For a moment I lay frozen, stupefied. Then screamed, "Please, Mr. Hallman, don't knock me with your head!" and submarined down under covers between the smell of my toes, crying for Mommy.

Though it wasn't for fear of the Headless Hallman that I insisted she come in the night to tuck me in tight but the still more terrifying Bellybutton Monster, that coiled out its long sticky frog's tongue from beneath beds in search of lint and other morsels in its victims' navels. Somehow I was convinced the tongue couldn't penetrate the percale barrier of sheets.

Describing its tongue, David entered a poetic trance of bumps curves slithers . . . childish pornography of explorations under nighties in whispers over breakfast cereal, until my eyes had become saucers and Mattie appeared, a dust of flour across her nose, scolding, "What you be worrying your little sister about now? You always up to some mischief." David evaded fingers clutching for his ears by slipping under the table — his fat grin compounded of fear of God and sympathy for the devil.

But David's descriptions! I was not frightened so much as fearfully excited in an amorphous, forbidden way that set little creatures tickling my insides. It was like the "bigger-bigger" game Mother sometimes played, drawing in pencil a line spiraling bigger . . . bigger . . . bigger, while I watched, barely able to contain my excitement. One night I learned more about all of this.

When I couldn't sleep — walls whispering too loudly and Mommy/Daddy out for the evening — I'd wander the upstairs. Adam wouldn't be home, so by hall light I could freely explore jazz records and bottles of liniment in his neat room. Open Mommy's door — didn't dare go in. I felt secure in the dim hall, for I'd convinced myself that the Headless Hallman could only get me in *my room*. Sometimes I'd stand in David's doorway and visit while he lay tossing and muttering in the bottom bunk. It wasn't necessary that he talk back. But this night I heard a moan as I passed. Hall light cut a swath through darkness to the bed, mixing there with shadows. David bucked and groaned. I could make out rapid movement, like he was fighting something. The Bellybutton Monster! A chill went through me. I crouched and sneaked closer, hiding behind the desk. I could see his covers were thrown back and somehow the monster had gotten his pajama bottoms down. Davie appeared to be in tremendous pain. My heart made hoofbeats in my ears. But this was *my brother*; I had to save him. I made my magic thumbs and crept forward till I was right behind the chair. David sighed, his fist whacked up and down like a piston. But where's its tongue? I wondered. Maybe it's invisible like Devora. Though I could see it was planted in his bellybutton and he was trying to pull it out. I stood stock still, feeling awful that Davie might die. But even if I could hit it with a book, I couldn't see it! Suddenly he gasped "Oh . . . OOOoooohhhh . . ." and his hand fell limply to his side.

Davie was dead. The heavy rattling of his breath had died away. He lay so still.

Then I saw it! The point of its tongue drooping over just below his belly, wet and glistening. Loyalty overcame fear. I stepped closer. "Davie — ?" I cried in a tiny voice as I latched hold of the tongue to yank it from his belly, noticing only at the last moment his features fixed in a million dollar grin.

David shot up with a hallelujah scream. I had a vise grip on his slimy dingus. He chased me down the hall — straight into babysitter Esther's arms as she came up the stairs, muttering over the top of a thick novel she was reading, "All right, you guys, what's going — GAWD DAVIE! Looka' you!" Her eyes round moons behind Coke bottle glasses as she stared down at David's thing and began shrieking, "Get in there, get y'r pajamas on — Davie!" I burrowed between her huge boobalas and David must've pinched one, 'cause she screamed, "I'm gonna brain ya —" And his feet scurried away, quick.

Next morning, between mouthfuls of Sunday bagelsloxgefiltefishmarmaladeonionherringstrawberriesandcream, David wagged a fist in my face, vowing revenge. I came home from piano lessons one afternoon to find my room blitzed: toys smashed, cottony insides of stuffed animals everywhere. David got spanked, then me for a tattletale, which seemed unfair — more evidence that I was a second class citizen in our family. When Dad came up the stairs like a chuckling Santa with a new batch of cuddly bears and Little Miss Makeups (and his shy smile), I curtly refused them all. His eyes hurtled panicky about the room — for this had become the one sure zone of his affection, these gifts on sickdays and birthdays — then he turned and walked back downstairs with his armload.

When I blitzed David's room he simply ignored me. Silent at breakfast and as we walked the half mile to the bus stop. After a week of this I said: "I'm not mad that you wrecked my dumb toys. Everyone thinks I'm still the baby in the family, but I'm not anymore." But David's stubborn frown seemed to promise that we would remain enemies forever and I would always be the baby.

So there I sat in the listless lap of summer, watching winged grasshoppers make helicopter dashes across the lawn and squirrels scold from treetops in a nervy chattering. Out back, the lawn sloped past Daddy's carriage house studio into an African veld of tall grasses, dense sumac and willow jungles, a line of pompous birches, finally the river. Africa didn't frighten me. Lions fully respected little girls in too big cowboy chaps who trailblazed through the scrub. One day when I was no taller than the burdocks, I secretly followed Adam and his girlfriend to the tall line of paper birches, where they lay down in a grassy clearing and began to neck and wrestle. I pulled my six-shooter to keep them covered and crawled closer, whispering a running narrative for my gang (who were invisible): how Adam kept unbuttoning her shirt and she buttoned it up again, like a silly game, which he finally won. Then they started all over with her bra. I told my buddies how silly it was when he talked baby talk to her breasts and she giggled like crazy. People never did grow up — even when they got bigger.

The riveriest thing about the river was its smell. It was too sluggish and clotted with algae and duckweed to swim in, and David said it would strip flesh from your bones like lye. On humid days, the river smell rose in a soupy fog, making walking fish of us. I rowed about in my skiff, racing water spiders, making friends with mud turtles who watched sagely from snags. The water moved so slowly — if I fell asleep in my boat, I always woke up before reaching the bend. I would lie drifting, inventing stories for frogs and dragonflies that belched and rattled response; though I understood that I was really only talking to myself.

Then something happened downstream, like they pulled the plug on the river. It began moving faster; duckweed and frogs and lily pads went with it. I could no longer safely dream in my rowboat and Agnes found it impossible to snooze in shallows that had become dizzy swirling eddies. That signaled a change in everything. True, Mother had already gone to work years earlier, but that was when David entered junior high and was preoccupied with growing taller, when Adam stopped talking to Dad altogether, and Mattie's daughter tried to kill herself, and when my body began its first rebellions against childhood, and Mother stepped up her campaign to make a "little lady" of me. "You shouldn't spend so much time with your brother and his friends," she said. "You should have your own friends, little girls!"

"I hate girls."

"Don't be silly, Nattie. You are a girl."

I regarded her suspiciously.

We still ice-skated for miles over bolting glass of the winter river and now, in summer, neighborhood bikes filled our drive. But river fog was swallowed up like humidity in a thunder storm. And some of life's magic went with it.

David and his buddies locked me out of the rock 'n' roll clubhouse of his room (those records! a cow barn full of bleating calves and milkmaids beating tin buckets; I became a devotee of the classical music Dad played in his studio while he painted). They called me tag-along-lulu and no longer wanted me on their bike expeditions. Now when one of the boys shoved me David didn't tell him to lay off. I asked Mattie why he had suddenly changed.

"Seem like men get a meanness in them," she said, "and he about reaching that time. Seem like they always be inventing wars and fighting over any little bidness. That's one thing, honey, make you thank the good Lord whenever you want to regret you are a woman."

Now I regretted it. I wanted in baseball games, wanted to hit a homer every time. When I told Ridsley to eat it and he dared me to say it again, so I said, "Eat it, eat it, eat it! Ridsley!" and he shoved me down, I wanted to get up and sock his ugly puss, instead of squirming and crying while he held me down in the dirt. And when David told me to get lost, he hated tag-along-lulus, I wished, like Adam, I'd been able to grab my shoulder pads and go disdainfully off to football practice.

Screw David. I could make up stories and practice chords on the piano. I read a million books and begged Mommy to buy me a guitar — which Daddy did, trying his shy smile again. Things were happening fast, maturity coming on like a mugger. In camp that summer of eleven I met Jerry, my first love, who held my hand and pirated kisses at the campfire circle; and I had never known anything could be so scary-illicit-wonderful as when his fingers made explorations and he vowed to love me forever. But then Jerry went home.

Then one Friday, a warm, soulful September evening, Mr. Cherry appeared in a shiny blue Oldsmobile. "I got wheels!" he cried, exuberant as anyone had ever heard him.

Dad poured out two tumblers of Scotch and chuckled his ingratiating chuckle, and Mattie's gospel tremolo vibrated the entire house through a twenty minute shower, and dapper long-boned Mr. Cherry never had to confront ferocious Book Jones, because somehow Mattie had conjured him away.

Though I always felt a little sorry for Mr. Jones, 'cause I know how it feels to get dumped.

CHAPTER TWO

MAXINE

I WALKED STRAIGHT TO A CHAIR IN FRONT, PAST THE TIDE OF AMUSED eyes. Class had started and Miss Pearlman regarded me with a little smile that had to work from a frown, chalk poised before a spaghetti tangle of lines on the board. "Natalie Bach," I muttered, finding a seat and glancing cautiously around. It was my first time in class since school had started. Miss Pearlman hunched eyebrows and spoke through a splendor of white teeth.

"Pink sunglasses with one missing lens! A touch we definitely need in this drab class."

My classmates barely suppressed giggles. I sat blinking at her, not sure she was someone I wanted to tangle with: not tall or big really, but compact, with roundnesses suggesting muscle and solid tan posts jutting from gym trunks. Zaftig. A hand cocked casually on one hip, a little like a gunfighter.

"Would you be so good as to remove the glasses, Natalie? I doubt the radiance of this class will be too blinding."

"I can't."

"You can't remove those obnoxious glasses?"

"No — " had to bite my lip to keep from tittering along with the others " — I have pinkeye. See, it passed right down the line of Bachs from my great-great-great-great-great-uncle Johann."

"The composer, I bet."

"He really lived in utter filth." (Everybody laughing openly now; life has been dull these past weeks without smartass Natalie.)

"All right, Natalie, we've seen the act. Now would you remove the glasses? Please?" Little tuck of a smile.

I folded them primly. "You will be fully responsible for any chromosome damage."

"Fully." She wasn't a gloating winner. Much later she would say: "In strong attractions impulses get tangled. You're not sure whether you want to hug or fight."

We played field hockey in a grassy swale just off Central Park West. Rather, I sat on the slope watching them play. A bunch of jerks chasing screaming after the ball like it was a matter of life and death. Miss Pearlman limped uphill and sprawled beside me, panting. She stretched the damp T-shirt from her stomach and let it snap back in exaggerated disgust. One of those sticky October days stolen from August. "Gawd, it's vicious out there. You ought to try it, Natalie. You're a scrapper." She smiled, trying to make friends, I knew, but pretended not to care. Her legs stretched out, so dark beside my pasty white I wanted to tuck mine underneath. She seemed to notice my discomfort — and workshirt tails slopped over my gym trunks, fingering the frayed hem. "Very nice. So dresses the daughter of one of America's foremost fashion designers." I shrugged. She gestured at my jerky classmates, shrieking after the ball like a troop of howler monkeys: one would smack it, the rest all tangle up, roll over the ground, laughing like crazy. "Why don't you play?" she asked.

I was engaged in a pastime I pursued as a kid in the suburbs: zipping off grass strips that parted crisply along veins. Except here it was mostly cig butts and dog doo. "I'm not in the mood," I said, extracting a cigarette from my breast pocket.

"What is this? Smoking in gym class?"

"We're in Central Park," I said.

"We have to test each other, don't we, Natalie? I've got to say, 'Step in line, soldier,' and you've got to say, 'Screw off, Pearlman; I've been here longer than you have.' "

I shrugged. She sat up, tucking one leg beneath her, the other forming a vertical post, polished at the knob — not exactly shaven, but not hairy either, just enough to signify independence from social form. She rested chin on knee, folded in a supple repose from which, at any moment, she might wing off like some tropical insect. Secretly, I studied her.

"Sooo, it's none of my business, but where have you been these past weeks while I mark zeros in the attendance book?"

"Sick," I mumbled.

"Doctor sick?"

"Sick sick."

"Ahhh —" her eyes made a dice roll around sockets and came to a dizzy stop "— that kind! Now I ask for a note, right? But we both know: I ask and you don't produce, nothing happens. That's why we're here at Whitman."

"Right." I produced a note, rattling the paper with a triumphant flourish.

Miss Pearlman studied Mother's concise longhand. "You can almost see the cut of Zilla's spring line —" huddling her chin "— Straightforward. Efficient. Snappy." She smiled up at me. "But you know what's best for your hypertension?" I shook my head. She poked a thumb at the girls. "Hard sweat."

Conjuring my serious-sophisticated look, I released a plume of smoke that hung on the thick air. "Sports are okay."

"Just not today?"

"Hockey is ridiculous." I frowned out at classmates, who laughed too ardently. You knew it was sex, not hockey (so did two black dudes captaining a hill in broad-brimmed gaucho hats, laughing and trading skin with palms of their hands). Everyone ready to take a tree, hockey stick, anything to cure virginity. But scared, too, the cure might be worse than the disease (except maybe Marty and Carol who'd already had it). Then the jerks would get serious, snapping orders and pursuing the ball like gladiators — who had to keep dodging dog shit. Miss P. watching with her small smile. "So *young and so untender*," she crooned.

"You aren't exactly Grandma Moses."

She laughed, waving a hand to disperse cigarette smoke, a gesture reminiscent of Mother. "I can't even quote Shakespeare."

"Do you write poetry?" I asked, my s-s look again.

"That's one thing you learn as you get older: every road can't be taken. Life is a process of elimination. Though the joy of being young is believing all roads can be. But I do write poetry, yes." Reaching back to loosen hair, which fell from a prim bun thick and dark over her shoulders.

Below, Lydia was screeching like a chicken (no one would ever guess she was seventeen) 'cause Marty had pinned Carol under her fat *derrière*. Carol shrieked like a rape victim, her face strawberry red, while Libby tickled her pits and Colleen — prima donna athlete — swaggered over in knee socks, swaying her shoulders like a boy, whining, "C'mon, you guys, let's play —" turning uphill and braying "— Maxiiine . . ." (*they* all called her Maxine). Miss P. shouted, "Hey, no dirties! Keep it clean out there." They climbed giggling out of the dog pile. "Jerks," I hissed, turning away in disgust.

Miss P. was on her feet in a flash, got a grip on my foot and started dragging me — "I'll play if you play!" — on my ass down the slope. Then mountain Marty had my other foot. Everyone screaming, me twisting, yelling, "I hate hockey!" shirt up over my head, scared shit any second it would peel off completely. On opposite sides, fighting like pit bulls over the ball. All of them just a backdrop for our duel. Chasing each other, panting over the field — *Nat's got it* . . . *Watch Maxine!* . . . *Nat's got the ball* . . . *Stop her, stop Maxine!* — chickens scattering when I came flying at the goal, hair wild as hawk's wings, leaping away with little shrieks as I swung the stick bat-style, running smack into Allie, who sprawled spread-eagled, mouth popped wide in a wounded "Oh!" Gathered around laughing, cheering after I'd scored five goals and dropped in a respiratory heap — my team having de facto a new captain. Creep Colleen in ducktail hair and striped socks eyeing me with hate profound.

Walking back to school, Maxine said, "I thought you weren't athletic."

"Something popped."

"God," she snorted, "a one-woman hockey league. You're dirty, too." She rubbed her ass, which had interfered with one of my slap shots. I laughed, near bursting with my new image, poked her under the ribs. "Pee-yew," she whinnied. "You could use a shower, kiddo." Lifting a sweat-matted fringe from my forehead, she planted it back in its nest of hair and smiled. "After you start smelling like an athlete, the rest is all downhill."

Maxine was leaving French class, having switched the sweaty American look for a Continental tight skirt and soft plunging blouse. Sophomore boys rolled their eyes in the wake of her hip-shuttling walk, and Teddy Katz performed a peristaltic wiggle. As she passed the junior-senior clique, giving that small enigmatic smile and a condescending nod, the girls made soft nnnns and wee-wees like a herd of semiliterate French shoats. I caught up to her out front by the memorial bust. "Hi," I said. She turned, eyebrows raised.

"Oh, Natalie! My star hockey player."

"I wanted to apologize for missing so much class."

"I'm really not precious about gym class. Which way you walking?" I said downtown, guessing she was going that way. "We'll walk together then," she said, reaching to take a couple of my books. But then stood lost in thought, staring at "Old Walt," Whitman's sandstone head on its pedestal — school mascot, sufferer of scale and pollution, eyes blackened, a corner of his jaunty hat broken off, beard grizzled with pigeon droppings. Really looking the part of the poet.

"It had nothing to do with you," I said.

She looked up. "What didn't?"

"Skipping class."

"Want to tell me what it had to do with?" Her eyes moved back to "Old Walt."

I shrugged. "It's a long miserable story."

Maxine smiled. "Growing up is a series of long miserable stories. I'm not sure how we survive it."

We cut through the park, dodging preppies whose ties dangled loose at open collars. On Fifth Avenue ancient dowagers, escorted by still more ancient maids, stopped to discuss each curb, mumbling precautions to one another. We entered the ragged army of commuters, mobbed at bus stops, pouring underground like wilted crickets, business suits limp on their backs. A bitter, defeated, disgruntled corps that made you wonder: if this is the top of the mountain, how bad is it in the lowlands of America?

While we walked, I spewed my life down the sidewalk in one gush, shouting over the pandemonium of evacuation, throwing out my arms, dislodging *New York Times*es stuck under businessmen's worsted armpits. All of it: ugly dinner scenes, Mother barging in on me smoking in bed, frowning beside me in the bathroom mirror, poking my bare butt (completely ignoring my flat belly) *I don't know how you can live with that, Natalie,* opening her robe to display, in bikini bra and briefs, her own trim body, turning side to side — I realized we were stopped midsidewalk, passersby dodging left and right in their panic to get past, Maxine's expression tense, troubled. "Sometimes I want to kill her," I hissed.

"How about coffee?" Maxine asked, as casually as if we were old friends.

We sat at a tiny café terrace table, viewing the parade from the happy vantage of escaped rush hour sidewalks. Women heel-clicking past, that hollow-cheeked sangfroid of Manhattan vets; the male of the species harried, sexless in chalk-blue suits, superfluous to the deeper life of the city. Except working men. Ethnics. Open-shirted, regarding passing women with horse trainers' instincts. Despite all its violence and aggression, New York is a feminine city. They know it and praise God in every wolf whistle celebrating a jiggling ass.

I sensed her studying me while I dismembered a book of matches, wanting to believe she shared the attraction I felt for her. "I went to see Mother's shrink a couple times," I said. "I just wanted to understand what was going on."

"You don't need to apologize, Natalie. I'm doing graduate work in psychology."

I fumbled for a cigarette. "I really do appreciate you listening to all this . . . stuff."

"Friends are for listening." Her voice quiet over the table.

She picked up one of my books, pursing her lips, an approving frown. "D'you like Thomas Mann?" I asked quickly. "I just read 'The Blood of the Walsungs,' about a brother and sister who sleep together."

"The *Catcher in the Rye* complex." Tilting an inquisitive eye at me. "What about that?"

"I have two brothers —" sending up a blue column of smoke "— I can't really think of them like that."

"What about sisters?"

"That would be pretty weird."

"I meant, do you have any?"

"Oh, I thought . . . No . . . no sisters, which is okay. I prefer men, really."

"So what's preferable about men, Natalie?"

In the plate glass window opposite, a thought line arrows across my brow. "Men aren't catty. They're more constant, you know. Dependable."

"I don't know. I don't even agree."

"I just mean . . . easier to talk to."

"So your friends are boys mostly?"

"No. Hey! What is this? The grand inquisition or something?"

"Only a minor one, called getting to know each other."

The waitress slapped menus before us as if we belonged to the clan of Capulets, a hemorrhoidal smirk. Maxine touched her arm. "We're on your side," she said. The woman stared — first at Maxine, then me, features coagulating towards a miserly mouth — then trudged off, muttering.

"You're amazing," I said.

"Because I come to the aid of wounded creatures? Listen, if you let opportunities pass you begin to slide and that happens." She nodded back at the woman. "It's entropy. The powers are all on evil's side."

The thought arrow again. "You sound like Tolstoy."

"No. Tolstoy couldn't accept entropy. Maybe Dostoevski. He had a healthy respect for the dark side of the soul. But we Jews understand it best."

I studied her a long time, while she mused upon the living river flooding past on the sidewalk. "Why do you teach gym?" I asked.

"I teach French, too. But why not? I teach gym because a job was open and I needed it. Or let's call it a predilection, like choosing whether or not to shave your armpits."

My chin pocking in the window. "I shave mine 'cause I can't stand the smell."

"I don't shave; I love the smell."

We laughed in that care-a-damn manner that elicits polite smiles. Next table, a gay couple exchanged a tolerant grimace.

"Besides —" Maxine leaned forward confidentially "— underarm hair is very very sexy. Listen, let's not talk about me. I want to get to know Natalie Bach. I'd like to know if — according to her formula that men make better listeners — she finds a more sympathetic ear in Papa than in Mama Bach?"

Not a question I really wanted to answer. "My father's busy," I mumbled, "business commitments, and his health is bad. He's got emphysema." She smiled gently. "Mine too."

Inside, the fat proprietor harangued his help in that vowel-harsh New York manner that makes a missile crisis of a missing mustard lid. The waitress ignored him, slamming cups on our table, but the black busboy appeared ready to break for the street.

"So tell me about the mysterious girl in pink sunglasses."

"All right," I conceded, "I'll discuss anything but Mother."

"You sound determined about Mother."

"I hate her guts."

I hunted quickly for a cigarette — forgetting the one already burning in the ashtray — flinching when Maxine touched my hand, snatching mine away. "Something I've learned," she said: "all the crap about women being catty, self-centered, unreliable, men have used for eons to divide the feminine house, keep us feuding amongst ourselves, vying for male attention. Look, I'm not blaming your father. It's bigger than that; men are victims as well as women. It's a cultural tyranny."

I studied the foam-encrusted rim of my cappuccino. "I don't know if I really hate her —"

"You can hate her, Natalie."

Wheeling on the neighboring table, I snapped, "Get your fat ear out of our conversation . . . creep!" The man who had been drifting towards us like a paper moon hunched an ironic eyebrow at his friend. Maxine grimaced. "You don't have to declare war on the species."

"They're not men anyway," I muttered. The two giggled gaily. Natalie Bach in the plate glass became obscured behind a dirty haze of smoke. "I've never really had a man stand in the way of anything I've wanted to do," I said.

Her brows knit. She studied me: a just-you-wait expression.

"Isn't it great that we can talk like this?" I cried. "When I first saw you around school, you know — so cocky and tan, like you spend your whole life under a sunlamp. Always wearing warmups like you just ran the Boston marathon —"

"Wait a minute!" She jumped up, modeling a madras print skirt and shiny cotton blouse.

"That's what I like about you: you're so up-front."

"I hope that's not a pun."

"I mean it's probably no big deal to you, talking to one of your students . . ."

"Don't underrate yourself, kiddo," she said, chin in hand. "Okay, my turn. You're very charming, Natalie. And even cockier without the pink sunglasses. But so serious —" imitating my knit-brow expression.

I laughed, overloudly. "Gee, I thought you'd say: You could be a lovely girl, Natalie, if you weren't such a slob. Mother's favorite line."

"All right, no more Natalie's mother."

We sat gazing at the blur of rush hour, not knowing what to say next, glanced at one another and smiled. She looked at her watch. "Oops! I gotta run. Listen," she said, getting up, "let's make a pact: you don't smoke in gym class, I don't teach outside of it. Okay?"

"Agreed, my deah." Extracting sunglasses from my cluttered purse, I slipped them on and peered about — seeing that mimic Natalie in the café window, one eye obscene behind a pink lens, leaving the other doubly naked.

"Definitely a born actress."

Our waitress watched the table like a hawk, frowning when Maxine plopped down a dollar tip. I plucked it up and gave it back to her. "Y'r right," she said, "I didn't want to leave it anyway. Listen, I can't ride the train home with you to the Village, but I'll walk you to the subway."

"I don't live at home anymore. I'm staying at Juli's on Eighty-sixth."

"Not at home? Things sure have changed since I was sweet sixteen."

In the window, that other Natalie stretched and craned back her long neck; a Yemenite necklace of hammered silver coins and tiny gems (Mother's castoff) jaunty against the clay-spattered shirt and corduroy trousers with a tear over the left buttock — which had our gay friends in a laughing fit. "Free at last," I heard her say. "I love it."

"And that's why you missed four weeks of class?"

I shrugged noncommittally.

"I'll buy it," she said. "Freedom is one of the best excuses."

CHAPTER THREE

ROSITA

MEN WERE NOT ONLY ABSENT FROM LIZ'S HOUSEHOLD BUT AS FAR as she was concerned, banished. Though it was impossible to look at Kitty without realizing that somewhere there were male beings. Kitty wasn't beautiful, and thirty pounds overweight — " 'Cause if it's between men and chocolate cake, I just about got to where I'll take that cake!" — but she was W-O-M-A-N. About her hung an aura that caused men on the street not simply to look but devour, and when she smiled her defiant tuck of a smile, throat stretched long, to whistle and "Hey mama" after her, while she swayed haughtily past. "Let me tell you about men," she said: "the first ten years, that was exciting; the second ten was fun; the third ten I commenced to get tired out; now the fourth ten, what you think that gonna be? I tell you, girl, wasn't one ten that was profitable yet." When I asked her, "Who's better in bed, Kitty,

black or white men?" she regarded me sternly and snapped, "They
don't come by the boatload, just one at a time."

Kitty adored John Kennedy and assured me that any man who smiled
like that couldn't have no doubts about his manhood. She was endlessly
clipping magazine photos of the Kennedy clan over the kitchen table,
holding them at arm's length with an appraising nod, proclaiming,
"That family has got class," before pasting them in her scrapbook along
with Malcolm X, Aretha, Jackie Robinson, and a wiseass young boxer
named Cassius Clay — smiling side by side with J.F.K. so that Kitty
laughed and said, "I don't know which of them got the biggest
teeth." Over her bed reigned the trinity: Kennedy, Martin Luther
King, and a blond/blue-eyed Jesus, like three brothers in the House
of David. When I tried convincing her that Jesus couldn't have been
blond/blue-eyed, she said, "Shoot, you don't know. You ain't even
Christian."

Kitty ran our household of women. When Juli asked her mother for
money, Liz snapped, "Don't bother me with that crap. Kitty keeps my
checkbook." Kitty would ask, "What you need this time? This family
can't keep doing like it's Rocker-fellers." Laugh at Juli's contrite blush
and hug her, saying, "This girl won't have no trouble in the world. She
could charm St. Peter out of religion." Open the worn coin purse she
kept in her bra and count out like a pawnbroker, wetting fingers between each bill.

I had the spare room between Liz and Juli. In the evenings, I typed
résumés for summer stock companies or practiced lines for the latest
school play — Liz's typing next door and Juli's foot unconsciously tapping the wall as she studied were welcome cover. Often I sat late talking
to Kitty, who gave me the long whites of her eyes as she poured coffee.
"You finished all your homework?"

"I can in the morning."

"You know, it mystify me how you study so little and my Juli sit up
till after I get in the bed — and both of you going to the same school."

I shrugged. "Juli wants to get into Antioch."

"Don't you fool around and mess up your chances."

We were doing *The Crucible* then. Everyone knew I should have
been Abigail, but Delacroix said he couldn't see me as Abigail, so gave
me Mrs. Proctor and blonde WASP Allie — who'd gone to finishing
school in Connecticut but came back with only her horsey nostrils finished — got Abigail. It soon became obvious there were internal poli-

tics involved, very internal! Mr. D. was more interested in fulfilling his own fantasies than Arthur Miller's.

Theatre was in my blood. I was *Streetcar*'s Blanche in the morning, Antigone at noon. I loved to Raskolnikov home from school along Central Park West, head bent, shuffling . . . just after he'd chopped up the old woman . . . or Lizzie Borden just before. One lovely fall day I saw two small boys fighting, surrounded by a gang of screaming kids. Since I was Alyosha Karamazov at the moment, I jumped in between them crying, "Don't fight, c'mon! Be friends. Love one another." Bouncing, my hands in the air, taking inadvertent punches before they stopped — little round eyes staring at this nutty-nearly-adult wonder as she finger-jiggled a Motown beat. Then caught on with smiles like sunrises over Israel. All of us rocking and rejoicing, bouncing down the hill. By the time I reached home I was Mrs. Proctor again, cutting winky-letchy doormen with a puritanical glare. Although sometimes I was just Me — hearing crowds cheering as I strolled along the park toward Liz's courtly apartment, swinging arms in exuberance, past doormen who nodded recognition, clots of men on porch stoops, whose eyes plodded like tiger's feet after my ass, their shrill whistles sticking on the sweet autumn air. I hoped cold weather would soon chase them inside.

I worried a little over my leapfrogging personality, but had Kitty's love of the Kennedys to thank for keeping the "Me" at its molten core intact, for I had to keep a constant eye out for newsstands and the day's fattest Hyannisport smile — looking as if it might deliver the world steak every night and no child born ever again with a cleft palate.

One October afternoon, when you could see winter's sharp knees coming around the corner, I had just arrived home when Liz came in from some political meeting and went straight for the liquor closet, stepping away as if struck. "Where's my hooch?" she demanded. "I had a fifth of Jack Daniel's —"

"What you want with Jack Daniel's?" Kitty asked, indifferently.

"You fucking well know what I want."

"You got no bizness with a drink at three o'clock in the afternoon," Kitty told her. But Liz had begun rifling cupboards with an energy unheard-of in her phlegmatic regime, spilling things onto the floor. Kitty touched her elbow. "Listen here, honey, we got an agreement. Now why you want to spoil it when you been doing so good?" A frying pan tumbled out with a huge clatter. Kitty snorted, "You sure not going to find it in this kitchen!" Liz on her knees, head stuck under the sink, dress riding over coffee stocking tops, purple veins snaking up milk white thighs. "Get up off that floor," Kitty ordered. "Ain't you got no self-respect?" Liz's reply was a Pyrex bowl popped back over her shoulder, a detonation of slivers.

"Get your ass outta my kitchen!" yowled Kitty.

Liz got up, bratty-faced, lumbering. She tiptoed through shattered glass and stopped to scowl at the latest Kennedy clipping, then up at me. "That prick tried to assassinate Castro and right this minute is getting us up to our asses in a shitty little war in Vietnam that the French lost for twenty years. Papa Joe Kennedy is Irish Mafia and Mama Rose is the biggest Catholic cunt since Isabella of Spain —"

"Cart your nasty mouth out of my kitchen," Kitty snapped, "so I can clean up this mess."

"I admit," Liz continued, "I was once a card-carrying Democrat: stayed up all night answering phones and wet my pants over every fuck who put *liberal* in front of his name . . . wasted my best years as a city councilman's whore. But you can't stay dumb forever." A grim smile. "I'll tell you something else. This *New Frontier* crap is a euphemism for *New Fascism*. Right now the Kennedy boys' Democratic Party won't seat blacks on its southern delegations. But *she* won't believe it. Shit!" Liz's spittle scattered towards Kitty in a Fourth of July spray. "If they were carting blacks to the ovens and said it was just to warm them up for a watermelon feed, she'd be in the front seat."

Kitty appeared beside me, nostrils dilated, eyes flashing.

"And as for that human tire pump Baptist preacher . . . after all the other Negroes in this country are melted down for soap, that putz will still be spieling his basso profundo Uncle Tom bullshit from the steps of the Lincoln Memorial."

"Out!" Kitty commanded in a no-mucking-around tone, a trembling finger speared toward the living room. Liz glanced at her — a plaintive look a child might give her mother. From the other room she called back, "At five I want a drink. Jack Daniel's straight up."

"That's the agreement," Kitty replied, her damp eyes stretched towards the door. "I just know she seen her ex at that meeting. Deep down she got the heart of a kitten; she be crying when the Rev'rend King speak, don't care who notices neither, and work on all those campaigns. Then all at once she get nasty, like she can't control herself." Kitty swept up the glass, and that little therapy returned her good humor. She grinned. "Oh, she burned it up now. Just in a minute, I'll bring her a cup of coffee: she be sitting up at her desk writing a letter to the congressman." Kitty shook her head. "Seem like all she think about is politics and alcohol; I gotta use one to cure the other. Shoooot! it ain't politics —" two sequined elves danced in her eyes "— I b'lieve that woman is got a bad case of empty pockets." Kitty placed forehead on folded arms and jiggled laughter.

One morning at breakfast Liz asked when I thought I might be going home. "I'm not pressuring you but I don't want trouble with Zoe." Her face as raw as the egg she had opened with a fork.

"Don't worry, it's my decision one hundred percent," I said, a little shaken, for I had assumed I would be staying at Juli's through the winter — perhaps forever.

Liz glanced up. "It may be your decision, but mothers are strange creatures. Juli can vouch for that —" baiting with that ironic twist of her mouth that had probably inspired Juli's play-it-safe style in the first place.

"Juli ain't so stupid," Kitty quipped, taking English muffins from the toaster. "She know some *par-ticular mothers* is very strange, and others isn't."

We laughed. Gravel rattled in Liz's throat. "Somebody's gonna get her overweight ass fired."

Kitty turned to me. "Last time this woman fire me, she stood up in the court for not paying her rent. Not to mention the kitchen caught fire cause somebody — not sayin' who! — left a roll of toilet paper on the 'lectric range. The woman is *incompetent.*"

"There are more important qualities than efficiency," Liz muttered.

"And lazy! Now she trying to figure a way to have me urinate for her so she don't have to climb out of the bed at night."

Liz eyed her. "There are two million black Jemimas in this town who'd love your job. They're not all named Kitty, but we wouldn't notice 'cause they all look the same."

"That last girl stay only one day. I know she about run outta here fast as she can. Then *She* commences calling me on the telephone: 'Kitty,' she say, 'I need you back.' And me stupid enough to come."

"You were starving selling pencils on the street corner."

"She just jealous 'cause she never was no good at business." The slightest dip of eyelids standing in as a smile. She shook a muffin on the air. "Nobody . . . I mean No-body gonna work here long as they got two legs and can crawl. Have to put up with this chaos-mess and the bad way it smell 'round here in the morning. Shoo-oot!"

Liz's face snapped up. There were off-limits, as with any old couple. They glared at one another across table with the contempt and contentment of familiarity, while Juli and I stuffed hands in our mouths to stop laughing. Kitty mumbled, "I must be crazy. Except my girl —" squeezing Juli's hand "— I'm just about crazy about my girl." Juli blushed, a ponytail hanging discreetly over each ear. I said it was different in the Bach household. We were at each others' throats for real. No playacting. Liz's eyes snapped. "Who's playacting?" She asked politely for more coffee and Kitty politely poured it.

"First thing I hear every morning is Mother calling me a slob."

"You are a slob —" Liz flicked ashes at the ashtray "— and your friends stink." She pushed long fingers back through thin hair and gloated at Kitty.

"Mother!" Juli protested.

"Juli's not a slob," said Liz. "She's a prude. It's terribly demoralizing when you've raised your daughter in an unwholesome atmosphere and she turns out a goody-good."

"Leave the girl alone."

Liz took a slug of coffee. "Stick it up your ass."

Kitty's round face expanded. "What kind of way is that? The woman should be institutionalized. She filthy mouthed. And alcoholic!"

"Who's alcoholic?"

"Drinking before She get out of the bed in the morning."

Liz appealed to me: "One little bracer to get me on my feet."

"And another half-gallon to stay on 'em." Out went her finger. "That God's truth. I do the shopping in this house: two dozen eggs and three gallons of bourbon whiskey."

Liz stared out the window. Central Park just visible beyond the adjacent building and over it the Midtown skyline, bone white in sickly morning sunlight. "Woo-hoo —" she yowled, waving a hand "— Halloooo . . ." We rose to see. A woman had opened her curtains in the tower across the courtyard. She slipped a negligée over her head and stood naked, offering herself to the city. Then dressed slowly in glossy lingerie. Liz snorted, "Women will do *anything* to get laid." Conversation lapsed in moody silence.

As resident guest, I felt obliged to cheer things up. I announced that

Mom/Dad had invited Maxine to dinner. Liz exchanged a glance with Kitty. "Aren't they lucky," she said. I looked at her. "What's that supposed to mean? Mother can be very charming, you know. She isn't always a bitch."

Liz squirmed and jerked in her chair like a kid trying to sit on a balloon, unable to get comfortable in the tropically flowered muumuu she always wore around the house (she couldn't tolerate constricting clothes). Finally, Kitty snapped, "Woman take your gassy self to the bathroom," averting her face as Liz rose in dour silence and Juli and I struggled to keep straight faces. "That woman got such bad gas. Some day she gonna blow up like a November pumpkin."

Liz wheeled around in the doorway. "Just don't give me this 'Mother is a bitch' crap, Natalie. Say 'Mother is a bitch around me.' That completes the equation."

Kitty nodded. "Oh, she always got direct dialing on the truth."

My decision to leave home for Juli's was a culmination of events beginning years earlier. I can remember the exact morning at breakfast: Dad arranging and rearranging bathrobe over his knees, Mother entering on brisk rustlings of her robe and a bouquet of bath potions, pecking first Dad, then me, then Mattie — who plopped a steaming bowl of cereal before Dad and went off muttering, eyes seemingly hollowed from her skull. The three of us exchanged a surprised look. "Mattie dear, what's wrong?" Mother asked. Mattie snapped, "Everything wrong, Mizz Bach, the whole world wrong."

After Dad had left for work, I eavesdropped through the kitchen door while Mother scolded Mattie for not providing her daughter with "protection," and Mattie asked if she studied on "protection" for me at thirteen? "Why it be different?" she demanded. "Because she a white girl and my daughter a black nigger?" Their voices lowered, I caught only key words — *bastard child, abortion* — a whispered code that brought moral night riders galloping: late night screams and tabloid photos of gory bathtubs. I remembered the upper-house girl at Whitman who had disappeared from school amidst wild rumors, returning a few days later with a new Mexican skirt and haggard eyes. The Russian doctor's name on a brass plate down a Village back street I often passed with my friends, someone invariably whispering: He's an *abortionist!* Our eyes lingering back in horror on his garbage can. In my schoolgirl mind, abortion was hardly a step above human sacrifice.

After her daughter's abortion, Mattie moped about not being home where a mother ought to be. I overheard Mother telling Dad that Mattie had changed. "She's not as cheerful as she used to be." Tensions mounted. Mother found the first of the missing buttons that were to haunt her through many maids. She became nearly hostile about pronouncements from Malcolm X in bold black headlines across crisp morning news. "What do you think of him, Mattie?" she asked.

"I don't have time for it, Mizz Bach."

"Well, I think he's a racist," Mother snapped, bewildering me, for I had always thought of her as a liberal.

A conspiracy of pain and rage seemed to develop between Mattie and me, though she still hushed me if I said a bad word about Mother. I begged Mother not to fire her. She laughed. "Where did you get that idea? Mattie is like one of the family." Though she looked shaken, as if I had picked her thoughts.

A few weeks later Mattie announced she was taking her daughter back to North Carolina. "This isn't no place to raise a child." It was all smiles, reminiscences and sweet tears then, but I knew Mattie was too proud — too loyal, I liked to think, to the memory of the Bach family — to want to be fired.

A succession of maids followed, beginning with a huge jolly black woman with a row of straight pins perpetually clamped between her lips; of whom Mother said, "I can't imagine what she does with all my buttons." Then a lean haughty coffee-brown woman. So it went — from fat to slim, lighter and lighter in complexion as if Mother were conducting a sociological experiment.

I befriended the maids, sat drinking coffee with them, passed on pieces of jewelry Mother had given me and waited for her to accuse them of stealing. "Blacks can't be trusted anymore," Mother said one night when the Freids were over for dinner. "It's all the black power stuff. Martin Luther King is putting crazy ideas in their heads."

"For example, being treated like human beings," I said, looking at Hettie Freid, theoretical friend, with her prim black bun of hair, tightly crossed legs, and Tricia Nixon smile. She copped a wary glance at the adults and wiggled up her chair to escape complicity. "Mother's a racist," I explained. "I bet you are, too."

Then came Rosita.

"She's a Negro, you know," Mother assured me. I shrugged. "So am I. Negro isn't the color of your skin, it's the color of your heart."

God help the person who called Rosita "Negro" to her face (only a freckle band across her nose hinted any black blood). She was Cuban. A *blanca*. A weasel, changing coat to match the social climate. For Mother she wore a furry little smile, a compliment always on her lips. With Dad she was vivacious, turning on the Latin charm, joking with him as he practiced Spanish, unbuttoning polished cotton blouses till her tits were two ripe plums hanging in his face as she poured coffee (until Mother suggested she wear something more ... circumspect). With me, Rosita had a disarming habit of parting her lips slightly when I spoke, like a disapproving librarian, revealing the little points of her teeth.

Fourth of July just sticking its head around the corner that summer of '63 and the city coiled like a snake — hot and slickly glistening. If you listened hard on sticky nights, you could make out a low moan rising out of Harlem (some said it was a war cry). Open warfare in Mississippi, Americans just learning those oddly melodic names: Da Nang, Haiphong, Mekong . . . but mostly a lighthearted mood — prosperity, Peace Corps, New Frontier, college and the future of your choice, led by a bright, attractive young president with a sense of humor. People played touch football and planned vacations, watched their dollars graze plumply on hillsides of the world. Beatniks writing smutty poems and some sour-voiced jerk who'd changed his name from Zimmerman to Dylan just added to the excitement.

I slipped into poetry readings at St. Marks Church, pinned Beatles lyrics on my wall, bought sandals and a serape, read James Baldwin and J. D. Salinger. I knew something had started, felt the external energy percolating through my inner being. Mother was worried. You shouldn't be so trusting, she warned, there are a lot of crazy ideas floating around.

At times fate is manipulated by an intelligence with chess players' proclivities. So it seemed anyway that summer before I moved to Juli's, with events leading to the final alienation from my parents. Beginning when I declined the invitation to join them on a Caribbean cruise: I had the theatre workshop, besides, couldn't imagine spending a month with them aboard a luxury ghetto. Though I dreaded the time alone with Rosita, I hoped things would cool out without Mother around. Wisely, I had invited Carol to come stay with me.

One night about two weeks before their departure, Mother had guitar club and I had rehearsal, leaving Dad and Rosita home alone. Don't expect me early, I told them, 'cause we were doing *The Children's Hour* and it took us forever to get through it. However, by chance, Delacroix got an emergency call from home in the second act and dismissed us. I came in quietly, keeping a low profile as always those days — astonished at hearing a clicketing rumba from the living room instead of Mozart. One of the folding doors was ajar, so I stood peeking in from the dark hallway, feeling sneaky, but overcome with curiosity.

Rosita dancing: a sinuous sort of march forward and back, arms pumping, skirt snapping about her knees, writhing like a restless adder. Dad raised his glass and called out, "You make a wicked piña colada, Rosie." She returned a smile full of playful insolence, blouse unbuttoned nearly to her navel. Perhaps men would find her sexy — dark angry eyes, man-eating curl of upper lip blanketed in dark down — mistaking her disdain for desire.

"Hey!" she cried, "you need 'nother drink, Mister Bach."

"Why not?" said Dad with a grin that made me tingle. "Won't you join me, Rosie? Sit down and relax a little."

She shrugged and threw her tiny apron at a chair. After a minute returned from the kitchen with two frothy drinks and sprawled on the couch, stretching out toes and spreading elbows like wings behind her head, revealing black whorls at armpits.

"Es delicioso," Dad lifted his drink.

"Está deliciosa!" she corrected him, pulling lips away from her teeth. He sipped the drink and whistled. Rosita put on another record, clapping hands overhead and kicking up legs, the rotation of her hips sending the skirt spinning above her waist, exposing tiger-striped panties. Dad chuckled. Fortunately, I couldn't see his face.

Rosita moved close to check his drink. She stirred it with the straw, which she then passed slowly between her lips. Her smile hung above him a long moment. "Fidel!" she cried suddenly, seeing *Life* magazine with the cover photo of Castro on the coffee table. *"Mi camarada —"* slugging out a phony fist. *"Viva la Revolución!"* She stooped beside Dad to pick it up, short skirt crawling up her legs. Dad turned in my direction, eyes watery. Looked as if he was about to cry. Sentiments affected him that way. Maybe even lust. He shut his eyes, as if about to leap into cold water, and slid a hand up her dark thigh.

Maybe I had walked into the wrong house? I considered tiptoeing back for a reentry, closing the door with a bang. But couldn't budge. Like the family's conscience waiting in the dark to be noticed.

Rosita shook a finger and clucked her tongue. Dad, suddenly aggressive, gripped her wrists and pulled her onto his lap. She mock struggled, her laughter filling the room with shattered glass as he nibbled at her neck. His hand slid into her blouse and she cooed "naughty naughty —" a small man-eating smile on her lips — and reached back to unfasten the tiny bra. I wanted to scream.

Dad started as if struck. His eyes flashed to the door. Maybe I had cried out.

If it's possible to feel both panic and relief at the same moment, I did. I froze, stepping back reflexively into shadows. Dad had gotten to his feet and was approaching me. Then I realized there was no recognition in his glassy stare. Perhaps he had just gotten up to close the door. It was Rosita behind him — standing, blouse open, skirt snagged on a nylon, cat's eyes narrowed to small slits — who saw me.

Dad stumbled drunkenly, hands paddling the air like lost swimmers, a foolish manlust look on his face. I didn't wait to see if he fell but padded back to my room and closed the door. Within minutes came a knock. I sat absolutely still in the dark, riding out panic. The door opened: Rosita silhouetted against hall light. "Don't think I so stupid," she hissed. "You don' tell nobody. Not your mama . . . Nobody!" She shook something — finger, fist? "You tell, I cut you up like tomato."

Afterwards, I lay in a stupor of fear, outrage, disbelief, obsessed with the drunken, undignified stumble of my father, cursing myself for coming in so quietly, until mentally exhausted. *But how can it be my fault? It's fate, like a curse, a knack I have for blowing it.* Neither quite awake nor asleep but in a moral torpor when a light snapped on and Mother's face popped in the door. She looked scared.

"Did your father have an attack, honey?"

"Attack?" I murmured. "No, I don't think so."

She came into the room, leaving the door open. I sensed Rosita in the semi-dark behind her, listening. "I found him passed out across the bed with his clothes on," she said, her face bunched like a worried snail. She bit at a cuticle. "Was he drinking?"

Cornered by her eyes, my mind racing for something to say, I could think of nothing — except the truth. I stalled, imagining the panic in Dad's eyes when she shook him awake: goggle-eyeing her like a guilty child, remorse pooling at eye corners. "I had rehearsal," I mumbled. "I really don't know."

Mother sighed. "I'd better call Dr. Solomon —"

"Oh, that's right!" I blurted. "Rosita's brother came over; they were drinking some rum stuff."

Her eyes pondered me, then relaxed a little. "He shouldn't drink like that. What's the matter, honey? Are you sick?"

"Kinda depressed," I said, relieved to be diverted from the living room scene. "I have to get up early tomorrow to memorize my lines. I couldn't face it tonight."

"What's wrong, honey?"

I shook my head, in no mood for her fickle affection.

"I remember those years —" Mother leaned against the doorpost, dreamy-eyed "— Boys and parents, every sort of trouble . . . growing up." She smiled. "We played blues tonight. Gee, Nattie, I wish you would come some night to teach us folk guitar. They'd love it."

I shrugged, just wanting her to go and leave me alone. "I'm really busy." Her face seemed middle-aged, swollen with betrayal, off-blonde hair and rouge in tiny hardened drifts under her eyes a desperate last grasp at youth. It was unbearably painful to look at her. I turned away.

"How was rehearsal, honey?"

I thought of Dad lying on their bed, spent. "It was okay," I mumbled. "Delacroix always gives me the wrong part, but . . . it'll be a good play."

"Gee, that's great." She bent to kiss me goodnight — frowning suddenly. "Should you be reading that?" picking up a paperback beside the bed.

"*Lady Chatterley's Lover!* It's a great book," I said. "Lawrence really cares about women."

"You know, everyone doesn't share his values. It's a pretty mature book."

"We live in New York, Mother. What I see daily makes this look like Walt Disney." *Like in my own living room with that Cuban cunt of a maidwhore.*

She turned the book over as if reappraising. "I like Lawrence," she said, head cocking birdwise. "Did Rosie go out?"

I shrugged and pulled the sheet up to my chin. Mother sat down on the bed. "I wish you'd try to get along with her, Natalie. You know, your father and I are very pleased with Rosie. She's clean and she doesn't steal. I don't think we've ever been more pleased with a girl. Of course we loved Mattie."

Words ganged up at my throat — a shout that bounced noiseless around the room. I didn't dare look at her. "Please, Mother," I managed, "I just want to go to sleep."

We gathered at breakfast next morning. Dad kept eyes on his cereal, tense as a cornered rabbit. Rosita was hyper, inventing a story about her brother bringing a fifth of overproof Jamaican rum. "And the fellas," she laughed, "I think they drink too much!" Mother chided Dad, then Rosita, who groveled and yes ma'am'd, her dark eyes slashing at me with a kind of satisfaction. I glanced only once at Dad — his gaze at half-mast as if studying Mother's chest, elbows stuck out awkward as harpoons in the linen jacket — and quickly excused myself.

Outside the sky a Spanish overcast, scalded with light. Walking along filthy sidewalks, I debated conscience: *You should have slammed the door instead of sneaking into your own home like a don't belong.* Yes, if only I felt welcome in my own home. *You should have cried out "I'm home!" like any other daughter and bounced in to look in the fridge.* I'm not any other daughter. I'm me. And not responsible for my father's actions. He would have found another opportunity.

Not fully realizing I was on my way to the synagogue on Fifth Avenue until I stood before the huge stone edifice, steps that seemed ancient in proportions, carved from Biblical sandstone. The heavy wooden doors were closed. I realized I had never been to temple — not once! As a Jew I was a stranger. What was behind those doors? The ark of the covenant? A courtyard full of nodding rabbis? Perhaps offices, meeting halls, sober chapels . . . isn't there some sort of sexual segregation? Maybe women aren't allowed inside at all. No one emerged to help me. And if they had, what would I have asked — how one went about praying? I backed down the steps.

Shortly afterwards, I passed a tiny church surrounded by lush plantings and flower beds. The doors stood open, candles flickered on an altar. It was shadowed, discreet, inviting. God wouldn't care which phone booth I used to call him.

I tiptoed in and sat in a back pew, alone but for an old woman near the front. But how did you do it? Folding hands seemed too Christian. I looked up at huge wooden beams knitting the ceiling together — perhaps God had a nest up there like a dove, hidden under the eaves — then looked quickly down. What could I ask for? I doubted that even

God could erase the past. The awesome somberness and damp quiet of the place oppressed me. It looked as if the bulge-eyed Christ, crucified above the altar, would begin to bleed any second — like those grotesque icons in Spain. Or might shout:

Jew infidel! Out of my Father's house!

A man hung on nails. Perfect symbol for our civilization.

On the way out I threw a wish at Whatever Was Up There: Forgive us both, Me and My Father.

Mother gave me a twenty to buy an antiquey ruffled blouse for the play. On the way shopping, I stopped at a street vendor for a soda and handed him the twenty, thinking it a one. As if reading my thoughts, he returned a dollar's change, but I didn't notice until I had reached the clothing store. I rushed back, but couldn't find him. I was panicked, had to have the blouse for dress rehearsal, considered calling Mother at the office, but the thought of getting the Zilla Bach y'r-a-fuck-up treatment right before opening night was more than I could bear. Instead, I went home. Making sure Rosita was in the front, sneaked back to Mother's bedroom — and the money stash I knew she kept under a jewelry box in her dresser.

I felt sick as I opened the drawer; I had never stolen from her. Kept turning around, heart a frog in my throat, unable to shake the feeling I was being watched. Eyes of the many Zilla Bachs in Dad's paintings around the room followed me — faces laughing or beckoning or sad . . . all suddenly shocked. What difference does it make, I reasoned, whether I ask or simply take? It comes from the same place. Still I felt nauseous as I snatched the bill and rearranged things in Mother's drawer, trying to convince myself she wouldn't notice, and if she did, was certain to blame it on Rosita. She would never imagine . . .

As I closed the drawer, I glanced up at the bureau mirror. Rosita stood in the doorway behind me, arms folded across her chest. I turned, hands behind my back. Her smile licked my bones clean and spit them out. I brought my hand forward, clutching the bill.

"Mother knows about this. It's all right with her."

She replied by putting out a palm. We faced off.

"Is that what you planned with Dad, extortion?"

Her hand stayed there. A smile showing her sharp teeth; I doubt Dad would have found it pretty. Me thinking I could jump her — go for her face . . . eyes! I had her in size, maybe strength. But she was older. Street-tough. Her stare menacing, and that polished scar under her collarbone like a badge in the open tops of blouses. I thought of how she tested knives with a scar-callused thumb before using them to slice vegetables. I took a few steps across the carpet, Rosita moved to block my exit. My heart kathumping; though I was more outraged than afraid, really. I closed my eyes very tight. "Get out of my way."

She rubbed a finger across her thumb as if testing a knife. "Don' be stupid," she said. "We share like sisters." Her mocking smile.

"Don't push me." I braced forward.

Out went her palm again.

I spit. It missed her hand, spattering on the door behind. Rosita stared for a tense moment at my spittle, her body crouched, feline. Then her eyes met mine. "Stupid," she hissed, *"muy estúpida."* Smiling. "I get you. You wait, I get you." She turned and left the room.

Tensions mounted those last days before the cruise. I expected Rosita to strike any moment. Instead, she taunted and teased, telling Mother she had sniffed marijuana in my room, or was cheerful, doing me little favors when Mother was around, which tortured me even more. I openly despised her. Mother scolded, "Y'r such a sourpuss. Give Rosie a chance. She's very fond of you, you know." *Right!* I thought, *one of us will be dead when you get back.* Mother didn't notice that Dad no longer joked with Rosita, hardly looked at her, or the knife-wielding smile sweet Rosie clenched in her teeth whenever I was around.

One day Mother collared me. "There's something I have to discuss with you," she said. "I keep a few bills in my dresser drawer —" I froze. Should I blurt it all: Me and the money, Dad's hand on Rosita's thigh? But incredibly she said nothing about the missing twenty, only that she was leaving cash to meet my needs while they were away. Instead of feeling relief, I saw my predicament: Rosita knew that I couldn't betray Dad. She was determined to make me suffer twice — for my own sins and for his. She could always find another job, but the Bach family would be left in a shambles.

It was a relief when Mom/Dad finally departed. Rosita became almost pleasant. My new friend Carol had come to spend the month. Sometimes the three of us sat at the breakfast table and Rosita told stories of her Caribbean girlhood. I alternated between hope she had

forgotten our feud and fear she would slip ground glass into my eggs. I
kept a cheerful demeanor. Someone had once told me it was street
savvy to strike when your enemy is down. I was never down.

August a nonstop party. Through molasses hours of sunny afternoons
we sat in Washington Square Park. Nearby, black and Puerto Rican
drummers palmed out cadences, hands a blur of movement, drumbeats
echoing off canyon walls, claiming the city. Whatever wasn't white in
our souls danced for joy. A crowd gathered about the drummers — in-
termixed, black and white, smattered with beards and eagerness, like
they had all just returned from Freedom Rides and lunch counters in
Greensboro, North Carolina, to the splendid new age Kennedy had
promised at his inauguration, with Robert Frost at his right hand. But a
tension, too, as if expecting at any moment police cars to come howling
in from every direction.

The insolent blondness of Carol's hair and willowy body, easy flight
of her laugh drew men like magnets — always older, often black. They
stood joking, grinning like boys around a magazine rack, slapping one
another's palms. And had plans for me too — as they always do for the
tag-along-lulu. I felt panicky, way out of my league.

We rolled up the living room rug and threw our bodies into the Motown soul of Aretha and Diana Ross, blasting full volume from the
stereo. Rosita joined us, adding salsa to the brew. But when our black
friends began dropping by her eyes flashed warning. From the depths of
her hybrid heart Rosita trusted nothing hybrid.

Every night Carol and I lay abed in the mostly dark, Carol moaning,
"Ohhh, I gotta get laid —" recalling her sexploits in a lusty singsong:
New Jersey drive-in nights, sex behind a boathouse on the Delaware
River, in the sand dunes at Cape Cod. . . . "What's it like?" I asked.
"Heaven," she sighed, "God's lollypop!" drawing what may have been
a penis on the air with her toe. "C'mon —" laughing "— tell me!"
Carol arched her back, whuffing down on a cushion of air. "Ohhh, I
can't stand it," she moaned. I threw a pillow at her. "It's not fair. I'll be
ninety-five before I ever sleep with a man." Carol sat up with a squawk
of springs. "Tomorrow Bach gets laid." Her baby doll nightgown luminous in light leaking from windows, breasts full moons. "By whom," I
demanded, "Karl Housman? I have a little handicap, remember? Even
God has a breast fetish."

The bed lamp snapped on. She crossed legs beneath her on the twin bed, her near-nakedness almost blinding. "European men really dig small breasts," she assured me.

"Right. And some men dig women amputated at the waist, so they can carry them around on a platter."

Her breasts swayed heavily. Me thinking it would be impossible to pilot the feminine ocean liner of her body. More WOMAN-ly than mine could ever be. "There are other things in life besides sex," I sighed, aping Mother's favorite line.

"Math," she said, "hemorrhoids, sour milk . . ." whumping me full-stomach with her pillow. "Hey! you haven't even tried." She collapsed backwards. "Maybe you're queered on men." Carol slid hands over her breasts, O'ing her mouth in a grotesque kiss. "How about a little Sapphic dee-light?"

I lay awake long after Carol had begun a regular breathing, thinking how often I lay like this, enstupored in a despair of desire, intensified by the restless, moaning city. Getting up before the wardrobe mirror, I would inch my nightgown down in futility: hope could not give me a cleavage. Only when the house had fallen silent, the nightmoan become serenade did I slip my fingers down to whisper consolation. I considered doing it now. Funny! Mother considered me promiscuous — a regular nymphomaniac. When my sole experience, if you could call it that, had been in movie back rows with Karl Housman, who kissed like the toad who never would be a prince, working my little titties like bread dough. He was a mountain climber exploring routes to the top — through sleeves, around my shoulder, under pants' band. Karl was a pest.

I was awakened by Carol yowling, "Hey Bach, it's D Day. Dork Day!" She stood bra and panty'd daubing an underarm with deodorant. "This is step one," she said, grabbing the girdle on my dresser, waltzing over and tossing it out the window.

The girdle floated flat on the wind, an armored hope, towards Sixth Avenue, tabs flapping over the rush of taxis, folded suddenly and Stuka-dived at an old geezer walking his dog. We grabbed each other and laughed. Then I jettisoned my bra. (Long ago, beside a sale table at Macy's stacked with two-tone trainers, Mother had said, "Y'r lucky. Small breasted girls don't have to bother with that." I only knew these nubs wanted desperately to be trained.) The bra snaked and wiggled, cups filling and deflating, while the old fart gaped at the girdle, which his dog shook furiously in its teeth, tilting up the hollow of his mouth just as the bra performed one last somersault and collapsed lifeless at his feet. He goggled, awestruck, at every corner of the sky, head swallowed into his shoulders. Businessmen hurried past, a few glancing back at lingerie stretched like rape on the sidewalk. The old man looked around the circle of onlookers and spread his hands. Carol and I leaned together, shrieking.

"G'morning New York," she bellowed. "It's Dork Day!"

Like mantises, we seized the first two dudes we met that afternoon. Mine tall, skinny, with sleepy eyes and protuberant Adam's apple. Carol's had wads of muscle on his shoulders. But "who" didn't make any difference, only "what." "I don't know if I'm ready for this," I whispered to Carol on the way back to the apartment. "Y'r ready," she said. "Long overdue."

The little toothpick sucking creep doorman, who usually greeted us with an "Afternoon young ladies" as he opened the door, now halted us with a raised palm — noticing my ragged cutoffs and workshirt, turning to our black escorts, whose eyes flew about the lobby then to us, hoping we knew what we were doing. "Just visiting —" said my string bean, doing a little backwards shuffle.

"Visiting who?" demanded the doorman.

"Me," I said. "Remember, I live here."

He eyed me up and down, finally settling on Carol's over-ripe T-shirt, and stepped back with a disdainful little bow. The important thing, I reminded myself, was that Rosita was out for the afternoon.

Making separate nests on the bedroom rug in curtain drawn half-light, we did everything but fuck — my drummer's hands like coarse palm leaves on my body. Taking cue from Carol: "Not yet . . . okay?" A pidgin of guttural cooings and flighty giggles, fierce pleas and the hiss of clothing mixed like water. We would catch our breath and go down, then relax, come back to the surface to share a cigarette.

Rosita returned with a bang of the front door, having conferred with the doorman. She didn't hide her scorn for my drummer, who looked even shabbier after the nonfulfillment of our love match, but wrinkled her nose, eyes hate-hot, and said, "You wanna fuck this trash, go on, go out this house. Your mama no want it in this house."

"Go to hell," I replied.

I had never seen Mother more relaxed: travel was her seltzer. Both of them in a high and happy mood that day they returned. We went for dinner, and they laughed like crazy when I described my dive-bombing girdle and the old man's astonishment. Mother took my hand as we walked back to the apartment, singing in step, her voice tapdancing out the high notes of flippant prewar songs. Dad clapped rhythm, himself again, hangdog guilt burnt off in the tropical sun. I was giddy, hoping we could start afresh.

"I even cleaned my room," I crowed as we rode up the elevator. Dad chuckled. The apartment door opened. There stood Rosita, a canny smile revealing weasel teeth, her voice dripping syrup. Dad cleared his throat. I cursed the greediness of the past.

I had kissed Mom/Dad goodnight and was returning to my room from the bathroom when I heard Mother in the kitchen asking, "What trouble, Rosie?" A guardian angel warned: Get out! tonight! Run. Without undressing, I lay down a minute to think things out, my feelings piling into each other like carnival bumper cars.

I was awakened by morning light in my face. I opened the door. Silence. Not even the weasel padding in her kitchen. No time for the bathroom — just go! I tiptoed into the hall. The kitchen clock read 7:00. From the rear came Dad's even snoring. I rinsed my face at the sink — and realized a flame was lit under the coffeepot. Where was she, the sneak? I turned quickly, hoping to catch her behind me. Then hurried towards the front door. As I passed the living room, Mother's voice caught me like a grappling hook.

Curtains drawn back from a wall of windows, room airy, nearly buoyant — with its glass tables and leather-backed chairs in near-white, a luxury liner on a sea of morning light. Mother sat curled on the couch in her robe, eyes ragged in the Caribbean mocha of her face. "Sleep well?" I asked, with a sad attempt at a cheery smile, which Mother didn't return.

"Where were you going?" she asked.

I lit a cigarette and concentrated all my will upon smoking it. "I really had a fantastic time last night."

Mother's gaze remained even, lips dry. "Were you going to see your boyfriend?" It took a moment to sort out her logic.

"Mother, don't be ridiculous."

"It's seven A.M.," she said, as if this was damning evidence.

"I wanted to avoid this."

"You didn't." Anger spreading from eyes to her smile.

"We haven't seen each other for a month, do we have to fight the first day you are back?"

"Who is this black boy you are seeing, Natalie?"

"Mother . . . I'm really not *seeing* anyone."

"You know, it isn't natural to want to go only with blacks. You ought to give the other fellas a chance." She rearranged legs under her robe. I sighed around the room. "Dr. Sternberg says it's a phase girls are going through now. But your father and I are awfully concerned. You know, these men are very *mature.*" Her mouth twisted into a mollusk over the word.

"One time —" holding up a finger "— I brought home a black guy!"

"Someone you met in the park?"

"I don't think that's any of your business."

"You know, sex is a sacred thing, Nattie. Nothing exotic. On our first date, your father put his hand up my dress. I smacked him one. 'Hey! what's the idea?' he cried. 'Other girls let me do it.' 'Not me,' I said, and he respected me more for it."

A hand over my eyes. "I'd rather not discuss Dad's sex life." Looking up at her. "I'm still a virgin, Mother, if that's what you're worried about. And Dad never stuck his hand up my dress."

Her voice tightened. "You can get a bad reputation, honey. Fellas will wonder why you prefer black boys. They'll think you're loose."

"Could I please go now?"

"What were you doing in there?" She gestured at my bedroom. "Why don't you entertain your friends in the living room?"

"I'm afraid they will come off on the furniture."

Mother slipped off the edge of composure, lips forming a little beak. I slipped with her, though part of me wanted to touch her, cry out: *Mom! remember last night? We could be singing together.* Her expression icy, appraising me as if I were a stranger. "This stealing business —" tears suddenly boiling out of blue deeps of her eyes "— I wish you could convince me it's a mistake, honey. You aren't that kind of girl."

I nearly cried out. I had expected this for weeks; still it came as a low blow. Suddenly, I wasn't sure I was not *that kind of girl.* I felt only anger . . . red fury. I wanted blood: Rosita's! Even if it meant Dad's too.

Mother tilted forward, mouth open, imploring, beginnings of old lady lines at corners. "I wish you could say it isn't true, honey."

Light hit the coffee table and exploded.

"She's a bitch," I hissed. "*Why don't you come out and accuse me to my face?"* I shouted at listening walls. *"Come on, chicken. If you want to fight, I'll fight."*

Mother paled. "Who are you talking to?"

"You'd believe her, wouldn't you? You'd believe it if she said I was screwing my own father. You'd believe anything she said. Wouldn't you?"

Mother staring as if she feared for my sanity. "I think you've come under a bad influence with your friends," she mumbled. "I hardly know you anymore."

"Don't look at me like that."

Her mouth hardened. "How long have you stolen from us, Natalie?"

"Once —" jabbing a finger "— I did it once." Emotions leapfrogging from anger to remorse. "I'm really sorry, Mother. I had to have the money. I almost came and told you."

"If I might say so, you don't seem very sorry. I knew someone was taking money. I thought it was Rosie. It's disheartening to realize your maid is more trustworthy than your own daughter. Were you buying drugs?"

I stared at her, dizzy, trembling down into a vortex I had struggled to avoid, but the weight of what I had seen that night weeks before had grown unbearable as I carried it around. What a relief it would be to be rid of it. "Could I just go now, please?"

"I would like to know what my daughter is doing."

"You're forcing me to tell you things that I don't want to say. I hope you understand that. I'd prefer just to leave."

Mother eyed me, wary, unsure of what my *friends' influence* might inspire next. "If you know something, I want you to tell me," she said spiritlessly. I held her eyes.

"Doesn't it seem strange that Rosita hates me so much?"

"You're not making any sense."

"You don't want to see, Mother. You're like those German Jews who thought they were being loaded on boxcars for a picnic. And now you're going to insist that I see a psychiatrist. It won't be Dad or Rosita who gets the blame — but dear daughter."

Mother smoothed the robe over her lap with uncertain fingers, dark eyebrows forming arched wrinkles up her forehead. "I really don't know what you are talking about. Your father and I are very pleased with Rosie."

"Sure!" I cried, "Dad is extremely pleased with Rosie —"

The silence left between us drained towards the rear of the apartment like a wave, leaving a low hissing ... Perhaps Rosita in the hall. Or Dad. Or both of them clinging together. In sunlight splintering against the coffee table, a vengeful demon clicked its heels and grinned at me. My gaze fixed on her until fear formed little dimples in her cheeks.

"What do you mean?" she asked, just audibly.

Somewhere in back I heard a door close — thought of how, as a kid, I had stood beside Dad at the sink while he shaved, lathered my face, pretending with a finger that I was shaving too — and realized I was crying. My betrayal was far worse than anything Dad, half-potted, had done. I spoke softly: "You know the gift you brought back for Rosita? I found it this morning in the garbage."

"Oh!" Mother said, puzzled, then a little hurt. She shrugged. "I guess she didn't like it. Is that all you wanted to tell me?"

I nodded.

"I don't want you to think you have to steal from me, honey. Why not ask me if you need something? I want to think we can trust each other." She leaned forward, eager: a woman who had reached middle age, had always been successful and had only begun to lose things in life. All at once I felt sorry for her.

"I'm not the one you have to worry about in this house, Mother." I touched her hand. "I'm sorry but I just can't live here any longer."

She sighed. "You really can't expect me to let Rosita go. Good help is hard to find nowadays."

"So is a good daughter."

CHAPTER FOUR

STEPS

MAXINE DRIFTED DOWN HALL TOWARD ME IN A TIDE OF CLIques — Allie and Ellie, the Bobbsey Twits, to her right and left talking at once, boys swinging their bulging briefcases and rapidly thinning on top. I said hello. Miss Driftwood floated me an aloof smile and kept walking. They stopped near her French classroom, laughing and trying to outpun each other; boys eagerly awaiting front row seats and Max sidesaddling the desk, conjuring French verbs from their lips. I waited, wondering what she saw in those creeps. Allie and Ellie glanced at me, glasses flashing hostility. Then Maxine asked in an abrupt tone, "What is it, Natalie?" I said, "I just wanted to talk to you." She spread hands like a cab driver "Nu —?" Allie rolled eyes at Ellie. I turned and walked away.

Later, at rehearsal, in the dramatic scene where John Proctor says,

"Your justice would freeze beer, Elizabeth," and me so far into my Elizabeth Proctor Puritan role I wasn't even in this century, I began to notice tittering amongst other cast members. I turned around. Allie was mimicking me. She clasped hands behind her back and sauntered off, whistling. "Lay off," I shouted, "unless you want your head broken." Delacroix told me to grow up.

Maxine peeked out, her door open just a crack. "Surprise!" I said. She seemed reluctant to invite me in. "It's freezing in here," I said at the gloom — scholarly funk, furniture littered with books and thesis notes. "No heat until November," Max said, returning to the book she'd left open on a chair. I sat on the threadbare carpet. From a poster, a woman rolled eyes at me through a psychedelic mist, squatting in the yab-yum position over the lap of a long-haired androgynous mate. I grimaced. "Is sex fun like that?" Maxine didn't answer. We talked — rather I talked, while she fidgeted and threw tense glances at her book, frowning into the gloom.

"Turn on a light," I suggested.

She put the book aside, her eyebrows mating like two dark caterpillars. "What is it, Natalie?"

I looked out at darkness creeping city streets, lights popping on, a near festive spirit as the city hurried home in a light rain. I had no desire to join the rush. "I just wanted to visit. I guess you have to study all the time?"

"Won't you be late for dinner?" she said into her book.

I shrugged. "I'm not hungry. Kitty can put a plate in the oven." I leaned back against the couch and closed my eyes, sensed her moving like a sea creature in the murk. From the kitchen came a clatter of cupboards. *I'm not leaving*, I whispered, *I just got here*. A light popped on. Maxine's voice behind me.

"Look, I have to study. I've got a seminar tomorrow."

"Go ahead. You don't have to entertain me."

She sighed hard, picked up the book again, sitting lotus-wise, bulky in sweaters. I thumbed through stacks of *The Nation*, *The New Republic*, other bulgebrain publications. Gave it up. Stared at crow glintings of Max's hair, fixed in a bun, strands falling haphazardly, giving a near harried impression as she bent over the book. I giggled. "How can you read with your hair falling down?" Her eyes came up. "Why are you harassing me?" I glared back. "I don't like being snubbed." She was bewildered. "In the hall yesterday," I said, "with the Bobbsey Twits and their creep friends."

"Jesus, you bear a grudge, kiddo. That's why you skipped basketball practice yesterday?"

I lit a cigarette.

"So what's wrong with Ellie and Allie? They're excellent students. And good dancers."

"Oh yes! Such distinctive personalities. When Allie's tired, Ellie yawns. They even take turns having their period." (Max fought a grin.) "So aca-dem-ically superior in their hotsy clique, such star material for Sarah Lawrence — where they're *all* applying."

Max smiled. "Natalie's jealous. I can't believe it."

"Oh sure. I wouldn't join their stupid club if they begged me."

Eyebrows crawled up her forehead. "Oh, I believe you." She returned to her book, marking key passages with the squeak of a felt tip pen. I watched a cockroach cruise the wall, wanted to ask if she had decided to make Allie basketball captain. Instead, I lit a cigarette. "I wish you were directing *The Crucible*," I said. "The only directing Delacroix is doing is between Allie's legs."

"Can it, Natalie."

"It's true, though. They deserve each other."

Maxine sighed, laid her book aside, and picked up a sheaf of French papers, correcting them with ritual movements of a red pencil.

"Sorry if I bore you," I said.

Her eyes flashed. "You are beyond boring, kiddo. Y'r a royal pain in the ass."

I was flattened. "I don't need that, you know. I'm feeling bad enough about myself. Last Sunday Dad took me to the Modern Art. When we got home Mother was all freaked out. She's so crazy possessive I can't even go for a walk with my father anymore. She thinks we're trying to sneak off and sleep together. Honest! Maybe it's menopause. Maybe she's nuts. She's constantly picking on me. We went shopping at Bloomingdales and Mother insisted I buy a skirt — looked like cockroaches had made caca all over it. She keeps peeking over the dressing room door and announces: 'Natalie, how can you wear such holey underpants?' I'm ready to murder her. When I come out everyone is looking at me. Mother crowds into the cashier line right in front of some fat woman who starts yelling at her. Mother looks her up and down and says, 'I think you have a problem.' I walked out of the store like I'd never seen her before in my life."

Max shakes her head, smiling. "Y'r a true Jew, kiddo. Either kvetching or full of remorse. Such a nudnik."

I smoked. Max worked. She did everything passionately, generously. None of the pinchfingered stinginess with which Mother approached the shortcomings of Natalie Bach. I studied the room, trying to solve the mystery of the rest of her life: weekends off in Connecticut or with her bohemian friends. When I invited her to Mom/Dad's for Sunday brunch, she would offer me a remote smile and say, "I have my *other friends*, too, you know." Made me mad.

"How can you stand that?" I asked.

She looked up. "French is a wonderful language."

"Correcting all that stuff?"

"It's money. And I wish you would let me do it. *Ferme-la!*"

Opening a highbrow periodical, I tried to get into an article about U.S. advisors in Southeast Asia. "I doubt Liz will want me around much longer," I mumbled into the magazine. Max's pencil kept scratching. "It doesn't seem like I can make it anywhere." The pencil stopped.

"Move home, for Chrissake. So it's a bit rocky ... *c'est la guerre!* Don't blow family. It's a lousy beginning. Believe me, family is all you can finally trust in this world."

Me momentarily confused, nodding my head, then protesting: "You don't know anything about it. My brother Adam had to get away from them, too."

"So how many black sheep does one family need?" Her pencil began moving again. I felt grubby, wanting to shed off the past like an old skin. Afraid she'd get the impression I was sour about my life, when, actually, things were looking brighter.

"I just wanted to say, Miss Pearlman, it's too bad you never met Adam, because you would fall madly in love —"

She slapped down papers. "Natalie! you've got to go now. I have mucho work to do. *Va-t'en!*"

"What time is it?" I leapt up.

"You can't expect to camp on my doorstep whenever things are going badly at home."

"I know, I know ..." I kept dropping things in my rush to leave.

Max helping me into my coat, smiling forgiveness, kissing me. In the greasy dinnertime smell of the hallway, she said, "If you're selfish you can wear out your welcome." Me miserable, wanting to crawl like a roach into a crack in the wall. "That's not very flattering to yourself," I muttered. "I came 'cause I like to be with you."

"Goodnight, Natalie." She allowed the last syllable to lie on her tongue one suspended moment before flipping it off. I bolted bareheaded into a drizzle that penetrated with an instant chill. Along Central Park West, car lights shattered into numberless droplets, despair hissed in the loveless flight of tires.

As I came in, Kitty said she had put a warm plate in the oven. "Thanks, Kitty," I called, dropping jacket and books on the table and moving on through the kitchen. "Girl!" I turned. "I know your mama don't permit you do like that at home." "Just one phone call," I said. Kitty shook her head and turned back to the sink.

I stood over the phone in its nook, imagining Max off to visit her *other friends* the moment I had gone. Tried convincing myself there was some legit reason for calling — I had left a book! Jealousy a snake slithering under the dial tone. Just seven quick flicks of the dial — I couldn't do it. The receiver grew hot in my hand. *She's not a boy, dummy. You're not in love with her.* I slammed it down. Flattening back in the nook as Liz emerged from her bedroom — too late! She turned and focused, boozy-eyed. "What inna hell is this? Now she's screwing my telephone." Liz giggled. "Or mebbe you foun' some way to lay y'r boyfrien's long-dissance ... I always wanned to do that!" Limping off on her laughter.

Females. They make life miserable.

I stayed up late studying my lines for the play. It seemed the only role I was playing in my life that had any chance of success. At two, Kitty looked in, wearing the maroon nightgown that looked like a choir robe. "You sure got serious about studying all of a sudden," she said. I went to sit with her in the kitchen.

She sipped brandy, impeccable in her gown. An entity of self-assurance. Smug continent. She studied me, one eye near shut, as if aiming. "How old you are, honey?"

"Almost seventeen." I lit a cigarette.

"And you still a virgin? Lord God! Free, white, and seventeen and you still ain't been laid!"

"You make it sound like something shameful."

"That's egsactly what it is. You missing half the fun of being young. What the matter, honey? You ain't even got religion to mess you up."

"I've gone most of the way."

"Isn't no place to go. You can do it anywhere you got to, don't have to be licking a postage stamp on it and send it off somewheres." Her creaky laugh. Then she looked hard at me, a devil's advocate expression. "I never see you bring no boyfriends around here —"

"Karl Housman." I shrugged.

"Shooot!" She cried, and I laughed with her, stretching my arms, bringing them quickly down when she glanced at my armpits.

"I'm really not that interested in men right now."

"You just about to get interested, though. I smell it. Isn't Liz I'm smelling." She wiggled around in her chair. Snapped out a finger. "Don't just be giving it away, neither. That valu'ble stuff. Men think we got heaven between our legs, isn't nothing they won't do."

"I'm kinda scared —"

"Seventeen years old and you scared? Shoooot!" Shaking her head at the stereo — Aretha. "You don't be scared long. But you gotta go out. You won't have no trouble, you a goodlooking girl." She eyed me like a horse trader for my fine points — and frowned, pinching my frayed shirt hem in her fingers. "Why you want to dress like that for, honey? Nasty old work clothes. Men get the wrong idea when a woman dress like that."

I was becoming depressed, couldn't stand it when she got into this. I said I might be moving home soon. Her face fell, then recovered. "I got Rosita fired." Kitty clapped her hands. "Now that's good news." She disliked Rosita instinctively. I explained how Mom/Dad had been bugging me (probably because Adam would be leaving soon and they couldn't bear to lose us both). "Last Sunday Mother asked if there was any way they could coax me back. She said they missed me. Dad said, 'We do, Nattie.' "

" 'Course they do," said Kitty.

"I said I was considering it. Then Rosita comes in with coffee and her typical sneer. I look at her for the first time in maybe two months. She's digging at her teeth with a toothpick, doesn't even bother closing her mouth. Suddenly I have a brainstorm."

"Tell me about it," cried Kitty, eyes sparking little flares of revenge.

"I say I'd really like to move back. Mother says, 'Gee, honey, that's great.' 'On two conditions,' I say. Her mouth kind of drops. 'First, I want to be able to have my friends here — who I want, when I want.' Mother sighs. 'And second — ' I look straight at Rosita standing in the doorway 'cause she can always smell trouble '— I want you to fire that bitch, Rosita.' "

Kitty shouted a laugh. "You didn't, girl!"

I nodded. "Dad has a coughing fit into the *Times*, Mother's eyes blow up like goose eggs, Rosita just keeps working the toothpick. Then — here's what's amazing — she smiles. The first real smile she's ever given me.

"Anyway, I talked to Mother last night. She said they weren't happy with Rosita any longer. She's been giving lip, stealing liquor, the usual garbage. Like it was their idea to begin with. 'We're getting a new girl,' she said; 'I think you'll like her.' Except now I'm not sure I want to move home. Mother's impossible. I don't know what I want to do."

Kitty studied me — that eye-cocked, leery expression. "Tell me about this teacher you always carry on over," she said. "Miss Pearlman. You girls make fools of yourselves over that teacher. What she teach that you always over there to study?"

"French. She tutors me."

"I know she teach French. I just wonder how much French she planning to teach?"

The heat was too high, air jelling, sitting on the back of my eyes — a gravy of heat and despondency. Kitty's broad plantation of a face seeming to spread across the room, eyes narrowed to keen points.

"I don't want you to take this wrong, honey. You know, people beginning to talk about you."

A chill cut right through the heat. My hand crawled for a cigarette. "What do you mean?" I muttered.

"I mean the way you dress and always around that teacher. You never be fixing up, never be going out on a date. What's wrong, honey? Don't you know it wonderful to be a woman?" Her eyes worried preachers; I couldn't bear to look at them. *I don't know what she's talking about*, I told myself. But she continued. "I got a bad feeling about that teacher. She remind me of a woman when I was a girl. So friendly and nice; first chance she get, her hands all over me."

"It isn't true," I cried. "I thought you were my friend, Kitty."

"Girl, if I wasn't I wouldn't open my mouth to speak. Watch out for

older women, honey. They love the innocent ones." She touched my
fingers on the table. I stared at her strong hand — wrinkled as a reptile's
back — and snatched mine away.

"You're an older woman," I mumbled.

"Don't trust me neither then." Her voice gone sour.

At five, I stared at my haggard outline in the mirror: hair straggling
forlorn, eyes yapping at their twins like snappy little dogs. Any understanding I had attained of Natalie Bach shattered to pieces.

When I went in for breakfast at seven, Liz's puffy face came up from
her grapefruit. "You look like shit," she said. "What was going on in
there all night — all that muttering and fidgeting?"

"Leave the girl alone," snapped Kitty. "She got her period."

"Is that all? I thought she was molested by the air conditioner. She's
going to fuck every goddamn appliance in the house."

It was a fierce workout. Almost impossible to get a shot over Marty,
who dominated the key like an oak tree with branches spread. Creep
Colleen incessantly trying to steal the ball. She fouled me as I was going
in for a layup and I elbowed her stomach. From then on it was open
warfare. Fortunately, Andrea, the human string bean, was on my team.
She could lie on the floor and dunk the ball with her long arms.

I sat panting on the bench, watching Max lead modern dance troops
through tortures of splits and grotesque facial ballets on the far side of
the gym. Marty sprawled limp and wet on her back beneath me, eyes
closed, tits heaving like mountains out of a formless landscape. She gave
off the sour smell of old sneakers. The entire clique out there (dance
was *the thing* that fall): Libby in lavender, kicking legs up effortlessly,
folding suddenly at the waist, hair brushing the floor between her feet,
sugar brown skin glistening; Maxine's tights sweat-painted on, leaving
no secrets — she moved without a kink and they all followed like baby
geese; Zack bare-chested, muscles jumping up white leotard thighs,
producing a chain reaction in his bulging schmuck; beside him, Wallace Bean with his hollow chest; the Twits, Allie and Ellie, panting like
puppies, movements in perfect sync, their bodies identical — long legs
and pointy tits.

Max clapped her hands like a cheerleader: all gripped toes and
stretched legs up behind as though trying to tear themselves in two,
sweaty, and Zack's dingus bulging-heroic (if they're all that big I'm

gonna be in trouble!), Bantuing faces into preposterous masks. I started laughing. Maxine shot me a dirty look. My laughter was contagious: Lydia giggled and mimed their constipated expressions, braces flashing like salmon. "Woowie!" I shouted.

"Take five," Max snapped at the dancers. Panting, hands-a-hip, she hobbled over and dropped on the bench beside me. I started to speak; she held up a hand and worked on breathing, stretched out legs delicately, as if they might break, the soles of her purple tights caked with muck, nearly worn through at heel. Marty lay stone-still on the floor, looking dead. Across gym, cliquies formed a pack, staring over in anticipation.

"So why are you trying to ruin our session?" Max demanded.

"I just couldn't control my enthusiasm," I cried. "I mean, they dance with such . . . bravura."

Marty burped a laugh.

Maxine snapped soggy tights over her tummy, trying to cool off. Her mouth corners fell. "So how long does this grudge continue? I should get down on my knees maybe and beg?"

I glanced from her knees to my ugly kneepads. "Okay," I said.

Marty flopped over onto her stomach, shorts crinkled across the dumplings of her ass. Over there, the Twits had begun coaching each other — hands extended primly, as if to say *here's how it should be done*, tilting chins and tiptoeing through steps. Tireless Libby did back arches. Barney appeared, stripped his shirt and pranced about making muscles he didn't have to general hilarity.

"Have you ever noticed that Whitman boys look like TB victims? Sunken chests and chicken legs," I said.

Maxine cringed. "Shhhh, keep it down."

"Except Zack."

"What about Zack?" Her dark eyes filliping at him.

I whispered. "You can see his balls. That's why he's in the clique. Not big brain, big balls."

Max fell back laughing, nipples erupting through her leotard like Zack's gonads. The Bobbsey Twits traded wary glances. Zack leapt up to a bar and began doing chin-ups, bulge bulging with his biceps. We laughed even harder, ducking our heads.

Allie took control of the class. Firming lips in a thin line, she pushed out her chest and waddled elbows like a duck, counting out steps.

"So tell me, who's in this clique?" Maxine asked.

I swatted a hand at them. "Who cares? The Twits, Ellen, Wallace Bean, Barney, Karl, Libby — she's okay — Juli sometimes, creep Colleen —"

"Natalie sometimes?"

"Oh yes. I just love to stand around in the park smoking and competing to make the *bonest mot.*" Glancing across at them — the Twits' perfected indifference. "Radical people despise conventional people," I hissed.

Her eyebrows arching their backs. "I'm having a problem with all this anger I'm hearing."

"What's wrong with anger? Mother's shrink says it's healthy."

She slapped hands on knees and jumped up. Every cliquey eye snapping towards her like pop beads on a string.

It took three of us to peel Marty off the floor. I sank three quick baskets. Colleen was out for blood. She guarded me close, grunting, showing her white teeth and jabbing at the ball like a horsefly that won't bug off — greaser hair lying stiff on her head. (It was common knowledge that she lacked only a Y chromosome of being in the marines.) In desperation, I passed the ball to Lydia, whose method of catching was to close her eyes and open her mouth as if hoping to dazzle the ball with braces. She spasticated it! The ball vaulted and hit Ellie in the head. Like in a cartoon, her head bolted forward, sweat flew, then came back upright on her neck and she shook it like a lightbulb that might need to be replaced. A hand went in slow motion to her mouth, taking a smear of blood from her lip. She stared at it, then showed it around, first to Allie, then the others, then opened her mouth and bawled like a four-year-old.

Chaos. Everyone screaming, examining her cut lip, me running over, saying, really, how sorry I was; Colleen and Allie shouting I'd done it on purpose. I tried to explain, but Allie shrilled like an alto sax. "You're such a dipshit spastic." I glanced at Lydia for support. She grimaced and dodged behind Marty. "Really, it was an accident," I pleaded. Maxine squinted at me as if she wasn't sure. Ellie wiped blood from her lip with a Kleenex and stared at it in fascination. "An accident . . . an accident . . ." Allie taunted in her nasal voice. "Your existence is a bad accident, *Botch.*" Someone giggled. I gripped hard at reins of my anger; it was hopeless.

"Why don't you shut up!"

"Now now —" Barney shook a finger.

Allie's eyes puffed up. "Me shut up?"

"I said you." I edged closer. Allie grabbed the basketball, slinging it overhead as if she meant to throw it. "Just try it!" I warned. Barney shadowboxed: "Fight . . . fight!" We froze there. I didn't know what would happen. Her breasts heaved, nostrils flared, armpits were dark blotches. If she threw it, I knew I was going to jump her. Maxine stepped between us, taking the ball from Allie.

"That's enough, girls."

Ellie's eyes rolled like twin Lazaruses returning from the dead. I asked if she wasn't overdoing it a bit. Max told me to let it rest.

"She's acting . . . it's obvious."

"Just can it!"

I stalked off to the girls' locker room, sensing three dozen eyes coming in behind me. I turned up the water hot as possible, ignoring the others — giggling and making lewd allusions to one anothers' sex lives. Marty commiserating at the next spigot that they were a lot of assholes. Everything about her oversized: her mouth, knockers, battleship hips, and the deep-sea garden between her legs. The Twits soaped each other's backs, boosting forward in magazine poses, breasts jutting out like ice cream cones. They kept shooting me glances and followed me out when I left — passing Max going in, a towel sari'd across the swell of her breasts, a woman amongst girls. "Feeling better?" she asked. I didn't answer.

I stood at my locker, trying not to notice how they whispered and nudged each other, or the others forming tense little clusters at the corners of my eyes. I sat hard on anger — *Why don't they just leave me alone?* — felt it coil up like a growth in my stomach. I had a creepy feeling, like the time everyone started laughing at rehearsal. *Ignore them. What do they matter? Just a bunch of preppy rednecks.* Didn't even notice the odd heaviness of my bra until Ellie threw a hand to her mouth and I was slipping arms through straps and the soggy disgusting stuff already leaking from bra cups, dribbling down my stomach.

"SHIT —" I shouted, scooping up a handful and staring at pastel yellow pulp as Ellie had at her blood. Sopping wet toilet paper! the bra filled with it. Around me a birdriot of laughter. Allie offered a poison smile, and I heard her say, "We thought you needed a little padding." Then I was stepping over benches towards her, my voice squashing laughter.

"You have a problem, huh?"

She turned away as if she couldn't be bothered, boosting chest forward shower style to fasten her bra. I grabbed an arm and slung her around.

"I want to know what you've got against me."

Allie recoiled like I was a worm. She curled a lip. "Can't you ever control yourself?" For a moment we simply glared at each other. Then, in a slow, deliberate motion, I smeared the handful of mushy toilet paper in her face, slamming her back against lockers. Her eyes leapt to the top of their sockets like carnival gongs, bra hobbling arms beneath prima donna tits. She slid down the lockers a little and propped there, legs out straight, sputtering toilet paper.

"Just lay off, you understand?" I looked from Allie to wilted, terrified Ellie and pug-nosed Colleen, who made a gesture, but thought better of it. I was shaking. None of them said a word. Lydia, who had at times been the butt of their ridicule, had moved in close, mouth hanging open, braces glinting like a string of flashbulbs. "Leave everyone alone!" I turned away. The other girls cleared a respectful opening. Maxine leaned against a far locker, hair dripping from the shower, arms crossed. "Very nice," she said, nodding her head, wearing an expression that was neither reproachful nor amused.

Juli and I waited for her beside Old Walt. She came quickly down the school steps into afternoon sunshine, skin gone taut over her cheekbones. As she approached, I could feel her impatience. She scarcely acknowledged the quiet good-byes of passing students.

"It really isn't a good night," she said.

"Okay, forget it."

She motioned me aside, hair black-glistening in sunlight, eyes both warm and cold at once. "Don't be a schmuck," she whispered. "My life is very busy; I can't always be there for you."

"I said forget it."

Her eyes fell hard into mine. "Listen, I got no time for post-adolescent theatrics. Wha'sa trouble, Natalie?"

"I just wanted to talk." I tried looking elsewhere.

She sighed. "Isn't there somewhere else you can go for a shmooze? Your brother's maybe?"

"Oh sure. And listen to his lectures about being a Jew."

"What do you want me to say? I'm frazzled. Sometimes I need to get away from school . . . completely."

"I'm not *school.*" (Max's hands rose in a referee's gesture.) "Don't worry, I can take a hint. I won't be waiting for you after school anymore." I turned to Juli, who stared uncomfortably at the sidewalk. Max gripped my arm, eyes half-closed.

"You humiliate your enemies, you're elected team captain — how much do you need, kiddo?" When I didn't answer, she smiled and brushed a bang off my forehead. "Listen, y'r too possessive. It's not the way to go about it. I looked out my window this morning: there you were waiting on the bench across the street."

"No I wasn't," I cried, into the full ivory of her grin.

"C'mon," she said. "Friends come first, right? What've I got to do anyway . . . but write a lousy thesis?"

Autumn sunlight washed buildings on the north side of the street as if tossed from a bucket. We skipped along, bouncing imaginary balls that popped like magic into the blue net of the sky, past a derelict whose face wore the drugged expression of one who has been drowsing in the sun. He was pissy as a subway corner. "Pee-yew!" I yelped. Max chided, "That wasn't really necessary." I looked back at him — shuffling on, mumbling to himself — stung with something like shame.

We strolled bright Broadway toward the Babylon of midtown, past mini-parks and old men on benches, mouths hanging open, as if expecting salvation to ring up off the skyline like a cash register tab, or hang-head, drowning in eternal sleep. Max exuberant, a fat smile for Broadway and the wide world. "New York is where Dickens and Dostoevski would live if they were alive today," she said. "I know," cried Juli, double-stepping to keep pace. Some nuns passed, faces lamb white under black veils. I remembered how I got it wrong as a girl and always cried out: "Mommy, look at the *nuts!*" Around a corner ahead, a man appeared as if Max had conjured him from a Russian novel. He staggered, ambling towards shops, then slipping downhill to the curb, as if drunk or lacking control of his muscles. Not a walk really, a mechanical shuffle, originating in some cripplecorner of his brain, working down in spasms and jerks through his twisted body to the leg held stiff in a brace, which he flung furiously ahead like a hockey stick. Head bobbing loose-hinged upon its neck. A thermos, hooked in the crook of a finger, jerking to his staccato.

When he stopped to rest his forehead against a parking meter in a painfully slanted "h," an old woman in an ersatz leopardskin coat regarded him suspiciously, then turned her scandalized expression upon us. He looked up toward the next meter — young, but furrow-faced as an old man, viewing the world with the severity of Ahab. As we passed, he plunged ahead in his reckless dance on legs about to buckle beneath him, nerve fibers appearing to snap and crack around his head like raw little whips. Juli's fawn eyes — all of us — mesmerized; Maxine's gaze intent, as if helping to steady him. Emotions warred in me, revulsion against concern. "Isn't he disgusting?" I asked. "No," Max answered, "he's very brave."

A black kid strutted toward us on a gone-from-here stride, pants bells washing like ship decks around his ankles, shades for eyes. Seeing the little man, he spun on a heel. "Damn!" he said. Two dirty-faced little girls under a movie marquee giggled and mimicked his gait with moronic hang-tongue expressions.

We had passed and nearly forgotten him — as it is in the city of everyday tragedy — when someone screamed. The little man had stumbled out onto Broadway, legs floundering, arms waving before him, desperate to clear a path. He fell hard. A bus roared down on him like he was nothing, a bag someone had discarded. No time to consider, I leapt into the street, grabbing hold — shirt arms anywhere. He was heavy as the world. There was a shriek of brakes, a blackboard screech of leg brace across pavement, my own yowl for help — seeming from someone else, far away. I stumbled backwards, hands tangled in his clothes. The bus loomed, driver nearly overhead, feet spread wide like a man plummeting from a ten-story building. Max and Juli were beside me. Out of nowhere, a voice barked *"Damnation!"* And in one miraculous surge we were at the curb.

I looked up into flashing shades, the black kid shaking his head, releasing fistfuls of clothing from the deformed body, that seemed hunched now in infant sleep, head pillowed on the curb. "Damn," the boy said again, sucking air through his teeth. The bus driver extended hands through an open window and called in a gullish Caribbean accent, "Hey mahn, I c'n no be blame for dem drunk —" Horns swarmed in the blocked street. A taxi squeezed around the bus, cabby waving us away with both hands. Max bent over the motionless form. "Can you move?" she asked. "Dead!" decided an old woman's lips — wattles of flesh wagging from an out-thrust chin, cologne failing to mask the sour smell of old flesh. Was it possible? I stared down at the little fetus-man, lying as if asleep in gutter trash. His face revealed nothing more than stoical cheek hollows beneath beard stubble. Suddenly, his papery eyelids opened wide and he stared up at me. He began to writhe like a bug on its back, a midget wrestler arching from the shoulders; with a jack-knife snap, folded at the middle and sat up. Juli helped him to his feet. He teetered, self-sufficient again, checking right and left to see if his clothes were torn, then glancing at the cabby, nearly atop us, ramming both fists on the horn.

"Are you all right?"

Finding Maxine, he answered simply, "I'll make it."

"Your forehead is hurt," said Juli. He mopped at it with a sleeve, re-garded the little blood smear with indifference, then looked again to-ward the fury of horns — cabby screaming like a lunatic, his face a malevolent howl of yellow teeth. "Y'r sick," I screamed back at him, turning to the ring of curious jaws glazed in harsh sunlight, shut tight in an accord of apathy. "What's the matter with everyone?" I demanded of a middle-gray face in a three-piece suit. His eyes widened slightly and he walked away.

We helped the little man onto the sidewalk. The taxi scraped the curb as it shot past; bus let an ethery fart and roared off. He shook the thermos — incredibly, still hooked in the crook of a finger — jangled it violently, as if unable to accept the clatter of broken innards. Enormous anger filled his eyes. He shuffled to a subway grating and poured out a stream touched with slivers of light. A scent of lemons puckered the air. He replaced the cap and, without a word, thermos bobbing from his fin-ger, labored on as though he'd had no dealings with us.

Maxine turned to me, eyes aglow. "I never knew a hero before, I'm proud —"

"We're all heroes," I blurted, holding a huge smile inside.

"I'm proud of all of us." She hooked my arm and Juli's and started off at a brisk pace down the street.

On a bench nearby, an old man leaned forward, his troubled eyes settled on me. The two little girls with dirty faces, who only minutes before had mocked and mimicked, stood now abashed. A tension in their bodies suggested they might chase after the little man to see what would happen next. Instead, they ran lickety-split down a side street, their pale legs flapping up either side like wings.

CHAPTER FIVE

ADAM

EVERY VISIT TO ADAM AND RACHEL SEEMED LIKE THE SAME VISIT. I found myself in the East Village amidst round-cheeked, babushka'd Ukrainian women, lugging baskets and bags as if they had spent the night in hopeless migration. Turning the corner onto Bleecker, I passed a bakery with braided loaves of challah and a Star of David in the window and felt I had rounded a corner back into my heritage. Though just before knocking on the shabby door of my brother's apartment my heart sank, and I knew — like it was a role I'd learned perfectly — that my visit would be futile.

Adam opened the door. Typically unshaven, wearing an old T-shirt. He knew it was me; they had no other visitors. He didn't exactly smile, he let me in. Inside it was perennially dark. I can't remember any windows. A floor lamp threw a halo around a big leather armchair (the one extravagance), upon it a book with Hebrew script — which seemed to me less language than ancient, mysterious code. As usual, he had been studying. Elsewhere in the murk was a bed, kitchenette, a print of *The Lovers* by Marc Chagall (the one adornment). There was an odd smell, a bit like an old library, and everywhere, mixed amongst Hebrew and Jewish history texts, were periodicals with alarmist headlines proclaiming rising anti-Semitism in America. They had pulled a dense fog around themselves and moved like indefinite shadows; never going out — except Adam to the longshoremen's hall each morning to wait in a long line of other men for daywork. They gave little thought to the present, saving every penny for the life to come, moving with haste as if there weren't a minute to lose. I often left that apartment with a creepy feeling that I wasn't in America at all, but prewar Poland, barely resisting an urge to feel my sleeve for a yellow Star of David. Though came to see their immersion in darkness not as shtetlish fear so much as cocoonish waiting — one life being shed, the new not quite ready to emerge.

Rachel was a Midwestern Mormon, slim and plain, carrying about her a homespun solid quality, hair caught back in a ponytail. Something Old Testament in her, in a wood-whittled American way, as if any place — whether Israel or Iowa — where there is too much sun and distance there is likewise too much God. "Scratch an American from the God Belt and you'll find a Jew," Adam said of her, with his proud smile. Birdquick on her feet, always ready to serve others. And that smile, first with her eyes, then mouth much later. Willing to grow old honoring the decisions of a patriarch husband. She would smile and say, "It makes life simpler for me." Dad blamed their introverted life on her, insisting, "That witch Adam married is medieval." But I knew it was Adam's inability to do anything halfway. He had given up jazz piano completely, saying, "Jews can't afford to waste time." A total fanatic.

I came to eat Rachel's chicken soup (mastery of which, she'd learned, is the first step in becoming a Jewish wife), rich in floating fat globules, and to discuss my plans to go into theatre, maybe art. When I finished, my brother would scoot forward and begin speaking precisely, as if I were still the ten-year-old girl beside him on the piano bench. There are two ways to live, he said: you can be a drone, obedient to what's expected of you, or you can take life in hand like clay and make what you want of it. I stared back into his eyes, blue as a desert sky, nervous, but

very excited. The hard part is knowing what you want, though I didn't
dare suggest this to my brother.

There are big gaps in Adam's *curriculum vitae* — pieced together
from Rachel's hushed recollections, a few letters. There was the West
Village time: playing jazz piano in smoke-filled nightclubs at eigh-
teen — marijuana and sex and cocaine and disgust soon with all that.
He bummed west, worked on a cattle ranch, saw himself as a Jewish
Walt Whitman. He won a scholarship to Stanford, but after just two
terms sent home one of his succinct notes to Mom/Dad from Palo
Alto:

Going to boot camp in California. Be home in six weeks.
                                                              ADAM

It was like he wanted desperately to take life by the throat, but
couldn't get a grip on it.

While stationed in Düsseldorf he met Pavel. In snapshots, Pavel always to the side, hollow-cheeked and sickly, with sallow, translucent
skin and liquid Kafkaish eyes, an inward Orthodox air about him. Ear-
locks and yarmulke seeming antithetical to his uniform. Strange that
this fragile man could have been the major influence in my brother's
life. Broad-shouldered Adam with his John Wayne jawline clenching
small teeth in a smile beside him.

Like Adam, Pavel quit college to join the army, telling his rabbi father that the Jews had enough rabbis; they needed warriors. Adam must
have seemed a great opportunity to him. One year just before
Christmas, we received word that Adam wouldn't be coming home on
leave. He was accompanying Pavel on a pilgrimage.

Mother took his letter straight to Dr. Sternberg. "We're planning
wonderful holidays. We invited Rachel up from college — and you
know that Jacob can't stomach the girl! — and Adam wants to tour
concentration camps with that Zionister golem, Pavel!" Sternberg
thought it healthy for an American boy to want to see what had become
of his European antecedents. "You've always been indifferent about
your roots, Zilla," he said. "Jew . . . schmoo! But it's not necessarily an
admirable attitude." Later, Mother complained that Sternberg was becoming a radical and threatened to find another shrink.

I remember a snapshot of Adam beside a small grim road sign: "Belsen." Eyes hollowed by sleeplessness, dazed, as if he had just stepped off one of those boxcars behind him. Then came letters that disturbed even Dr. Sternberg: *Eichmann was not in an Israeli prison, he was selling ties in a haberdashery in Bonn, pumping gas in Bremen, and Adam had seen him sitting in a Brauhaus in the little city of Regensburg with beer running down his chin.* Twice he had picked fights with German civilians. His unit, he said, was riddled with anti-Semitism. "A Jew should trust only fellow Jews is Pavel's advice," he wrote, "and I think he's right."

Mother raged about this "Pavel babble." "I don't see how Adam can go along with it. He's a leper, this Pavel character." Dad assured her the army just had him nervous.

When it was finally discovered that Pavel had leukemia it was too late to save him. Adam helped place his friend's shriveled body on the plane that would take it home to Brooklyn. Afterwards, he threw himself into his work, writing long letters to Rachel, whom Dad had already dubbed "that witch from Wisconsin . . . or is it Iowa?"

Then, while anticipating his imminent discharge and arrival in New York, we received another of his terse notes, informing us that he had flown to Israel and surrendered his American citizenship to the consul in Tel Aviv, fulfilling a promise he had made to Pavel to help achieve the dream of a Jewish state — for both of them.

But it was soon obvious from letters — now addressed only to me, since Mom/Dad refused to communicate with Adam until he returned to his senses . . . and the USA — that something had gone wrong. For the first time in his life, Adam was having trouble with a language. Strange sibilants and gutturals tangled his tongue. Mother, always greedy to read his letters over my shoulder, dismissed it with a wave of the hand. "He's homesick," she said.

Adam wrote:

Israelis are a thorny breed, tenacious as desert scrub clinging to crevices at Masada. Israeli-born are called sabra, *after the prickly pear and its fruit encased in a thorny hide. I have not yet discovered the tender heart said to be hidden inside. I am jostled and elbowed in markets and bus lines. Sly old* saftas *are not above jabbing me in the balls.*

I have taken to walking desolate expanses north of the Old City, beyond Damascus Gate, along wadis forming a no-man's-land between East and West Jerusalem. At times I encounter Israeli gun emplace-

ments and patrols that warn me away. I have discovered a place where I can peer down at walls of Old Jerusalem, and I believe if I could get down there and stand at the Wailing Wall I might have a clearer understanding of my duty here. That is impossible. . . .

I come in dismay upon a roadblock where Jewish soldiers stop and search Arab cars, insulting occupants and shoving them about with rifle butts. Once (I hesitate to write this to my sister) I saw a Jewish soldier pull a Palestinian woman from a car by her skirt, raising it to the amusement of his buddies. I ran over, shouting, "We aren't Nazis." The soldier trained his carbine on me, but I slapped it away. Perhaps he thought I was a dignitary, for he began apologizing in perfect English. He was an American from the Bronx. You see, even we Jews find Jews of our own to kick around.

Adam's sleep was restless. He despaired of learning Hebrew and quit his studies at the *ulpan,* traveled south to Elat, north to Akko. "Such a tiny country," he wrote, "I must duck my head and turn around cautiously. Nowhere can you get more than a stone's throw from an enemy. Beaches are beautiful but tar-clotted. Girls in the skimpiest bikinis — wow!"

His final letter was from a place called Rehovot:

I am working the orange harvest. I sleep in fields a small distance from where a group of Arab transients have a fire and lie listening to the warble of their strange tongue, wondering what they are debating so fiercely. Maybe whether to murder the dirty Jew over there. They dispute nonstop. Each has his sovereign opinion, much like the Jews, who've formed a separate party for every Knesset member. They are good neighbors. Each morning one of them pours me a thick cup of Turkish coffee from the pot over their fire. So you see, there is hope for Israel.

Adam returned to Jerusalem and, within weeks, arrived quite unexpectedly in the States. It was some time before I learned what had happened.

In Jerusalem he had slept on park benches, not able to afford a room. Not knowing what to do next. Seeing an Arab beggar one day with flies eating his eyes, lacking strength to brush them away, Adam became terribly depressed. Could this be Pavel's dream? Maybe he had gotten off the plane at the wrong place. Wandering in King David Park, at very bottom, he decided to return home. He would go into PapaBach's business, marry some Park Avenue ophthalmologist's daughter who would wear MamaBach's designs, vacation in the Catskills, and participate in all the other liturgies of assimilation that he despised. Life was the dream spoiler.

No, he would kill himself.

From amidst other belongings in a locker at the Y, he took a pistol he had bought from a soldier with most of his harvest earnings. At the time he'd thought it a whim, but now it was obvious why he had bought the gun. As he walked toward his favorite post above the Old City, with the gun tucked under his shirt, he passed a bench where an old man raised a cane just perceptibly from its perch between his knees and said, "Sit here, ben Yaakov."

Adam stared at the old Israeli in the dusk, wearing the black caftan and fur-rimmed hat of the Orthodox. He was imagining things.

"Adam ben Yaakov —" the man smiled, using the Hebrew name which Adam had been reluctant to use.

"Do I know you?" he asked.

The old man tapped fingers on the bench and began speaking. To consider taking your life is nonsense, he said. Pavel had been right: Israel is where Jews should live, and it would need young men like him to survive. He reached forward to grasp Adam's biceps in bony fingers. "Like a bull!" he smiled. Then shook a finger. "Strength to defend, never to persecute. You have seen how our soldiers abuse the law. *Our righteousness is as a filthy rag.* Wisdom is greater than strength, ben Yaakov. Never forget."

Adam stared at him, astonished. Could he have mumbled his plans aloud in passing? It was possible. Then, with a shock, he realized the old man spoke in Hebrew. "Why shouldn't you understand?" The sage smiled again. "This is also your language." He instructed Adam, now dumbstruck, to "return home and marry the girl you love." "Better a righteous Gentile than an indifferent Jew. Learn and prepare, ben Yaakov. Then you will return." He rose on his cane and tapped away into the night.

Within a week of returning to the States, Adam had convinced Rachel to marry him and emigrate to Israel. Considering his loud arguments with Mom/Dad late into the night — me slamming my door so they'd know I couldn't sleep — I can imagine what Rachel faced with her Mormon parents back in Iowa. They tried bribes, mentioned a possible house for Adam and his bride on Long Island, while he chain-smoked Lucky Strikes and said they were making it impossible for him to honor the fourth commandment, finally shouting that he didn't want their fucking money, only their blessing. Mother told him they couldn't give it, and he stormed out, insisting Israel was all the family he needed. They all wanted to strike a bargain of duty and love, but no one could find it.

Adam waited beside Old Walt, broad-shouldered, tan and almost boyish, wearing a frayed T-shirt and jeans nearly worn through at knees. I was going home with him to prepare a surprise birthday dinner for Rachel, who was working at the nursing home. He tiptoed up — as if not tall enough already — and tentatively waved a hand. I ran back to find Maxine, crying that this was her big chance to meet my brother.

He cocked eagerly forward as we emerged, a gesture reminiscent of Mother, lips forming a tight, uncertain line, looking with his sun-bleached hair more like a sturdy Ukrainian peasant than an American Jew about to migrate to Israel. They shook hands almost shyly. "Your sister is quite a fan of yours," Max said. My laugh turned into a blush. Adam's chin puckered, eyes hopping sideways at her; I knew what he was thinking. Christ! what a knockout. He seemed overcome with adolescent awkwardness, not knowing what to say. "I understand you're a jazz fan," she said. "So am I."

Adam relaxed a little. "Who do you like?"

"Oh, Eric Dolphy, Coltrane —"

"Thelonious Monk?"

Her eyes grew wide. "Wow! a mind reader, too."

Adam shrugged. "You're the Monk type. After a while you can tell."

"Adam has his own group," I interjected.

"Had!" His eyes snapped. "I don't have time for that now."

Maxine met his seriousness. "What's now?"

"I'm going to Israel —" gesturing down his chest as though his clothes were testimony: kibbutzim, another way of life.

"Sounds exciting. Courageous."

"It's kind of a dream of mine."

I stared at him, astonished. This wasn't the brother who never revealed emotions. Together they were playing a whole keyboard of charm. I felt like three's a crowd. Maybe I should drift off with the passing kids — who glanced at Adam as if he were from another planet. Max mentioned a group of friends who jammed together Saturday afternoons. "We could use a good piano."

Adam brought out the small pearls of his smile. "Who said anything about piano?"

"Heard it from a fan." Max nodded at me.

"You never invited me to your jam sessions," I sulked.

"How do you know I'm any good?" Adam asked, playing the gallant, a role I thought alien to him.

"You're good. After a while you can tell."

Their eyes held. Color oozing under his tan, bringing up bronze. She half-smiled. He shook off the mood, tautening lips and looking away. "I don't have a piano now." His tone flat and final.

"We do. It'll be a chance for you to play again."

"I'm out of practice."

"All these excuses! You're as bad as your sister." She laughed; then Adam, a short shuffling giggle. A miracle: Adam laughing. Incredibly, he threw an arm around my shoulders. "I might make it," he said. "Once!"

"I hope so. Listen —" touching his arm "— I have students waiting. But I'll see you . . . okay?" They shook hands with a rapid, artificial formality, Max trying to catch his eyes, which were focused almost bashfully on the ground. With a wink, she touched a kiss to my forehead and ran off. Adam watched her move up the steps. As he reached to take some of my books, he seemed troubled, his good mood spent.

"Will you go?" I asked, feeling oddly depressed.

"No," he said sharply. "I'm finished with all that crap."

CHAPTER SIX

ULYSSES

$\mathbb{D}$AD AT THE MINI-BAR POURING DRINKS AS I ENTERED THAT SELF-conscious atmosphere of glass and off-white, warmed by vying fragrances of Scotch and the turpentine on his painting smock. He wore a distant smile, beyond distraction, in that artist's realm of profound detachment. Mother and I discussed *The Crucible* — Salem Village and witchcraft, which fascinated both of us. Maria, the new maid, passed through with a shy smile. She was Rosita's opposite, quiet and self-effacing and so plain I wondered how much Mother had surmised of Rosita's flirtations. "She's really a sweet woman," I said. Mother's eyes trailed her. "I just wish she would talk a little. I keep coming across her mumbling over those rosary beads." Hunching her shoulders. "It gives me the willies." I sighed. Dad fidgeted the smock over his knees and slurped Scotch like a small boy. Mother asked if I'd given any more thought to colleges.

"I'm still just a junior, Mother; why should I worry about college? I don't even know if I'll make it through high school."

Dad chuckled. Mother said I should learn to plan ahead. "Mills in California is a good school."

"Mills —?" An impression of WASP blonde Allies seated primly in short skirts and knee sox, hair forming yeasty buns atop identical round heads. I went across to the *Britannica* on the bookshelves. *MILLS COLLEGE, Oakland, California. Established 1852 as a young ladies' seminary. . . .*

"What do you want me to study, Mother, Immaculate Conception?"

Humorless, she struck off on her fingers the ducks already dead: Vassar, Skidmore, Sarah Lawrence, Smith.

"Isn't this something she should decide for herself, Zoe?" Dad asked in an ambassador's tone.

"Natalie can't decide where she wants to go to school."

I corrected her. "You mean where *you* want to go to school."

She squinched her lips, reluctant to fight, afraid I might leave home again. Me back in the nest just a week now and patience already ragged between us. Mother and daughter like two cloths beaten and chafed together. Nothing ever changes, despite all our heady resolutions.

Dad poured them another Scotch. Ice cubes clinking in glasses with a happy-go-lucky sound that wasn't convincing. He removed the painter's smock and sat on a lip of the couch in tie and gabardine slacks with crisp creases, which he pinched obsessively. A succinct white part, dividing his hair down one side, lent the impression of a middle-aged fraternity boy. "College is a wonderful time, Natalie," he said, gazing into dreamy distances. "The best time of our lives." His eyes sidled at Mother, who regarded him suspiciously, for she hadn't been to college.

"I'm not even sure I want to go," I said. "Why should I? To become a schoolteacher or a dental hygienist? Maybe I'm not in such a hurry to give up my dreams like everyone else."

"Do you know what she's talking about?" Mother asked.

"I'm talking about Israel and painting naked Polynesians in Tahiti . . . or maybe becoming a second Joan of Arc."

She paddled a wary, baffled look between Dad and me, curling her upper lip a little as you might at a growling dog.

"I want to live *life*, Mother. Not some middle-class soap opera."

She waved a weary hand at me and said I was beginning to sound like my brother.

"Maybe it's a whole generation."

Mother sighed. "I wish we could just decide about college."

Dad proposed we drop it for now, offering me a tense smile. Uncomfortable in the role of arbitrator between his warring women.

"I've only been home a week, and Mother is already hassling me about where I'm going when I leave. Really makes me feel welcome, you know."

"We're delighted to have you," he crowed. "I think we should go to Chantilly tonight and celebrate." Beaming at Mother.

"It's okay, Dad. I know *you* are happy."

Mother stared at the green glass lip of the coffee table. "I don't think that's fair, Nattie."

They drank. I looked out at the drizzly city, restless rain streaking windows, and sighed. "Think I'll go out. I hate rainy days." Mother wondered if I would ever finish unpacking my things, as if I'd already gone. Dad's conductor's hands patted pianissimo on the air. "Nasty out there," he suggested.

"Climate in here ain't so great either."

He chuckled. She asked where I was going. I shrugged, stopping at the closet for my jacket. "Tell Maria not to hassle dinner for me. I'll pick something up."

Mother's eyebrows hitched high up her forehead. "I wish you'd tell me. This is still New York, you know." Reluctant to issue an ultimatum. I preferred her old style. It was written all over her face anyway, like a case of sour stomach. I volunteered something about basketball practice, a cast party later on.

"A busy life." Dad smiled. "Going to visit Lydia?"

"God . . . Lydia!"

Assaulted last night on the subway. Three girls came up behind, threw her onto the floor and beat her unconscious, while passengers escaped the car from both ends — emptied it! Like rats escaping a burning warehouse. Beanpole Lydia — braces and blush of eager innocence, guilty of nothing more than being born to a family of "haves" (Maybe that's crime enough?) — versus scowling black hatred.

I said I'd like to bring her something. Dad fished a bill from his wallet. A fat one. "Something from all of us," he said. I told them I really didn't care about basketball practice anyway. I had only wanted to see Maxine. Mother slid me an utterly suspicious glance. Dad's smile a cod that had come up from deep water with no business on dry land.

"How goes the French?" he asked.

"*Bon. On y travaille.*"

Nearly dark, streetlights throwing oily light when I knock on Adam and Rachel's door. It opens and light floods out into the areaway, for a moment I think I have come to the wrong apartment. Rachel is alone, delighted to see me. A dress pattern across the bed, material for an entire new wardrobe stacked on the kitchen table — bright, sunny colors. She makes tea and we talk idly, a bit of the Rachel-without-Adam peeking through. A loneliness huge as the Great Plains. "How are Mom and Dad?" she asks, her needle working deftly in and out of a button. I shrug and ask about Adam.

Her head comes up. "Didn't you know? He jams at your friend's on Saturdays. I'm happy about the jazz for him. He needs it." Clutching her arms to illustrate tension. "I wanted to thank you for arranging it, Natalie."

"It wasn't really my idea."

She looks at me, bewildered. "I thought so —"

"I mean . . . it kind of was."

"I'd like to meet your friend." Rachel smooths back her straight hair, an unaccustomed cattiness in her voice. "She sounds like an unusual person."

"What does Adam say about her?" My interest piqued.

A sharp little laugh. "You know Adam, not much about people."

"You should go with him some time and play flute."

"I'm not invited." Then quickly, "I can play flute any old time." Looking up into the lamp, she closes her eyes, skin stretching over her cheeks in a taut smile, light catching hard edges of her face. "Next spring . . . in Israel!"

Adam arrives as I am leaving, sweatshirt rain-pasted to shoulders, hair sprawled like a drowned cat over his head. He isn't happy to see me. Conjuring my super-serious expression, I tell him I'm thinking of getting my own apartment. He pulls off the sweatshirt and begins chinning himself on a bar in the kitchenette doorway. Clipped words coming out between huffs. "You expect me to say that's great or something?" I shrug and light a cigarette.

"How's the jazz going?" I ask.

Adam's feet land flat on the floor. "What jazz?"

"Maxine's group. Rachel said you've been going . . ." My voice trailing off, I looked back and forth between them.

His eyes and forehead bulge as if he might seize us and ram our heads together. Without a glance at Rachel, he plods to the bathroom door, presses palms against doorjambs and heaves like Hercules. "I study at the library Saturday."

"I thought you played piano —" Rachel's voice a whisper.

"Once —" he spins on her, eyes fierce "— I played jazz piano." The sound of a palm slapping his bare chest clings a moment to the walls, leaving a dreary silence.

I feel awful — my fat mouth. After a time, Rachel turns to me with her sad smile. "I'd better get going," I mumble, taking the last of the cigarette and glancing at Adam who consumes his in quick, angry drags.

"I'm really sorry," I whisper, kissing Rachel's cheek as she hands me my coat.

"Be careful out in that jungle," she says, patting my shoulder as I go out.

In the drizzle again, starting for the IND line. Black toad of a night. Adam comes flying out behind me, bare chest glowing. For an instant I panic, consider running. Then he is on me — the whites of his eyes. Words chopped short. "Tell your friend to stop bothering me. I'm getting out of this fucking country. Tell her I've left that crap behind." He swivels on a heel and returns to the apartment, bare feet kissing wet pavement, leaving iridescent footprints against the dark sidewalk. I start off blindly, bumping into things as I go.

Down into the drippy steaming underground world, air thick with unhealthy exhalations — shared by man and machine — pasty sublunar light and damp walls, hissing snaketangles of graffiti. What tonight, sick city? My eyes slide past other passengers, that eye-evading dance to the bump-lurch of the train, blink with fluorescent lights over a track weld. I lean back into the bump-a-bump stutter of movement, vague, incessant comings and goings as the city rearranges itself. Forever uprooted. Faces — Oriental, Hindu, Teutonic, Latino, Ethiopian — jostling in uneasy peace, finding common interest only in adverts overhead. A clash of body odors. I close my eyes. Head on into guilt . . . or rage. Why do I blow it every time I open my mouth? *Is it my fault that it's a disease to be honest?* The train lurches, leaving me a sudden trenchant memory of that creep with a gold tooth I used to see riding home from school. Once he sat right beside me and lifted the scudsy surgeon's smock he always wore, revealing hairy legs and yellow women's panties stretched sheer over his big coiled thing. The Great Slime and Cockrot Express, Carol calls it. Old farts with Saint Bernards' eyes fondling themselves. On rush hour mornings some Mr. Narrow-Striped Tie and Button-Down Collar pretending to read his paper while thrusting his frustration into my teenage ass. Hopelessly, I fight retreat through cozy indifference, reading its *Daily News.* That big lie called "humanity." Subways, true realm of the Bellybutton Monster.

Hey kid! you can feel good about yourself. On the way to cheer up a friend in the hospital. I imagine Lydia: face swollen, one puffy livid eye creeping beyond its bandage, lips turned inside out, not pleasant, lying cheek down on the pillow, staring at my knees as I present the two pound box of chocolate creams. "Wha'd you get 'em for? I can't eat 'em," she mumbles woefully. Me quacking like a Chaplin-footed doctor, throwing Kleenex parachutes and gauze streamers across the ward, while she stares straight ahead, morose. Something about Lydia that makes you want to slug her.

Someone farts nearby, a sickly sweetness that blends with gravel in the conductor's voice, announcing stations: "Forty Second Street/ Grand Central!" I am off the train — not on my way to Mt. Sinai and Lydia after all, but taking the shuttle to the West Side. Later, walking up Broadway, I pass a Szechwan restaurant and rub, desirous, at Dad's twenty in my pocket — chalky, accusatory; if I want to eat, I must spend it. Thinking, as I enter the restaurant, I will call Lydia. It's almost the same thing.

Barely time to consider the menu before a face is smiling down, pencil poised on pad. I want to relax, I explain. He motions at customers lined up like livestock at the door (they enter, are smiled, teaed, served, chopsticked, fortune cookied, and exited). I am annoyed. He throws me a dark smile and disappears. I consider the phone up front, boxed in by the crowd — a face like Lydia's, peevish and gleaming with silver. A woman slaps down a teapot. Tomorrow, when there are ten billion of us, life will be one big Chinese restaurant. But the food won't be as good. That phone seems as far away as Mt. Sinai Hospital.

A second waiter, gray at temples, asks if he might take my order . . . *please.* "I haven't decided yet." I glower. His book flaps closed. He signals a couple from the crowd and invites me out with a curt bow. I can't believe this. I drop my napkin over an outstretched arm and exit past a Chiang Kai-shek torture squad in white linen jackets. My replacements smile. He wears a mohair sweater; she, a Cosmo face and tits like two large olives.

I hadn't wanted to eat alone anyway. I have enough for two.

I pause undecided before a subway entrance. There is still just enough time to visit Lydia. Facing me, at a newsstand, a bright Kennedy smile, promising the world an end to Old Fogyism. I think of Maxine, whose JFK fetish equals Kitty's. On the back page, Caroline is seated on her pony, Macaroni — America! where every good thing becomes a gluttony. Front page headlines:

KENNEDY HOPEFUL ABOUT NUCLEAR TEST BAN TREATY

My eye is caught by a smaller article: *Advisors seeking to dissuade the President from a swing through Texas, where, last week, Adlai Stevenson was manhandled by a hostile crowd in Dallas. . . .*

I hurry on, past a bank of phones, leaving Lydia behind.

Glancing back over a shoulder, I slip into Maxine's foyer and ring the buzzer. A voice explodes from the speaker.

"Who dat? Dat you, Daudert? You black bastard."

"It's me . . ."

"Who the hell is *me?* That you, Paynor?"

"It's Natalie."

"Nat-a-lie —" the voice nasals. "Hey, Mama Brodie, your star student is here. The girl with the sweet ass!"

Heels click across room. "Shut up, Richard."

A maniac laugh. "Owwwahhh . . . let me get my teeth into that kid's rumpus." I consider fleeing. The speaker goes dead, then on again. Max's voice is even, predictable:

"Hi Nat. Hey! this really isn't a good time —"

"I have to talk to you."

"Maybe tomorrow, huh? I have friends in. Okay?"

The speaker goes dead. I buzz again, no answer. The bitch.

As someone leaves the building I duck in. Inside Max's door, low voices and laughter. I falter, indecisive between fear and determination.

My visits to her always uncertain pilgrimages — her kinky friends and shifting moods, odd moments of distraction, as if she's forgotten I'm in the room. The door opens immediately after I knock. A lanky, intense man with sharp, somehow cynical features and wire-rimmed glasses perched on the curved spine of his nose mock bows. "Welcome, love, to the den of utter iniquity. I'm Richard."

"Shut up, Richard."

She means it this time, makes scurrying motions at sea creatures afloat in murky shallows of the room. Their stalk-eyes, aglow in candlelight, follow me voraciously. Something in the sticky closeness of the air, bitten with marijuana, suggests they have been furiously screwing and haven't bothered washing themselves.

"This is Natalie . . . my student," Max announces in an ironic tone, met by an ungenerous titter. I cringe at her tight-lipped smile, humiliation a gorge in my throat. Richard throws an arm around my shoulder. He reeks of garlic and tobacco. "My *star student!*" He leers, eyes bloodshot and blissfully depraved behind granny glasses. I am repulsed. And strangely excited.

They have soon forgotten me. Maxine's bohemians. Artists and unemployed intellectuals who regard their noncalling as the one legitimate calling. My eyes adjust to bluish gloom between yellow halos of candlelight. Sand sharks loll on backs and bellies in shallow water at my feet, scraping thick hides together in argument, led by a red-bearded fat man who discourses on the Cuban missile crisis. A slim blonde woman sits beside him on an arm of the couch, skirt tented far up thighs. Her mouth corners stretch downward, almost scornful — an expression which seems oddly familiar. "Power trips, Jerry," she says. "No matter who lays them down."

"You got it." His stubby index finger taps her bare knee. "And we better have a president who's damn good at them or we got trouble up the wazoo."

Richard produces a thin yellow cigarette, lights up and inhales greedily, then passes it to me. Max steps between us. "Absolutely no!" she says, pushing the joint away.

"I've smoked," I insist.

"Not in my apartment you haven't."

"Great friend you are. I came to invite you out to dinner." But Max's attention is suddenly elsewhere. I turn, sensing dogfish eyes watching us.

"How can I rap intelligently with a chick who just wants in his pants, for shitsake?" Mr. Fat demands of a dark, large-busted Jewish woman, who shakes her head, repeating, "John Kennedy is a humanitarian, not a Machiavelli . . ." He finger-drums now on the taut skin of the blonde woman's skirt. While she glares at me like a bad-mannered child, crossing her arms in a shivering gesture.

Confused, I try a smile.

Richard bends low, leaking smoke from nostrils. "It's theatre," he says in a raspy voice, "Jackie and the Nasal Tones." Straightens up, disposes of them with a wave of the hand: "Fucking politicos."

In my bewilderment — between Richard's flirtations and the blonde's hostility — I ask about the jazz group. "Defunct," he snaps. "Some dude came in on keyboard, showed us up so bad I haven't touched my horn since." He frowns at Max, who has taken flight across room. I recall the message Adam asked me to deliver, but mutter, "I really don't know anything about it . . . ," wishing I could believe that.

Then he has taken the burning end of the joint in his mouth; he bends over the blonde woman, hands resting on her naked thighs, and exhales slowly, seductively swaying shoulders, filling her up with smoke, while his hands slide under her tented skirt. I gape. Max touches my shoulder and motions me to follow.

In shabby hall light her eyes snap. "Always call first —"

"I've always come. I never called first."

"Just do it. These people aren't for you."

"Am I too embarrassing? *My student!*"

"You are my student, Natalie." She ducks back inside, features hard. "I need a little room for myself. Do it for me. Okay?" Leaving me with a peck on the forehead, a closed door, peeling wallpaper of the landing. I pummel #3-B with a soft fist, kick and shout until all is silent inside. Then limp away.

I wander vaguely downtown — streets abandoned, foreboding. Find myself, with a little thrill of fear, on Columbus Avenue. Loneliness stains walls in dark misshapen blotches, slides down to stalk me, forlorn streetlights glisten on wet pavement. My footsteps echo, instincts scream: *Got to have a destination*. Throw feet straight ahead, through this outback of strangers. I escape no-man's-land for Broadway. Down the city's spinal column, past Greek spoons and wino eyes. Safety in crowds, even mongrel crowds of urban half-breeds, central casting from half-remembered dreams. Castoffs like me. Wind penetrates my jacket and I shelter in a coffee shop. Sit through a movie until conscience grabs my nose like a nasty aunt and I rush out to phones in the lobby. Too late to call Lydia. Hours too late. I continue downtown, half relieved, half remorseful, past long-necked cranes looming over Lincoln Center, sullen and Lydia-like.

Down a long subway ramp lights flicker torchlike across urban cave scrawlings. I stand straight-backed on the near vacant platform. Emptiness is deadly in this town. Mother's first commandment: *Thou shalt not ride the subway alone at night.* My eyes scamper like mice amidst garbage between the tracks, slice at a subway troll sitting on urine-stained pavement, filthy dress frowzed up bruise-blue thighs, her pitted face with its huge beak in constant animation. Life has been reduced to this: humans competing with rodents for pizza rinds. Though maybe they serve another, higher, calling: pointing a finger at passersby, cursing us for regarding ourselves so highly. Like the blind pencil vendor on Eighty-sixth Street, pricing souls by what they drop in his tin cup. Mine not worth a nickel till I stopped and dropped in a quarter. Then he smiled and said I would go to heaven.

Down-platform a couple cuddles under a single poncho. Village types. The woman has that bleach-blonde straight-haired "blowin' in the wind" look — tight jeans, knee-high boots. The man sports a goatee, which brings his lean sharp face to a perfect point. They talk and laugh loudly, as if all the world is a stage. But I am glad they are here, and when the light comes fast-jiggling down its corridor I follow them into a car.

Bump-jostle of the train like the rocking of a memory ship. A start of recognition as I catch my reflection in the window across, leaping subway stanchions: hopeless dimples and tender little lights, mouth that can't keep shut, need that won't fill up, gifts neither purchased nor delivered. Maxine finds it a nuisance. How can I blame her? The air is gritty under my clothes, foul tasting. That face . . . ugh! If only I could scratch it off and toss it under the seat. Look quickly around: Village couple giggling under the poncho. A black dude puzzles down as if seeing his own reflection between his feet, rainwater jewels nestled in raffia hair.

The face floats free. I smile; it smiles back. Shy. Not so bad looking. Not beautiful in the way that catches its reflection off men — thank God! Too serious . . . *for a woman.* Eyes gigantic. They could swallow the world in one gulp. "Zealot eyes," Max calls them. In the lights of a station graffiti screams a warning. For one awful moment I see Lydia's head on the floor. My heart bumps. It's only the bag of a man who came on last stop. Sweat crawls under my blouse.

The face floating again, eyes drooping in a trance of movement. I stick out my tongue at it; it sticks back. I look up, startled, at the Village couple, who laugh and ogle me. He says something and she titters, almond eyes sidling at me. A chill grabs my shoulders. It's been a lousy night, a night of betrayal. But I am going to change. No more opening my fat mouth at the wrong moment. No more Lydias disappointed in hospitals.

Lisping noises insinuate down the aisle. The goat man is doing obscene things with his tongue, his eyes fixed on me like small demented flowers, while he strokes and fondles his beard. Screw him! I swear if he comes close I'll kick him in the balls. Her too.

The train slows at Fourteenth Street and the black kid moves to the door. The goat man regards me with satisfaction, like a fisherman sizing up a trout in his net. At the last instant, just as doors are closing, I spring from the train behind the black kid. The goat man's face lurches away in the window: an Oooo of surprise.

I stand a minute on the platform, eyes shut tight. This foul, desecrated city. If only that next train could carry me down under the ocean and away — for good. It stops too soon. Somewhere in the rocky toe of the island. *Mannahatta* . . . no wonder the Indians sold it so cheaply.

From an advertisement, a doctor waggles his stethoscope at me, and I realize the day has been too hard won to lose it now. I run upstairs, cross over the tracks, and catch the train back uptown.

On Eighty-sixth Street the blind pencil vendor is working late, Sphinxish on the top step of the subway exit, rattling pencils in his cup. He draws up and clutches the cane in his fist as I lean close. "It's all right," I whisper; "it's only me." His head tilts in an attempt to remember. I reach into my pocket and stuff the handful of remaining bills into his cup. His face lights at the rustle of paper. Lunging out, incredibly quick, he grabs my hand, the milky dead discs of his eyes attempting to find my face.

"A blindman don't never forget," he rasps. "Here, gimme a kiss, sweetheart."

He pulls me down, his breath full of garlic and decay. Other hand coming up, pinching and squeezing my breasts. I wrench and twist like a bird in a snare, neck arched, thrashing my head to avoid those lips, but his grip is iron. His kisses fall by concession to my throat, where a scream quavers and dies. He smiles, teeth like urine stalls.

With my free hand, I bring my purse down atop his skull with all my might. He squeals, pearly eyes popping wide. And I flee, his curses pursuing me like a bat mitzvah blessing.

CHAPTER SEVEN

SLEEPING WITH HERSELF

FROM THE STREET I MAKE OUT A SOFT GLOW IN HER WINDOW. THIS IS crazy, she may be entertaining a lover — all of them entertaining lovers. The lobby door stands unlocked. An omen. I go quickly up and listen at her door. Quiet. I knock, too softly to hear over the tide of blood in my ears. Nothing. Hover anxiously, trying to coax myself to split. Knock harder. I have begun tiptoeing away when a wary, sleep-husky voice asks who it is.

"It's me . . ."

"Natalie!" a tidy laugh. "You pick some visiting hours, kiddo."

"I can go —"

"Listen, don't be so hurt. Zheesus, it's after one." Beyond door panels, I envision a silhouette, disheveled to match the voice.

"I'm not hurt. I'm over it now."

A standoff silence, broken by the tumble of locks. The door cracks to the limits of its chain, as if she fears I might break into her life. Her hair forms a wild aureole against a soft red glow within.

"I just wanted to talk."

"You must, *meshugah*." The door closes then opens wide. She tousles my hair, leads into a living room junked with wine empties and overflowing ashtrays. She scoops up a bra, other clothes littered in a trail across carpet, drops them in her bedroom and shuts the door, then squats in a half-lotus. Her face, shadowed against the sunset glow of Japanese lanterns, seems older, features somehow disarranged. "Can you make it fast?" She glances vaguely over my head, making me edgy.

"I don't know where to begin. I was thrown out of a Chinese restaurant, then some blind creep tried to rape me —"

"Listen, do your parents know where you are?"

I light a cigarette. "It's really none of their business."

"And you wonder why you're having trouble at home?"

I touch my forehead where subway grime lingers. "Remember when you told me that our parents expect us to fulfill their own dreams? Today I fulfilled all of Mother's nightmares."

"I do believe it — crashing parties, kicking down doors . . ."

"I got upset."

"Upset! You got destructive. And I wish you would keep your eyes off my twat."

I giggle. "You're sitting there with your robe wide open."

"Zchgee . . . Can't I be comfortable in my own apartment?"

Max fidgets the robe over walnut dark thighs, fingernails tapping a dead-soldier wine bottle. I lean against the couch and sigh. "Do you always get horny before your period?"

"No, I always get horny," she says, and we laugh. Suddenly, fingernails fall silent against glass; she sits up, tense, hands gripping thighs — an animal listening. "How about I call you a cab?"

"I just got here!"

We sit in an uneasy truce. I don't quite look at her.

"Can I ask you a question?"

"Since when do you quibble over permission?"

"Do you think I'm a rotten person?"

Her face lights, then frowns. "What kind of question is that?"

"Sometimes you act like you can't stand the sight of me."

She looks off, holding a small grin. "I wouldn't say rotten. Y'r a real pain in the ass. How's that?" But even as she twists my nose, reaches for cigarettes, she is distracted again — listening.

"I thought you didn't smoke."

"I don't —" letting vapor trickle out her nose "— but there are times when nothing else makes it."

"Like after making love," I say, stretching my arms.

Max fillips a wry eyebrow. Her eyes leap up behind me again. She draws at the cigarette as if trying to get it all in one drag.

"Why are you so nervous?" I ask.

She touches my knee. "Listen, I think you'd better go." Her eyes remain on the bedroom door, an expression nearly of chagrin. She sighs and hunches shoulders as if to say, What could I do?

I turn around. A figure stands in the doorway, startling me. A pale, nearly luminous outline against darkness. For a moment I imagine it an apparition. Molasses quiet — disturbed only by the tinking of Max's nails against glass. After a small eternity, I hear my own voice, high-pitched and unnatural: "Gawd! I didn't know you were there."

"You do now." The voice is slivered ice.

As the figure emerges into the lantern glow, I recognize the blonde woman from before — hair matted, haggard — astonished I hadn't identified her earlier: Max's friend Lucy, lower-house humanities teacher at Whitman. She stares at Max, mirthless, adamant, clenches a London Fog raincoat closed with one white-knuckled fist and fumbles a cigarette, fingers visibly trembling.

Me an intruder in a ménage that makes no sense. Don't dare look at the woman's eyes, sunk deep into Maxine, who stares into empty space, her posture tense, closed up as if in pain. Each waits for the other — like schoolgirls balanced on a seesaw, toes just touching ground. Max claps palms to thighs. "Gee! I should hang out a shingle, maybe. Everybody bringing me their troubles middle of the night —" Her smile shabby, peeling at corners. I sense Lucy's scouring glare; try to return it but bump hard against her anger and glance about the room in confusion.

"How about coffee? Looks like a long night." Maxine starts for the kitchen. "Want to give me a hand, Luce?"

"I'll help." The words leap out of me. Max closes her eyes. Lucy grinds cigarette in ashtray, eye whites pink in lantern light.

"I'm going," she snaps. "I'm not into slumber parties."

Max rests cheek against kitchen doorpost and shuts her eyes. "We were about to celebrate blind beggars and faithless —"

"I'm leaving . . . all right?" Lucy's cheekbones hold a billiard-ball glaze. Her rancor, I know, directed at me, but I refuse to be intimidated. She slips on shoes and crisply ties the raincoat belt. Max follows her into the hall.

Rapid, tight-curled whisperings. Maxine's fingers pale hooks around the apartment door. She dashes into the kitchen for a paper bag, disappears into the bedroom and emerges with the bag full, handing it to Lucy — gripping her hand a moment before closing the door with a nearly inaudible click.

She stands, deep in thought, worry wrinkles indelible on her forehead. Then conjures phony cheerfulness. "So where were we?"

"What's her problem?" I shiver. "She gives me the creeps."

"I think you're making too much of it, Nat."

"She made too much of it. I can see you if I want."

Max's mouth twisting in an ironic pretzel of a smile. She puts on Segovia and stands before the stereo stretching leg muscles (dance class warm-up routine), begins grinding hips and serpentining hands in a manner both restrained and sexually insinuating, Oriental and incongruous with the guitar's Latin *agitato*. I realize, a little shocked, that she's a poor choreographer, and from the red animal glow of her eyes that she's stoned out of her mind.

I shout into the music. "She's a weirdo."

Max cups hand to ear, unable — or undesiring — to hear.

"Her and her obnoxious lover, Richard."

She sprawls on the couch, robe butterflied over thighs, her nakedness spilling out. I attempt not to notice. "What's all this lovers stuff?"

"You told me."

"I did?"

"You said they make a perfect pair: she's a prune and Richard's a banana. All pecker!" I giggle.

Maxine frowns. My eyes drift again to her open robe, a zaftig muff of dark dense curls. I look quickly away.

"What was Lucy so pissed off about?" I ask.

Max's eyes reach for the ceiling. "Didn't anyone teach you not to be a noodge, for shitsake? Lucy's got troubles . . . all right? Things you wouldn't appreciate yet." She leaps up. "I'm gonna make some Spanish coffee." Turns mid-stride, typical Max, always stopping in the middle of things. "How do you get home?"

"I thought we were having Spanish coffee."

"No —" eyes stab at her watch "— definitely time to call a cab."

"I could sleep here . . . on the couch."

"Not a good idea. No, that's out!"

"Do you want me to get mugged, like Lydia?"

"You should've thought about all that before coming."

"C'mon."

"Look, I'm not getting into this. I know how you take to motherly advice." My eyes beg; she sighs. "I'm not comfortable with it, Nat. Students don't spend the night at teachers' apartments. Not even at Whitman."

"I'm not a boy, you know."

Her mouth puckers, forming little crinkles like dried mud.

"I'll call Kitty if you're so uptight. She can tell Mother I'm staying over there."

She frowns, eyebrows backing together. "You insist on remaining naive about this, don't you?" Spreading hands in a Pilate gesture. "I give up. Do what you're going to do. Sleep here on the couch, in the bathtub. I don't care." She goes to the kitchen.

As the phone rings and rings, confidence lands like a lump in my knees. I imagine Liz answering, realize the time.

"Shooot, I can't be calling your mama at this hour," Kitty says, sleepy-voiced. "Don't you worry none. I'll tell them. Now you make sure he put that sock on. Don't let him be crawling in there with bare feet." Belting a husky contralto laugh.

The receiver fits back into its cradle, a trigger click of malaise. I conjure up an image: the knit of Kitty's brow if she knew where I really was. "Did you call them?" Max asks from the kitchen. "It's okay," I mumble, wondering if I should just go.

The fumes of the coffee alone stone me. Floating in a rum Barbados, Max's book-crowded Caribbean, lush ferns, spider plants, bohemian frowze — sweet island refuge in the swells and foamings of the city. Crash of a bottle below on the sidewalk, nickering of the wind coming off the Narrows, carrying with it the bellicose snaps and cracklings of wet sheets hung from countless Brooklyn clotheslines, wino mutterings, drizzly-headed and inconsolable, carried over from Broadway. I lay my head back in the lap of the couch, secure. Max sits meditatively, legs folded beneath, holding the coffee mug in both hands, staring into it between pensive sips as if crystal-gazing. A contemplative mood settled over the city with the rain. Her features vaguely troubled, yet hinting a smile, hair nested in a disheveled raven's wing, light from a candle softening her features, time-washing them so that she seems nearly Biblical. Esther, beautiful and good-hearted. A mensch who comes to the aid of waitresses and cripples. My friend.

"You look very Jewish tonight," I tell her.

She looks up, a preoccupied smile. "Thank you, Nat. I feel very Jewish — like I just stepped from a mikvah of sorts."

I'm not certain she isn't being sarcastic. "What's a mikvah?" I ask, expecting some crack about my shiksa upbringing.

Maxine smiles tolerantly. "A mikvah is the ritual submersion Orthodox women must take before having sex with a man, legacy of medieval misogynists who fear female contamination."

"Have you ever had one?"

"Only emotional mikvahs." That wistful look fading, replaced by a tautening of her mouth.

I smoke reflectively. "I've never felt very Jewish. I can relate to living in caves sometime in the past, but the thought of having roots in an Austrian shtetl seems absolutely foreign."

Max laughs. "Not too surprising for someone raised in a home that never celebrated a seder."

"We celebrated things."

Her derisive little smile. "Like maybe Brother Adam's exodus to Israel. I'm sorry," she says, "that was nasty. Somehow I can't imagine Mama Bach throwing out the leavened bread. But I wish you'd quit peeking at my snatch. I feel like Gypsy Rose Lee."

"I'm not —" I giggle.

"Y'r absolutely immodest."

"Me? You sit there with your robe wide open."

"Can't I relax in my own living room?" We laugh. Max produces a Baggie of grass from her robe pocket and rolls a joint, sealing it with a pink swipe of her tongue. She inhales deep and long, then passes it to me. I am dumbfounded.

"I thought you didn't want me smoking."

She shrugs. "It seems to be a night for breaking rules."

The grass backfires, bringing me down instead of up. Out somewhere in that huge wound called "Manhattan" a siren wails as if the situation is equally hopeless at both ends — a bathtub full of abortion or a junkie burning up in the building he has torched for its fixtures. I think of Adam's rain-pocked shoulders, glistening in Alphabet Block gloom — as though fanatacism were one of those diseases which cause the body to produce its own luminescence — the message he instructed me to deliver. All those resolutions of needy-mouthed Natalie stillborn. I attempt to sound offhand.

"I hear my brother has been coming to your jam sessions."

Eyes mute, she studies me. "It's a mystery to me how Adam, coming from his background, developed such a passion for Israel," she says.

I shrug. "I don't think he loves Israel so much as he hates America."

"He's very good, you know."

"Good?" I stare at her.

"The piano, dummy." She gooses me under the ribs.

"You know what Richard says —"

"Richard says a lot of things." Shifting legs beneath her. "I've never met his wife. Rachel, is that it?" A suburban pretension in her tone. "I'd like to have them over for spaghetti before they leave."

"You never invited me for spaghetti." I sulk, half-serious.

"I don't have to invite — you stay!"

"I'd like to know what he's got that's so great."

"Plenty, kiddo." Chucking me under the chin.

I shake her off, annoyed. "How would you know, Miss Pearlman?"

"I see it in his eyes. He's a powerful guy. Very attractive."

"Married!" My glare digs in. "And my brother."

Opening her hands. "I don't see the connection."

I would prefer to let it drop, but a dybbuk has taken control — a compulsion. "Adam was here this afternoon, wasn't he?"

"Would you stop being so fucking nosy?"

"Too bad you didn't meet him sooner. Except I really love Rachel. I think you'd make a stinko sister-in-law."

"Ben Yaakov and me! Are you kidding? Last of the double Y chromosomes, Herzlean Marine Corps . . . Whoo-eee!" She laughs over-ardently. "I'd make a crappy Zionist; I'm into rational solutions."

"I don't think it's Adam's machismo that turns you on, it's because he's married. Très dangereux. But you better watch out. Rachel has a black belt in karate."

Max frowns. "You're very provincial, Nat. If you gotta know, it's not the sister-in-law who frightens me. It's the brother. He's Old Testament; you delve in with a little . . . awe." My gaze remains fixed on a wine bottle draped in many-colored layers of wax. "Listen," she says, "this conversation has a bit of the Grand Inquisitor about it. How about we discuss one of your male friends? Karl Housman, maybe."

"Are you sleeping with Adam?"

She leaps up for more coffee, twists my nose in passing, mock-cheerful. "Mind your own business. Matchmaker."

"You wouldn't even know him if it weren't for me," I call after her.

She turns in the doorway. "What's the problem, Natalie?"

Anger comes hissing and slithering down about my feet. "I'm jealous," I admit.

An incredulous chuckle. "Jealous? Of whom?"

"I don't know." Averting my eyes. "Both of you."

It's a while before I chance looking up: she is staring off into some private involvement. The words come; there's no stopping them. "He asked me to give you a message." Her eyes pop up. "He wants you to stop bothering him. He said he's through with all that garbage. Whatever that means."

"Me! —" she pokes her chest "— bothering him?" An enraged snort. "Wow, that's some incredible vanity."

"That's what he said."

She stares, hand pinned to breast like a carnation, a fading prom corsage. The first time ever I have seen her composure truly shaken. I'm sorry I have spoken. But nothing can be done. It is a day for stepping in where I don't belong.

Returning with coffeepot and rum, Max is taciturn, remote, as if internally her head keeps shaking — *Me* bothering *him!* My emotions have settled. I want to make restitution, cheer her up. I begin telling about Karl's party: how he'd closeted me in his bedroom, too wine-soused to fight him off; Karl an octopus, everywhere at once, whispering over my bare boobs, like Adam with his girlfriend long ago at the river.

Max isn't listening, not really. Although she laughs dutifully. Hugging her knees, a lingering, almost wistful smile clinging to her lips. The usual thing: off on her own star. I ask why she's always distracted when I talk to her. She tilts her chin. "It's a great story. Very erotic," she says, pumping dark eyebrows. But realizes I'm not appeased. "Listen, I've got a lot on my mind now. Dad had another attack. His lungs rasp now when he breathes, like insect wings chafing together. I love my father very much. Maybe you can't appreciate that."

Words huff out, sullen and gravelly, "My father has emphysema, too, you know."

"I do know," she says. There are tears in her eyes.

Suddenly, I am talking about Dad — how he's an artist, really, and it's his drawings people like (though think it's his clothes designs). He has an artist's sensibilities, and there's no place for that in the wasteland of business-before-beauty America, not even here in New York. Staring a moment at a low-guttering candle, tiny flame atop a volcano of molten wax, I mutter, "Even his marriage is falling apart." Then the whole Rosita episode is pouring out, from the moment I stepped in the apartment that summer night: these months of secrecy and guilt; the fear of betrayal building a fence between Dad and me, through which we sniff at each other like cautious dogs. I am crying. "I haven't told anyone. I'm afraid it will get back to Mother." Max beside me on the couch arm, caressing my hair, saying it's too much weight to carry alone.

I rest my head on her shoulder. "If only I'd slammed the door coming in, it wouldn't have happened."

She daubs at my eyes with robe sleeves, bends and kisses the tiny bald spot atop my head, the hub where hairspokes meet. "It isn't your fault, Natalie."

I look, hopeful, into her eyes, good dybbuk Devoras. Our faces hold for what seems eternity — sun and moon trading light and warmth back and forth. "I'm sorry about Adam," I whisper. She shakes her head. "That was inevitable, too." Leaning forward, she kisses my forehead, her breath smelling of sweet rum. My eyes fall to the robe, parted nearly to her waist, spilling breasts round as Japanese lanterns, nipples the dark sides of Kabuki moons. For an instant, I want to lay my cheek there . . . to touch them. A fever of trembling seizes me, my eyes flee past a small sad smile which seems to intuit what I am experiencing.

I leap up from the couch.

To the window, ignoring a Natalie Bach reflecting back at me — through her lips brows near aquiline nose, a car, like some Ray Bradbury beast prowling the side street — sensing behind me her gaze that observes the rag-shaking of my knees. In time the room stops shuddering. My stomach settles. Max claps her thighs.

"Time for the sack, kiddo," she says. "I'm frazzlehausted."

* * *

Confusion is narcotic. Slipping from clothes like a thief when she has gone in the bedroom, beneath a ratty old blanket; furniture floating in the feral glow of the city. Think of Lydia as I close my eyes and the day rushes at me like a snorting horse: Dad's twenty, Adam's bare feet, subway tongues, blindmen's kisses . . . a whispering from the bedroom. My eyes focus on a wedge of light from her unclosed door, though sleep sits on them like a fat Buddha. Between drifting furniture, Karl shuffles on knees, his shlong slung lucently; with a small boy's grin, he fondles himself. Me slipping off panties: "C'mere quick," I hiss, "before I change my mind."

Karl humps rhythmically. I open my eyes but can't see him. "Karl . . . ," I whisper, realizing at once there is no Karl; I am at Maxine's apartment. Though he pants and creaks bedsprings — faster faster, louder louder, filling the apartment with low gasps and moans, furious insect humming. Is it possible that someone else . . . maybe Adam? Then, alarmed, humiliated, I realize what she is doing. Oh God! I duck under the clammy blanket, plugging my ears like a frightened kid, stung by my own sharp sweat-stink. Throw the blanket off; seeing I'm half naked, quickly pull it up again. *Why can't she keep it to herself?* I fight for breath, suffocating in air thick with her shamelessness. She wants me to hear! The thought makes my skin crawl. Lewd noises crowd around me — debauched imps and succubi doing unmentionable things. I should get out . . . flee. But realize I am strangely fascinated by the sliver of bedroom light. Beckoning. Mortified at a growing desire to tiptoe over — just to peek! I lie motionless, battling panic.

Then a long low tear of breath, jagged moan continuing, continuing like a train pulling in at station. Then nothing, but an occasional hiccup of breath. Her light snaps off, leaving cat's eyes, little demons of the dark. The apartment sinking deep into thick, ominous quiet, transited by bizarre erotic fish, darting out from subconscious trenches, eel-slithering over the floor. Me drowning in fears. Absolutely creeped. Got to leave — now! I slip into clothes and move soundlessly to the door. Hesitate, realizing I have no key to lock it from outside; hate to leave it open, but there's no choice. The bolt turns with a loud POP. Blood thunders in my ears.

Max's voice cracks the dark. "Natalie, is that you?"

Without answering, I tiptoe back to my couch.

* * *

Maxine stands at the blackboard in gym togs diagraming basketball plays in dotted line figure-eights while the break bell jangles in my ear. At the door, the Bobbsey Twits whisper passionately. I start to laugh. Max spins around, clothes cut away in front, leaving her unabashedly naked.

"She's right here," I hear her saying, "right here on the couch. She's fine, Mr. Bach . . . a little cranky. I'm really very sorry, I had no idea. . . . Would you like to talk to her?"

I sit up to gray-faced dawn, molester of dreams, leering in the windows. Sweat-basted, blanket-itchy. I wave away the phone, hovering above me like a cobra, and hear Max hang up. She stands glaring down. The look in her eyes is nothing to wake up to. In the raw, pornographic light, she is bare naked and piss-pregnant. I avert my gaze, intimidated by her sexual luggage.

"That was your father," she informs me. "He and your mother have just spent a pleasant night calling cops and emergency rooms, worried sick about you." She makes a crude attempt to cover herself. "You little shit. Don't you have any consideration for anyone?"

"Leave me alone," I answer, turning face-down on my pillow.

Dad was the retriever in our family. Once on vacation in Pompano Beach he and Adam had a big fight. Adam took off and Mom was hysterical. Dad went looking for him through the local bars (though Adam was only sixteen), returning hours later, droopy-eyed and deflated, with his oldest son, who stared wordlessly ahead, square head fixed upon fullback's shoulders.

He came by taxi to retrieve me, exchanging cordialities with Maxine in a farce of strained politeness. I was no fullback, but sleep-sour, feeling the family's temperamental blood thickening in my veins. Max touched his shoulder as we left — as though her first loyalty was not to me but adulthood.

Beyond a milky Plexiglas mugger screen, the Latino cabbie demanded, "Where you wan' go, mister?" Hair planted in glossy black plugs, screwed firmly into his scalp. Dad ignored him, fixing me with an uneasy smile, his own wavy hair so staid and civilized — no boomala-boomala-boom in that fine weave. What remained of it. The trench between his brows had deepened with fatigue, like some Olduvai haunted by personal bones.

"I doubt we should go back just yet," he was saying. "Your mother had a pretty tough night. Dr. Sternberg prescribed a sedative." He chuckled, interpreting my frown as concern. "She'll come around." He disregarded the importunate cabbie, turned now completely in his seat, losing patience.

"How about coffee?" Dad asked.

"You said no when Maxine offered coffee," I reminded him.

Dad's Levantine eyes licked me, damp as dogs' tongues. He waved off the cabbie. "Go ahead," he barked, "anywhere you like." The driver slammed the accelerator, muttering Spanish. I felt an urge to embrace my father, tell him: *Take it easy. God numbers every hair on our heads; there are so few of your number left.*

Seated in a café on Bleecker Street, he breathes as if it's a public affair. "I know you don't like this much," he says, "and I don't either. Feels like I'm checking up on you."

I knocked the ash from a cigarette. "Well, aren't you?"

Gold sparkled across teeth crowns. "I think it might be best if your mother didn't know you were at Maxine's."

I stared at him blankly. He had called secretly, on a hunch, he explained, without telling her. "Zilla has misgivings about your friendship which I don't share. Your mother is a little possessive." He chuckled.

"You mean a little sick."

Wrinkles accordioned up his brow. He stared at my hands on the table. "I understand the attraction. Maxine is an intriguing woman, very bright." A darting look of his brown eyes seemed to insinuate more. I cringed, revisiting memories of the night before.

"I'm getting really tired of everyone being down on Maxine."

"Down on her?" Dad asked, bewildered.

"There are two things I can't stand: being spied on like this and Mother's paranoia. Maybe it's menopause. I don't know what it is. But I really can't live with her suspicion and ambivalence anymore. And I can't stand it when you go along with her."

Dad spread hands in a helpless gesture. "It isn't easy to grow older, Natalie. We all have to be patient."

A red bright ass of anger. "At least I'm not a hypocrite. I don't play goody-two-shoes while I neck with the maid behind my wife's back."

Dad's face drained of all color. Ashen. His eyes darted about like cornered fish and he began to wheeze. Fearing he might have an attack,

I gripped his wrist, slopping a little coffee over our fingers. "Don't worry, I won't tell her," I promised. His eyes gone watery as I explained that I just wanted out — my own apartment. Not imagining that what I proposed was blackmail.

Silence followed us home. When we arrived at the apartment floor, while Dad held the elevator door for me, I assured him that if Mother gave me any crap I was moving out for good. "I'm old enough to live like I want to live."

In a tissuey whisper, he promised to get me an apartment: the grim I'll-do-my-duty resignation of a father giving his daughter away in marriage. I kissed his apple-red face — its vaguely medicinal odor — and did a little jig out onto our floor.

"It may be best," he said. "You'll be able to come and go as you please."

At the door he straightened his tie, as though to eradicate any signs of affection.

Mother sits in a beige robe on the beige couch, keeping her weather watch like an old captain hanging out a storm lantern in the pilothouse of a Conrad story. When she isn't dressed before nine o'clock — squall warnings! She looks right through me.

"Where did you find her?"

"At a friend's," I answer for him.

"Which friend?" Her eyes like the burnished aluminum reflectors used in photographing her models.

"I'm going in to take a shower. I slept in my clothes and I kinda —" lifting an arm and flaring nostrils for Dad's benefit.

Mother starts setting out breakfast things as if that's all there will be to it. Though I see in the sleepless deeps of her eyes that she is savoring it — nothing like a good fight for breakfast. Peace at table be damned. We are liberated Jews.

"Where's Maria?" I ask.

Mother regards me as if I've pushed the right button. "It's been a pretty lousy morning. To begin with I didn't sleep last night . . . Natalie! Then I had to let Maria go." Her tone implying that I am somehow responsible for both events.

"You fired Maria?"

"She was stealing —" her face changes mid-stride "— actually, maybe she wasn't. She came in wearing my blouse again. She denied it and insisted she had bought it herself. I can't tolerate that sort of cheek from my help. I let her go. Just now I was doing a wash and I found my blouse in the basket. Oy! I felt awful."

"I'll bet she felt worse."

She regards me, cold and flat. "You know, Natalie, you could have had the decency to call so we didn't sit up worrying."

No question, I've really bought it this time. I try not to look at either of them. "Kitty promised to call."

"You were at Juli's then?" A cheery, reassured tone.

My eyes brush vagrantly with Dad's. "Why not?" I mumble.

Hard to interpret Mother's expression — pained astonishment, like the look she gives fatties on the street. "How's Lydia doing?" she asks thinly, as if the question has gone sour in her mouth.

I light a cigarette, murmuring unhappily, "Lydia —?"

Her flame blue eyes close briefly. "You see, Kitty didn't call. I called. Liz was drunk. Listen to me, Natalie! She said, 'Your girl isn't here, Zoe.' Although I could hear Kitty prompting in the background: 'Sure, she been here all evening.' Liz said — I believe her words were: 'Bullshit! I won't have these girls using me for a cover every time they come into heat. If I wanted to go into that business I'd do it for profit.' " She clasps a hand over her forehead and seems to struggle to control herself.

"You called Lydia?" My question barely a whisper.

Dad grimaces. "It was embarrassing, Nattie."

Silence that weighs the world. Mother's eyes bulge through a Miltown glaze as if she's going to cry, her voice squeaks. "I can't trust my own daughter anymore." I feel suddenly gritty under the skin — as if subway grime has penetrated my clothes and continued working inward. Mother sniffles and sharply shakes her head.

"Was she with her black boyfriend, Jacob?"

"Don't be ridiculous."

Dad remains tensely silent, anticipating the moment she loses it completely and Sternberg comes to shoot her full of Valium; she'll be comatose for twelve hours, then Dad will take her to dinner. Same old thing. Life starts over Monday morning — and by Sunday she'll be coaxing creamed herring on me and chiding about my weight. The weekly round, from coma to calories. I've had enough.

"I'd like to know who my daughter is sleeping with —"

"She's sleeping with herself."

Dad's gazelle eyes urge calm. I wish he'd step forward and punch her nose.

"Could we just drop it?" I propose.

"I think Nattie's right." Dad shoots Mother a glance. Her eyes snap at him, but she moves silently off to the kitchen to prepare breakfast, astonishing us both.

"I was at Maxine's," I confess suddenly as we sit to eat, unable to banish a peevish note from my voice, like a child tattling on herself.

Mother eats a minute, fork tearing pink meat of a grapefruit. "You know, it won't win our blessing for your friendship to conduct it clandestinely."

"I got stuck. Really! It was too late to take the subway."

She flaps off this lameness with a hand. "Maxine is too sophisticated for you, Natalie."

"She's a good friend. She respects me."

Mother sets aside papery skin of deli sable and regards me evenly, eyes flecked with orange detritus of the sedative, tiny flakes of fish clinging to her lips. "Quite frankly, that seems peculiar to me. It's healthier to have friends your own age. Like Lydia."

She places a bagel on my plate. I put it back in the warmer.

"Why does everything have to be so healthy? Mental health, physical health, spiritual health. All this health makes me sick."

Dad does his egg routine: scooping a yolky sunny-side-up into his spoon and swallowing the whole schmear in one gulp. Mother butters the bagel. She sighs, as if about to call a truce.

"All the same, it isn't healthy, and I wish you would see less of her socially."

"I try to see as little of Lydia as I can."

"Always a wisecracker."

"I wish you would stop picking on my friends so maybe I'll still feel like coming over here on Sunday mornings after I move out."

Her head snaps up, straining on the long neck that Max says is the secret to her fashion success, swiveling goose-like from Dad to me. This once her paranoia is justified.

CHAPTER EIGHT

NOVEMBER 22, 1963

I PUSHED THROUGH A MUDDLE OF BARE BREASTS BUTTS BELLIES
in all sizes, armpitty shirts and sneakers ripe enough to run by themselves, past Marty, standing mid-aisle, arms akimbo, giant economy
sized drooping almost to her navel, nipples like Dad's palette knife
smearings, an Irish smirk for Carol who had discovered a torn seam in
her gym shorts. "Wear them anyway," advised Marty. "Sure! —" Carol
laughed "— give the Parkies a thrill." Maxine stood with one foot on a
bench tying her sneaker, flanked by the jabbering Bobbsey Twits in
twin undies. For each of Allie's assertions, Ellie's tits jounced enthusiasm.

"Guess what, I got wings," I cried. "I'm getting my own apartment!"
Faces turned towards me, a quick murmur of excitement. "I owe it all
to you, Miss P." Engulfing Maxine in a bear hug.

She shoved me away, yanking at the elastic band of her shorts.

"Just what do you think you're doing, Natalie?"

I formed my hands on the air, voice fading with my grin. "I'm trying to tell you. If I hadn't stayed over at your place Saturday night I wouldn't —"

"All right —" Max cut me off "— let's go, girls. Move it! Natalie. Get dressed down — pronto. You're late." Her eyes murderous. She swatted my ass, leaving a brand that tingled for minutes.

I overtook the others midblock, November air ballooning cheerily from their lips. Juli raised a victory salute, Marty a fist. "Do it, mama!" she shouted. Carol jogged along beside me. "Who's your roomie?" she asked. I excused myself and sprinted after Max's head of jet black hair.

"Hi!" I said. She dropped to a walk, letting the others pass. "I was just feeling good, you know. I wanted to thank you —" Max touched my arm. A warning. Her eyes reflected sharp white morning light, breath coiled slowly around us and disappeared.

"What goes with you?" she demanded. "Exhibitionism gets you off? Is that it? Or are you just making my private life into a show-and-tell adventure . . . huh? A personal triumph?"

I said I had no idea what she was talking about.

Rage a beast contorting her features, ready to leap at my throat. She managed to control it. No more announcements about weekends spent at teacher's apartment, she warned. No manic public affection and grandstanding her personal life around school.

"I'm your friend —" I protested meekly.

"Don't do it . . . understand? Never again." She had seized my arm, sinking a clawish thumb deep into muscle.

"That hurts, you know." She released the arm. Watching the red imprint fade slowly from my biceps, knowing it would form a bruise, I found anger.

"I'm sick and tired of people telling me not to be myself. Natalie's too nutty, Natalie's too outrageous . . . Bullshit!"

We faced off. Max's nostrils horse-dilating, leaking vapor on the chilly air, mixing with mine. She stood glaring at me, and I felt suddenly disoriented before that anger coiling out of her like a snake. I turned and ran after the others. Max calling as if nothing had happened: "Tuck in your shirt. I think even Whitman deserves some kind of dress standards."

"Screw you, Maxine," I answered, running backwards. "You want to see something really outrageous —?" I pulled the sweatshirt off over my head and spun it like a lasso — cold air slapping my chest, a goosepimple thrill. I raced into traffic on Central Park West, bare tits bobbing. Brakes screamed, faces turned in delight, a dapper black bystander whistled. Me feeling so high. Birdfree. Sprinting down into our hockey valley to wild cheers of my classmates. Max in pursuit, waving my discarded shirt like a battle pennant, shouting: "Damn you, Natalie. I'll break your ass."

On Tuesday I composed a letter.

Dear Miss P.
    Miss Propriety
    Miss Prissypants
    Miss Poisonarrow
    Miss Prunehead
    Miss PastFriendofMine:
Do not, in the future, address me in public or private. I am from now and forever and ex post facto not your friend. If you do address me I may feel the urge to throw up. . . .

All my life, I wrote, people had urged me to sacrifice what I was for what I wasn't, as if God had cursed the whole idea of *Natalie Bach*. At first I thought you were different. Now you say: "Nat, be tactful, exercise please a little propriety —" i.e., be a big phony, make tinsel smiles and rinse your mouth with lies, be as milksop mediocre as everyone else . . . and don't dare stick out! Never sing or flap your wings; if they're reading Fitzgerald this year, by all means read Fitzgerald (even if he stinks). Keep shut your fat mouth and keep brushed your kike hair, and don't you dare knock on my door without calling first (fuck Hillel and Jesus and the rest of my principles). Do all this and you get the booby prize for boobies, get to pin on an orchid on Mother's Day and join B'nai B'rith, make a jolly WASP smile and play golf with your friend at the country club, complain about hemorrhoids and the kids' grades . . . and finally have your uterus removed to spite them all.

But first! Gotta drop those brats like spent bullets — that is, what's spent in you, what dreams you once dreamt and hoped life would be, but wasn't! So you gave it up and surrendered life to your children, hoping in your mouthwash way that they would do more with it —

knowing they wouldn't. And at the rate things are going in this shitted-
up world they might have to work twice as hard just to accomplish your
failure. Then, one day, to utter in bewilderment: "The children find me
contemptible. . . ."

Not me! When I was five years old, one bright-star summer evening,
Hettie Freid and her parents came to Huntington Park for a barbecue.
The adults drinking daiquiris and watching us, much amused, as we
played — at least, as I played in my Roy Rogers outfit, while Hettie
stood watching in a minty green dress. I remember Miriam Freid smiling her square teeth: "What are you playing, cowboys and princesses?"
They thought that was very funny. I wandered out back and called a
conference of fireflies. I told them solemnly that I would be different. I
would never join those voices of my family and their friends, murmuring in the background.

Wednesday morning, as I passed her classroom, Max said, "Shalom,
how's my favorite stranger?" I handed her the letter. "So she doesn't
talk but she does communicate. Prolifically!" Thumbing through the
many pages. "Natalie —"

I continued walking. Caught up to Lydia, who had just returned to
school — one eye a sick pansy, yellow and violet, face swollen like a
puffer fish, lips crucified on a mouthful of braces . . . Ugh! Hard to
imagine anyone being that sadistic just for fun. I took some of her
books. One damp eye smiled gratitude.

"Nat-al-lie!" Max repeated. Lydia turned. I seized her elbow and
steered on down the hall.

At Friday lunch Karl and Barney were doing their Kennedy brothers
routine — *'Cause it's my football, that's why* — from the record. General hilarity as Zack did his underwear number: schlepping around with
the elastic band pulled high above his pant waist. Across room, Maxine
placed her fishwich onto Barney's tray as he made the rounds of the
lunchroom, demanding, "Tickets please —" I wondered what I had
ever seen in her. God designed her as a La Leche League model — all
bust and no heart. Pathetic, with her jerk friends.

At the faculty table under the clock sat her good buddy Lucy and the
whole crew — Delacroix, Hilma, Melanie Tibbs, Ron Groat the scrag-
beard. Typical private school bunch. Bulgebrains and oversensitives.
Mostly chewing with mouths open and Groat crying out: "Where did
you get that? Where in hell did you read that?" He and Lucy were con-

stantly sparring; Carol said, "They're just rubbing intellectual gonads."
Delacroix galumphed, Hilma let go her Teutonic giggle, Melanie
Tibbs' laugh was a tinkling mountain stream, and Lucy clipped her
sentences as if chopping vegetables. I had managed to avoid her since
that certain night, until, on Wednesday, we passed in the hall. I
squeaked out a "Hi" and she gave me an Oh! what a sick smile. Mrs.
Samson, lone black faculty member, sat at the end of the table with a
forget-me-not smile, writing as if she were keeping score, though everyone said it was poetry.

My popularity quotient had risen five hundred percent. Overnight,
getting your own apartment had become a Whitman fad. I wasn't rushing into anything, I told them. It had come down to a choice of Village
or Upper West Side, near school.

"I'd go Village," advised Marty, who considered herself a beatnik.
"That's where it's happening." A fish flake stuck almost delicately to
her chin.

"Naw," said Libby, waving a cigarette (she'd been suspended four
times already for smoking in the lunchroom), "too many weirdos down
there, too many old jerks who walk around like this —" making a face
that cracked us up.

"We's goin' up to Harlem, ain't we, sister?" cried Carol, trading skin
with Libby. "We gonna show them some real class."

"Class my ass. The only way the bloods wanna see a honky up in
Harlem is flat on her back."

"Right on!" Carol snapped her fingers and did a little shimmy.

Libby asked who would be rooming with me. I followed her lead and
lit a cigarette. A little giddy and uncertain with my new social power.
Actually it had come to a choice between Carol and Libby (Juli had no
reason to move from home) — though they didn't know it. "If someone
wants to join me . . . who knows?" I shrugged.

Down the table, Allie jeered, "Whoooo knows . . ." frogging out her
cheeks. Ellie croaked hyperthyroid laughter. Colleen nearly spilled her
ducktail haircut into the chocolate pudding.

I turned to Allie slow and deliberate as a movie tough. "Some people
have lousy memories." My eyes threw her across room as I had that day
in the locker room.

Allie removed her glasses and rubbed at little purple dents either side
of her nose, which lent a bruised impression to her eyes. I despised her.
Barney whacked fist into hand and made grunting noises, egging us on.

Lydia's good eye leapt back and forth between us like a grasshopper. It was rumored that since our last encounter Allie had been taking judo lessons. However, her whole face was chickenshitting now as if she hadn't heard me. I watched a balloon of cigarette smoke drift across table and said, "At least in my apartment I won't need twin beds."

Hilarity. Teachers turned at their table. Except Maxine, who still, after twenty-four hours, hadn't acknowledged my letter. Melanie Tibbs made crushing signals about our cigarettes.

Suddenly, Dr. Lang's voice came over the loudspeaker, asking all staff members to come "without delay" to his office. He sounded rattled. "Wow!" cried Barney, "the mad bomber is loose and about." I squeezed far down in my chair as Max passed, but her eyes snagged me. She smiled fleetingly. I knew the showdown would come at basketball practice.

Teachers gone, Carol loudly mimicked the voice from the film we'd seen that morning in Hilma's Bio 2 class, nearly achieving that effect of words echoing down a blue ice corridor, while Karl and Barney did rhythm: "*Freshly oxygenated blood enters the left atrium through the pulmonary veins* (thump-thump thump-thump) . . ."

Maxine burst into the cafeteria, face a mottle of emotions, panicked. Then Delacroix, hair frazzled over lobster-red forehead, raising his hands for silence, his shouts running head-on into pandemonium.

"The President —" his voice cracked "— President Kennedy . . ." Just as a radio voice burst over the loudspeaker:

"*There was blood, a great deal of blood on Mrs. Kennedy's suit. She had been sitting beside the President. . . .*"

The emotion in that practiced voice hushed us.

"*We are waiting — a nation and a world — waiting for news from the operating room at Parkland Memorial Hospital in Dallas. The President was rushed from his motorcade after a sniper's bullet . . . President John Fitzgerald Kennedy shot by an assailant while riding in a motorcade in Dallas, Texas —*" He repeated over and over as if not believing his own words, or as if the repetition were a form of prayer, public invocation. Or hoping it might reveal more: How Mrs. Kennedy was not hit, but ran in beside her husband's stretcher . . . But Governor Connally . . . and JFK had been rushed into surgery, he repeated, as if we wouldn't believe him, because we didn't really. Then switching to Washington to make sure that what was true in Texas was true across the country.

A sudden outcry of voices in the cafeteria. Chaos. Resistance. Delacroix hunched over a transistor radio hugging his knees; Lucy leaning against a wall, arms clenched tight in that shivering posture. Me numb, caught up in the devastating tension. Tomb-quiet alternating with fearful outbursts. "He's going to die, I know it ––" some voice kept insisting. I hated it. Creep Colleen rested her James Dean hairdo, comb-furrowed and smelling faintly of hair tonic, against my shoulder and snuffled. I comforted her, kept assuring, "He'll be okay." Thought over and over of Kitty and her picture album. Dreams. The waiting went on forever, while voices droned over the radio.

Maxine pacing the room, frantic. Suddenly, unable to bear the suspense, she broke for the door, heels clicking, skirt chafing like the wings of a captured insect . . . her father's lungs. Her most profound emotion: Escape. Moist eyes stretched against mine as she passed. She bent swiftly and kissed my forehead.

The Dallas voice said, *"The President is dead. Let us pray."*

A wail that had no beginning and end, border or boundary, that tore our hearts wide open.

CHAPTER NINE

DEAR NATALIE:

DAYS PASS, I KEEP MY VIGIL BEFORE THE INSATIABLE ELECTRONIC *eye, gawping at an empty White House lawn, riderless horse . . . those sovereign symbols of grief, and more human ones: the old black horse trainer's anguished face, small bewildered visage of John Jr.; does his filial duty, throws the white rose down onto daddy's casket. I eat endless Chinese takeout, feel like a necrophiliac voyeur: peering in at widow's grief, the wiry, scar-faced assassin shaking a fist at the world's spiteful eye, LBJ's bleary basset hound's face. Watching, all of us, in thrilled horror this ex officio version of The Mummy's Tomb, watching as the State's seamless shroud comes unraveled.*

My ferns reach out to me: "Water us, please."

Leave me alone. I got no time for life.

How fragile hope must be that it is obliterated by a few well-placed

*rifle shots. I try comforting myself with Pollyanna banalities (His mar-
tyrdom was necessary, etc.), knowing damned well there have been
more than enough martyrs already. Even after six million Jews Moloch
soon has hunger pangs again. You are too young to remember smoke
rising from Ethel Rosenberg's head as they pulled the lever again and
again; she wouldn't cooperate, didn't seem to understand that she had
been selected. Something Mayan survives in us — that need to propiti-
ate with live sacrifice. What are martyrs but bad luck cases tossed whole
to history?*

*"He was cocky," Lucy Cynica tells me. "He knew if he went to
Texas some cracker would take a potshot at him. He thought the guy
would miss."*

What can be said to that?

*Nu, our rebellion against the tyranny of new money and old men is
spent, the world delivered back again to cranky prostates. Outside, I can
hear it returning to its feet. Nothing can long halt the régime of bank
and bakery. No Holocaust, no Hiroshima, no Kennedy.*

*But wait! Friend Natalie tells me she is no partaker in politics. Ex-
cept on the personal scale, where she is a regular majority whip of the
poison pen, throws elbows like Huey Long on the basketball court,
when there's trouble at home, secedes from the Union. Kiddo, you
don't fuck around. Would it appease you to say I am sorry? (Not so
much for acting as I did, but for arousing in you so violent a reaction.)
If you'll suffer a little advice: the politics of personal survival isn't all a
matter of declaring war and independence. Love is what's most
wanted — and most radical! — in this world. Natalie sitting cross-
legged comforting Colleen: that's enlightened politics. This is my
friend, I thought, who's going to make a big crater in the moonface of
indifference.*

*Listen, ma chère, friendship is no tap we turn on and off. No deals.
No Mishnayot. The one law of friendship: You say what you need, I say
what I need. A real friend knows when to keep her distance. Why must
you embarrass me over my need to protect myself? Remember, I am
still your teacher. There are taboos. Don't you, too, have drawers that
aren't for everyone? How should I say this? — it makes me blush almost — Beyond affairs platonic, there are affairs hormonal. Call them
what you want: love affairs, fuck affairs, clitoral adventures. Who needs
you peeking from under the bed every time I entertain a lover? Or
sprinting into gym class announcing, "Guess what! . . ."*

And the crap about Brother Adam meaning more to me than Sister Natalie! For shitsake, kiddo, I scarcely know your brother. However, I do wish you could empathize with your parents' grief over Adam's departure. Perhaps it's impossible for those of our parents' generation, children of the depression, to understand why a young man would throw away security for a foothold in the desert. Zionism I can't buy either; ghettoization gives me the willies. I'd prefer to believe the world needs Jews and Jews need the world. Neighbors gossip, but they get along. There should be such a proverb.

Let's laugh again after school and rescue cripples from under the wheels of buses. I forgive, you forgive: a deal? After all, you didn't hold the first colloquium with fireflies. I beat you to it.

Let's be friends.

LOVE, MAXINE

Max's letter arrived just as I'd found the apartment on Ninety-first, off Amsterdam. A bit rough, in need of fresh paint, but pure magic. I wandered around in a kind of trance, touching walls and cupboards, barely recognized myself in the cracked bathroom mirror. So what if the toilet smelled a little, I was free at last. And annoyed when Carol and Jerry clomped upstairs with a load of her stuff. "Whooo-eee," he was shouting, "Fun City!"

I was so moved by her letter that I posted it on the school bulletin board (*sans noms*). Later that afternoon, a very dour Maxine stopped me in the hall. Lungs Lang had summoned her to his office, she said, and demanded an explanation for a letter "that leans too far towards Henry Miller even for my permissive outlook." Max assured him that she hadn't posted it.

"I assume you wrote it," he snapped. She nodded woefully. "There are two typical causes of teacher dismissal, Miss Pearlman," Lang had warned her. "First, neglect of duties; second, lack of circumspection in one's personal affairs. As regards the first, you are home free. A damned fine teacher . . ."

Maxine eyed me dolorously. "Y'r friendship is no bargain, kiddo. Seems like I can't keep it without risking everything else."

"So don't keep it." I shrugged, bluffing.

She shook her head, still unsmiling. "Then I'd lose your ratty old shirt and grouchy disposition from my basketball team. I couldn't live with that."

A few days later, Adam and Rachel departed for Israel. It seemed more than simple coincidence — as if they understood that America had lost its last good captain and was about to sink. The Jewish State provided plane tickets and an address, a kibbutz near the Lebanese border.

Initially, Mom and Dad refused to see Adam off at the airport. But at the last minute must have changed their minds. From where Juli and I stood on the observation deck, I saw them running up to a chain-link fence as passengers walked to the portable boarding ramp — imagined Mother (with a son going on *aliya* to Israel) pleading her way through El Al security.

They were calling out, waving arms frantically overhead, a white handkerchief fluttering in Mother's fingers like a last minute surrender to love and loss. Tears glistened like Passover wine on their cheeks. Their firstborn son, with his wife, went straight ahead in a huddle of passengers as if not hearing. Though at the last moment, just before ducking into the plane, he turned — giving them a wave that was more like a salute.

PART TWO

DUET

CHAPTER TEN

ST. MARKS PLACE

HOLDING THE ROBE TIGHT TO MY STOMACH, I SPRINT THROUGH the living room. Richard sits straight up on the couch, begins to rise, goggle-eyeing every which way, expecting fire or thieves, cock swaggering between his knees. "Just the phone," I tell him, catching one hard God-forbid-the-phone-has-rung-middle-of-the-night breath.

There is no one on the other end. An insistent hum.

I sit defeated at Richard's feet, knowing I will not be able to cross the tender boundary back into sleep. Giggles make a peristalsis down tucks of his belly, ending in spasms of the wilting cock. His eyes slit, satyric, sleep crumbs packed at corners. "They always find you," he says.

"Give me a cigarette, Richard."

Light gleams from book spines, muttering — the whole word-wasting choir of them — a monotone of remedies and passions. I refuse a glance at my own failing attempt on the desk. *Nu, you want to be a writer . . . what have you accomplished?* they mutter. I ignore them. I could agree with Richard in a cynical mood: they amount to nothing, *moins que rien!* Library of failed attempts, for them who haven't courage to witness life directly, from them who haven't adequately explored it.

His clothes form an untidy scramble on the floor, scrotum a mound of conceit. "You've got great tits, Pearlman," he coos, and wonders why we haven't slept together. It does seem remarkable: these many nights he has camped on my couch, afraid to penetrate the DMZ of his neighborhood after dark.

"Because we want to remain friends." I cover myself with the robe.

"You're too udderish for me anyway," Richard smirks. "I like trainer bra titties; like your friend, little Bach."

"I won't get back to sleep." I light the cigarette. Richard shrugs, squatting in a coat hanger lotus, foot soles together, knees pointing out, intending perhaps to keep watch with me.

"I have a job interview tomorrow," I remind us both.

"You don't want the job, Pearlman. Remember? You want to be a prizewinning journalist."

"That kind of sarcasm I don't need right now."

He scratches his balls in profound unconcern.

"You got no modesty, love." I snuggle into a couch corner. There is the faintest lingering persuasion of sleep, like a hiker far ahead on the trail. I despair of catching it. Richard roots at his groin (he wouldn't bring crabs to my couch?). Heat pours in open windows, swelters . . . I remember Rome, our sluggish odyssey between Colosseum and *aranciata* vendors, Natalie forever dumping cupfuls of water over her head. She is out somewhere . . . New Hampshire? Her second summer stock season. Up against lonesome truths of America. (Just maybe out to call from a phone booth across the road; fireflies blink, a dog howls somewhere; she decides too soon there will be no answer and hangs up.) Richard slides toes up my leg, sniffing at the underbelly of a thigh. "The boy is hungry," he whispers, his foot a concupiscent grub, parting my robe. I slap it closed. "The boy is presumptuous."

Richard sighs. "What a beautiful snatch."

It becomes a standoff: I grip the foot, all muscle and sinew; his grin like the slow growth of his pecker, stretching flaccid skin around his mouth, foot stiffening gently as toes press into me. "I really don't need this," I mumble — preferring it to sleeplessness that awaits me in the other room. "You have the tits of a Shakti," he whispers, his gritty cat's tongue circling a nipple.

Later, I consider Lucy. Not exactly remorse. Richard thieves my thoughts. "Just something that happened," he smiles. "One look at those Pearlman thighs and it was all over but the shouting."

I laugh. "You're proof, love, that the seat of male intelligence is in the genitals."

"Hey! it's okay by this boy if you and Lucy are sleeping together. I can appreciate the attraction . . . both attractions."

I tell him I suspect he's confusing us for one of his pornographies, a masturbatory fiction. "It earns me a living." He shrugs, instantly horse grins. "How about Natalie with the sweet ass? You still tutoring her in raunchy French?"

I seize his midriff in a scissors hold. "I give, I give —" throwing hands up at once. He is on his knees, chihuahua eyes sniffing again at my cunt, his half-tumid cock an eager wagging little dog.

"You can't do it again —"

He must, of course. Putz long as a Henry Moore phallus. Only when he has crumpled sideways, his ragged snores filling the apartment, do I fathom my frustration. His cock still rouses raw hunger in me — though it's sedation I want, not pleasure. I demand that suppurating Lazarus rise from the dead. He tastes of rotting shrimp, paws at my face with unconscious fingers; limp, drooping at a pompous, self-satisfied angle. Furious, I straddle him, grind like a cowboy into the saddle of his hips. Sink my teeth into a bare shoulder. Richard comes up bucking, eyeballs forcing wide the slits of satyr eyes . . . back in his own apartment, where a junkie disembowels his dreams with a knife.

I was briefly tempted to keep Richard around. Not love, mutual convenience: so often he couldn't go home and I couldn't sleep. Insomnia the bin where all the day's unfinished business collected. It seasoned into rugs and wainscoting of that dark apartment, sat on a bed corner whickering as I tossed and moaned. Insomnia was my incubus; it fucked me good.

Dad was worse. I knew from Mom's *Cherry Orchard* peevishness and his compensatory gruffness. "She's becoming a goddamn nag," he complained. "She stands right outside the fucking door when I go to the bathroom like I'm a goddamned kid." The more he cursed, the more he gasped for life's breath. Their sparring — her worry and his, expressed in contempt for hers — contributed to my sleeplessness, trying to imagine life without him.

Money worries, too. Writing worries that wove like an endless tapeworm through dreams, gobbling up what meager nourishment short sleep provided. At times, whole novel plots and episodes quickened willy-nilly in my spotty sleep, and I woke in a panic, scrawling huge words page over page in the dark, frantic to get it down — to no avail; for the tapeworm, after it had consumed sleep, consumed itself, leaving only the rustlings of cannibal half-words, like cockroaches scuttling in the walls. While my mind hatched anxious tomorrows of zombieish half-consciousness, dragging body and soul like a gallows weight, ending in yet another sleepless night. The logic of insomnia: chronic continuity, the barking of a moronic hound.

Lingering half-dreams filled the night with images, implicitly sexual: the acid smell of a great oak near where I slipped into Lake George one adolescent morning, deliciously naked, bushes filled with the Peeping Tom eyes of animals; the suburban scent of grass clippings at twelve, when summer gave clothing to my mons veneris — exotically, glisteningly black — and with it neighbor Teddy Katz peeking in my window one Friday night, yarmulke slipped to the back of his head like Moses coming down from Sinai, eyes swollen twin tablets. I stripteased in view of the curtain crack, stepping away just as I unhooked my bra, beginning a thwarted romance that lasted until the snow fell. Serially, I dreamt of the women's locker room at the Danbury Racquet Club, where, as a child beside my mother, I stood gaping at tan lines and loose tummies, breasts that were a garden of blossoming flowers — from perky, athletic poppies to sprawling, imponderable water lilies — my gaze so nakedly uninhibited that there was soon turned to me a row of bleached and dimpled asses, at which I began to giggle; while Mom blushed, helplessly scolded, finally seized me by the elbow and dragged me away. Every door of sleep leading to the vaguely sour smell of that dressing room. Teddy Katz's eyes lingered in the first snarl of commuter traffic as I brooded hollow-eyed over dawn's coffee, wondering why I couldn't dream up a good novel plot, instead of pre-menarche pornography.

I tried masturbating myself to sleep. I ached, burned (from what I later realized was the vibrator), stood naked at the open window in night air rank with restless life. Traffic edged past on the street below, the building across claimed insomniacs of its own in many lighted windows. The city a speed freak with a hypodermic jabbed in its heart. I fell back into an armchair, switched on the lamp and had sex with myself before all the Teddy Katzes of Ninety-eighth Street. Floating in muggy release, my own sweat, neither satisfied nor despairing, but visited by pricking anxieties about the day to come, it occurred to me ironically that I had chosen the role of observer in life — secondhand woman, recording voyeuse. Writers don't act but record the actions of others. Yet I had always considered myself action oriented. Seeing my reflection in the window, frowsy in a yellow penumbra of light, I understood that the ultimate action is surely rebellion, the ultimate rebellion is against one's own nature. Strangely comforted by that observation, I became deliciously drowsy and fell asleep with dawn's light full in my face.

Time had come to move. I convinced myself that insomnia was like the gloomy northern exposure, a given of the place. Moreover, I could no longer afford the rent as I could in teaching days. I began looking in Richard's Lower East Side: walked filthy streets past stripped, derelict cars, monuments to urban anarchy and the cynical indifference of law and order, parking tickets stuck like flags to the looted carcasses. Clusters of tawny young men tilted brown-bagged bottles to lips, outdoing one another in mongrel insults and piercing wolf whistles — which only fools could imagine women find complimentary. I could live with it. I needed low rent and time to write.

Richard admitted me through a reinforced street door. "Sounds like Maxine," he shouted from inside, "but junkies are blue jays; they can mimic anything. Besides, not even Mother Courage Pearlman has the balls to walk this neighborhood alone —"

"For Godsake, Richard!" Trying to keep my back away from the street where a gang of curious kids had gathered.

"Aw fuck it. Probably is Pearlman." His eye appeared like a small bird in the door crack. "Are you fucking crazy?" He pulled me inside, slamming the door behind. As we climbed the stairs, threw me scrutinizing glances, as if still unconvinced.

The stairwell miasma of piss and vomit percolated into his apartment: shabby fortress, with barred windows and a meat cleaver embed-

ded in the nightstand, stark bare and peeling walls. I shivered, though it
was airless and baking hot. "It's Auschwitz in here. How can you stand
it?"

"It's Auschwitz out there." Richard sat edgily on the studio cot,
cracking his knuckles. He gestured about. "You probably think this is
some kinda nudnik racial fascination, right? Hey, this is numero uno
ranked block in the city for homicides — the whole fucking city! Last
week they found a cop in a plastic bag down there, chopped up in little
pieces."

"You're kidding?"

He stared, pan-faced. With Richard you couldn't always be sure.

"At first I dug the neighborhood," he said. "Alphabet Town. I
shmoozed Spanish to old men on stoops, kissed babies, loved those
Rican Lolitas — ohhh what tits! I mean it oozed romance. But that first
night I came home the place had transformed: grade Z *West Side Story*.
Even the punks were scared to be on the street."

He seemed offended by my laughter. I conceded I might try elsewhere. As he walked me back to First Avenue, I said, "Get out of here,
Richard. The violence outside can't be half as bad as the violence
you've brought in."

Richard focused straight onward like a condemned man. "You think
I don't want out? You think I wouldn't move tomorrow if I had the
bread?"

Ahead, children splashed in a jet of water from an open fire hydrant.
A berry brown boy with a mop of black hair cried "Mira!" and de-
flected the spray at us. I ran through, laughing. But Richard froze mid-
spray, turning to face the boy in slow, mechanical movements, clothes
disheveled by the spume hitting him full stomach. The boy's fingers remained planted on the hydrant nozzle, defying fear, while Richard
glinted maniacally at him. "Little cocksucker," he hissed, starting for
the boy. Mothers squawked alarm from their stoops, faces turned. I
strode back into the stream, hooked his elbow and marched on past a
gauntlet of anthracite stares.

"What is it with you?" I demanded when we reached the corner.
"Have you lost your mind?"

Richard hung his head, both remorseful and childishly truculent,
hair a damp ridiculous rag over his forehead. "It's making me edgy," he
grumbled, "this fucking neighborhood." His eyes flailed wildly at a
passing black boy toting a basketball under his arm, staring back at us in

our limp, dripping clothes, his hot, troubled eyes burning klansmen's crosses in our foreheads.

"Listen, I'm not going to let paranoia bite a hole in my heart no matter where I live." I turned and walked away, leaving him standing there on the corner.

A few days later, I found a fifth-floor walkup in the East Village, territory of Ginsberg, Kerouac, and Gregory Corso. Just up the street in a dingy brick building W. H. Auden had his winter diggings; in the basement Trotsky had published his *Novy Mir*. Solid writers' country. I felt immediately at home. Besides, I was anxious to be done with looking, the most petty of the things I had resolved to accomplish (with writing articles and finishing work on the M.A. and the novel that hogged desk space and a disproportionate territory of consciousness). I had been reading Gurdjieff and had decided that I, too, must seize authority over my own destiny.

The morning I was to move I sat midpoint of blond oak floors of my new apartment, delighting in its white-walled bareness, light streaming in windows. I would furnish with absolute austerity, a few mats on the floor — leaving stuffed furniture behind for fear insomnia had crept roach-like into the cushions — and would live stripped down to essentials like an urban yoga and sleep the sweet sleep of the unburdened.

The entire crew came to move me. They formed a fire brigade, schlepping boxes upstairs, where tireless Lucy organized my new life. Richard stood midstreet with sweat dripping from his nose addressing a gang of neighborhood kids who seemed to be sizing up the loot, his T-shirt wrapped around his head like a pirate's kerchief. He was saying:

"She's a writer, man. Another Ferlinghetti come to sing benisons of depraved verse and immortalize your dreck-dingy — but *escúchame!* redeemed through the scarfy pen — your neighborhood, fellas! Aren't you delighted?"

The Puerto Rican kids watched him. Two old Ukrainian women had stopped to rest a moment from their ceaseless wanderings, setting down webbed shopping bags and exchanging sibilants in a gobbling tongue. Richard turned to them.

"She's come to inspect the stains on your underwear and ferret out the breed of bugs in your armpits. *You must be delighted!*"

Paynor laughed; the neighborhood punks eyed Richard hostilely; from beneath flowered babushkas, the Ukrainians flashed devouring glances at us. I smiled and snapped, "Shut up, Richard." They gathered up their bags and trudged on.

"Right, pop! That's her window." Richard pointed for the benefit of an old black man whose skull was covered in a tight cotton nap. "Think of the opportunity. You could stand right here and dictate a whole fucking book." Richard demonstrated, megaphoning hands around his mouth, while the punks laughed and mocked the old man, who grinned agreeably and mumbled, "Tha's right."

"Everything you've been holding in, pop, every dirty bit of gossip about the world. These fellas here will be your Greek chorus. The Athenians of Avenue B."

"Tha's right."

The punk who appeared to be top honcho tilted his head and eyed Richard obliquely, running a thumb along the ridge of his nose. Richard threw hands to chest. "Hey! if you don't like the script, take it up with her —" nodding at me "— I got nothing to do with it."

"Can't you shut him up?" I asked Paynor.

"Shut him up! I love it."

I pulled Richard's elbows down like pump handles. "Could we get this crap unloaded so I can get on with my life?"

The young gang leader flashed a gold tooth. "I help you get on, baby."

Richard had turned back to the old man. "You're sharp, pop. You notice a bit of the *beat-nik* about her. Don't let it worry you, man. Beatniks are just white nig —"

Lucy had materialized and in one deft move stuffed a coffee-colored bra into Richard's open mouth. His jaw worked as if trying to eject the mouthful, arms thrashing like windmills, straps dangling ridiculously over his chin. Lucy whumped him towards the van with the heel of a hand. Street punks whooped. The old man, one eye dull and cataract clouded, repeated "Tha's right . . ." And just then the bottom fell out of my manuscript box which Brenda was taking from the truck.

Pages hit the ground in one huge flock and scattered to the wind like seabirds. I flew after those cartwheeling towards a subway grating — all of us! Richard, my bra like a pennant around his neck, Lucy moving cat quick, Paynor nipping up pages in fingertips, Brenda, our classical musician, flurrying ineffectually with gasped "Oh my God's"; but it was Angel and his gang who really came through, displaying the advantages of quick feet and tight organization.

Afterwards, we sat around my novel in a helter-skelter pile on the apartment floor, guzzling beer in the dousing heat. "Hope we got them all," I sighed. Paynor shrugged, emitting a faint aura of cloves, glancing coquettishly at gangleader Angel: a handsomeness pocked with sheer arrogance, T-shirt sleeves rolled in tight, fastidious bands. Brenda arched thin blonde eyelids and demanded of Paynor, "What is it, exactly, that you have against fiction?" He batted eyelashes at her; it was a discussion they'd had many times. Angel downed a beer in one guzzle, turned to me and promised, "Nobody bother you in my neighborhood, baby." I smiled gratitude, wondering what he expected in return. Richard grinned. (He would say: *It's your strawberry shortcake knockers. Every young man longs to bury his head between the twin hills of Jerusalem.*)

Paynor ogled Angel. Pure infatuation. His passions, beyond science, were chess and cock. Once, according to Richard, Paynor had proposed sex to him. "I said Why not?" Richard later told me. "But it was the worst blow job I ever had — all precision and applied physics. So I said, 'You gotta get passionate, man. Soul. It's what your race is famous for.' Paynor started blubbering. I mean it was fucking ridiculous: two grown men, bare-ass naked, holding each other's schlongs and discussing a blow job." Ever since, their relationship had been much like Richard's friendship with Lucy: testy and charged with pubescent urgency.

Now Richard glanced at the door. "Welcome to Breadloaf," he cried, turning to Angel. "I want you fellas to meet one of the sweetest asses in New York City."

In the doorway stood Natalie, with Lydia, Marty, and Carol, who made straight for the beer. "Perfect timing, girls," smirked Lucy; "we've already finished the work."

I leapt up to embrace Nat. "Natalie! My God, you look ravishing. Gee, it seems like ages . . ."

She was transformed: a bright Mexican blouse, tight jeans accentuating her thin waist, Oaxacan sandals and huge hooped earrings, hair billowing loose over bare shoulders, *au naturel,* fluffing free and zapped with energy — that flamboyant razz-ma-tazz and cultural apocalypse of the hour. At last she had found a fashion of her own. She begrudged a blush; then grumbled, "I had mono for a month and you never came to see me." Holding her hands, I beamed at the sleek new profile.

"Whatever you had agreed with you."

"I had mono!" she insisted.

Marty hadn't changed (not even her shirt): a small icon, a pudgy Mao smile, on each stubby collar wing of a wilted flannel shirt, alkaline sweat moons under the arms. But Lydia had leapt from braces directly into womanhood: full-hipped, nearly busty, wearing fashionable granny glasses; home from Bennington for the weekend. Jolly blonde Carol twisted a chair around and straddled it, skirt bunching about her waist. Underneath she wore green panty hose, nothing else.

"For Godsake, Carol!" I muttered.

Plucking a beer bottle from the floor, she stuck it between pea green thighs. Richard hooted, the girls laughed, Angel's cronies traded skin and slid moist smiles at her.

"Fiction," Paynor said, nostrils dilated in that dark, expressive face, "is for people who can't see life as it truly is."

"Like Dostoevski maybe? Or Balzac?" Brenda's ginger eyes snapped.

"Did you know I quit teaching?" I asked Nat. "All that youth was giving me a bad case of adult blues."

"Gee, aren't you aging a bit fast?"

"Wasn't much fun after your class left. A word of wisdom: Jobs are good finding and leaving, in between is shit."

"How about it, Pearlman?" Richard demanded. "Daudert says fiction's dishonest —"

Paynor batted eyelashes, his brow rippling silkenly upward. I was annoyed. "I can't discuss literature with someone who hasn't read any."

Paynor's fingers butterflied to chest. "I've read Shakespeare, James, and Karl Marx."

"Karl Marx!" cried Richard. "You fucking shlemazel."

Brenda sat up like a squirrel. "Shakespeare is dishonest?"

Paynor blinked at Richard, insulted, nostrils flaring regally. "I am compelled by verifiable fact alone, you understand?" Depositing the phrase before us and tapping a long slender finger on the floor. He spoke with put-upon superiority, tilting head back and regarding listeners over his smug chin, batting eyelashes emphatically.

"Oh Christ!" Musician Brenda lit a cigarette and snubbed it right out. "Don't you ever *feel* anything?"

"Certainly I have feelings. As a disciplined scientist, I've trained myself to mistrust them. I acknowledge what may be verified and duplicated, nothing more. Feelings don't fall in that category."

"And you've read Shakespeare?" Brenda demanded.

"Certainly."

Angel tapped my arm, inquiring, "Who's the faggot?"

Seeming not to apprehend the menace in his voice, Nat hissed: "No artist would invent a hydrogen bomb. It takes a repressed Teller creep to do that. Scientists are destroying the world. If people were smart, they would exterminate all the scientists."

"Lynch the fucking boogie scientist," howled Richard.

Angel crinkled a beer can and tossed it in Paynor's lap. "Hey fairy, suck my dick!" I touched his elbow.

"You're my guest here, you know. And so is Paynor."

Angel mock bowed. "Whatever you say, beautiful."

Paynor breathed with wounded hauteur. "You don't know what you are saying. Without science there is no art. No rabbit skin glue, none of your acrylics. The sciences subsume everything known to man — and unknown. Even your irrational behavior." His smugness such a taunt I wanted to take a swipe at it myself. Natalie held his eyes, smoke leaking from her nostrils.

"I think you're an overeducated moron," she said.

Richard screamed approval, seizing Nat's hand and rubbing it vigorously between his own. Lucy's December gray eyes froze on her. "Must you always play *enfant terrible?*" Turning to Paynor, "I don't think Natalie's hostile so much as frustrated that you won't acknowledge the expressionistic outlook."

"I am hostile. 'Cause he's a simian parading as a bulgebrain, and the kind of sleazo queer that makes me want to throw up."

Paynor threw a wounded hand to chest. Richard cried, "Hey Daudert, she's got you pegged, man." Angel released a piercing whistle, while his buddies shifted restlessly about. Lucy was furious. "Can't you ever control yourself?"

Nat wheeled on her. "And you're an even bigger fag than he is."

Richard roared, raising her arms champ style. All of Lucy's anger transferring instantly to him. Paynor remained motionless, one fey hand pinned to breast, and I realized that the persona he intended to present the world was that of steely, virile intellectual. "Now you see," he muttered hoarsely, "I don't become hysterical."

Marty surveyed us from droop-lidded, bloodshot eyes, Promethean mouth curling down at corners. "It isn't a question of whether we need arts or sciences; we have them. It's a question of who they serve. Now they serve the corporate elite. We need art and science that serves the people."

"Hooray!" cried Brenda with a little fist flourish.

"Talk talk talk . . . drive me crazy." Angel tuned his portable radio to a sizzling Hispanic station and began rocking on his haunches, bumping shoulders to the beat.

Paynor turned to Marty, addressing a dazzle of buttons — "Peace Now," "God is a Gook," "VIRGINS SUCK" — at eye level across her triple-D bosom, while she gazed distractedly off at Angel and Carol dancing a pelvis-grinding twist: she on supple green legs, he lifting feet high and thrusting them down, jeans tight tight.

Paynor left soon, complaining of a headache. Nat joined Richard in spontaneous celebration around Angel's radio, throwing her hips at the music. Lydia wiggled breasts like bait before the punk with a scarlip. Nat's arms winging out, face contorted in fierce solipsism; Richard's pelvis aching toward her, his own features twisted into a concupiscent grin. He planted hands under her small breasts, hers went down to meet them, holding them there. "Little cunt," I whispered, confronting emotions too disarmingly like jealousy, realizing for the first time that friend Natalie has become a woman.

Natalie was a volatile spirit, litmus of emotion in the atmosphere. Just to have her around was adventure. Twirling on the stone rim of the Trevi Fountains in Rome and falling dizzy into the water, coming out dank as a sewer rat but spirits high and dry and dancing hair-plastered and sturgeon-eyed down the piazza to the delight of small children and horror of their mamas. In Crete, tumbling head over heels in love with a hairy-chested sailor, only to dump the poor man when he tried to make good on her flirtations. Nat, the child who is never satisfied, and when told it's a sin never to be satisfied, replies, "I'm not satisfied with it being a sin." No one a bigger hassle on the Europe trip — not even Marty McCoy, spilling sexual favors like heady Irish stout; or Carol, knocked up by the kitchen steward on the ferry from Trieste to Ancona (an abortion later in New York). Nat was a natural catalyst: always the one to hit the switch just as the light bulb goes. Something to do with a penchant for illogic, rebellion against the given order of things. Full of Quixote highs and Molly Bloom broods. Windmill chasings and regular throws from the horse. Just as I have decided that discontent and depression are endemic to her, Nat wings off in ecstasies over the play of moonlight on the surf, or the voice of a fisherman singing from his skiff.

Artist absolute. That roller coaster temperament with its dizzy dips and giddy climbs.

Nat inspired radical reaction, never indifference. Lucy despised her. Their mutual aversion escalating to full scale war on the European tour, while I, caught in the middle between Lucy's impatience and Nat's jealousy, told them to get along or get lost; my income for escorting eight nubiles through a Greek Passion in the most fertile estrus of their lives didn't cover feuds — especially involving my co-counselor.

At times now, I would see her wandering Village streets aimlessly, or sitting alone in Washington Square Park, a book open but unheeded across her knees, absorbed in people around her, face flipping through emotions as if discovering humankind's poorly kept secrets. Sometimes sweet dopestruck Carol sat beside her. The girl had become a walking Casbah: colored feathers in her hair, bells on her toes, jingling exotic scents. I worried that Nat, too, was being swept up in the maelstrom of dope, disillusionment, and sidesaddle sex, the John Lennon Grateful Dead Hey Hey ElBeeJay stone your head on brown rice through the looking glass poster paraphernalia of the hour. She balanced in indefinite status between student, artist, lost soul.

Gradually, as my eyes adjusted to the gloom of her apartment, a personal holocaust emerged: clothes scattered in flight, dirty laundry mingled indiscriminately with cat food tins and Kleenex wads, a pestilence crawling over the floor and up onto furniture. Nat sprawled on the couch, as if part of the general calamity (with what panache you live like a slob when your mother is among the ten top names in American fashion). "To what do I owe this honor?" she asked.

"Just a visit." I tried a smile. "What goes on here? The place smells like a Bowery flophouse."

She shrugged. "We're a little overcrowded: four people in a one bedroom apartment — including Suzie from the New School." In the near-dark I thought I made out a frown.

"Listen, the *pas de soleil sans ombre* shtick may be romantic to you but I find it depressing." I opened a paper shade. The sudden flux of light setting teeth on edge.

"How's things?" I asked.

A tabby cat leapt to her lap, purring while she stroked desultorily. The cat shook its head, mewling when she lit a cigarette. Within a brooding smoke cloud, her eyes were swollen, outlined in red. "I might drop out of school," she said, seizing the cat and dropping it to the floor. "I hate cats." Those eyes nipped at me like small fish. "I thought our relationship would change after I graduated, but now we hardly see each other."

"A college woman." I immediately regretted the patronage in my tone. "You haven't changed, Nat. Except maybe more hard-core on the smoking."

"When we talk on the phone I get the feeling you're trying to avoid me. You're always in some huge rush and you have a million excuses for not being able to see me. I don't want that kind of second-class friendship in my life anymore." An intensity that is almost embarrassing. I think of those young women Rossetti painted: pale, ethereal, yet a fierce capacity for devotion. A *Jeanne d'Arc* hunched but majestic on horseback, smothered under the weight of armor.

I spread my hands. "New Yorkers are busy people; we don't have a lot of time for socializing."

"Don't tell me about New Yorkers. I was born here, remember? Not out in Connecticut or someplace."

"*Touchée*, Natalie."

Then in one of those Natalie Bach flip-flops, she blushed an entire zodiac of red and invited me to stay to dinner. I glanced at the detritus of four young lives that wouldn't have passed the Board of Health. "Sounds risky. Don't you ever clean this dump?"

"Marty just messes it up again." She sat up, hooking a pair of ragged nylons on a toe. "Suzie's!" she grimaced.

In the Calcutta Hole of a bedroom I could make out only two pale shapes. "Do you share beds?"

"Marty never sleeps here; she just uses it as a litter depository. And Suzie has appropriated the couch. The woman's a nympho. Really! She's majoring in sleazo sex at NYU, always bringing home these creeps she meets in front of the Waverly. Then they hang out and try to score with the rest of us. It's a real drag."

"So why not bail out?"

"Sure! on my income? Mother refuses to help with the bucks unless I move to a dorm. She says I only see them as money bags. She's been saying that all my life." Nat frowned, then her face brightened. "Remember Clarence from next door?"

"The graduate student. Social work or something?"

"We're lovers now." Very serious, smoke winding in coils from her thin nose. "A while ago he offered to initiate me to lovemaking whenever I was ready."

"How generous of Clarence."

"He's much older, a very gentle man, and I knew he would be going back to California; so it seemed really perfect." She wanted me to have details: no pain, Clarence was sweet and solicitous. "And when we came together I thought the walls would crash down. I heard Bach's *Magnificat*. Then we smoked some grass and I kept giggling. Last week he went back to Los Angeles. I probably won't ever see him again." She stretched extravagantly.

"You sound delighted."

She shrugged. "There aren't any complications this way."

"Sounds like a psychology experiment."

Nat picked up a guitar and began moody strumming.

"I have a breakthrough of my own to announce," I said. "I may have placed an article with the *Voice*." (Her limp smile; she couldn't care less.) "I won't believe it until I receive a check. Editors still aren't ready to hear women's anger. They want us cheerfully Bloomsburying, arranging verbal bouquets."

"Women are copouts," she snorted, thrumming hard into a Dave Van Ronk tune.

"So tell me, what's the trouble with school?"

"They don't teach anything — except what the IRS wants you to know."

"I can't identify with that. I liked college. I got no bones to pick with that order of things."

Her head dipped, fingers flew, jaw set into the music. She muttered at the ceiling, "Won't be anything left when we graduate anyway; our parents' generation hogged it all up."

Slogans of the hour. Not easily refuted with an ugly, senseless war in Asia and much of the world hungry while the few gorged. Her friends dropping out, bumping lover to lover, job to job. It was a generation of dropouts.

"They always say: 'We're doing it all for our children; we don't want them to suffer what we suffered.' What they don't say is that in return they expect their kids to live out their fantasies. It's Mother's fantasy to go to college, not mine. Our parents aren't satisfied with only one shot at life; they're greedy to live ours, too."

Natalie sang at the ceiling, a Beatles song — exorcising me along with her mother.

"I could find more glamorous places to be ignored," I said.

Nothing. Words breathed upward.

"So, I'll cook. I was invited for dinner and for dinner there must be preparations. Nu?"

In what passed for a kitchen, cockroaches cruised walls, garbage laid siege from a corner. Occasionally, when it got to smelling bad enough, they threw a bag of it out the window into the Gehenna of a backyard. The fridge was empty. I glanced in at her anemic face, near phosphorescent in the gathering dusk. "Listen, I'd love to take you to the Szechwan on Broadway." Her eyes lit, but she suggested dutifully that I couldn't afford it. "Very true. But when you get hungry enough —"

My eye was attracted to a neat stack of hardback books in a corner. She said they had been "liberated" from the bookstore where she and Carol were working. I should let her know if I needed anything.

"Good Jewish girls are stealing books now?"

"They're real rip-offs," she cried. "They don't even pay minimum wage. And their prices are ridiculous."

"Stealing is stealing."

Nat plucked discordant chords. "What makes you so superior? You're no saint."

"Clearly. Perhaps I'm working on it. We can liberate ourselves, you know. Beyond the big issues there's social progress on a personal level, becoming what we believe is right. Like your brother Adam."

"Maybe it's arrogance," she sulked.

"It takes a certain arrogance. All our Gandhis and Kings are morally arrogant. It also takes courage. You become exceptional by willing to be exceptional. It doesn't happen by chance. You must look outward, beyond yourself. Listen, if we're eating Chinese we'd better hurry; I'm busy later."

Nat fiddled with a tuning peg, then launched into a Hebrew folk song (perhaps one Adam taught her), voice lilting over soft consonants.

"Very lovely, Natalie," I said when she had finished.

"Adam says I could sing in Israeli nightclubs. I don't know. I might take some art classes, or just commit myself to theatre."

"Wow! Art, theatre, nightclubs. I'm impressed."

She flushed. "I'm not a dilettante. I really love all the arts; I just don't know which one I love most yet."

"Listen, the vital thing is that you decide for yourself. Not for Adam, or Mama or Papa, or, for chrissake, money! You have to learn what *you* want out of life. Most people never do. They allow expectations or circumstances to decide for them. Life's numberless little go-alongs."

She put the guitar aside, engrossed now. "How is Adam?" I asked. She didn't appear to notice my awkwardness.

"He invited me to the kibbutz. Sun, hard work, fresh fruit, and hostile neighbors, he says. I'm starting to think, since life's a battle anyway, you might as well know who the enemy is. Adam knows . . . he really does."

"Right. Your brother sees himself as a Biblical precept: *Men must be soldiers*. That's it! No pussyfooting around."

"I think you're still in love with him." Nat smiled.

A startled laugh. "You're very generous with my affections."

"Maybe Adam is right. Jews should be true Jews, you know?"

"Listen, it's not Israel or Orthodoxy that makes a Jew. To be part of our tribe is to doubt that things are perfect in this world, or perfectible; yet to cling to the hope of perfection."

"Hey! I like that," she cried.

"We're eternal skeptics. Thus we've produced our Freuds, Marxes, Einsteins. It starts there: first doubt, then curiosity, then you go after the truth. No doubt, no curiosity, no truth! We're obsessive machers for improvement, we Jews. Makes our Christian neighbors nervous. We won't sit still, lousy boat rockers. They think us cynical because we won't accept the Hereafter myth. We aren't cynical; we simply realize that no one longs for righteousness when they expect a fairy tale ending."

Nat thrust out her hands excitedly. "That's just what I was trying to tell Richard. Exactly!"

"When do you see Richard?" I asked, alarmed.

She angled forward confidentially. "He wants in my pants."

"Does he?" My eyes wandered to the window and snapped back. "Stay away from Richard, Nat. He's not for you."

"Thanks, Mother." Nat held my gaze. "If I slept with all the men you two think I sleep with my yoni would fall out."

I bolted laughter. "Listen," catching my breath, "Richard is a goat."

* * *

Giving up on dinner, I take the train to 125th Street. Leroy leans against the frame of the open door in a sleeveless loose-knit T-shirt as I come up the stairs, affecting cool, but tense and mirthless, blocking entry. His eyes take an easy stroll up my body, a smile edged with disdain. I manage to speak before he does. "I don't always feel comfortable coming up here. Maybe you haven't noticed, but I'm lighter-complexioned than most people in the neighborhood."

He taps lazily at a button on my blouse. "Oh yeah, I noticed, baby. I also noticed —" he glances at a watch spread flat and heavy across his wrist "— you are late. And this man don't like to be kept waiting."

He pours drinks, easing the cartridge onto a Charlie Mingus record. The room is instantly charged with music, lights dim instinctively. I sit on the bed and unbutton my blouse, knowing he likes to begin by invitation. His palm judges the line of my chin, a finger flirts at neck hollow and lazy on inside my bra, around the bell of a breast, pinching the nipple erect between thumb and forefinger. His eyes a little menacing. I shudder. "You're all self-confidence, aren't you, love?" He answers by sliding a hand under my skirt.

"Take your clothes off, baby."

"Hey, slow down."

He frowns and slips his shirt overhead, expecting a shiver of light over pectorals, kiss of mansweat on the air will open my legs. Often it has. "Not yet . . . ," I whisper. He leans back against the headboard and lights a joint, hitting long and watching with one eye closed before offering it. I fasten the blouse. It's as if I've slapped him. "Hey baby — " Opening his hands. I touch his moist chest. You see, I've lost my bearings amidst ethnic bits and pieces, cultural catchall — part Harlem, part Africa — tiger-striped bedspread, conga drums, dashikis, soft lights embracing a grass-skirted Afro beauty with conical chocolate-nippled breasts; facing her, a feverish Malcolm X; tacked to the bookcase, a tiny Lee Harvey Oswald, fist raised (which I don't dare ask about).

"It's not you, love. I'm just not comfortable here tonight."

He snorts contempt, hands moving slowly as if parting waters between us. "This pad *is me*. You understand? We're one and the same."

I slide a dry hand over his bare shoulders. "I just want to wake up at home tomorrow. Is that so strange?"

His mocking smile. "The woman don't want to fuck soul tonight."

"She wants to fuck *you* tonight."

"She wants to fuck black but don't want to fuck soul. 'C'mere boy, into my boo-dwah and give me some nigger stud.' That old number —"

"You want I should beg? Please, Leroy, come home with me."

"— Moment she is satisfied, starts in screaming: 'Rape! Rape!' Shii-it . . ."

"I really want to go and I probably won't without you."

"Way downtown, baby? That's enemy territory."

"Puerto Ricans everywhere." I sigh relief when he laughs.

All repeated at my apartment: music, drinks, I remove the blouse completely; he steps from slacks, bulging in tight underwear. Desire is an elf licking between my legs. We open and swell with it. Nerve endings giggle and tingle back to that childhood place, discovery. His lips tease a nipple until it stiffens against his tongue. I trace his cock, under sheer nylon — The phone rings. "Fuckinay," cries Leroy, pinning me on his lap. I snag the receiver: it is dumb habit.

A silence that listens and is unnerving.

"Who is it?" I demand. It waits, without breathing."Listen, there are eight million New Yorkers. Harass someone else."

Leroy snatches the phone. "Look here, this shit don't go down."

And I realize who it is — can nearly see her stretched out on that shabby couch, torn between need and shame, dreaming of Chinese food. Leroy slams down the receiver and turns on me.

"What in the fuck you laughing about?"

"No . . . nothing. A private joke."

"Whole damn night is a private joke." He sits stiff as a boxer about to spring from his corner. I touch his hand.

"Have you ever had someone idolize you, someone younger?"

"Every day, baby."

"I mean excessively, as if you're an extension of themselves?"

"Now you're talking bullshit." He glances at the phone.

I shudder a little. "It's a big responsibility."

When he speaks again, his voice is strained and untrifling. "I don't know where you are tonight, baby, but I'm right here, and I am about ready to be impatient."

Incredibly, he is still erect, cock about to burst through thin nylon. A moment ago I would have taken it in my lips. But desire has fled. I get up to replenish drinks, seeing in the mirrored cubby a limp open bra, dangling and slattern, tits spilling full and swollen with desire. I remove the bra. My waist is too thick, thighs outlined beneath the skirt. Mine is a body to mattress upon. A receptor's body. The thought makes me chuckle. Leroy (in the mirror) is a Hannibal or Genghis Khan studying the lay of my ass. Men plot entry; women plot possession. We deal in a separate physics: theirs of space, ours of time.

I stand before him, drinks in hand. In one deft motion he slips off his briefs. Cock lustdrunk between his legs. And when I laugh he takes it for invitation, seizing my ass. I gasp at the silky whistle of fabric as he raises the skirt and pulls down my pants. Lifting a gentle foot, I press toes into his desire, until he pulls me close and buries his face inside me. While ice clinks in glasses shaking uncontrollably in my hands.

And the phone rings. I let it ring and ring, checking an impulse to answer, but at what is surely the last moment, break away from Leroy and snatch it from its cradle.

A voice I don't recognize. A nurse, she says, at Danbury General. "Your mother asked me to call. We've admitted your father —"

"Is he all right?"

"Your mother would like you to come out immediately."

"Fucking idiot!" I scream — perhaps at myself — realizing now who had been calling the first time.

Throwing a raincoat over my nakedness, I run for the door, passing Leroy whom I have already forgotten — a naked stranger sitting rigid and angry on the lip of my couch, his eyes menacing scraps of glass. "What's this shit?" he demands.

"I have to go —" fumbling with buttons "— my father's dying." Leaving him there, naked and cursing in my living room.

"Danbury . . . Connecticut!" I cry, sliding into a cab.

The cabby's head rolls back on his shoulders. "Lady, there isn't no Connecticut in New York City."

"There isn't time to screw around. North. Danbury!"

Throwing a hand to his heart. "Do I look like a bus driver? This is a New York City taxicab, lady; it don't leave Manhattan."

"Listen, my father is dying. I have to get to Danbury General Hospital."

His eyes are tiny, barely intelligent bites from a face that is one huge moronic pastry, crowned and seemingly inspired by a Yankee baseball cap. "My condolences about the father," he says. "Believe me. But this particular taxicab don't leave the city a New York under any circumstances."

"This once, please! I'll pay whatever it costs."

Calmly he steps out of the cab and opens my door. "Out!" He thumbs.

My hand mines in a pocket — realize I haven't brought my wallet. I taste panic. An inspiration! I smile and slide a coat flap across my leg. His porcine eyes walk up my bare thigh.

"I don't trade, sweetheart," he says flatly. "Get da fuck outta my cab!"

I pull the coat closed. "The law says you have to take me."

He lunges into the cab.

I howl "RAPE!"

He leaps back, grinning at passersby. "Little misunderstanding."

"I'll pay double," I mutter (not knowing how). He inhales, staring hard at canvas stretched taut across my knees. "Triple," he snarls.

"Anything. Just hurry . . . fast!" He gets in and leaps around a corner of traffic, muttering that he must be fucking crazy.

I shoot past nurses' stations to the room where he lies, a Medusa of tubes hooking him to life. Mother rises from the bedside, taking my hand. I gasp at sight of him: shriveled, it seems, under the sheet, cheeks caved in, a baby blue haze across his forehead. His eyes come weakly open when I kiss them. Dad motions me close with a nearly imperceptible gesture and I realize, a little startled, why that ash-gray face seems so naked: it is missing the cigar that has grown from one mouth corner ever since I can remember. His growl is barely a breath. "They wanna put me out in the daisies." His cheeks quaver protest, and for just an instant those pale eyes are more desperate than I have ever seen them. I pat his face and mouth, "No, Daddy." His heavy lids fall closed.

Mom takes my elbow, begins giving hushed details of the attack: how he'd gone to the bedroom, "in one of his moods," to use the respirator. "You know Daddy's moods."

"He's going to be okay." I kiss her. "Listen, I have a cab waiting; I'd better pay him."

"A taxicab . . . from New York?"

"I had to get here. I ran without my wallet."

"How much is it?" she asks, pulling lips away from her teeth.

"Two hundred and forty dollars."

"Oy favoy!"

Though we have been whispering, Dad's eyes pop open. "Jesus!" he mumbles, and Mom sinks into a chair, laughing. "Oh Maxie, that's the best therapy your father could have."

* * *

I stayed two weeks in Connecticut in that great sprawling château, helping Mom "with things" while she nursed Dad — or rather reinforced a nurse in the losing battle to keep Hyman in bed. At times he disappeared completely; they would find him in some linen closet, unused in years, chewing a cigar from a secret stash they never found. "She was afraid —" Dad grumbled as the nurse bullied him back to bed "— if she hired a young one I'd feel her tits. So she hired this old shitbag." Scowling at her. "Good Christ, are you ugly." She regarded him sourly. He was enjoying himself like a fucking kid. But for me, no fun, no sex, no inspiration in that dreary winter palace. Many days Mom and I didn't share enough words to fill a poem. Two weeks of it and I escaped back to the East Village.

At St. Marks Place, Master's thesis in dead heat competition with magazine articles and growing political urgencies. I wrote for neighborhood newspapers about civil rights and asshole landlords. Some mornings stumbled nakedly into my living room to discover neighbors had spent the night (could scarcely recall inviting them): Hispanic women, evicted by landlords or deserted by husbands, lives crawling with bawling, inconsolable *infantes* — lovable-detestable black-haired urchins pissing on the rug and rubbing graham cracker goo over typewriter keys; until, desperate, I evicted them from my life, their sad eyes drinking me up as if for the first time fully understanding their predicament. Life is a series of evictions. Later, awful fits of conscience. But I had my needs, too.

Through a summer of torched cities and black militancy, Leroy despaired of life in the North and moved back to Atlanta. I landed a job with a textbook publisher proofreading psychology texts. It was money. Richard appeared at my door on one of those get-to-work mornings when life seems as hackneyed as a coffee commercial. "I was just on my way out," I told him. "I was just on my way in," he replied, moving past me and sprawling on the couch. He shaded sleepless pink eyes with a hand. "I gotta tell you about the kid," he said. "Last night I ask if she wants to ball. You know what she says? *Richard, you didn't have to ask.*" Laughter squealing out. "You didn't fucking have to ask!"

"Why," I demanded, "are people always presenting me the erotic history of Natalie Bach?"

"Watch out! Pearlman is jealous."

"Natalie's got enough troubles without you, love, believe me. And so do I."

It took a moment for him to see that I meant it. His face flared with something like a smile. "Y'know, that's why I always avoided you, Pearlman. You're a goddamn ball-bust right down to the core."

"I just want you out, Richard. I don't need the rest."

I saw little of Natalie. She had dropped NYU and begun classes at the New Art Institute, her life choices edited down now to painting and sculpture, with Israel on the horizon of possibility. It represented to her approximately what it had represented to vastly different Jews of another generation who had inhabited the Lower East Side in those vastly different days when it had been a teeming immigrant village, where bearded men sat over tea reading the daily *Forverts* and discussing Bialik's poetry and the fine points of the Zohar. It represented hope. When all else fails, there is Israel. Like the Messiah — who surely comes, but only if we make too great a mess of things. Hope, too, that the New World, New York, the dreams of youth . . . might offer a lasting solution.

But now there were new stirrings in America, and Nat as excited about them as the rest of us. I saw her at Village coffee houses and St. Marks Church poetry readings featuring Le Roi Jones and Allen Ginsberg. A new energy in the air, legacy of the old but pursued by a generation that knew nothing of immigration and celebrated its opposite. All of us felt it — from Puerto Ricans who came across Tompkins Square Park to Beat poets who wrote about them. A living lab where people played possibilities: Zen, sex, and chemicals. You felt at the heart of it just walking streets — garbage littered, dog shit filthy, but charged with the incessant hum of conversation, from cafés, bars, sprawling furniture nude lofts and shotgun flats, where revolution was stashed under floorboards and death lurked in the eye of a needle. Poetry howls, ecstasy moans. Every day more appearing: runaways from every backwater of America discovering themselves in long hair and yeast infections and Bob Dylan and Lucy in the Sky with Diamonds, in seemingly perpetual beatitude amid the unblessed gray hulks and urine stench. A miracle incarnate. On every street corner a chapbook of poems announcing it. Right here! An Israel around us.

Natalie, like the bellwether of a generation she claimed to repudiate, made leaps that left me dizzy, caught up in the catharsis of cool despair, imminent apocalypse, and sexual divination. So much the seeker, lop-eyed celebrant, impressionable tabula rasa upon which the moment could etch its havoc.

One day she appeared at my apartment in plaster-spattered jeans, hair splashed out in a great nimbus. Her eyes glowed; she was perhaps high. Beside her was a blond beautiful creature, real pretty boy, with refined, nearly feminine features and transparent blue eyes. She had come to show us off to each other.

"This is Claude," she smiled, innocent as a spring flower, wholly in-cognizant of the sun's infidelity. And he offered a smile that was all sex and narcissism.

CHAPTER ELEVEN

A DUCK AND
A DINOSAUR FOOT

MARTY HUNG A SIGN OVER THE TOILET:

DON'T DUMP RICHARDS IN THE JOHN

The fact is, I had danced with him so often to Drums of Passion, gotten sweat-sticky and itchy-sexed rubbing eyes with him I thought he would never ask. Afterwards, when I bent down to kiss his tuchus — really the best part of him — Richard shot up, frantic, crying: "No you don't. I don't need another ball-bust!"

Richard was nuts.

Generally, I couldn't get frantic about sex. Occasionally I joined Carol on the Saturdayniteprowl, sitting at the Figaro, keeping a cappuccino alive while she singlehandedly flirted guys at the neighboring table, leaning over, braless, to accept a light, dazzling them with her amusement park eyes, talking talking as if sex had gone verbal. Until finally one of them noticed me and asked, "You Italian, too? Italian chicks are hip." And I lassoed him with cigarette smoke and said, "No, I'm an aborigine nun," sliding sideways out of the booth. When Carol caught up with me on the street — despairing out her arms, "Why don'cha talk? The woman's a regular oyster" — I explained that I despised collegiate types with faces like botanical gardens for exotic species of acne.

Some days I could barely squeeze in my apartment door. The place was a disaster zone. There was a smell of cats. Marty dumped her frowsy life on the living room floor and Suzie appropriated my bed, scattering cosmetics and her ruttish paraphernalia everywhere. I threw it all out; and when Suzie came home and freaked out, I shouted, "This is *my* bedroom . . . remember?"

"Be cool," said Carol, "everything is mellow."

She passed a joint. Weed had become her lover — *Cannabis erectus!* A way of life. Running cherry-eyed to jobs or an occasional class (Marty worked at the Forty-second Street library, Carol modeled at the Art Students League). Rock 'n' Roll and latebeds and sex. Jerry and his friends appearing at any hour, sitting around a gurgling hookah, smoking and laughing in a sandalwood haze. I joined their regime half-heartedly, often found myself protesting, "There's more to life than dope and sex." Carol just laughed, but Marty agreed. There were political imperatives — like putting a bullet in LBJ. She was buddies with the Columbia students downstairs, who considered themselves urban guerrillas and measured the year not by Christmas or Yom Kippur but Watts and the march on Washington. Often, I met them dashing up the narrow stairs in fatigue jackets and makeshift helmets, clutching leaflets in their fists; they regarded me dubiously. Passing their door late at night, I heard the same endless conversation: Is the American working class ready? Was Malcolm X a revisionist?

I sensed what was in the air as keenly as anyone — Vietnam and Mississippi, the Free Speech Movement out at Berkeley. Not that I kept up in any read-the-paper sense. No need. News flashed along the grapevine of women's room graffiti and midnight rap sessions that grew on the air like a lush flora. The best way to discover what was happening was to read the latest change of buttons across Marty's flannel shirt. On the night Malcolm X was murdered, I remember footsteps pounding down an empty street in the Village, leaving Carol and me their portentous echo as we stood frozen, knowing something had happened. It was a time when most anything could happen.

There was the huge civil rights march through Harlem, thirty abreast, black and white together as far as the eye could see, belting out "We Shall Overcome" and accompanied by ten thousand Matties screaming wet-cheeked from tenement windows; their little ones, hair in neat cornrows, raining down tissue paper flowers and smiles big as Africa; at times the spry cheer of a wino — standing on a bench, waving madly as we passed. A miracle. My first real plunge into Sixties euphoria, thinking: My God! it really is possible. . . .

Though talk was the true elixir of the time. All other activities seemed superficial by comparison. We couldn't exhaust it. I would meet Carol and Marty after class, and in a blue haze of coffeehouse smoke we would rap as if we were the final generation of humanity. It was up to us to determine what had gone wrong.

Mostly I couldn't agree with Marty's outlook. Life seemed too rich to be reduced to political abstractions, and my own apocalypse more engrossing than the one on the street. Then again, I couldn't embrace Carol's shallow pothead hedonism. I skipped classes, haunted museums, played guitar, sat in the park drawing. I remember reading a D. H. Lawrence passage about life being enough of a struggle, we don't need all the wars and revolutions. We have our own personal politics to work out. I quoted that passage a lot.

One day I told Marty that her politico friends were like the pebble in Blake's poem, their interest in others distant and abstract, just hollow rhetoric. She eyed me, unblinking, vaguely bloodshot, shook her head and suggested I read Frantz Fanon and Trotsky to learn what was coming down in *this* century.

"We need *personal involvement*," I said with passion.

"What personal involvement? You think spreading your legs for a black brother makes the revolution?"

"What revolution? There isn't any revolution."

"Don't be so self-righteous. You do your thing, I do mine. Except I still don't understand what you do."

"My involvement is art." I glanced at Carol. "I mean my philosophy is as an artist." Carol nodded, accepting this.

"An artist?" echoed Marty, her big mouth puckering sarcastically.

"Listen, artists are the true revolutionaries. No one protested against the materialism and brutality of bourgeois society more effectively than the German Expressionists."

"The *Blaue Reiter* bunch!" Marty smirked. "Lesson numero uno in how art fails to achieve its objectives."

I blew smoke into the air. "What do you mean?"

"I mean the munitions makers had the last word. Ask Franz Marc. Painting is difficult after you've been blown to bits by a fragmentation shell. *Bomb makers aren't stopped with paintbrushes.*" She spoke as if to a child.

"His paintings outlived the bomb makers. And so will mine!"

"If you survive to paint them, or —" her eyes twinkled "— are permitted to paint them."

Carol sighed. "Maybe if we stop painting wars, wars stop happening."

"Don't you have that backwards? Art copies life, remember?"

"That's what's backwards," I cried. "Life should copy art."

Marty gave me an oversized frown.

There was college. Three semesters at NYU. It would be an exaggeration to say that I was a student. College was to me what it had been to Adam: something to do while I decided what to do. Occasionally I went to class or opened a book to Pavlov drooling over his dogs. When I explained that I'd already read *Beowulf*, my instructor grunted and said it didn't count since it had been assigned by someone else. This was Higher Education?

From my very first brush with academia I knew it wasn't for me. I had bounced into the office of my academic counselor (also speech therapist and drama coach) to obtain his approval of my course list. He was a chubby little man with cropped teeth protruding beneath a dainty moustache, seemingly stuck in his lower lip in a permanent grimace, making it impossible for him to open his mouth more than a clipped sibilant. A wave of hair rolled glossily backwards off his forehead and broke into many smaller waves. He sat very straight behind a steel gray desk in a stark institutional office, where even index cards puckered in their files. Briskly, he shoved a passage at me from Shaw's *Candida* and snapped, "Read it, please, Miss Buck," cutting me off halfway through with a flap of the hand. "That will be enough." He jotted quick cuneiform on a small pad like doctors use for prescriptions, tore off the page and thrust it at me. I wondered if I had mistakenly wandered into the clinic. "You will require two semesters of speech." He smiled. I laughed.

"You're kidding!"

"I most certainly am not kidding." His eyes mirthless as the tiny buttons pinning down his shirt collar. "You have a lisp," ejecting it as if the word tasted rotten.

"Are you nuts?"

His eyebrows leapt. "I assure you, Miss Bick, I am not . . . nuts."

"How could I have a lisp? I'm an actress."

"Hard to say. Perhaps you were born with it, or emulated someone's faulty speech habits."

I stared, incredulous, realizing he was serious. "Wouldn't I know if I had a lisp all my life?"

"These things aren't always discussed. Speech one and two. I would suggest you get them out of the way right off." He smiled those buckteeth at me.

"I'm not taking your stupid speech classes."

He grimaced as if trying to remove cold grease from his shoulder blades. "Then you shan't matriculate from this university, Miss Back."

"*Bach!*" I snapped.

"You say that you have no lisp. Repeat the sentence for me, please: I slipped, sliding down on the slick unshoveled snow."

"*I slipped, sliding down on the slick unshoveled snow.*"

"You see." His smug smile.

"See what?"

"You have lith-ped terribly, Miss Bosch." His eyeballs popping.

"Oy! I didn't *lithp*. Is this some kind of nightmare or —"

"You see. You do it every time."

"Lisp Lissp Lisssp LISSSSP . . . ," I howled.

He shoved specs up his nose. "You confirm my evaluation."

"Then how do you say it?" I demanded.

"I say —" he uttered precisely "— I do not have a *lip*."

I stared at him. Laughter welling, gurgling, bubbling, boiling up out of me as his eyes widened. I grabbed my course packet and retreated from Dr. Strangespeech's office. Outside sat a middle-aged secretary whose hair formed a close gray cap over her scalp. Her eyes waddled at me with a severe case of Association of University Women interruptus. I went out, slamming the door.

Adam's decision to trade college for the army, which had always mystified me, began to make perfect sense. Like my brother, I had no desire to be processed in the name of *liberal education*. "College isn't for artists; it's for accountants," I told Mom/Dad when I had decided to drop out. Mother's face curled up. "That may or may not be so," she said. "Nonetheless, you aren't an artist, Natalie."

"Oh yes I am, and I really always have been."

What mattered most in my life was the plaster dream slowly taking shape in the basement of the New Art Institute. *Natalie's nude. Nat's Woman Rising.* Though I titled it "The Descent." Eight feet high. Biggest hunk of plaster anyone had ever draped over an armature in that studio, said teacher Rafael, who eyed it bemusedly each time he passed, saying only, "Looking good, looking good."

Rafael, with his Zapata moustache and twinkling eyes, short but ox-shouldered, wrists like tree limbs, face pocked but ruggedly handsome. I was a bit in love with him. Mostly in love with the idea of carving. "Most people wait a little, do some clay sketches," Rafael had said that first week of class when I told him I wanted to start right in on something major. "I can't wait," I said. "The idea is leaping out of me. I'm afraid I'll lose it." Rafael shrugged, gave me a hammer, and I began building the armature. Nails bent, pieces came out too short; those wood and chicken-wire bones, that *woman* I had hoped would soar began to squat. Which was okay. The piece was defining itself. It wouldn't be avant-garde but classical: a woman stooping down to draw a jug of water. Ruth. After Carol helped me apply plaster in a great white immobile snowdrift to the armature, we ran leaping ecstatic down the street, red eyes peering owlish from plaster-mask faces.

Each night after work at the bookstore I went to the studio. Soon the arch of the back had become a saddle and the soft curve of her ass stuck raggedly in the air like a tail. I began to suspect I didn't know what I was doing. No matter. Art is discovery. Hadn't Michelangelo found form in the stone itself? My shoulders ached mercilessly; I started wondering if women were made for such work. Late nights were best — alone in the building but for the janitor and Ludmilla, the old black bag lady, New Art stowaway, subsisting on pizza scraps left by sympathetic students, who found in her a living metaphor for the artist — never quite collared by The Powers That Be. I would hear her rummaging rat-like in the storage area, find her eyes watching me from the dark behind plaster castings. It was a little creepy.

Then one evening I came exuberant downstairs to find a woman standing before my work, hands-a-hip. "This yours?" she demanded.

My heart sank. I waited for her to inform me she needed the space (though too striking really for a teacher; teachers are always somewhat commonplace). She had the classy look of an Uptown patron. "Culture cuños," Rafael called them. Madonna dark features, a sensuous Italian mouth and bold Roman nose, short but built — as Richard would say — like a brick shithouse. She wore faded jeans and a frayed sweatshirt.

I nodded yes. She looked me over with something of Rafael's irony and said, "All right." Turned and approached a huge block of sandstone against the far wall. Soon she seemed to have forgotten I was there, studying the stone and a clay model beside it, bending at knees, frowning — while I pretended to study my own work, fighting a panicky feeling that I wouldn't be able to hold a chisel with this stupid . . .

Clapping her hands peremptorily. "You have better light," she said, a simple observation. She went to a turntable that had materialized in the room with her stone and arranged a stack of records, then returned to the block, touching it as one would a lover, running fingertips gently into a fissure. "Be good to me," she half-whispered. "No secrets." And, pulling a mask down over her nose, began to work.

I took little snailbites of plaster, chisel wide and unwieldy as a church pew, wishing she'd leave me to work this out by myself — secretly studying her. She worked with decision, a deft, nearly slow motion rhythm, mallet to chisel, that fascinated me. Faster when an Eric Dolphy record dropped from the changer. She began to talk without looking up. "Imagine playing the sax, gripping fingers down hard on the stops and blowing. All rhythm, see —" throwing her hips "— Doo-wah Doo-wah Doo-wah . . ."

I looked around to see if she was talking to someone else. Didn't say a word. She went at the stone: dust and chips flew, nearly obscuring her, turning glossy black hair a dull white. And before my eyes, like a miracle, form began to emerge out of that stone. Still just a suggestion, but form.

Barbara came every night. Soon I relaxed and we talked in little spurts between the intent silences of serious work; we laughed over Ludmilla and Lizzy the dyke. I continued to study her furtively; while she, one night when I arrived late, threw her arms wide, crying, "There she is! I was afraid you weren't coming. Y'r a worker, that's eighty percent." I couldn't deny being flattered. She continued teaching me through the music. All metaphor. Nothing asked, nothing answered. Thelonious Monk and Charlie Parker. Barbara understood that I had come to learn *how* to do, not *what* to do, in a scene where most had it backwards. One night she brought Aretha Franklin and we got nothing done — dancing around our work, clicking heels on the concrete, waving hands in the air. Later, as we sat cross-legged on the cool, chip-littered floor, she confided in her clipped manner that she had become a sculptor and, moreover, that she worked to jazz because they were male-dominated forms. "First I learn what the men know, then I go beyond. Because I know something they don't know. I learned it at hospital delivering Jamilla. You sculpt with your gut. Push —" she hissed to the beat of the music "— push . . . push!" I glanced at her piece in the corner: abstract, even more brooding and earthstuck than mine, though more confident. It looked like the padded, imponderable foot of a brontosaurus.

Rafael staggered in, throwing out his arms. "My two *escultoras!*" Kissing first me, then nuzzling Barbara's neck, copping a feel. "Hah-ah, I love them both." She shoved him off, and he stumbled drunkenly, giggling to himself.

Immediately, she returned to her work. He stalked her and seized a sinewy arm. "She's short . . . but look out! Guineas is the worst. Once she hit me, you know, with a mallet —" patting the side of his head "— two weeks in hospital."

Barbara shook loose. "You don't cart your ass outta here, Suárez, another two weeks —"

"*Me* get out!" He grinned at me. "Ain't that some shit? My studio and she telling *me* to get fucking out." I stared back and forth between them, dumbfounded. Rafael lamented in the direction he took to be God: "You see the crap we got to live with?"

Barbara raised the mallet; he jumped back, tottered. "Jesus! See what I mean? Mamá, the broad intimidates me."

They faced off, sizing each other up. I muttered, "Gee, I didn't know you two knew each other." They turned in unison and laughed. "This little beauty is my wife," crowed Rafael. "My one an' only."

Next day he appeared with a raw claw mark down his cheek. He shrugged, "Anyway, she missed my tongue," wiggling it out at me. "*Seguro.*" Barbara came in that evening with a livid eye swollen into her cheek. She put a stack of records on the changer and worked in brooding silence. Midpoint in a John Coltrane number she said, "Last time this happened we were both in the emergency room and we made a pact. No more studio sharing, no critiques, no brawls — with all that dangerous shit around. Last night he broke the pact." Her dark eyes flashed. "He said my work is like a dead wop: it stinks too bad to be buried."

As our friendship grew — and my "Woman Rising" squatted closer and closer to the floor — I realized that with each imperative throw of her arm Barbara chipped away not only at that dinosaur foot.

I brooded over my work, doubting I would master it. Besides, I had begun seeing a new therapist and dreams often colonized entire days. I was avoiding people, letting everything slip aside, reading Hesse and van Gogh's letters, taking a plunge down inside myself. One night when Barbara didn't show up, I despaired of working and went upstairs for coffee. The lounge deserted but for Lizzy the dyke and some new girl she had cornered. Lizzy talking, exuberant as a street punk in a black leather jacket. I slipped back out, behind me heard Lizzy call, "Hey ya, Plaster, what's happening?" In the hall I met the girl from California: her blonde banality and perpetual tan, wearing terry cloth even in November. "Is she in there?"she whispered. I nodded yes and she gritted white teeth and tiptoed away.

I returned to the basement, past rooms where students were busy over easels and linoleum blocks. Restlessness a hungry beast in me. I worked without conviction. When Barbara finally appeared, she was so down she barely mumbled hello; went at the stone, raising a little yellow cloud around her. "Everyone is down today," I mumbled. "It's like that in New York; bad moods are shared like the weather." She muttered something. Meanwhile, I studied her, mesmerized by the rhythm of the mallet. Nearly jumping when she barked, "Work on your own piece. You don't need my troubles."

But I got them — in a dreary monotone that had discovered my talent for listening: Rafael's boozing and screwing around (currently a friend's seventeen-year-old daughter — "Jailbait!"). After she had composed herself, she said, very quietly as if it explained everything, "I'm thirty-six." Her chisel skittered across the floor, clattering amid steel cabinets. "Balls on this. I'm going to a bar, the first man I see I'm taking home and fucking his brains out." She grabbed her jacket and left me to work on my Ruth.

I was determined. I coaxed, whispered — though mine was no Michelangelo Christ, it didn't reply. I had found the best rhythm of the night, swinging from the gristle hinges of my knees — chink chink chink — mumbling encouragement to my blade, when a voice behind me said, "I like your style."

I swung around, startled. Claude Charles, the graphic artist, leaned against the door post, arms crossed. "I was working upstairs and heard you tapping down here," he said. "I thought we should get acquainted. How about coffee?"

I blushed furiously. "I was talking to myself."

"I do it all the time. It's a mark of self-involvement." He shrugged. "I'm the most fascinating conversationalist I know. How about that coffee?"

Claude might have been a dancer. I thought so anyway the first time I saw him, waiting for a taxi — very erect, eyes hinting at Mediterranean blue, shadowed beneath a fedora snatched from a Fitzgerald novel. A heavy tweed overcoat skirted pointy Italian shoes. His dandified style seemed piecemeal, put together from Canal Street bits and pieces. His eyes stalked me as I approached Institute steps; illumination from streetlights cut cleanly by the inclined blade of his jaw but his lips remaining mysteriously in shadow. And I had thought: *This man is a creature of the night. I am going to sleep with him.*

Over coffee, Claude did the talking. I didn't so much listen as plunge like a moth into the flame of his vanity. Consumed. He was an illustrator, was learning Swedish (because American art would soon be the thing "over there"). "We're the only ones doing anything now. The avant-garde in Europe ended with the last generation — Munch, Chagall, Kandinsky . . . that bunch. When Duchamp moved to New York the geography of art changed permanently."

"Picasso?" I asked, though I wasn't really paying attention, but pondering the sexy little beak formed by his upper lip. There was something, I realized, a little foppish about him.

He dismissed Picasso with a wave. "A borrower," he said, "a mongrel. And please don't mention Salvador Dali."

"I love Munch," I said cautiously.

"Munch! Do you realize that Munch advanced the art of block printing as much as Rauschenberg is advancing silkscreen today? Munch is wonderful. Who else d'you like?" He pushed back a shock of blond hair; his seawater eyes brushed past me, hunting the waitress, holding his cup aloft for a refill.

I took out a cigarette; immediately he produced a light. All of his movements dramatically abrupt. Consuming things quickly, including the waitress's round breasts as she poured coffee. Little smiles flickered across his face, and he continuously swiped loose strands of hair off his forehead — a sort of nervous tic. But he was charming. I told him I was trying to avoid strong influences now, finding who I am as an artist first. He said, "I know who you like. The German Expressionists. Van Gogh. Jewish women are into van Gogh. WASP preppies love Cézanne. Italian chicks are still hung up on the quattrocento. English women dig muddy landscapes; English broads are a drag. Germans and Scandinavians are hip. Have you ever seen Dürer's self-portrait? He looks like someone you might meet in the Village."

"You're very International." I exhaled blue smoke.

"Actually, I'm a New York chauvinist. I love Rauschenberg, de Kooning, Jasper Johns. Jasper is a personal friend of mine."

"I'm not into abstract — I mean, I'm not against it!"

He shrugged. "Women are basically conservative." His smile could have charmed the fury from Alice B. Toklas. He withdrew a Frenchish long cigarette from a case and, holding my eyes, leaned across the table to mine for a light. Just that small contact churned tidal action in my stomach.

"You have lovely eyes," he said. "Sansui eyes: a ring 'round the iris. It means you are a sensitive lover."

I was suddenly talking compulsively, as if a small dog were nipping at my composure, about my work and how art students don't understand creativity; whatever Lucien or Grunewald do they all follow behind like baby geese. Artists should open and close their own doors (making a fist). It takes courage. When I had finished, he said, "I like strong women. I want to get to know you." Leaving it at that, as if expecting me to propose something. I simply sat, staring into my coffee, hoping my trembling was only on the inside. When I looked up, he no longer sat across but stood beside the table, mining into pockets of jeans that clung like cellophane, his balls jutting out. I tried not to look.

"Are we going?" I managed.

"I'm very embarrassed," he answered, "I intended to buy you coffee but I'm flat."

"It's okay . . . really. It will be my treat." I smiled. He helped me into the heavy Oaxacan sweater that exhaled plaster dust.

Outside he smiled and promised, "Next time it will be on me. I insist."

As we walked back to the Institute, I first noticed Christmas decorations in shop windows, could nearly smell holly on the crisp air. Beside the steps he said, "I really have to split, but this isn't good-bye." I nodded. Our eyes held a moment, then mine blurred and by some miracle I had plunged like that moth down into his kiss, his tongue ramming hard between my lips, on and on until my legs were water and we came up gasping, and before I could master wits or courage to invite him home he had spun, his heels castanets — foreign and fiercely proud — clicking along the sidewalk as I watched the retreating back, swish of overcoat, fathoming my disappointment.

We met the next night as if by arrangement. Me coming up from sculpture, Claude down from lithography. He took my arm as we walked past jingle-corners of Salvation Army Santas, windows frosty with aerosol snow and the pink-cheeked delight of manikins. Joy brewed like eggnog in my veins. My heart ached like a kid on Christmas morning, seeing so many gifts in his smile. As we got on a bus he asked, "Can you cover me? I don't have any change."

Our lovemaking began with the anticipations of fingertips, jouncing on that bus, a kiss that began at his apartment door and didn't end until we lay naked on the couch and Claude inside me. But he was no Clarence. Skittish, abrupt, as if sex were another thing borrowed. Within moments, it seemed, had spilled himself, screaming out in solo flight, leaving me not so much frustrated as confused, feeling inadequate. Convinced it was my own failure.

Afterwards, as we lay together, I teased the hair around his nipples and he shut his eyes, jaw set. When I touched him, hoping to arouse him again, he shuddered and moved away.

"Are you all right?" I whispered.

He turned, holding me with those agate eyes, a blond sheaf of hair splayed across forehead. "Would you mind going now?"

I was too humiliated to reply. I dressed, hopelessly trying to compose some reaction — even to comprehend one. He lay studying me, arm crooked behind his head. "Will I see you tomorrow?" I managed, my voice creaking betrayal like old stairs. Claude bequeathed me a smile and touched my knee. "We'll see each other —" was all he said.

* * *

Those next nights my work went abysmally, possessed by an impatient dybbuk. No sign of Claude and hope could convince me of nothing. Barbara worked steadily, humming — now to Beethoven string quartets. "Antsy?" she asked one night without looking up. I told her I was expecting someone. Her eyes came up, chuckling: "Sandy blond, a delicate jaw; cheekbones aren't bad, a solid touch. Can't forget the hat, snatched from Humphrey Bogart's prop library."

"How did you know?" I demanded.

She cherished a smile. "Doesn't everyone know Claude Charles? Be careful —" eyes peeking over her piece "—some men break every heart they enter. Take it from an old pro."

I crushed out my cigarette and went up to the lounge. Just to get some air, I told myself, though detoured past lithography at the last moment. No Claude. I nearly felt relief. Upstairs, the crew sat at the usual table near the coffee machine. I slid into a chair, shaking a little dust storm from my hair. Carol grinned. "Some blond dude left a message for you. Said he hoped you vacuumed before coming over tonight." Everyone laughed, except Andrea, who it was rumored had had an affair with Claude. I frowned.

"This place is more gossipy than the suburbs." Not looking at Andrea.

The girl from California banged through the door. "Aach!" she cried, coming towards the table. "She gives me the creeps."

"She's merely in love with you," said Andrea, in typical monotone. "She's lovelorn. She drools." We cracked up.

"Hey! Lizzy's got style," cried Carol. "Last week she emptied this duffle bag of stuff out on the table, Andrea was there. First comes her potting tools, then out comes this huge dildo —" Carol spreading hands as if to measure the biggest fish "— economy size! and a leather harness, the whole megillah to stud herself up. She winks at me. 'Didn't think I was so well hung, didya?' she says. I'm thinking: Wow, I gotta introduce this chick to Suzie."

"C'mon!" I laughed.

"God's honor," insisted Carol. "Lizzy says her big fantasy is to fuck a pregnant woman . . . Y' know, those Siberian gray eyes! Then she leans close to Andrea and says, 'Y'r not pregnant are you?' " A perfect Lizzy imitation — one eye hitched higher than the other, like Ahab. We screamed laughter. Except Connie Kline, who muttered, "She's sick."

Andrea shrugged. "I didn't take it too personally."

"Sure it's personal," cried Carol. "She goes to work on your little quim with that monster — it's gotta be personal."

"Would you shut up?" said Connie Kline.

"We should tell her she isn't welcome at our table," proposed the girl from California.

"You can tell her. I'd prefer to move," said Andrea. Carol laughed. Connie snapped, "Just drop it!" Glasses balanced precariously on her thin nose.

I was just about to leave when Lizzy came in; stood squat and stocky in black leather jacket and clay-sheathed jeans, ginger hair furrowed back in a glossy ducktail, surveying the room, squinting as she found us — all watching! A swaggering irony similar to that expression she wore when we didn't understand her jokes, just before bellowing laughter. She strode, boots whomping, key chains jangling, towards the coffee, while the girl from California nudged me with an elbow, hoping I would make her disappear.

Lizzy sat, propping a boot on our table. "How's it hanging, girls?" She began scraping dry clay from under fingernails. The g. from C. poked frantically, whispering, "Tell her to leave."

"You tell her!" I said out loud.

Lizzy's eye came up. "Say what? Hey, plaster caster, I seen your work down there. Real sweet." I cleared my throat in response. "Smell this!" Lizzy thrust clay-daubed fingers in Connie Kline's face. "Damn, that's pungent. Ol' Lucien musta shit in that batch." Her laugh boyishly husky and missing a front tooth. Connie threw a hand over her mouth and fled the room. "She got a problem?" Lizzy demanded, squinting after her.

As Connie went out, Claude's head came in — and popped right back out again. I looked away as if I hadn't noticed. "There goes New Art's number one pussy," scoffed Lizzy, yammering, "Oh my! Such pretty, faggy little drawings."

Words leapt out of me. "He draws better than any of you do." Lizzy stared. Carol clipped teeth together. Andrea sussed out breath, "Oh Jeezus . . ." On my way out I heard Lizzy asking, "Is everybody on the rag today or what?"

The steady chink of Barbara's chisel nearly reproachful as I came down into the smell of plaster dampness. Two women stood by my work. The lanky one with a brash New England face gesturing as if she found it offensive — halting mid-sentence, slicing eyes at her companion. They sidled past, silently; though as they started upstairs I heard one of them say, "People should know what they are doing before starting something so monumental." I gripped mallet and chisel . . . but my hands wouldn't work, my heart as sluggish as the water in my Ruth's urn — had she held an urn. I knew that other students ridiculed my work: called it "Bach's duck," and one cocky creep quacked when we passed on the stairs. Though their doubts troubled me far less than my own growing conviction that I was incapable of visualizing in three dimensions. "Shit!" I yelped, making my first cut far too deep, losing an ear.

"Forget them," said Barbara. "They envy your ambition. Artists are as petty and gutless as anyone. They're the worst."

"You know what they call this thing?" I demanded.

She stopped working. "Let them call it. Art is made not born. You have to try. It's lots of faith and heartaches."

"Maybe they're right," I sulked.

"Get out of here with that horse shit." Her eyes flashed. "Your work upsets people; that's a good beginning."

I tried again, but she drove me nuts with her disciplined klink klink klink. Finally, I said I'd had enough. Barbara nodded, giving me her sad sororal smile.

Picking my way over an icy sidewalk, hunched from wind that was a death rider galloping the streets. At the corner of Seventh Avenue, feet came crunching behind me, Claude's voice. I threw arms around him, squealing, exuberant with kisses. "My hat! Watch my hat!" he muttered, clamping a hand over it.

At the apartment, we smoked a joint, listened to the Supremes, kissing on the couch like naughty children. I grabbed his hands to dance; he pulled me into his lap and nuzzled. Carol arrived, trailing a *Helloooo* like cheap cologne.

"You have a roommate?" he groaned.

"I already told you, three roommates."

His eyes closed. We went to the bedroom, behind its sprung door. A whump in the other room and Marty had arrived. Her Liberation Front bellow: Ten thousand new troops to Vietnam. Who's going to napalm that Johnson asshole? Claude pulled away, his eyes bright eggs in a wedge of light. I kissed his neck, he lay like a board. Enter Suzie and one of her schlemiels. A political fête in the living room: Marty calling the guy a fascist because he was ROTC; him trying to shout her down, "I'm a law student, I know people resort to invective only when they have no argument." Claude groaned. I stroked his hair. "How can you live like this?" he demanded. "It's a public urinal."

When I tickled he got angry. I think he felt it somehow anti-modern to laugh. He lumbered atop me like an old husband with a garden-hose erection. "This doesn't happen to me," he groaned. "Just stage fright," I assured him. "No one's watching." At last he fell asleep in my arms. I nestled against his hair, smelling faintly of after-shave, dozing off in something like bliss.

Very early, I awoke to him slipping on clothes in the dark. "Are you going?" My voice squawky. Claude mumbled something. I snapped on the bed lamp and said I'd make some coffee; Claude's eyes mercurochrome, jittery. "Look, I didn't mean to wake you."

"You were just going to sneak out of here?"

His mouth twisted unpleasantly. "Hey —" kissing my forehead "— it was sweet. See you later." And he left, leaving everything unanswered.

No work on Bach's duck that night. I sat home, imagining how we'd go for Chinese food. But by eleven he hadn't come. I found his number in the book. A woman's voice answered. "Claude?" she asked curtly. "Who are you?" I hung up. Tried reading, but not even Dostoevski could convince me he knew more about despair. I went to the bathroom mirror and despised what I saw.

A knock on the door. I virtually flung it open. Richard stood, cupping in his hands a tissue paper poppy, the kind sold by disabled veterans. "I've come with flowers," he grinned.

"Richard!"

He stepped past me. "A slasher is loose in midtown emptying peoples' stomachs with a machete. I won't go near my neighborhood. When one maniac lets go, others get ideas. Let me get this in water." Filling a dirty cup in the kitchen, he plopped the poppy in head-first. "Can I sleep here tonight?" he asked, colonizing the couch. I explained there was someone else in my life now. "I don't think I can sleep with you."

Richard's palm whumped the couch, raising dust. "Sleep here!" he shouted. "What is it these days, something they put in the water that's making you chicks so arrogant?"

I made an omelette and we discussed the art scene in New York. "A lot of queers graduated from Yale, determined to lay their no-comment fiats on the world," Richard said. "That's the art jam in Amerika. All slickness and style. And you girls don't fit in too well, 'cause everyone knows you have a tendency to wax emotional. But worse, you don't possess the *Big P*. The *Big P* means *Power* and *Power* is what Amerika is about. Today's art is button-down, with an affinity for Chivas Regal and Mercedes Benzes. None of that funky anti-bourgeois shit."

"You sound like Barbara."

Richard dumped the paper poppy on the table — grotesquely swollen petals dripping red dye. No Georgia O'Keeffe blossom suspended in dry desert air but a soggy Mekong rose in a small bloody puddle. "Would you get rid of that thing?" Richard looked at me and started laughing like a lunatic.

Somehow, we slept together that night. But it was Claude who had my thoughts, even though Richard was more solicitous than Claude would have been. Really a simple, natural man who couldn't tolerate frustration and armed himself with theories for everything. The city kept him wound up to near breaking. I asked why he didn't leave. He said, "I know other places exist — maybe better places. For me, the attraction of New York is that it raises certain questions that other places don't raise at all. Just because you leave doesn't mean they have been answered."

Suzie padded in on bare feet, clutching a dress over her bare tits, eyes wasted as Richard's poppy. She squinted: "Not the blond tonight . . . someone else. How sweet." I told her to get out.

We woke early, feeling we had wrestled all night, our heads trying to share a single pillow. Richard didn't look too good in the morning, a little like a miner who has brought some of the dust of sleep up with him. I hated myself for wishing he was Claude. When he had gone, I asked Carol why we didn't get out of this circus and find an apartment together in the Village. "This place is exotic. I have friends who won't even come here."

Quickly, often working half the night, Barbara had finished her piece and hauled it away to a gallery downtown. I had the studio to myself. My piece had become a fixture, a monument — the very building seemed constructed around it. Her hope had been to capture some essence of life in a corner and take a chisel to it, knock off any rough edges. *Irreducible form!* she would say like an Ave Maria of her Catholic past . . . a faith. But I couldn't believe in abstraction. Life just can't be reduced to a few simple lines. Though on its own my piece was becoming an abstraction. It was demoralizing. "No problem," Rafael said, "you got the plaster talking to you." But the more I carved the less certain I became. "Bach's duck" had become anorexic. In places, chicken wire of the armature broke through like some spindly cancer.

I refused to despair. If you lived like an artist, I decided, art would surely follow. I rode buses in sweat-hardened plaster dust that made my arms crinkle as I moved; fellow passengers swatted angrily at their clothes as I brushed past. I crawled each night into sheets stiff as potters' jeans. *You should change them in case Claude comes,* I told myself. But dust was a residue of despair. I wore it with Marty's fierce pride. Art and filth: my politics.

Wore it to those early sessions with Dr. Kaufman — whose number Dr. Sternberg gave me, saying: She's the best in town — into her Fifth Avenue lobby past Hispanic doormen who furled upper lips, sliding me their flunky suspicion as I ducked past like a spy from the world of the deprived . . . or depraved. *Though this one she not as crazy as the other one* — who always came out as I entered, making a run-run-leap across the lobby out onto the sidewalk in plum leotards and high rouge-apple cheeks, launching doormen into orgasms of rolled eyes and fingers wound around ears. Oh yes! *muy locas.* All these fucked up white girls.

Dr. Kaufman greeted me warmly, taking my sweater at the door of that office/living room arranged like a baroque painting: Japanese prints and Malayan masks, book walls, a Persian rug in rich peacock blues that shimmered a little off the floor. Although there were large windows the outside didn't intrude. Real life, that room said, is interior. Dr. Kaufman herself lacked the charisma of Maxine or fire of Barbara, but was a steadfast, soothing presence as she rocked in her leather chair, dark eyes never straying from me. A no-nonsense, vaguely Semitic nose, gingered lightly with freckles in a lean angular face — always bronzed and sensibly healthy, as though she'd just returned from a vacation in Mexico. Black hair iridescent with flames of carmine, spun into a neat chignon at back. She wore conservative tartans and British tweeds; only knee-high boots suggested anything unconventional about her.

For the first five minutes we made light conversation — psychic stretching exercises before getting out on the track. Then, rocking gently like a boat impatient at dock, she slipped on glasses — vaguely schoolmarmish — and began to tap, with a yellow pencil, knuckles nested on a legal pad in her lap as if tenderly cupping an egg. This was the signal to begin. And I always experienced a moment of panic. My psyche raw-blistered; between sessions there wasn't time for it to heal.

We were working on my relationship with Dad. I had told her about Rosita — reliving such rage afterwards that I couldn't see him at all. Dr. Kaufman dug and dug into my feelings, until I began to suspect that she thought there was some deep dark secret I was repressing. It was murky, unsettling stuff, and one afternoon I told her I wanted to move on: "My problems aren't with Dad anyway; they are with Mother." She sat, nodding sympathetically, then bent intently forward and asked why it had been so painful to accept my father's flirtation with his maid: "Really a rather innocuous incident —"

"It wasn't innocuous," I shouted, surprising myself. Her eyes held me, a tender, nearly pained expression.

"You're very jealous of Rosita, aren't you?"

"Jealous!" I stared at her, snorting a small laugh. "How could I be jealous? I despise the woman."

"You say that you took afternoon naps with your father as a small child. Do you remember why you stopped taking the naps?"

"I don't know. . . . He didn't want me to anymore."

"And he never displayed physical affection — never touched you — not even during those naps? Did he kiss you goodnight?"

"When I was little."

"That stopped . . . when?" Her pencil tapped.

"Maybe about six. I really don't know."

"Did your father ever spank you?"

"I told you! He never touched me . . . in any way."

"In any way?" Her eyes unflinching. "Tell me, Natalie, was it your mother who forbade you to take naps with him?"

"Mother?" I was confused. "I don't know . . . yes . . . maybe." I was sweating, could almost smell my armpits — furry little skunks (I should shave them, I thought, they would smell less). Glanced at my watch, reminding her time was almost up. She sat waiting, like a hunter, lips touching with just a hint of anticipation. Or of a smile. But her sternness Promethean, like Mother's. Intimidating. She spoke with professional delicacy, like a surgeon delivering bad news: "Even though it may be painful, we must go deep. We must learn to trust each other." Her hand opening as if letting that egg roll out of it.

We remained stalemated for several sessions. Dr. Kaufman obsessed with the Dad stuff; sometimes shotgunning questions, at others just waiting. We could sweat out the whole hour with hardly a word — as if I'd only come to sit and smell the bitter varieties of my nervousness. "Why would a father be afraid to touch his daughter?" *It's just the way he is.* I began wondering if it wasn't all a waste of time.

Christmas approached. The city rising to typical holiday frenzy. Though for me it was a season of bad dreams and depression. I continued going to the studio by rote. Any hopes that Claude would appear had vanished with all hopes for my *duck.* At home, cheery messages from Mom/Dad piled up on the phone stand, finally spilling over to the floor. I ignored them. It had been weeks since I'd shared Sunday brunch with them. I couldn't bear it. Claude's rejection was even harder to bear. At last, deciding that pride is for masochists, I signed up for Grunewald's life drawing class, though I'd missed two months of lessons.

Grunewald had an unvarying method. He sketched, then erased all the lines with a kneaded eraser. Sketched again. And erased. Until the newsprint was a chiaroscuro disaster of scoured charcoal and rubber litter, paper worn completely away in places. All his students worked just the same — heads bobbing, little eraser balls bouncing across the floor and piling in corners. While the model scratched her twat and yawned, maybe wondering why Grunewald didn't just stick a board with a wig up there, if all these shmucks were going to keep erasing her. But Grunewald wasn't what attracted me to life drawing.

When Claude came in that first day, I smiled orphan-shy up from my table. His blue eyes widened, he gave a startled nod and veered at an oblique angle across the room, taking a seat in the far corner. Claude was the one exception to Grunewald's method. He simply drew, deftly exploring shade and shadow, working with loving care around a hip or the hollow of a thigh, while the model smiled gratitude at him. And I kept glancing over, torturing myself with his absolute disregard.

The third day in class, Grunewald stopped at my desk, seized my drawing pad in both hands, bringing it almost to his nose. "What in hell is this s'posed to be?" he roared. The entire class work-halted, watching. "I'm drawing the model," I explained in a near whisper, turning my embarrassment away from Claude. Grunewald grabbed my eraser and went madly to work nullifying lines I'd just sweated bullets over, raining me with rubber and thick spittle. "I believe in movement! Not a lot of static crap. Do I look like Poussin?" Though cowed, humiliated by his huge head that had swollen even bigger in red rage, I stuttered:

"I don't agree with your method."

He scowled, eyeballs small fish swimming in white bowls of incredulity. Jabbing a finger toward Claude, he shouted, "When you get that good you can have opinions in my class. This . . . *dreck!*" He tore the pad completely in two. The class buzzed gleeful scandal, grins flashing at me like cheap coins. While Claude continued to draw as if nothing had happened, glancing from model to pad. I despised him.

Outside the classroom I burst into tears — suddenly noticing Ludmilla's head, a snake-tangle of hair, dodge behind a fortress of shopping bags. "They don't know anything about art. NOTHING!" I hissed, as she peeked out from her Lord and Taylor asylum, fear in her scavenger eyes softened to something like empathy.

About then, Rafael appeared drunk in the studio one night and cornered me against a workbench. I squirmed and dodged his wet kisses and a hardness pressing into my groin, managed to shove him off only after he had torn my shirt open, his sculptor's hands chafing my breasts. And worse! Lizzy was getting chummy; she seemed to appear whenever I went up to the lounge.

"I been keeping track of your work downstairs," she said. "It's got balls. I got a feeling you and me could really get down and communicate." Shuddering inside, I kept those wolf eyes at bay with a smile. Lizzy took a deep drag on a cigarette, and what may have begun as a cackling laugh ended in a hacking, smoke spilling cough. "You're all right," she growled, gesturing fiercely at others in the room. "These people impress me for nothing. Isn't one teacher here I haven't fucked. Rafael, Jennifer Hanes . . . Lemme tell you something —" she squinted an eye "— I could put the make on you anytime I'm ready. Right now I'm not interested." With a mumpish lip-curled smile, she tucked the flannel shirt into her trousers all the way around.

I told Dr. Kaufman about a dream in which I'd opened my closet door and found Lizzy inside, wearing nothing but men's jockey shorts, bulging hugely in front. That dream shook me up so badly I didn't go near the Institute for days. "What do you think it means?" I asked her. She minimized it, saying it was merely an anxiety dream. I wondered if she wasn't just feeding me line, like a fisherman playing a fish.

After the session, feeling lonely and morose, I thought of visiting someone. But whom? Adam and Rachel in Israel, David off at medical school in Chicago, my roommates busy doping and dorking, Max never home — though I could walk right in (to Max locking an apartment was bourgeois paranoia) to a clutter of books and unfinished manuscripts, her deflated diaphragm on the bed stand like a Duchamp found object, an impression of life lived on the wing. No time in it for our friendship. I decided to visit the Guggenheim. Art is the best friend.

I was just going up-ramp to the Kandinskys when I saw Max ahead, studying a Francis Bacon triptych: raven black hair against a brown and white Peruvian poncho, her attention riveted upon charnel house bishops — gobbets of coagulate blood and flesh peeled away from teeth. I dodged behind an ovoid Arp, arousing the suspicion of a guard. Recalled our chance meeting on the street just days before. "How goes it at the famous New Art Institute?" she'd asked.

"Everyone's into abstraction," I said. "They all eat, sleep, breathe, and shit abstractly."

"At least they're dedicated."

"Now they're jealous of me 'cause when I set out to carve a person it comes out more like a duck. I have natural talent."

"I think you do."

"Coming from you, Miss P., that's a compliment. You have an eye for talent."

I asked about her father. She said that while staying in Connecticut she had done some soul searching. "I realized that even though Dad's death might be more painful, losing Mom would be more devastating to me. I tried starting a dialogue with her out there. Hopeless." Max sighed. "It all seems like a lousy, overplayed Greek tragedy. Instead of resolving things, people have children. All the residual dreck with their own parents gets passed on intact. You see it all the time: the mother's ghost lingering in her daughter, now a mama herself. Maybe it heals in a way. The mother has grandchildren to love unconditionally, as she had hoped to love her own daughter, and the daughter has done her generational duty by passing the misunderstanding down the line. Seems like a miserable fucking bore."

"Well, I'm not having any kids to screw up; that's one thing I'm sure of," I said. Max regarded me like I was some kind of freak.

Now I followed her up-ramp. Once she glanced around and I faded behind a cluster of sporty Westchester types, discussing their museum jaunt as though it were nine holes of golf. Max had become lost in a

Käthe Kollwitz print. And me, giggling inside like a clock about to burst a spring, tiptoeing up behind and grabbing her elbow.

"Freeze! Y'r under arrest!" I barked.

She gasped and twirled around. I cried out. Shocked. Mortified! It wasn't Maxine at all but a total stranger.

We stood staring at one another as if mired in a dream — she holding a hand to heart and breathing, livid sagging pouches under her eyes; me muttering hopeless apologies, sensing the guard hovering close. I spun and walked rapidly away down the ramp.

I entered Dr. Kaufman's office the Thursday before Christmas raw and disheveled, eyelids inflamed and scratchy: "I can't take this," I blurted; "I can't sleep, I've had awful nightmares all week." Dr. Kaufman sat, calmly crossed her legs and began rocking. She asked about my dreams. I was too agitated to sit, tensely pacing the room.

"First I was in the shower and heard someone in the apartment — in the dream I mean — and I started to panic. The door opened. It was like that scene in *Psycho* where the camera angle is from outside and I could see myself through the shower curtain. I threw the curtain aside and there was Rosita with a huge knife. She smiled and said she was going to cut me for breaking our agreement. She raised the knife, I grabbed for it, and we fell down wrestling in the bathtub. Streams of blood mixed with water were guttering down the drain, and when I looked I saw it wasn't Rosita at all. It was Mother lying like a white fish on the bottom of the tub."

Dr. K. scratched with a pencil, though her warm eyes hadn't budged. "Go on —" she said softly.

"The dream switched. I was a little girl shaving beside Dad at the mirror—except instead of using my finger it was a real razor and kept nicking my face. Dad kissed it and put a bit of toilet paper on like when he cut himself. But the toilet paper got red and stiff and was disgusting."

"Was your father naked?" she asked.

I glanced at her from the window. "No . . . in his robe."

Her eyes didn't disbelieve me, they remained, tense and cobra-like, glasses throwing cold shards of light, pencil tapping against her teeth. "Never? He wasn't ever in the bathroom naked?"

"That's right!" I blurted out. "Once he was."

It was a flash of searing light in thick darkness, a step off into a yawning, depthless unknown, heart thudding, the smell of my own sweat. Amorphous dread. Yet territory so familiar — slimy walls and Headless Hallmen, snickering books and scampering dust-mice, voices whispering in the night. The Hydra-headed horrors of childhood. Dr. Kaufman's lips moving: "Go on —" she seemed to be saying "— you can remember." I felt a need to sit in the blue recliner, closer.

"It wasn't dirty. . . . I was just curious. Really! You have to believe me. I asked him what it was. I remember his voice seemed very high-pitched and unnatural — strange. No! He wasn't shaving. Now I remember. His hair was dripping and there were drops of water on his shoulders —"

"You're doing beautifully." She smiled.

Then I could nearly see it. I felt oddly calm, relaxed, leaning back with my eyes closed as if recalling a family vacation. "I know now. The door was unlocked and I walked in just as Dad was getting out of the shower. First I noticed his bony shoulders and white stomach, then saw this thing hanging down. I had seen David's little pecker, but this was so huge and dark I thought it was some kind of creature. I went right up and started talking to it and playing."

"He had an erection?"

Her question shocked me. "It wasn't like that. It wasn't sexual. Just a . . . discovery."

She nodded.

"He was holding the towel in one hand and just kind of frozen, staring down at me with this strange little smile and chuckling nervously. He didn't know what to do. Then his eyes were flying all around, very frightened. I think . . . maybe I kissed it. And I was amazed by his balls; they were like some kind of fruit. I was holding them and . . . Oh God! —" I sat straight up "— the door crashes and Mother flies in. She's naked. Hysterical screaming, her hair sticking out like a wild savage. She snatched me away by my hair and slapped Dad. A loud whack like a bullet. I thought she had killed him. I was pulling on her leg, crying, 'Mommy, please don't kill Daddy . . . Mommy!' Terrified. Then I heard Dad sobbing and pleading, while she screamed filthy names at him. He looked so old and hunched up. Then Mother dragged me by the arm into her bedroom. I remember her face was moist and very red as she knelt down beside me on the rug and hissed never to tell anyone what I had done. Never! I was huddled up, staring at the floor — and saw that she wasn't wearing any bottoms and that she had hair, but no penis. I thought maybe she had cut it off. I didn't move. Her fingers dug into my skin and I was crying. I knew I had done something terrible and she would never forgive me. Might even kill me. I was terrified of her —" looking into long yellow eyes of an Indonesian mask on Dr. Kaufman's wall "— and I've been afraid of her ever since."

I felt suddenly dejected. Drained out. "For a long time after, Dad wouldn't come near me," I told her. "Whenever I got near him, he fled. I didn't have a father anymore."

Dr. Kaufman's demeanor was startlingly beatific, as though she had reached a different conclusion. "That's one door you won't have to keep closed any longer." She smiled.

"I'm still scared of her," I said, shuddering. "Even now. Like she might come bursting in here any minute."

Barbara kissed my cheek and invited me in, placing my gift under the tree with the others. I felt abashed by the Christmas cheeriness of the place — tinseled tree and brightly wrapped packages. I took off my coat, telling about the new apartment Carol and I had found in the East Village, leaving the old to Marty and Suzie, and how, while other people celebrated the holidays, we were scrounging furniture and painting walls — our lives piled helter-skelter over the rough wooden floor. "I'm not getting any sculpting done but it really feels good to move. The old place was a bad movie."

"Speaking of bad movies," she said, "my show flopped. Not a single piece sold. I was the token woman in the group and the dealer gave me a back corner, near the urinals." Making a who cares expression, but the cost of it in her face. "I'm touched that you came to see me. All any artist needs is a few friends. Critics, public . . . fuck all!"

"I'm really sorry," I said.

"Actually, it's done wonders for my marriage. Rafael stays home all of two nights a week now." A self-mocking laugh. "They always throw us broads some kind of bone."

"How is Rafael?"

"*Quién sabe?* You probably see him more than I do."

I flushed, remembering that night in the studio. "He's going to lose you," I snapped. "And I think I'll tell him."

"Oh, he'll be impressed. *Muy desconsolado.* I'm sorry —" giving me a wry sad smile "— I do appreciate your concern, Natalie. But men like Rafael, their only loyalty hangs between their legs."

I was a little shocked that a wife could talk this way about her husband. Barbara brooded on daughter Jamilla, sleeping in the beautiful cradle Rafael had carved: smiling Barbaras and Rafaels bouncing the happy baby on their knees. Dream family.

She poured brandies and I noticed Christmas cards strung across one wall — too conventional, middle-class suburban for that high-ceilinged artzone, suggesting other tensions. "I'm not celebrating Christmas this year," I said. "All my roommates went home, but I can't handle my parents right now."

"Christmas? I thought Jews didn't have to put up with that crap."

"My family always observed Christmas. I've never even seen a Hanukah candle."

"Then you can appreciate what it is to be an artist. We're like kids running down Christmas morning with high hopes — and there isn't anything under the tree. For women it's even worse."

Jamilla whimpered in her cradle, cheek nestled against a pink teddy bear that seemed to be sleeping too. Barbara once had said: "She's all I can find to love about Rafael anymore."

"It can't be that bad," I protested.

Her eyes flashed. "What do you know? Come back here in ten years and tell me that." I just looked at her, vowing never to become this bitter. Instantly, her expression changed; she smiled down at Jamilla, who'd just opened her eyes, scooped her out of the cradle, gently cooing and patting her bottom, while the baby girl looked about with a cranky, sleep-pinched expression.

"I'm thinking of quitting sculpture anyway. I don't really have any talent."

Barbara frowned. "You have talent. You may not have courage."

"Somebody has been leaving notes on my work," I sulked.

"Notes? You mean critiques?"

My face gone oven-hot. "They're pornographic."

"Really! These must be some notes, to make you give up your work." She wrestled Jamilla, who had begun to writhe and whimper, rearranging her little daughter and stilling her restlessness with a kiss, like a maternal wizard. The baby sat peacefully on her lap, staring at me with big dark eyes, while Mommy brushed chin across her hair.

"They're disgusting notes. I think it's Lizzy."

Barbara's laughter was contagious. "That place is a zoo," she cried.

"Fucking artistic ape house. To hell with them all — the Lizzys and Rafaels and Grunewalds. All the bomb-out shows. Who cares what they think? It's not for them we become artists. Keep it up!" She made a firm, insistent malleting motion, muscles leaping up her right arm.

Leaving Barbara's Spring Street loft, I walked up the Fifth Avenue showcase of Christmas glitter and fashion to the Institute. Long-striding, forcing myself to be cheery in that unconvincing eggnog of honking taxis, frantic last minute shoppers and jostling office party drunks. All the tarnished merriment of the city seeming a tawdry pretense in the face of ragged dead-eyed bums and old women taking Christmas Eve dinner by themselves in greasy spoons. There is no loneliness like Christmas alone in New York. But Barbara had inspired me. I just wanted to see if my *duck* was redeemable — to hell with all the rest.

The Institute was dark and quiet, the front door locked. I had started back down the steps, hearing the tinkle of a Salvation Army bell on the cold air — its devastating solitude — when the door opened behind me. A voice jingling out:

"For the beautiful and talented the doors are always open."

It was Claude. I threw my arms around him, giggling delight.

We left together — neither of us knew for where — caught up in the giddy atmosphere. "You were working on Christmas Eve?" I wondered. "I'm an aesthetic Scrooge." His eyes playful. "Actually, I was waiting for you. We had a date, didn't we?" And I realized there was a kind of symbolic truth in his teasing: both of us outsiders on Christmas Eve, amongst the emotional needy. He recalled the Grunewald incident. "You were marvelous," he said. "You really made an ass of that stuffed shirt."

At an intersection he leapt from the curb to clear a patch of ice; his heel caught its slick tail and he fell hard and lay moaning in the filthy gutter. I knelt over him, not certain how badly he was hurt. For a moment he didn't seem to hear me, then was sitting stiffly, holding out an elbow for me to help him up. "Fucking back! Out again," he grunted, skin stretched taut over his cheeks. We tried walking, but he groaned and hunched forward as if the pain were unbearable. He refused to go to a hospital, claiming butchers staff emergency rooms. So I helped him into a cab and took him home to St. Marks Place.

Thus, inadvertently, Claude came to live with me. He had my bed and I bought a heating pad, which was all the therapy he said he needed. I helped him to the bathroom and cooked his meals; and when I returned from work in the evening, with groceries and lotsa cheer, he said: "Hey, I never had a friend like you. It was worth fucking up my back to get it on with you." He'd grab my hand and pull me down on the bed, kissing all over. "You know what I've needed all day?"

I would giggle. "You can't make love."

"Do me," he would beg. "C'mon, take pity on a poor cripple."

Afterwards he stared at the ceiling and talked about Ricky, ex-lover, who had sapped the juice from him, evicted him from his own apartment and now, he suspected, was entertaining lovers on *his bed*. "I lie here torturing myself about it; then my back aches so much I have to let it go." I would ask him, Please, could we talk about something besides his old girlfriend? Then he'd throw out his hands, adamant: "Look, that's finished . . . all right? She's a man-eater. Who needs it? Now I've seen what real friendship is all about. As soon as I can get around I'm liberating my clothes out of there. So no more about that cunt. All right?" As if I'd brought it up in the first place.

Except it wasn't easy finding something to talk about. When we talked painting we disagreed about everything. Finally, he would tighten his thin lips. "Women don't understand art. Ricky was unusual that way. Very hip. She thought like a man." His eyes knocking on the door of his apartment, leaving me more hurt than angry.

All day he lay and drew, head propped on a pillow. "What are you drawing?" I finally asked. "Self-portraits," he answered. I could fix a mirror for him. No, he didn't need it. And he showed me the pad filled with sketches of his penis in varying stages of arousal. "It's the only live model I have," he explained. Claude's two passions: his pencil and his prick.

At night, as he moaned and tossed on the narrow bed, keeping me awake, my thoughts often went, oddly, to Mother. In that late-hour truce between warring city noises, memories whipped across my mind like old sheets, keeping me awake. Just a few years earlier I had brought her chicken broth when she was sick, adjusted pillows and stroked her forehead, and when she told me how nice it was to be mommied I couldn't hide my joy. Then one day she had pulled aside the towel as I stepped from the shower and cocked her head, saying, "You're becoming a woman!" From that moment things had gone sour between us.

Sex is the Indian giver: boasting the most and giving only the most heartache.

* * *

Just after the New Year, Claude visited a chiropractor who elimi-
nated his back troubles, presto! — in that wizard's way of realigning
vertebrae and disciplining discs. He was spry as a spring goat and
wanted to retrieve clothes from his old diggings. That's it, I thought: he
leans on my compassion a few days then walks out of my life. Won-
drously, he returned with a suitcase. I didn't ask about his Ricky.

A honeymoon began. Long mornings in bed — and so what if you're
late for work — endless movies, coffeehouse raps, strolls on frosty evenings. I could walk on air; I knew the sweetest secrets of the moon,
which is earth's sister. Life too rich to bother with art. My duck sat untouched in its basement. Even the correspondence with Adam, which I
had resumed since his return to Israel, was overlooked. Sunday
brunches wholly abandoned (though I kept thinking one of these days I
would take Claude to meet them). It was a volatile, purely magic alchemy. It couldn't last.

The moment Marty was alone with Suzie in the old apartment she
suffered a fit of sensitivity and threw her out. Revolutionary as she was,
she couldn't bear the woman's one person revolt against all propriety.
Suzie came begging at our door and big-hearted Carol couldn't turn her
away. Seeing that sultry glance she slid Claude as she walked in, suitcase in hand, I knew there would be trouble. Within hours she was
sprawled over the couch in see-through lingerie reading Henry Miller.
Candidly, behind his back, she warned me: "The dude's a real prick,
he's gonna bring you grief." My glower delivered the message: *Keep
your hands off.* And when Carol insisted her stay would only be temporary, I replied, "The only thing temporary about that bitch is her love
affairs."

One night I cooked a huge pot of spaghetti and Claude convinced
me to put marijuana in the sauce, saying it was a natural friend of tomato sauce. Soon Carol left for class and Claude and Suzie smoked a
joint, giggling like school kids. Suzie opening her fleshy fish lips, ready
to swallow him whole, laying down a path of suggestive eye flashes, her
soprano titter building to such a pressure in my head I thought something would snap; while he threw me dark three's-a-crowd glances,
coming on to her like a tiger paced through his endocrines. I imagined
them fondling each other under the table — viewing the scene in sullen
silence as if from offstage.

Suzie yawned, breasts flattening against sheer blouse. "Time for my beauty sleep," she singsonged, eyes teasing blond, sloop-eyed Claude, who despised me for standing between him and that big uddered cow. Not giving a damn for tact, he mumbled something about the bathroom and followed her. When I entered the living room they separated reluctantly, like partners in a modern dance, standing in the dark at a tense angle to each other.

Suzie went into the bedroom and began undressing in brash yellow light. As she reached back to unfasten the bra, I started toward her; she caught the door with a bare foot and nudged it closed. I fell back on the couch, slipped off sailor's pants and arched my pelvis up towards Claude, who shifted about uncertainly.

"Come 'n get it, baby," I cried.

He stooped over as if to fake a sore back. Instead, whispered "Not here —" Eye whites moving to the bedroom door.

"Here, now!" I snapped. "Or get out!"

Claude insisting he couldn't get it up with my roommate right in the next room. Me saying he'd had it up all night, now he was going to use it. Why couldn't we go to his place? We could relax there, he pleaded. I looked up into the lunar sincerity of his face, kitchen light faltering on the trough in his forehead, and said I thought he no longer had a place. "I don't know when to believe you."

"Please, baby, let's go uptown. You know how much I dig you."

As we rode up in a nearly empty subway car, he cooed and kissed me behind an ear in a manner that seemed sham and almost mocking. I shoved him off. "Don't kiss me. Just ball me. All you're good for is a fuck."

His hand, as it hit my cheek, slapped those grungy walls hard and flat, brazed the dripping blood of spray paint graffiti and brought passengers awake. I was at the door before its clarity was lost in the scream of wheels. Shouting back, as doors opened and I leapt off the train at the station, that if he ever hit me again I would kill him. The train lurched away, leaving me the image of a black mother, perhaps Haitian, in a colorful kerchief, shielding her small son's eyes — her own stuck on long white poles.

There was a salt-metallic taste of blood in my mouth, and by one of those miracles of coincidence I was only blocks from the Institute.

My heart a runaway horse, emotions sucking like flies at the decomposing stuff of my self-respect. Only vaguely sensing what I was going to do, I ran to the school, darted past the few voices chafing like rice paper wings from studios, and down stairs to the basement and *Bach's duck*. It had been weeks since I had seen it and the failure of my conception hit me hard. The piece was a monster with a quacking overlarge skull and bomb crater eyes, navel like the idealization of a Bellybutton Monster's desire. I seized a long, heavy crowbar from Rafael's workbench and in one furious swing squashed its head, which swiveled like an owl's on a two-by-four neck. Again I swung, sinking the claw deep in its plaster stomach.

Maybe I was screaming. A little crowd had formed, coming down from upstairs. Onlookers dodged aside as I leapt about, with sledgehammer now, systematically crumbling plaster from chicken wire — from dust to dust again. A teacher appeared with camera, whirring and clicking pictures as he ducked and loomed, crying: "That's good . . . fuckinay! That's marvelous!"

I left splintered bones, dust smoking up off the corpse, shoved through spectators — who ogled me and conversed in hushed, solemn tones — wiped my hands on a rag and went home. (Weeks later, Grunewald would stop me in the hall and tell me he would have taken the piece for his backyard. "Best thing that's come out of here in years —" indicating the studio "— process, pure process.")

When I arrived home, depleted, nerve-shot, there was no sign of Claude. I went directly in to Suzie, who lay with her mouth open, cheek buried in pillow, ass in the air as if she'd fallen that way from heaven. I hesitated a moment before her sleeping innocence, then shook her awake and warned that I couldn't live with someone who made passes at my man. She peeked up at me over covers like a child, with frightened mascara-bruised eyes.

When I returned to the living room, Carol had come in. "How's your mother?" she asked. "Did it come out negative?"

I stared at her. "What are you talking about?"

Her eyes widened. "Didn't Suzie tell you? Your dad called this afternoon. They found some kind of lump in her breast."

CHAPTER TWELVE

THE LANDLORD

RECEIVE A CALL FROM JACOB BACH. HAVE I PERHAPS SEEN NATALIE, HE wonders; he's not been able to reach her. Her mother goes into surgery tomorrow. A prolapsed uterus. Nothing too serious, but still . . . Oh yes, a little lump in the left breast near the nipple. Most likely a cyst; we're a lumpy family. He chuckles. But the mammogram and other tests weren't one hundred percent. They'll do a biopsy just to make sure. His voice stumbles. I will drop everything, I assure him, and find Nat.

"I just don't know where to look," he apologizes. A father whose daughter has belly-flopped in the feculent brine of sixties young adulthood.

I begin at a St. Marks Place walk-up wedged cheek by jowl amid mottled brick buildings, the uneasy harmonies of salsa and jazz spilling

from bohemian flats, tenements for last century's sweatshop East Europeans, who have left a remnant of burnt blond hair and ruddy cheeks.
In Tompkins Square Park, Ukrainian men play cards, women sit bundled in sober rows along paths stinking of urine; they cackle in their impossible tongue or nod under prim babushkas. Ubiquitous Puerto
Ricans weaved among them in a colorful weft. Another of New York's
refugee camps for the disinherited — mongrel, filling now with junkies,
gays, winos lying face-down on filthy sidewalks. A neighborhood of the
defeated and displaced, destitute and depraved.

Two black men sit on the stoop breathing warmth into cupped
hands. Suzie answers the door, sleepy-eyed, a funky robe clutched to
chest. "Seems like I'm always getting you out of bed." She misses the
sarcasm. I inquire about Nat.

"She's crazy possessive, says I'm after her old man. I'm not interested. He's an A-number-one prick." She jabs out her lips. I resist the
temptation to say he sounds like her type. "I've been kicked out twice in
one month. That's bad karma," she sighs. "Real bad."

I ask again about Nat.

"I don't know where they hang out," she snaps. "They can't be at his
pad 'cause his former lady lives there." I pat her arm and continue my
search through Village coffeehouses.

Nat's life a jubilee swath cut through the DMZ of the time. Claude
moves in with her; I am thinking, the girl is a fool, he has nowhere else
to go. The type who has always forgotten his cigarettes, and if you don't
offer he is sure to ask. A misogynist playboy. Friends stop visiting: her
fits of brushfire jealousy keep us away. She verges on manic-depressive,
volleying between carefree highs and gutter lows, haunting extremes of
impressionability.

One evening she called, sounding far off in an exile of depression. "I
had a talk with Claude," she said. "I told him how much he meant to
me and he freaked out. Says he can't handle clinging women and all
that stuff." A pause, then tears in her voice. "I don't know why I always
have to blow it."

"Telling someone you care for them is blowing it?"

"I haven't seen him for three days. When I go to his apartment no
one answers the door."

I wanted to tell her to let him go; instead I commiserated. A few days
later she called back to tell me he was in her life again, that things had
always — basically — been good. A little stormy but that keeps life ex-

citing. "Claude isn't an easy person. That's what makes him so dynamic. You don't really know him."

But I know him well. The *gonif* who fucks you over and you say, "At least he's not dull." He kept her spinning like a top, burning like slow phosphorus, hardly sleeping or eating, red-eyed, anemic, losing weight. And the flip side! At the top of the Ferris wheel kicking her feet, spinning with the aerobatic wingflashes of a sparrow. A master of manipulation.

I imagine her father's unanswered messages, Nat scarcely glancing at them in passing. *Mother was healthy. Just some little minor thing. Maybe she would visit her in the hospital. No! she hated hospitals. She would send flowers and call.* But at the moment she was obsessed with health and happiness — or unhappiness. They couldn't expect a young woman in love to get morbidly preoccupied with her mother's plumbing.

After checking neighborhood coffeehouses I went uptown to the New Art Institute. Those I asked regarded me with amusement. A stocky woman in a leather jacket, hair slicked back to a sculpted tail, worked a finger in an ear and sized me up. "Yeah, I know her," she said. "She did a righteous number on her masterpiece down there. The chick's got balls, y' know." She laughed and reamed her other ear.

I'd had enough Nat hunting. I had plenty troubles of my own.

With articles I had written for neighborhood newspapers and my appearance wherever tenants were organizing, I'd become somewhat famous on the Lower East Side as a tenants' rights activist. My own landlord, Sally Scotto, had targeted me as a troublemaker. I was prime agitator over the building's old boiler that heated like a candle in an ice storm, and when we called a strike the bastard shut it off completely.

An old Ukrainian woman upstairs, whose cheeks were incandescent apples in the cold, recalled that years ago they had rent struck against Scotto Senior, paterfamilias of the current bloodsucker. He had commandeered the top floor landing, throwing down bricks at tenants who tried to dodge across hall to the common toilet. Though it required he break down a wall to obtain bricks. His young son stood at his side learning tricks of the trade, laughing in delight when old Mr. St. John was hit in the back and tumbled downstairs.

The son had learned well. He had scrawled the rental amount in pencil on my original lease, saying he would type it in later. The second

month, when I handed him the rent check, he bellowed: "Naw naw —"
snatching lease from his pocket, jabbing a thick finger at a doubled
amount and yowling Brooklynese that chops words in two, ejecting
them between nose and palate "— You can't read or somtin'? T'ree
hun'd dollahs. It says right heah in black 'n' white." I was incredulous.
"We agreed on one-fifty. Here's my check." He snatched it from my
hand. "Wanna see wat I think of dat fuckin' check?" He tore it in two
and told me to pay up or cart my sweet ass outta his house.

Every morning for weeks I was startled awake by Scotto's fist pounding my door. Through the peephole his eyes floated in subaqueous hall
light, a cold fishbelly gray. Go away! I screamed. He at me to get da
fuck out. Each month, as legal aid had advised, I placed my unaccepted
rent check in a special escrow account. Thus the rent strike had started,
inadvertently. But soon spread through the building. My apartment was
Strike Central and Sally Scotto beyond fury. I knew it was only a matter
of time before he hit, though he had long since stopped hammering at
my door and no longer even came to collect rent.

One morning as I left the building a junkie fell in behind me and
began muttering. Accustomed to neighborhood freaks, I didn't pay him
much mind — though this one was very insistent, selling dope I supposed. After three blocks, with him tagging me like a sticky dream, I
spun around. He spoke excitedly, throwing hands about. An absolute
babble. I took him for a halfwit and started on. He seized my arm. The
sign in a city where all is permissible between strangers — except touch.

I froze, turned, looking closely this time. Realized it was Jesús
Muerte — evil-faced, with the peeving, spiteful eyes of a neglected
child, features crammed too closely together. Everyone in the neighborhood knew that Jesús Muerte had earned his nickname one Palm
Sunday by stealing a church offering and stabbing the young priest who
tried to stop him. Though a jury had acquitted him for lack of evidence.

"Remember what I tol' you," he snarled, backing away and leveling a
finger at me. "You remember!"

By the time I returned home that evening I had forgotten the encounter completely. I was fumbling for keys in the gloomy hallway outside my apartment door when I heard a click downstairs. I listened.
Nothing, except a rapid scurrying which I took for mice in the ceiling. I
had just turned key in lock when a voice leapt out of the murk, almost
beside me. "You remember what I tol' you?" I was inside cat-quick,
body wedged against the door as he shoved. By some miracle of adrena-

line got it shut. Must've been screaming at lungtop. There was a com-
motion in the hall: upstairs voices, downstairs Jesse shouting, "What's
the shit, huh? What's happening?"

They coaxed me to open. Brown solicitous faces, a concerned babble.
Perhaps I had imagined him, I suggested. "No, you don' imagine. He
working for Mr. Scotto." "*Madre de Dios!*" I moaned. Our eyes crept
the hall, seeking the crack he had slipped into.

I spent the night at Lucy's. She tried convincing me to buy a Mace
gun. "Listen," I said, "I can't cop to that kind of reactionary reflex. At
this rate everyone will be packing weapons."

She escorted me home next morning. Danger is emetic. I locked myself in and wrote up a fury, warming fingers between thighs as I groped
for metaphors. Later, I went to file a complaint at the precinct. The
desk sergeant, bottom teeth exposed like a row of dirty exclamation
marks, told me there was nothing they could do. "If we locked up every
one of 'em makes a threat there'd be more in jail than there is on the
street."

"This one meant it."

The sergeant nodded, eyelids at half-mast, as if to say: Whatever it is,
lady, I heard it before.

When I came in that night, depressed and cautious, downstairs Jesse
opened his door. He ground fist into palm as if pulverizing a worm.
"Just say that one word, baby. I been wanting an excuse to step on that
motherfuck."

Ox-shouldered, with a small oval head, wire-rimmed glasses, and an
intellectual bearing that added mystique, Jesse transited easily from
street talk to Oxford English. He was a photographer for UPI, away
most of the time; so it wasn't much comfort to have his protection. I
had tried early to sell Jesse on the rent strike, but he had shrugged. "Pay
the man his money. You never saw a monkey mean as he has on his
back." When the rest of us struck and the heat went off completely,
Jesse broke open a sealed fireplace and built a fire. His rooms filled with
smoke, fire engines roared in from every direction and Jesse came over
as an ardent striker.

I touched his arm and said, No, I didn't want anyone getting stepped
on, but I was glad to have him right downstairs.

Those next days were the paranoid phase. Always jumpy. Looking in
both directions — like a kid crossing the street — before sprinting to

the subway. Convinced the guy walking behind me in the bustle-jumble early dark on my way home was a maniac, running upstairs, slamming the door on my fears — to find them perched like a cat on the fire escape. Deeply moved by the courage of my city sisters who face fear as a daily commodity. Resenting men. They aren't harassed on subways. No one tries to cop a feel or strike up innocent conversation. Landlords do not leap so quickly to take advantage. Men, invariably, are the oppressors. Never women. For centuries they have terrorized our planet. God created Adam, then decided to try again. Not because Adam would be lonely, but because he was a botch. So God created Eve — and left out the cruelty.

On the morning it happened I was late for a job interview at a publishing house, striding down the street still mentally brushing my teeth. It was some time before I realized Jesús Muerte had fallen in behind me. Something flashed in his hand.

I took the corner of First Avenue and slid into a tiny drugstore. "Can I use your phone?" My face giving it all away.

"Something is the matter, dear?" asked the druggist's wife, looking not at me but at Jesús Muerte peering in between window displays. "This man he is bothering you?" The two customers were quickly uninvolved, but the old druggist motioned me to the phone, muttering something in Yiddish, as if fearing Jesús would overhear him. His wife stepped in front of me and gestured towards the window with flabby, waddling arms, scolding her husband. "The lady is a good customer but this one is a bad one."

I stepped around her to the phone, reached a bored dispatcher who told me he had no car available. "He has a knife," I pleaded. "I'll see what I can do," he promised.

I waited. No cops. The wife muttering to herself, eyes unflinching from Jesús, who paced before the shop, reluctant for some reason to enter. She approached me in a wheedling whisper, glancing at the feeble druggist. "We wish we could help you, dear. But we do not want this one should come in. Is an old man, my husband." Spreading her hands toward the street as if appealing to Muerte rather than me.

The white haired druggist waved dismissing fingers at her. Taking my hand, he led around the counter, bent slowly down, and came up purple-faced with what appeared to be a child's baseball bat. Very short, but when he placed it in my hand, lean and effective. I slipped hand

and bat inside my coat, thanking him. He smiled, just barely, eyes remaining glued, rheumy but fierce, on my pursuer. "In the nose ... SHWACK!" he spittled.

Brisk, walking through the door and down the sidewalk, shaking fiercely. Muerte beside me instantly, walking step for step.

"Hey cunt! You give Sally hard time, huh? You don' wanna pay no rent. You see what I got, huh? You no wanna be cut up?"

He had my arm again — but the wrong arm. My speed astonished me. Splat! across the face. A knifed impression: grin cut cleanly in half, one eye forced up, the other down, bat landing between with the destruction of his nose. Blood spurting in a little spray. And I ran, turning only as I took the corner. Jesús was squatted on the sidewalk, hands covering his face, leaking blood.

I ran straight to Jesse. "You're okay, baby," he promised. "I caught you now." He rummaged in a drawer and produced a stubby pistol, turning it over in his big hands.

"I don't want this. I'm sick to my stomach."

Jesse pushed shells into handle clip. I touched his arm. "Please put it away." He looked hard at me. "See, it isn't no fucking fairy tale. The dude comes in here there's gonna be blood — *his* blood or *your* blood, you understand?"

I nodded my head, disbelieving. "Maybe I understand ... in the stomach. Why don't I just get out of here?"

"Because you're not one of those people who walks in and gets people in trouble, then walks out on them. I know you're not."

And I wasn't. Word on the street was that this mama is dead. But word also that Angel — who had visited occasionally since the move and still hadn't despaired of sleeping with me — and crew were protecting me. Jesús Muerte had never been liked in the neighborhood. Now his respect had dropped to zilch. Esmelda said, "Some kid gonna scratch him to earn his letter." Nonetheless, for days I bolted myself in and paced the floor, cataloguing sounds: fear in a door slammed downstairs, a footstep in the hall ... remembered how I had ridiculed Richard's paranoia. When Lucy brought me a Mace gun I threw my arms around her and wept gratitude. Nothing happened. It was spooky. Word was that Scotto was dissatisfied with his thug and wanted his money back and that Jesús had split the neighborhood.

Gradually, I began going out again. No sign of Jesús. But one day I found eviction papers crammed under my door. I tore them up. The rent strike had step-stoned along the block to other Scotto buildings. First of the month he couldn't have collected five hundred dollars from his six buildings combined. His voice came capitulating along the halls, announcing that the plumber would be in to repair the boiler. Though stopping at my door, bellowing: "You I want out . . . OUT!" Hammering with a fist until I thought he would break it down.

Mirabile dictu, we had won. I gloated. When it came to a good fight, Sally Scotto was bullied by his bank account. "Not so fast," said Jesse. "The dude is just catching his breath. He'll take all the count we give him."

A few days later Scotto posted a notice downstairs:

> *Rent is due on first day every month no exepsions.*
> *No more garbage cans I provide. No more exteminator.*
>
> THE MANAGEMENT

Mothers began a lament outside my door. I knew its meaning. Previously, Scotto had been tolerant when welfare checks were late (as they invariably were); now he would stick to the letter of the law. Three days late was grounds for eviction. I waited inside, leaning forehead against the door, despising my callow idealism which had engineered such a hollow victory. Esmelda's voice rose above Gatling gun Spanish and bawling *infantas*. What had set her against me? Envy? Jealousy over my friendship with Jesse? Pettiness reigns supreme in this world — those tawdry little human shittinesses outclassing all our great ideals and hopes.

Opening the door I faced a ragtag of mamies and dark *infantas'* eyes turned curiously toward me. Esmelda's glower holding the knife with which Jesús Muerte had bungled. She waved Scotto's note in the air. "*Mira!* What you say now, smart lady?"

"It's not easy standing up for what is right," I said, going for their hearts and sullen, dubious eyes, but sounding like a Young Republican. "Until many join us we are vulnerable troublemakers. Landlords can say, 'Get out! I can find a hundred others to eat my shit. The city is full of shit eaters.' I know it's hard. But it's our only hope not to be bullied the rest of our lives." My words soaking into traces of onion and cabbage in greasy walls, wrapped about with baby yowls, Esmelda's voice cutting through:

"Big mouth, talking talking —" flapping fingers at me "— What do she care? She got lossa money. She don't be thrown out."

I threw up my hands. "Sure, what do I care? I don't care." I slammed the door in their abashed faces, sat down and started work on an article about Sally Scotto and the St. Marks mob.

When Jesse read it he blew out a long bullet of air, concentrating on a spot across the room. "Now you bought it. This mother *is* Mafia. You hear what I am saying?"

"Somebody's got to tell it. We can't let these bastards walk all over us."

"Some-body's-got-to-tell-it. Shee-it, baby. Who do you think you are? First you pull a rent strike, then you assassinate the man's assassin — that's all right, that maybe earned you some respect — now you want to mess with his pride. You don't understand these people. You can't push them that far."

I was quickly losing my nerve. "He probably won't read it."

"Somebody is gonna read it. You'll hear from the man."

Friday night. Some of us meeting to determine a response to Scotto: bundled in layers, which we kept stripping and putting on again. The heat quixotic — never knew whether we would freeze when the boiler couldn't get going or swelter when it couldn't stop. Old upstairs Jesse, a former mason, was explaining how to make the chimneys functional again so we could burn wood scraps from neighborhood dumpsters. As we were breaking up, someone rang my bell, steady, insistent. I went down.

Nat was at the door, eyes wild, nearly bowling me over to get inside, screaming back at two men, calling sexual insults and laughing from the street. I had a galvanizing flash of Jesús Muerte. My legs went mush. Jesse came down the stairs followed by two other men. "Open it wide," he shouted.

"Hey motherfuck!" Feet slapping the street.

Nat clung to me, gasping for breath. "I hate men. Creeps. All of them," she snarled.

Upstairs, the others had gone. Nat shed layers: sweaters, a pair of woolen navy trousers, jeans underneath. "Have you gone hobo?" I asked. "Pee-ew! you smell it, kiddo?"

She shrugged. "I couldn't bring a suitcase. I told Claude I was going to buy cigarettes." Hard to recognize in those pink pothead's eyes and cracked lips a happy young woman in the trillium bloom of first love, or the irrepressible Nat I had known at Whitman. I lugged her castoffs to the hearth.

"I'm afraid they might combust spontaneously."

"I don't feel too humorous now." She lit a cigarette, taking it in quick violent drags. "Claude is fucking up my whole life. He just hangs around. He doesn't want to be with me, but he won't move out. He hates being alone, can't even make his own coffee. So I thought maybe if I left for a while he might —"

I shook my head. "Running doesn't work. When you want him out, you'll say *out!* He'll know there's no mucking around. It sticks out all over that you can't decide."

The cigarette shook in her fingers. It was the Natalie I had first known — vulnerable, none of the psychic armor of adulthood. She stared ahead, voice nearly caving in on itself.

"I've decided. He's an asshole. He pushes my friends away. If I talk about my work he gets bored in ten seconds, but expects me to listen to him all night. Sex is the only way we relate. And if I'm not instantly available he'll go somewhere else. Suzie. Or his old girlfriend, Ricky." Her eyes glistened. "He's an asshole."

"Welcome to womanhood."

"Could I stay here, Max? Just a few days till I figure things out?" A small voice, touching in its uncertainty.

I shook my head. "Sorry. I really couldn't live with your bohemian beach boy camping in my living room."

"He doesn't even know where I am."

"Listen, I can't stay myself. I've been evicted."

Staring a moment, those van Gogh big eyes. "It wouldn't work anyway. Mother would freak out. She thinks you're queer."

"That's presumptuous of Mother."

Nat's eyes slid elsewhere. "To Mother everyone's queer. I'm queer, her maids are queer, even Dad's queer."

"How is your mother? Did you ever get in touch?"

"She was in intensive care, all kinds of tubes and stuff up her nose so I couldn't talk to her."

"Intensive care?"

"She's fine." Nat shook her head, annoyed. "Mother is strong as an ox."

"What about the breast?"

"Nothing. Just a precaution. They shined some kind of light through and weren't satisfied, so they cut a piece out. They're butchers, they love to cut. Look, Mother isn't the cancer type."

"You can be scared, Natalie. There's no rule against being scared."

"You're the one who's scared," she snapped. "I'm just . . . Claude has me all fucked up."

"All right —" touching her "— just a little nervous."

Jesse stepped in, wagging a bottle. "I thought we should celebrate having some heat in this dump, 'cause you never can be sure how long it's gonna last." He laughed, coming in and taking Nat's hand. "We almost met downstairs, but I was going out in a hurry and you were coming in in a hurry. Isn't that the way life is?" Turning to me, "Why you been keeping this lady a secret? She's the best news I've had all day."

Nat's face a sunrise of bashful delight. Jesse uncapped the bottle, tipped it back, then handed it to her. "Thirsty," he gasped. "I had a little race around the block. All things being equal I b'lieve we would have won. Indubitably, fear makes men run faster." He chuckled privately and approached the record changer. "Does this thing work for a living? Let's have some sounds."

I gestured at the records and he began thumbing through.

"Mahler's Eighth, Béla Bartók . . . You know we can't boogie to this shit. Oh, she's got some soul here. Otis Redding." Swinging around to Nat. "You like to dance? I'm going to have to go and locate some of my magic. She can't help it —" nodding at me "— she's so square, no matter which side you put her on she won't roll downhill."

Jesse returned with records. Ear blasting electric guitars, wailing on and on like desire is an elastic stuff. Dancing, all of us, passing a joint, falling into melodic holes between guitar riffs. Tropical heat rose off radiators, Jesse doffed his shirt, sweat forming a pool in the dent of his chest, muscles jumped to the hard pulse of the rock. He winked at me. I felt suddenly needy. Too hot. Unbuttoned my blouse and dropped it on the bed. The buzzer ringing. Natalie off before I could move, as if expecting someone. She returned, triumphant, with Claude.

He removed the pretentious hat and belted overcoat, his blue wash and wear eyes licking my bra. They were Narcissus pools. A man deeply hooked on himself. And my tits. I killed the overhead and lit candles. Jesse cried, "Right on, we got a party now," hips taking the music. He handed the bottle to Claude, who furtively wiped its mouth on his scarf before tipping it to lips. I whispered, "You dazzle me, kiddo." Nat merely smiled — and seduced her lover into the music.

Dancing, who with whom impossible to say, libidos broken loose from moorings. Claude's eyes followed me while Nat tried to interest his hands in her (the girl who'd just finished with him for good!) and Jesse mumbled, "Right . . . mmm-hmh." The record ended. In a bright voice Nat announced, "Time to change partners."

"Ohh yeah," said Jesse. He put on Jimi Hendrix and slunk toward her with a slow rhythm of hips. The little bitch was all over him, his hands moths in the candlelight, voice opening like a creaky door: "You got a bee-yoo-ti-ful ass, baby. You can come visit me any time, you know right where I live." Though I understood what was happening only when Claude pioneered with his tongue behind an ear, coaxed a nipple to life with a circling finger, mumbling hosannas for my breasts, whispering how good we could be together in that spin-the-bottle darkness.

Removing his fingers, I warned he shouldn't take curves so fast, though my heart shambled like a horse losing a shoe. A heavy metal lust that matched the music, imagining all four of us in a sweaty pile on the rug, my hips replying to the heat and hard of his crotch. Nat and Jesse no longer beside us; I expected any moment to hear consenting bed springs. Instead, a premonition of disaster, Jesse's booming whisper: "Let it go, baby."

A God-awful squawk as needle raked record. Jesse moaned.

Claude's hands everywhere at once, squeezing my breasts, mauling. A kid hooked on destruction. I shoved and he undercut at the knees like a tree and toppled onto the couch.

Lights on. Party over. Nat's anger primordial, *the very first anger!* Thick as smoke in the room. She didn't quite look at me.

Her lover popped up from the couch, grabbing coat and dandified hat, moving past Nat, whose face seemed about to shatter into vitreous fragments. "I have to be going. It's been nice —"

"Yeah," said Jesse, grinning at the bulge at Claude's polished crotch, "you could use some fresh air."

He was gone, leaving us dazzled by the bright chrome of his cowardice. The clinging silence he'd left behind broken at last by Nat's voice, nearly bitter, "I'll buy you a new record."

"Let it go. It isn't my favorite disc, y'know. You needed it worse than

I do." Jesse chuckled softly, grabbed his shirt, hesitating toward me a moment as if about to speak, lips forming a puckish smile at my near-nakedness, then shaking his head. "I'll be leaving you ladies to your own devices," he said and followed Claude out the door.

Nat turned the record over and started dancing, transposing rage to movement — a peristalsis beginning at shoulders and working downward. The room was hers: eyes closed in agonized celebration, palms tilted skyward like a monk lost in God-struck meditation. I was banished from her universe of release. Watching, a voyeuse of her catharsis, seduced by the abandon and raw energy, feeling all that pain. Until, exhausted, she sprawled over the couch, catching her breath.

"Only masochists love people committed to hurting them," I whispered.

She crossed legs beneath her and stared at linsey-woolsey soles of her tights, one pink heel peekabooing. Her eyes snapped up. "Are you making it with Claude?"

"You're kidding! No secrets. You were right here, you saw how far I let it go."

"Could we talk about something else? I really don't want to discuss this right now." She lit a cigarette.

"All right. Let's talk about Richard."

She stared. Looking away. "I'm not interested in Richard."

"You're certain?" Locking eyes on her, feeling suddenly ungenerous, almost vindictive. "Natalie?"

"I don't take sex so lightly that I would sleep with just anyone."

"Just men like Jesse whom you've known five minutes or so?" We played the stare-you-down game schoolgirls play. Nat juggling a long cigarette ash, as if wishing to defy the laws of gravity.

"Hypocrite," she hissed. "It's fine if you sleep with someone —"

"What makes you think I'm sleeping with Richard?"

"I have a peephole in your wall."

"Your peephole won't show that Forty-second Street beach bum of yours. I wish I could convince you to drop that phony blond Narcissus. Men like that are cloned at L'Uomo and turned loose on the world."

Her eyes smoldered. "I never trust people who tell me that."

"Listen, I can't help it that I feel protective, big-sisterly, towards you, Nat. You might not like it but it's there."

She studied threadbare patterns in the rug as if reading something there, scarf rolled in a neat taut band across her forehead, back under the drift of hair. Letting go a girlish squawk, she struggled to control her voice. "I love him. I really do. Our last fight he hit me. Then just disappeared for days. I wanted to kill myself. I really did. I'm just a doll he uses for jacking off. He's taken over my life. I don't even exist anymore." Her voice coming apart completely.

I sat beside her on the couch, stroking her hair as she sobbed. What was there to say? You are not the first woman to be abused by a man. Some other platitude? She placed her forehead against my bare shoulder. "I'm afraid to go home," she mumbled. "I still love him . . . I hate him. He probably won't even be there —" speaking as if to herself "— then he'll show up in a few days and we'll act like nothing happened."

"Sounds like you have a lot of self-respect."

"You don't understand about men. You just get these studs to service you. You never fall in love."

"That's good to know." I pulled away a string of hair magneting to a tear on her nose. Nat toyed distractedly with the tiny silk rose between the cups of my bra.

"In everything else you seem to get what you want. But not with men," she said.

I gestured, annoyed, at the wall above my desk, papered with rejection slips (of which Paynor says, "I couldn't accomplish anything with all that *no* staring me in the face"). "Right! All my dazzling successes."

Nat wiped wet cheeks with the palm of a hand. "Whenever you're having an affair you seem really animated. Then you throw him out and go around in the dumps for a week. After that you're back to your old self again. You have love affairs like other people have colds."

"I don't want a *man*, if that's what you mean, Nat. I do want to get laid sometimes. That doesn't have to mean *friend*. I don't mix those concepts up, because that's where you can go wrong. Friendship grows out of trust, not sex. Sex is a small jar; it holds only so much. Friendship is bottomless. And friends don't have to carry penises. I despise the type of woman who wears a tie to the office and goes out drinking with the boys — only the boys! Those secret woman-haters. Relationships are supposedly wonderful things, I know. But you can't stretch out in bed. If you talk to yourself, he gets jealous. I prefer being on my own. I trust myself."

"Maybe you just don't trust men."

"Maybe for good reason." I glanced at my raincoat over the chair, Mace gun in pocket.

I got up off the couch and put on Olitunja, began an old Whitman dance routine. Stretched hard left, both hands to the floor — vertebrae popping into place up the fuse of my spine like Chinese firecrackers, pop pop pop. We shared a joint, music gathering behind me, a restive wind, Nat frowning.

"I still don't think you're so down on men."

Laughing. "I like men. Come dance."

Launching ourselves on the rhythms, Nat seizing release, whooping, muscles spasming an epilepsy of delight. Steam hissed from radiators; any second I expected the ancient boiler to go. Her red turtleneck had a burgundy stripe down the chest.

"Take it off," I suggested. "Go ahead."

She glanced at my breasts. "I'm not wearing a bra." Turning away, she pulled off the top and tossed it. Danced nearer the bass speaker as if to let the beat conduct directly up legs to her round tight belly, small breasts spinning in tiny circles.

"You have lovely breasts, Natalie."

"What?" she mouthed, cupping an ear. Smiling, sliding back into the music, eyes closed, chin puckered in concentration, electric spasms working out to tips of her outstretched fingers.

I put on Greek folk dances. We jogged through steps, forward and back, touching palms. "It's a swamp in here," Nat cried, unbuttoning Levi's and kicking them across the room, where they caught a corner of the desk and hung like an abandoned virtue. Nat giggled. We linked elbows, spinning faster, faster, pulling away from each other but eyes touching in sheer delight, until we dropped side by side on the couch.

Nat sprawled, childlike, candlelight teasing her features, shimmying in her eyes, one leg hooked wantonly over a couch arm. She seemed nearly happy. Sighing, she stretched out and rested her head on my belly, spreading arms luxuriantly. Seeing the nests of hair at her armpits, I remembered our first conversation, years back. "Very sexy," I said, teasing damp coils. Bending down and kissing her forehead.

Getting quickly up, I stood before the long mirror, lowered my jeans and looked, profile, grabbing a handful of belly. "I'm getting fat. I don't get any exercise."

"You look good," said Nat, lying on her side. "Sophia Loren."

I unfastened the bra and rolled panties over my hips. "How about a shower, kiddo?" Her eyes skittish; I caught them for only a moment amidst shadows, skittering away like rabbits. She shook her head. "You don't want I should scrub your back?" I peeled socks and threw them at her. She rifled them back with the furor that had made her dodge-ball terror at Whitman.

Her mood squandered. Stretching out, she pulled the fusty blanket up to her chin. "I just don't want to go home right now and find him fucking Suzie on my bed."

"Let him fuck Suzie," I snapped. "He deserves her."

When I returned, wrapped in a towel, she lay asleep, head crooked at an impossible angle against the couch arm, groaned as I slipped a pillow under. I sat watching her a moment, stroking that thick hair until she breathed regularly again. Wondering why I shouldn't invite her to stay.

Came good writing days. Though time was heavy with matters unsettled. A sensation exacerbated by a visit from Angel, who leaned at a reckless angle in a chair, pointed shoes crossed on coffee table, each sentence chipped off in a little rain of sparks, telling me Jesús was *muerto* for real — slashing a finger across his throat. "Sally Scotto make him a nice little home in Red Hook."

I stared at him, envisioning an industrial pit junked with scrap cars, a sinewy hand clawing up through frozen muck.

I walked carefully through the days.

Returned home one night from a late movie. Just fishing for keys when I realized my apartment door was ajar. I backed off, sprinted downstairs and banged on Jesse's door. No answer. *I could flee*, I thought, *abandon this sinking shittub for good. No, Pearlman. Your manuscripts are up there — every scrap you've ever written.* My heart sank. I went back up those steps, Mace gun readied at eye level.

"All right. I'm coming in —" My voice a mere skeleton. Shoved the door. Resistance. I squeezed through.

Thought at first, in the overhead glare, that a bomb had exploded: furniture splinters and cushion stuffing mixed with torn clothes and gutted books, record changer crushed, speaker innards intestining over the floor, best Deutsche Grammophon records impaled on a decapitated lamppost; the couch had burst and sprayed homey comfort across ceiling and walls. Heart rattling, I waded to the desk over my savaged life, groaning, *Bastard! fucking wop bastard.* It was demolished, split by an ax. Typewriter lying hunched on a shoulder. A wounded bird. I stooped down, lifting it carefully in my hands. Thank God! it looked repairable. Saw pieces of my manuscript box (like running down to the mailbox, you *do* and *don't* want to know the news), realized this confetti I stood upon was my work. Four solid years.

Moaning, on all fours, pawing through, gathering scraps in my fingers, wet from what I realized — looking at my hands — was ink. And a smell, familiar but elusive, indelible in the gray subway stairwells of memory. Smelling hard, I realized was urine. The pigs had pissed on it. Crying . . . laughing at once, for they had botched it: torn some in two, wetted others, but only top pages stained beyond legibility. Dumb incompetent assholes hadn't succeeded with the one irremediable hurt, not appreciating the power of the word even when it had hurt them. Scuffing on my knees, clutching reeking pages to chest, laughing, spitting out words — dumb-pig-shit curses — like a dazed kid. *And the phone rang.*

I stared at it. The one thing in the room untouched, inviolate on its stand, gloating like a coconspirator. Evil thing. Another of man's devices for reaching long-distance to torment an enemy. As I answered, my eyes crawled up-wall to the only other possession left in place: a photo of me, flanked by Richard and Lucy at Jones Beach. A steak knife stuck in my bikini crotch.

A long silence on the other end, then gravel rattling in Scotto's throat. "Now you unnerstand? You got no respect. I don't gotta steal like a nigger. I say fuck y' filtee money."

My voice slicing through — not a laugh exactly, a fierce braying monkey shriek. I tore the phone from the wall, looking down at my clothes (the only intact ones remaining to me), ink-smeared, ruined. Rising off them, infused and enduring, the reek of urine.

CHAPTER THIRTEEN

CLAUDE

AUNT BERTY AND DAD SAT TOGETHER IN A CORNER OF THE WAIT-
ing room, heads nearly touching, Berty whispering in a gravelly voice
that filled the room and clattered out into the hallway, Dad hunched,
hands squeezed between his knees. They looked up together, as if fear
were a family thing, and for a moment I wanted to turn and flee; tried
seeing around where the hall made a jog-trot turn and disappeared into
an infinity of sickness and death. White linen jackets flitted, carts
creaked as though pain had seeped even into inanimate things. Then I
rushed forward and kissed Dad. Berty hugged me, whispering, "We had
a close call, honey."

"Close —?" I sank down on a seat beside her.

Berty explained how they had taken a biopsy of the lump in Mother's
breast. At first, they thought it malignant, and the surgeon brought

Dad in to describe the procedure, if the breast should have to come off. Then the lab pronounced that little core of flesh benign and they proceeded with the hysterectomy. "They scooped everything out, ovaries too. She had a rough time."

Dad stared straight ahead, elbows on knees, as though he could see around the bend in the hall. He had been up at Mother's side all night, holding her hand. In his sleeplessness he looked very Semitic, as if reverting back. My emotions tangled like cats. I wanted to hug him for the first time in years.

"A butcher," Berty was saying. "What's another tit to him? The bastard wanted it so bad he was drooling." From her station, a candy-striper regarded her in horror. Berty's horn honk voice. "You should'a heard 'em describe the surgery, sounded like a football game: four pints of blood, three hours under the knife. Nifty job. *Nifty!* that's what the turdhead called it."

A nurse trotted in, buxom, flushed, eyes stuck on Berty — but speaking to Dad. "Maybe she could use a sedative, huh?" He nodded. That abiding faith in the Wonder Drug. *Our Father Which Art in Valium.* Berty threw up a hand like a traffic cop and the nurse backed off. I sat chain-smoking.

She seized my arm. "C'mon, honey, we'll go up."

We waited in white antisepsis outside her door, while nurses clicked down polished halls, wearing dice on the heels of their shoes. A cartful of flowers clickety-clicketed into Mother's room: love in the blush of poinsettia, condolence from gawping Bird of Paradise mouths and orchid tongues. When the nurse emerged, I reminded her, "I'd really like to see my mother."

"We'll see —" A smile that offered aspirin.

Berty growled, "This is her daughter, for chrissake." Smunching her cigarette into the floor beneath a no smoking sign, lipstick forming a red nipple around the filter. The nurse shook her head and walked away.

"How's things?" Berty asked, lighting another cig and handing it to me. I told her that Carol had moved out; she didn't get along with my boyfriend (truth was whenever she took a bath Claude needed a shave, stood ogling her in the mirror; "He's a maniac," she said; "his eyes say *rape!*"). Berty frowned. Then her plastic mouth spread ear to ear in an unholy cherry-red smile. She glanced down the hall in both directions. "C'mon honey —" Planting a hand in my back, shoved me into

Mother's room, hunching shoulders like a naughty kid and closing the door behind me.

Mother was propped on a mound of pillows, eyelids closed, vein blue, needles feeding into backs of hands; a tube extended from under the sheet, draining into a pouch. Her lids begin to flutter — papery as insect wings — and finally open, eyes glazed but miraculously blue against wax white of her face. She extends a feeble hand and I take it, kiss her cheek beneath bruised eye sockets. Her lids open and close; she floats above pain on a thin pool of analgesia. I ask how she feels. She floats. Her consciousness like driftwood coming to me from some eddy of the past — Pompano Beach perhaps, where I chased sea gulls . . . or really chased David chasing sea gulls in that salt air, while Adam stood by himself, staring into the arcing eternity of ocean, and Mommy like a fifties cover girl, arms akimbo, head tilted coquettish for her-man-Jacob with his Kodak, almost busty in a cashmere sweater in that breast-crazy season when men thought heaven was between a woman's knockers. A safe place.

"Nattie dear —" she whispers. Tears roll down her cheeks.

I sit in a chair at bedside and caress her fingers. Mother, who has never had time for sickness, lying there. I feel cheated, realizing she is not invincible. She smiles, struggling to keep eyes open. Does anyone know this woman? She fought the union when it tried to crack *Bach-Fashion*, and I never believed — as she claimed — that she'd done so because it insisted she pay lower wages. The same woman who, one day, seized the arm of a wino tottering precariously on the lip of a sub-way platform, crying, "Hey, watch it! Jeepers —" pulling him to safety while others ignored him: eyes slit, squinching her nose as she turned back to me. "Golly, he stinks."

Suddenly the nurse bursts in, shooing me out with her hands, scolding like a starched white hen.

When finally I got home, Claude's blond suitcase had disappeared without a good-bye. I sat a minute in the gloom, resting forehead against kitchen table. The super's door was ajar as I went downstairs, but her dog didn't worry me.

Saturday night: stacks of Sunday *Times* blocking sidewalks before newspaper stands, whisking cabs fared with happy people, hippies shopkeeping on blankets, a bum with his face stuck in a carton of ice

cream, a band of Neapolitan across his forehead. Everyone prospers on
Saturday night. In the hornbleat and voicetinkle I pretended my heart
was off for a carriage ride through Central Park. It knocked wildly in
traces.

Richard sat at his usual table at the Figaro, in the politico-lectual
patter; men with graying beards leaning intently towards one another in
the smokehaze. We kissed. He patted a chair beside him and I sat. "My
life's falling apart," I said.

Richard shook his head, his eyes going to a frizzly-haired woman
whose tits stuck out like *Playboy* fantasies. "If it was all up we wouldn't
know when we were high."

"Will you come home with me?"

He grinned. "I wouldn't mind. But the boy's a little shaky about your
blond boyfriend. I'm expert at spotting psychos."

"He's gone . . . really. If he comes back I'll throw him out."

Richard guffawed. "You sound like an O'Neill character. Full of undecided decision."

"You won't regret it."

Richard rubbed hands together. "Oh yeah?" Grinning at Miss Su-
pertits like a snake at a frog. "Ohhh yeah . . . "

As we entered my building the super's dog began a staccato barking.
I grabbed Richard's arm. "She's a loony," I whispered, telling how she
left her door open so the dog could stick its muzzle through an accor-
dion fence and snap at us. "It's real narrow there, you have to slide
along the wall —"

"Dog?" Richard demanded, attempting to see past me.

"It's a Doberman."

His eyes rolled. "Holy fuck!"

"She's racist," I whispered.

Richard's chin jutted forward. "You expect me to go in there past
some demented fucking bigot and her Nazi mutt?"

"Shhhhh —" I cringed. "It isn't so bad. Just scary."

Buds of sweat sprouted over his forehead, but he followed me, tiptoeing along the wall. I peeked around her door. She sat at kitchen
table, oblivious. The dog shifted nervously on its haunches beside her,
ears flat over the snake skull, muscles shifting under sleek blue skin. He
looked right at me. Then sprang forward, toenails clipping tiles. We
stood frozen, backs and palms flat against the wall, gaping at a streak of

slick dark movement and white teeth. The Doberman crashed against the flimsy fence. Richard made a bird sound deep in his throat. Again and again, the dog leapt and snarled, teeth slashing the air; Richard tweeted; the fence bowed perilously; I expected it to give way any second.

Then she had the dog's collar; her knee caught him hard in the ribs and he deflated like a popped balloon. "You again, is it?" Her puffy Irish mug leering out. "He don't care much for kikes." The Doberman whined, muzzle forced through the gate, leathery black scars criss-crossing head and back.

Richard seized my hand and made for the stairs. Behind us, she barked "Fresh meat!" Her insane squealing laugh. At the landing he stopped and screamed back: "FUCKING BIGOT! We'll sic the JDL on you, we'll —" I pulled him inside.

Later he couldn't relax, lay tossing, scratching himself, finally sat up and lit a cigarette. "I don't know which makes me more antsy," he said into the dark, "that dog or your psycho boyfriend."

I laughed. "C'mon, he's not so tough."

Richard realized that the super's apartment was directly below us and began leaping up and down on the bed, bringing up the muffled yowling of the dog. Really enjoying himself.

In days that followed, we talked art and theatre, made spaghetti, Frisbeed in Central Park on Saturday afternoons, stopping to squawk at gulls and ducks perched side by side on the reservoir ice. "Why don't they fight?" I asked. Richard's shout echoed back from a wall of buildings along Central Park West: "FIGHT, C'MON! NONE OF THIS COZY SHIT. KILL EACH OTHER." Through the long afternoons at work, I had begun looking forward to our evenings together in a way I never could with Claude. No sudden disappearances.

I propped my easel at the living room window above the chorus of St. Marks Place — as I had never dared with Claude's sharp tongue around — Mom/Dad's wedding portrait pinned to a wooden upright. Standing late before that frosty window, soul wide to the grinding night music of the city that cannot sleep, watching entranced as their faces formed themselves on my canvas — like they'd been there all along, just waiting for me.

On Mother's birthday — sitting on the beige couch in her blond parlor, still echoing Rosita and other wars of a recent past that now seemed ancient history — ice tinkled in glasses. Mother shouted "*L'chayyim!*" pledging, "I'm through with all that now. I detest middle-agers who become obsessed with their bowels." Whenever Dad looked at me, I tried to smile: fearing my teeth would click together. The latest maid soon appeared to announce dinner, regarding Mother almost tenderly. A heavy woman with ample features and dented eyes, more Mattie-like than any maid in years. I realized with a shock that I didn't know her; I had been around so little recently. All of us gathering to help Mother up. She gave a teenish smile and said, "I'll go with my Jacob —" taking his arm "— and my Nattie, too." Her giggle was contagious.

After dinner she overrode Dad's protests, insisting on a walk. We passed a pet shop on Eighth Street, spilling cold light into the night. A tail-wagging Chihuahua puppy with bulge eyes and a bark like the chuffing of a teapot leapt against the glass. I pressed my nose flat to its chilly surface, starting a love affair. Mother wanted to buy him for me to celebrate her recovery. So I carried him home in a pocket, his wet nose sticking out — yapping, frantic, as I passed the super's closed door, bringing her into the hall with the Doberman, shouting, "Take him right out! I won't have no pets disturbing my tenants."

A few days later Richard returned from a trip to Vermont. He regarded little Marcello suspiciously that first night, demanding, "What's he doing in here? Dogs don't sleep in beds." I explained that he was short-haired, he got cold. "Cold!" Richard's eyes bulged like the puppy's. "The dog has fleas, man. Look at him scratch. I'll bet he's the sneaky type that pisses pillows."

"He's my friend. When I come home from work he gets so excited he jumps around and pees on the floor."

Richard squinted. "You got some fetish about dog piss?" He got hold of Marcello, wriggling like a rat, and dropped him on the floor, where he sat whimpering. Richard covered us fastidiously with a blanket, but Marcello wasn't fooled (certain unmistakable sounds and smells, I suppose); he yapped and tore about in furious circles and nipped at blankets. Managed to scamper up on the bed, breaking the climactic surge of our rhythm.

"Hey, your little mutt is humping my leg," Richard cried. "Fuckinay! your dog just shot his lousy little wad." Sticking his ass in the air like a dog biscuit, Marcello grabbed it, Richard shrieked. "He broke the skin ... looka' that!'' His face red-blazing, he grabbed for Marcello, who had wiggled down under the covers. Me laughing so hard I was afraid I would pee.

We lay sharing a cigarette, while Marcello strutted about the room like Julius Caesar. Then Richard was staggering bowlegged to the phone. Coy at first with whomever he'd called, saying he was at a friend's — a close mutual friend. "Hey, why not join us? No, kid, it ain't Lucy. Come on over why doncha. We'll have a party, a fucking Ginsberg Howl!" I had leapt from bed, on my way to the phone, when his voice crumpled. "Looka' that! She hung up on me." He held out the receiver for me to hear.

Me shouting, "What are you doing, Richard?"

He shrugged. "Thought it'd be fun — a little threesome."

Claude opens the door, using a key which had traveled along in a raincoat pocket as he sampled half the pussy between Bethune and Bowery, right in as though he pays rent, past Richard strumming guitar on the couch and into the kitchen where I stir chicken soup, begins nibbling behind an ear, whispering hellos. Richard strides in behind him, hands outstretched like a referee. "You don't live here anymore, remember?" Claude regards his disheveled hair, thin lips pinched in disdain.

"Did you ask the grocery boy to stay for chow?"

I shake my head. "I have to sit down. I can't handle this."

The two men stand, not squared off exactly: Richard's hands shake, eyes intent on fringes of Claude's scarf; Claude half turned away, patting a hand over scalloped hair. Me suspended between like a dizzy tightrope walker, unable to take a step. "I wish you would both just go," I manage. Richard's eyes cut me with betrayal.

"I get it. It's a pawn shop: the man has returned with his ticket." He kisses my forehead. "It's been sweet, babe."

I stand watching as he starts for the bedroom and his clothes, but stops as if snagged by a hook and comes back to Claude. "I understand you're buddies with the super downstairs."

Claude dips a spoon in the chicken soup. "Don't be a sore loser."

"You could be Irish. You have the sullen choirboy look."

Claude slowly turns his head, fingers crawling towards a meat cleaver on the chopping board. I touch Richard's arm. "You're a sweet woman," he says. "I'd hate to see you get involved with an asshole like that." He glances at the cleaver, spins and leaves the kitchen. Minutes later I hear the front door close. I consider running after him — if only this were a world that honored the better man.

Claude's hands making immediate assumptions. I shove him off. "What happened? She threw you out again?"

His prima donna smile. He shrugs. "You wanted me back, I'm back. That's what matters." He clutches my chin and presses his mouth fiercely against mine. I break loose.

"That hurts, really."

He takes another spoonful of soup and I nearly shout: "I'm not just living for your convenience." Claude shuts his eyes in mock pain, shaking a hand in my face.

"Let's drop it."

Later, I read Hesse, while his eyes prowl from me to drawing pad. He showers and appears with a towel around his waist, sits cross-legged in the armchair combing his hair. Marcello sniffs his foot and backs away, tripping over his own feet. *Dog sense*, Max would say. My feelings seethe.

He asks to sleep with me. "Do what you want," I tell him. But when his hand pioneers the valley of my back I refuse him. "You can't just walk into my life." My voice lacks conviction. He rolls over onto his stomach and falls asleep. This is how it will be: cut-rate sex in the morning, alienation in the afternoon — the in and out of his love. I am awakened by his penis prodding my belly like a finger, legs sliding over the sheets; he clutches my ass and burbles unintelligibly. "Claude?" I ask the dark. He flops over beside me, asleep. His spermdrizzle matting my pubic hair. Dreams are boats slipping past in the fog.

Next night he doesn't show for dinner. I lie on the couch wondering which excuse it will be this time: late theatre audition, art dealer who'd taken him for a drink . . . knowing I share some complicity in his deceit since I insist he bring an excuse as a ticket to my bed. He would be content to say, "Wow! this little honey I met gives great head." I am asleep on the couch when he arrives and wakes me with a peck on the forehead. "Anything to eat?" he asks, "I'm famished." I point at the trash.

Adrift again on a ship from nowhere to nowhere. Each port of call in my life — art, work, school, friendship — equally arbitrary. I can make no plans, expect nothing. I spend my money on grass and forget to call home when I have promised, lose entire days and miss appointments with Dr. Kaufman. While Claude is complete, self-content. A Hopper conception: cold light on a nonchalant background.

Sometimes, returning home from the art store where I've landed a job, I sense trailings of another woman, an intuitive knowing: heat leavings, a spot of blood on the bottom sheet . . . blood spreading behind my eyes, the Rorschach of jealousy. Our relationship parasitic: each night he doesn't appear I lose a little self-respect, Claude gains a little power. Despair comes the night he moves to the couch — allergic, he claims, to my nasty little dog. Though I know it's not Marcello dander, but love and need and any kind of caring.

Mom/Dad invite us to dinner at Peter's Back Yard. Berty comes, too, wearing a soft pastel-blue sweater that is too tight — her nipples jutting out like copper pennies — and a muffler of furry animal tails that keeps slithering off her shoulders. Mother is in blond mink. Together the two New York sisters are a wildlife society. Dad shakes Claude's hand, glancing at the sculpted hair, and Claude turns gallantly to Mother, taking her hand and saying I have a beautiful mother. She offers a tepid smile and kisses me coolly. Berty imposes: "I'm Aunt Berty . . . since nobody else is going to introduce me." Extending her hand and a lippy smile.

Through dinner Berty drinks and flirts, finding any excuse to brush her tits against him, teasing with puppy-playful eyes. While the rest of us make determined conversation and Claude posts his patrician schnoz high on the air, inclining his head mallard-wise, as if to emphasize that this is his natural habitat.

Berty accompanies me to the ladies' room, bellowing brashly from an adjacent stall. "So how's things with y'r gorgeous goy guy?"

I am trying to pee.

"Whatsamatter, honey, another gal? There's always another gal with studs like him. I've married four of 'em y' know."

She's at the sink coating her lips in frostpink when I emerge — each side curling up from the little phallic stick in a momentary arc — smacks them together with little pucking sounds. "Well, there's lotsa fishes in the ocean." In the mirror Berty studies me as if pondering something. "Y'know, I hope y'r not seeing any more of those dyke friends of yours."

I recoil. "You don't even know my friends, Berty."

"Some people you don't gotta know."

A toilet flushes.

"Just drop it —" I whisper "— before I get mad."

A woman emerges from a stall, impeccable in wool suit and ruffled blouse. She looks first at me, then flares nostrils at Berty, who sticks out her tongue in the mirror. The woman pretends not to see, quickly exits without drying her hands.

"I gotya this little pamphlet —" Berty rummages in her purse. "Y'r the high risk category: Jewish, small-busted, and affluent. Don't take chances, huh?"

She hands it over: *A Guide to Breast Self-Examination.*

In the taxi home, Claude says it's strange that Berty should be so well-stacked when Mother and I are small. "Padding," I assure him. "That's not padding," he says. "The woman was all over me. She played kneesies under the table. She's definitely hot. But Jeezus, what a cast iron voice."

"You could always gag her," I suggest.

In bed he is a trapeze artist, suspended above me like a Flying Wallenda, sending me shrieking down dizzy toward the net of orgasm; making me wonder if I am not Natalie at all, but perhaps Berty . . . Mother, the Coney Island Avenue Sisters side by side, girdles hobbling knees . . . or a composite, Mrs. Potatowoman, with endless stick-on possibilities: Berty's boobs, Ricky's lips, Suzie's snatch. Imagination's manikin, the ultimate in erotic hardware. But *Everywoman* is *Nowoman.*

Dr. Kaufman studies me, her eyes set on the horizon of glasses, continuing to rock in her chair. Mother and I have fought again, I explain. When I told her I was afraid Claude might leave me, she said, "Gee, honey, I didn't know you cared so much for these fellahs." *This fella!* I had snapped, sick and tired of her belittling my feelings. Then she suggested I might be spending too much time with Maxine. "Y'know a man gets insecure if his girl spends too much time with her girlfriends. He can get the wrong impression."

"Wrong impression?" asks Dr. Kaufman. "What did she mean by that?"

"Mother wants him to get the wrong impression. Remember, I told you she used to call me a tomboy and say I didn't like being a girl because I wore cowboy chaps and played baseball and liked doing the things my brothers did. Why not? I didn't have anything against being a girl. That was Mother's problem."

Lifting her chin slightly. "Tell me about that problem."

I shrug. "To Mother everything is in types: the *tomboy type*, the *I'm all woman type* — like people are precooked and packaged in cellophane. No in-betweens or subtle shadings. She doesn't really know *me*, only the packages she's tried stuffing me into."

Dr. K. dips her head, a slight smile, eyelids drooping — a code which means she isn't satisfied. I suggest that Mother doesn't want me competing with her as a woman. "Secretly, she didn't want me to be a girl so she tried to confuse me. The older I've gotten the more insecure she's become, and the more she's tried making me believe I don't like my own sex. She says how thrilled she was to finally have a little girl, but I think I was an accident. Sons were easier. Her ego just can't handle a daughter. Even when I was small I knew she didn't want me around; I felt guilty just for existing. Now she says, 'You need to see a woman analyst, Natalie. You could use the role model.' She doesn't even realize the irony."

"You disagree?" Dr. Kaufman's boots creak as she crosses them.

I look at her, eyes scratchy-bloodshot. "I think it's irrelevant. Everything is screwed up, everyone is miserable, we all need daily doses of drugs and therapy just to keep going. No one knows who they are or what they want anymore. They're too busy using other people to love them. What can you do to change that? What could anyone do? You can't change the world. Or make Claude be loyal. No analyst can do that."

"No," she says softly, part moved, part wounded. "I'm sorry." Her hand moves on the pad, doodling hieroglyphs, mysteries. "I'd like to get back to Maxine," she says. Waiting with fisherman patience while I smoke a cigarette.

"Max is a few years older than me. I guess that's s'posed to be sinister or something. Actually, Mother is jealous 'cause I respect Max more than I do her. People resent other people who aren't ground down by life; since they know they've been ground down. Besides, Max is brilliant and beautiful and really knows what she wants. Very strong. I think she would make a fantastic shrink. I mean, she always knows more about people than they know about themselves."

"This doesn't sound like a real person to me."

"What's wrong with having a hero?"

"Heroes are fine. Gurus worry me a little."

"Actually, you remind me of Maxine. That's why I chose you for my analyst."

She doesn't respond, letting my observation become swamped in the ticking of time, dripping seconds. And I realize that, in reality, her lips are ungenerous, eyes lack radicalism — nothing overdone, everything in medium sizes. Perhaps it's the solidity that reminds me of Max.

"Lately," I blurt, "she hasn't wanted to see me."

"Why?" Her eyes focus, nearly hypnotic. I admit to having suspicions and ask if it will destroy her image of me if I tell her. Dr. Kaufman touches fingers to lips. "Excuse me," she says. "It just amused me, the idea of an analyst put off by a client's revelations."

Then I am talking about the night at Maxine's — stripping to undies in the steamy apartment, dancing together, my voice going brittle. *But it wasn't what you think.* "Go on —" says Dr. Kaufman. I tell about Max standing naked at the mirror asking if I wanted a shower. Parallel lines form a quick shaft above Dr. Kaufman's nose; she smoothes the skirt over her lap.

"Didn't it seem at all odd to you that a grown woman would ask another grown woman to shower with her?"

Her question shocks me. "I don't know. I didn't really think of it like that."

"Yet you didn't take the shower?" (Just the clock and her pencil tapping its rubber foot on the pad.) "I agree," she says, "I wouldn't have either."

All at once, I am overcome by the sensation I'd experienced that night — suspended, watching from beyond myself: Maxine's loud nudity as she stepped from panties — completely, whitely naked — unshaven legs, full moons of nipples, athletic smudges under her arms. Later, pretending to sleep as she sat on the couch arm, chin-a-hand, gazing down at me. Trembling inside, afraid she was going to kiss me on the mouth.

"It didn't mean anything," I mumble. "We were sweaty, enjoying the music. Haven't you ever had a friend? It's like nobody else has ever had a friend they love."

After a time she asks, "Is this the first time you've suspected that Maxine might want something beyond a platonic relationship?"

"Maybe she thought I needed a shower." My voice lacks conviction. Emotions tangle in my stomach like cats.

"Would you be flattered if she did desire you physically?"

I shudder, something in my head about to burst. Dr. Kaufman's boot heels stick sharply out at me from their perch on the coffee table; I can't look at them. A ray of sunlight shatters on a crystal suspended in the window and speckles fawn spots over her face and the trophies of knowledge and culture on walls behind, each a tiny rainbow. "We didn't do anything," I protest.

"It isn't such a criminal thing," she says softly. "I know we are taught that it's more than criminal. Subhuman. But all of us experience these feelings and must cope with them, even if we cope by sweeping under the rug. Now that it's out, you can run. Or can be very brave and say: *Yes, these are my feelings, I want to cope openly.*"

Words so incredibly heavy, weighing on my tongue till I nearly despair of getting them out. "I love her. But not that way."

Her face etched with delicate sadness. "Yet you do find her attractive?"

"I can't imagine making love to a woman. It's disgusting. I wish you would believe me."

I remember suddenly the morning I had arrived at Max's uptown apartment to pick up a French book and Lucy came out of the bedroom wearing one of Max's nightgowns. I knew they had just gotten up, kept touching one another. I wanted to vomit. It's impossible, I told myself, they're both very feminine women. Everyone going queer — as if feeling cheated by nature's choices, like some final human rebellion. Icarus's last flight. *And maybe I'm one of them.* The clock's heavy ticking joins the other accusatory voices: Mother, Kitty, Berty . . . now Dr. Kaufman. I have a panicky feeling she is going to just turn me out now — time's up! — as she has with other quandaries. I couldn't take it. I stare at her leg bobbing up and down, hinged on the knee of the other. A tiny gash in the skin of one boot, a wound; the flesh inside chicken white, obscene. I start talking rapidly:

"I had a dream that night I slept over, as I was waking up; it seemed so real. I dreamt that we were back at Whitman again, in the girls' locker room. Maxine told me to sit on her lap, and I realized that she was naked and I was naked. I was terrified, I wanted to run out of there. But it was like she had some magnetic power and I was pulled towards her. When I opened my eyes I had the eerie feeling that the dream was really an allegory of our relationship. I was creeped, I had to get out of there."

"I keep hearing Maxine as the aggressor. Yet you say since that night *she* has avoided *you*. I feel I'm getting conflicting messages."

Shaking my head, my voice a hoarse rasp. "It isn't true. It really isn't. I didn't ever come on to her like that."

Dr. Kaufman's eyes unwavering, twin suns above glasses rims. "Tell me —" she pauses "— do you fantasize about Maxine?"

Sweat trickles under my shirt. "It's ten after already," I remind her. But that solar gaze doesn't budge.

"I have a watch, Natalie. I know what time it is."

My voice emerges, scampers away from me, a small thing that could be crushed underfoot. "Maybe I am queer, maybe Mother's right about me. I just haven't accepted it. Isn't it true they can spot each other — even in someone who doesn't know they are yet? I think Claude knows. Maybe our relationship is an attempt to run away from the truth about myself." Tears; I let them come.

"Have you ever had a homosexual experience, Natalie?"

I tell her about Heidi who slept over with me as a girl.

"That isn't what I'd call a homosexual experience."

"It almost was."

"Almosts don't count."

I peek at her. "Maxine says Mother is a latent homosexual."

Dr. Kaufman frowns. "There's no such thing. In that sense we're all *latent homosexuals*. You aren't any more than I am."

"Really?" I cry for joy.

"This is a common fear at your age, Natalie. But you've found a strong role model in your mother — even though you may deny it. It's nearly classical for homosexuals to reject the parental model of their own sex."

"Last week you said I was searching for a mother figure."

"You're a demanding person." She places tongue against upper teeth as if debating whether to continue. "Homosexuality isn't just a matter of sexual preference. It's an emotional underdevelopment, fixation at a narcissistic, masturbatory stage. Ultimately, it's not about sex at all but about commitment and identification. A naughty rebellion against the demands of growing up. With lesbians, rarely a lighthearted rebellion.

An occasional homosexual fantasy is nothing to be concerned about.
Nearly universal. I wouldn't worry about it, Natalie."

I smile, I beam at her. Emancipator, custodian of nightmares. Feeling suddenly expansive, I give the other secret I have been hoarding,
telling her that last time Claude left me I almost killed myself. Her eyebrows arch, but she attempts to sound unconcerned.

"You're full of almosts. Almost had sex with a woman friend, almost
killed yourself. If we were responsible for all our almosts we would all be
ax murderers."

The apartment stank of dog poop. Dustmice copulated under the bed.
I ignored Marcello's cheerful hopping against my leg and considered
cleaning up, but couldn't muster the necessary self-respect. Began snoop-
ing through the drawing portfolio Claude had left in the living room —
perhaps seeking a clue to his other life. A new series of prick portraits.
These included lips parted in fellatio, eyes peeking coyly over the sump
of his belly, the blonde-bitch smirk of his Ricky. Then reversed. A
woman's breasttips, foreshortened belly, frizz of pubic hair — and
Claude's tongue extended, looming toward her like a space probe.

I flipped through the entire gallery of 6's and 9's: Andrea, other New
Art faces, including a pretty boy smile buzzing over Claude's glistening
stamen like a honey bee with empty eyes. Finally Suzie. Her Bronx
cheerleader simper and moist Russian mouth. In a fury I began tearing
them up *No! not art.* It was him I wanted to tear — lips from teeth,
cheeks from bone.

Not knowing what else to do with my despair, I napped. I was awakened by a knock on the door, a light, insistent rap. I got up groggily,
asking who it was. His voice, so close through the panels, made my
heart skip. "What do you want?" I demanded. "I want to see you," he
said. I eased a breath, staring into the door as though it were a mirror,
composing my face, opening: to the full sun-turning heliotrope dazzle
of his charm, the strained sincerity. He proffered a flower from Hare
Krishna chanters on Eighth Street.

"Why are people always bringing me paper flowers?"

Claude glanced at my bare breasts, then at a fresh Marcello lump on
the floor — into which, squinching his nostrils, he planted the flower
upright. "I haven't cleaned," I admitted. "I've been depressed." He
turned to prick portraits spread over the couch.

"Hey, fantastic! Hey, I'd like to do some of us."

I cornered his skittering eyes. "I'm sure you've planned a whole series: Grunewald, Lizzy the dyke, Aunt Berty . . ."

Anger flared his nostrils a moment, then he plunged hands deep into raincoat pockets. "At least you didn't trash them."

I held up the drawing of his pretty boy friend. "Are you gay?" I demanded.

Claude regarded me with an affected smile. "I'm bi."

"You mean you enjoy it as much with a man?"

"Often more."

"I think you're a nymphomaniac. You would probably fuck Marcello if there was no one else around."

He laughed too explosively. "You are a very funny lady."

"I mean it. You're totally hedonistic. Out for yourself."

"Just like everyone else." His smile straining at edges. Then suddenly he was animated, said he'd come to invite me to a Jud Biggs opening at a gallery south of Houston (SoHo he called it) where he might have a shot at a show. I shrugged and got dressed.

Old warehouses, an industrial loft redeemed by white paint and track lighting, wine in paper cups, tinkling voices, women in miniskirts, men in Ginsberg beards and smelly armpits, the few in tight jeans looking Claude up and down, eye-corner connoisseurs, a smattering of stumble-bums off the Bowery for the free dago red. "She's the honcho," said Claude, nodding at a tall predatory woman, blouse unbuttoned to navel and a horsy smile for every weed in her pasture. The one he would have to convince about a show. He smiled at her as convincingly as possible. Everyone furiously knowing everyone else — some faces I recognized from art magazines. Obviously, no one had come to see the work; they paid no attention to it. I turned to what seemed to be trash, slopped over the floor like cardboard mush in the gutters outside.

"That's s'posed to be art?"

Claude regarded me in amazement. "That's a Biggs installation. Biggs is art."

"I think it's a piece of shit."

Claude's eyes widened. "Jeezus —" touching fingers to forehead, he turned quickly away.

"Now what's wrong?"

"That's him —" he mouthed sidewards "— that's Biggs!"

I swiveled. A vaguely middle-aged man was watching me: paunchy, with a monk's fringe of beard. He raised his wine cup in salute. I turned away, but Claude had merged with the diaspora of American talent from Lansing, Michigan, and Medford, Oregon; expatriates of ambition — which is too often mistaken for ability — preening and finessing on a branch set apart from the common flock, disdaining and disdained in turn. Jud Biggs brought me a cup of wine. "You stand out," he said, making a sweeping gesture at the roomful of envious women. "Flesh, that's all. Cunts!"

I walked on, perused paintings on walls behind the Biggs installations. They were flower ghosts, silhouettes, a negative impression of flower ghosts. Biggs followed me around the room, his huge belly nearly bumping my elbow. He stank of tobacco, turpentine, and perspiration. "I got nothing against serious women," he growled. "Once I fell in love with one. She read T. S. Eliot while we balled." I looked directly into the twinkle in his eye. He repelled and fascinated me. I was certain he could explain the relationship between filth and modern art.

"You a painter?" he asked. A flash of gold teeth and cut-to-the-quick eyes. I nodded. He gestured at the walls. "Painting began as a record of fact. Straight stuff. Then for a couple millennia it got hung up on truth, beauty — that kind of shit. Religious propaganda. Today it's a fucking entertainment. Look at 'em —" sweeping a beefy paw to incorporate both people and paintings, "— That's no social critics. Fucking jinkapoos for the corporate kingdom. Gawddamn court jesters." His laugh boomed out, bringing up smiling faces. "Culture clowns!" he spat, one eye screwing up.

I moved on to a wall of abstract: art that said nothing, then furiously copied itself. He was right of course. At my elbow Jud Biggs asked, "Do you fuck?"

I looked him over. "No," I said, "I'm a nun." Walking away from his roaring laughter.

At the wine table, a svelte woman with long blonde hair caught back by a leather headband sporting blue-tipped fox tails said hello, vaguely amused, as if regarding a zoo oddity. Her face was familiar. "Do I know you from somewhere?" I asked. "Not exactly," she replied. As she walked away I realized it was Ricky.

In a side room Claude talked to the horsy woman. Her long teeth chomped words just inches from his face. Flighty and unsure of herself in the way of pederasts with a weakness for pretty boys. Eyes as jeweled as her hopes — and his ambition. She smiled/he smiled.

She gripped his hand/he nodded. Then she kissed him savagely on the lips.

I started for the door; I hadn't come to be humiliated. Someone tapped my shoulder. A statuesque woman. Valkyrian. Her face coarse-skinned and somewhat flushed, fierce black eyebrows and eyes that were small cups brimming with irony. "You're a painter," she said. "Takes one to know one." She blocked escape, jabbering on about the Old Boys' Club. "None of them can do anything anymore." Me nodding politely, attempting to edge past. I glanced back at the dealer, one hand crimped light as a mothfoot over Claude's arm, looking as voracious as he did victorious. "You can't trust her," the big woman said confidentially. "She makes promises that don't happen." Whispering, "Secretly she hates women."

"Excuse me," I said. "I really have to go."

"C'mon over, why don't you. I'd like to show you my work."

Surprised at first, flattered. Then it dawned on me: dark fists of her nipples under the T-shirt, her smile floating like the leer of a cartoon cat. "Leave me alone!" I snapped. Her smile buckled in on itself. And Claude had a grip on my arm.

"I saw you talking to Biggs!" Wide-eyed, excited. "You're not leaving?"

"Why? Did you have more humiliations in mind for me?" I made no attempt to lower my voice, glancing in at horseface. "She looks like the Wicked Witch of the West. I thought you could do better than that." Inside, some continued with conversations, while others stared unabashedly and the Valkyrie's mouth hung open. Claude made wormish little movements of his head. I glared at him. "You're a cheap whore," I hissed. "You'd do it for a boiled egg in the morning, wouldn't you? You make me sick."

Back home, I slipped out of the Bachdress, dropping it in a wad beside a mound of Marcelloshit. Nylons hissed as I slid between cool sheets. Feeling devastated, absolutely alone.

Some time in the night Marcello woke me with his snippy bark, leaping and snarling on the pillow beside my head. In icy lunar light leaking in from the street, I could just make out a figure hovering over the bed, frozen, as if reluctant to come closer. I barely breathed. "Get rid of your dog," ordered a voice. The bed lamp snapped on. Claude's face a glazed, savage moon, hair blasted, eyes bloodshot — drugged it seemed, demented, not the giggling blue I had known. He was shirtless, a jaunty scarf around his neck the only vestige of debonair Claude. He stank of booze and animosity.

"Please don't hurt me," I whispered.

In response, his hand chopped out, catching Marcello in the ribs and knocking him to the floor. The puppy landed with a yelp and ran shrieking around the room. I started up, screaming, but he pinned my stomach with a sharp knee. Unbuckling trousers and dropping them to his knees, he stared down at me, his expression blank, lacking joy or pity. Cock jutting out like the most obscene, violent weapon. I was transfixed with fear, helpless. He clambered atop me, reaching down, got hold of my pantyhose and they parted with a cruel shriek. Then I was struggling — planting a palm under his chin and shoving. We rolled, sweating together like wrestlers, his cock stabbing blindly for my vagina, fingers clawing at my thighs. Then he had pushed inside, penetrating just barely against my clenched muscles. Like a hot knife, a searing blade. Me screaming, trembling, bucking fiercely from the thighs. Almost immediately he came — an exploding, quick-shout ejaculation that sapped him completely. He collapsed atop me as if lifeless. A fever of revulsion shook my body. I heaved and Claude rolled away like a corpse, while the puppy yapped and nipped at the covers.

At once his ragged breath stalked me. I whimpered, my fingers groping for his spent shmuck, finding it, as he groaned and shuddered, huddled up fetally. Squeezing that soft manhood in my hand, I thought of sharp scissors in the bathroom. Slipping from bed, I gathered little Marcello in my arms, kissed his quavering brow and went in to sleep on the couch.

I woke to a rat gray Manhattan morning and found him slumped, arms butterflied like a desperate swimmer, a small bald spot amidst wispy blond hair — a window in his vanity. Gingerly, I touched my breasts. In dreams one had been amputated, leaving a bloody socket that bled and bled. I was at the mirror palpating in gentle circles (according to diagrams in Berty's pamphlet) when Claude groaned, blinking hard, as if astonished to wake up in the bed in which he had fallen asleep. With a moan he sat up against the headboard, lighting a cig from my pack on the nightstand and watching me. He puffed lips into a frown.

"You're always obsessed with something, aren't you? Look at this dump! You never clean up the dog dirt. You must have a low opinion of yourself."

I held his gaze in the mirror, my fingers continuing on tiptoe around a breast, my voice steady. "I was going to castrate you last night."

His eyes widened. "Me! What are you talking about?"

Spinning around. "*You raped me!*" I screamed. "That's what! I ought to turn you in to the police."

"I raped you —?" Claude snorted, an incredulous half-laugh.

"You really hate women, don't you? You're a sadistic son of a bitch."

Claude shook his head, as if I were an annoying insect — or as if I, not he, had gone berserk. He relished a prolonged exhalation, smoke trailing from his nose, wrapping around him like a snake. He said he couldn't remember anything of the night before.

"You don't remember slugging Marcello? Look at this!" I grabbed up the demolished nylons from the floor, stretching them open like a ragged oyster shell, tossing them at him. "I suppose you can't remember doing that?"

Claude spread his hands. "I don't even remember coming here." His eyes blue innocence; a deep furrow cut his forehead. "It sounds unlikely —" reaching with a flashy smile for Marcello, who shied away "— I'm not a violent person. Believe me. Forcing sex on you just isn't my style."

"You're sick," I spat into his incorrigibly tan face. "You need help."

He ignored me. "I do remember an unpleasant little number at the gallery. After you took off I didn't feel like hanging around. I bought some THC from a spade dude in Washington Square. Except it wasn't THC. Brought me down, way down. I visited someone. I was horny, okay —" combing fingers through his hair "— I admit it. It didn't work out. We had a disagreement. I started drinking. Things space out after that . . . very unclear. I thought I crashed on her couch. I was surprised to wake up here just now."

"You came *here* last night," I shouted, "and you *raped* me. Didn't bother taking off your pants. Y'r a sick sadistic creep faggot. That's what gets you off, isn't it? Buggering people. Violating them. I don't want any more to do with you and your sick garbage." I had pulled away the covers. He stared down at his white nakedness, astonished at the jeans still tangled around one ankle. He looked up at me, intent, suddenly boyish, a straggle of straw hair over forehead. Nearly frightened. Picked up the nylons, fingering the ragged tear.

"I really did that?" he asked softly. "I'm sorry, Natalie. I apologize. Jeezus!" His face knotting in puzzlement.

"I mean it! You should get help."

Solemnly, he nodded his head. "Really, I was all fucked up, didn't know what I was doing. It's very vague —"

I sat on the bed looking into those blue eyes, wanting to believe him against all better judgment. Taken by some blind last-chance hope . . . or sympathy. Those many words built up over months of pain and need congealing, gushing out. I felt eloquent, excited, holding one of his long hands in mine and brushing distended veins with fingertips. And for once he was listening, a deeply sincere expression. *You're hostile,* I said, *because I'm not totally blown away by your vanity. You have to constantly, totally be desired. Really, I think you're frigid — like a woman who only endures sex, uses it to get what she wants. There could be so much more to our relationship — can't you see? — if only you would open up.* . . . Claude's blue eyes gone almost gray. I sensed the desperation in him, the loneliness, gripped his arm with white-knuckled passion, all my rage converted to motherly solicitude. "I know you're afraid. You can't admit you're needy, but you are. Everyone needs love. And part of you really wants to give it."

Claude nodded, eyes mesmerized on my lips. "You're right," he said. "You're a beauty. A good friend."

"I am your friend and I know you can change."

"I want to try —" nodding, gazing off into nothing "— I really do. If you would help me —"

"I will, baby," I cried, hugging him, kissing that bald spot, like a tiny stigma atop his head.

He threw covers aside, patting the sheet and making needy noises. I got up. "I'm late for work; I gotta go." I dressed quickly. When I slid past the bed he grabbed for me and I ran out, giggling. "See you later," he called gaily. And I froze at the door, filled with sudden dread. Knowing it was a mistake to leave — now! when I had finally gotten his attention. Knowing, too, I couldn't sacrifice everything for him.

That evening when I got home Claude had cleared out all of his belongings — for good, I knew. I had touched him: that one unpardonable sin. Not that he moved out completely. He would stop by occasionally to leave dirty underwear in a corner, picking up what I had washed, by rote. I considered changing the lock but I couldn't afford it. Instead, I placed the bread knife on my nightstand and warned those four walls that next time I would kill him.

Beneath a movie marquee — BERGMAN in six-foot letters — I swallow two more of the little blue pills Claude left behind. The top half of my body remains connected to bottom by mere threads. The movie comes out to me: the moonscape of my depression where clocks tick and wood floors hold an icy sheen. An audience emerges, cold rushes at me from Sweden inside; I feel, overwhelmingly, that alienation which is our communal taking, the sad certainty of our civilization.

I wonder if Richard might be at the Figaro. Realize Max was probably right when she said long ago that I could handle only one friend at a time. Find myself strolling Eighth Street, where the Sixties pokes up its frazzled elation in a new head shop and health food store amidst the genteel bookshops and delis. Not home, but directly on up St. Marks Place to Maxine's, feeling less afraid of sexual ghosts than needy of a friend.

But the note I had left beneath her bell days earlier is still there. As I puzzle over the sooty envelope, a young Hispanic woman comes up the front steps, looking me over with sullen dark eyes not unlike Rosita's. She flaps a hand in the air between us. "She don't be here no more," she says.

I squint. "What do you mean?"

She simply shrugs, unlocks the door and lets herself in, barking back from inside, "You jus' wasting your time. She not here. She gone —" throwing a hand and good riddance "— she move." The door slams. I regard it in bewilderment.

I go straight to Barbara's, expect to find her working in that scruffy Spring Street ark that is studio-kitchen-nursery: dust in coffee, dust rising from couch cushions, dust caking corners of Jamilla's huge eyes, beside Mama in the long since outgrown crib. New York in her blood. But Barbara's is quiet too. About to walk away when the buzzer rings me in — a long, moronic whine. I ascend a plaster peeling staircase that reeks of stale urine. Why is it, I wonder, that we Jews and artists always seek sanctuary in the slums? Her door appears to open by itself. Cautiously, I duck my head inside. No one there. I hear a shuffling and look down. Stretching as high as she can reach, Jamilla has the knob in both hands; she shuffles backwards on the hem of a filthy nightgown. From the bedroom comes Barbara's voice: "Who is it, Jamilla? Who's there?" The little girl says nothing, staring up at me with madonna big eyes.

When I answer, Barbara cries, "Come in . . . please. I'm so glad —" In cold blue bedroom light I find her like an anguish-curled child in a Käthe Kollwitz lithograph — hair scattered across pillow, tears cutting creases in her cheeks. Jamilla curls at once like a dog at the foot of the bed, crawls under a blanket, and goes to sleep. Barbara reaches out to me. I hold her hand while she abandons herself to a nearly sensual grief. "He'll be back," I repeat like a litany into the cluttered room, illuminated only by the dawn thin nightlight. "They never come back," she murmurs.

I shiver in the heatless loft. "Get into bed," Barbara whispers, pulling covers aside. I shake my head, perplexed by her blue nakedness, snatching my eyes away.

"Do you have an extra blanket?"

"Don't be silly. Get into bed."

Warm-damp, smelling of a woman's body. Something — my closeness? — triggers a new spasm of grief. Barbara shudders and moans. I lie beside her, whispering, stroking her hair. Then I am crying too, lost in her bereavement. And my own. So I couldn't say whether I grieve because Rafael has deserted Barbara or because Claude has deserted me. She lets go a horrible caterwauling, sobs so violently that I become frightened. I mumble courage and hug her. Something seems to have broken loose; I've never seen such pain, my cheeks and shirt drenched in it. She throws arms around me, clinging as if for life, and wails, a low deep surf coming up from her chest. I return her embrace, squeezing tight and cooing, feeling her breasts flatten against mine, heart a small fluttering bird. I pull away, suddenly panicked, needing air. My fingertips graze the upright stem of a nipple — galvanic tremble of her skin releasing a scream in my soul. I stare down at those full, dove-colored breasts, afraid I will lose grip and plunge headlong into a pit of writhing cannibal emotions.

"Let go of me!" I cry.

She jolts as if I have slapped her out of hysteria, blinking up at me. I flee from her sad blue smile and betrayed eyes. Turn my back and hunch, trembling, at the edge of the bed, my voice remote, artificial. "I didn't know you were naked."

Barbara squeezes my hand. "Don't be ridiculous. I needed some comfort." Her grip loosens and I snatch my hand away, hugging it to chest like a wounded sparrow.

A forever silence. An agony in which things break loose and spin towards the moist vortex of her eyes. I slip from bed and stand awkwardly mid-room, mortified, disoriented; cannot bear to look back at those eyes that reach out for me, causing a near physical sensation. Nausea. "I'm going now," my voice breaks.

"You're being foolish, Natalie."

Shaking my head to dislodge her. Then another sound: animal whine building slowly and overwhelming thought, spilling over into other senses. I realize it is Jamilla. In the fragile dusk, she claws marsupial-like toward the pocket of warmth near mama's belly. Barbara takes her in, hugging, brushing away stringy hair and kissing her crab apple cheeks. Suddenly I begin to cry. I go to the door.

Behind me, Barbara warning, "You can't go home at this hour. I wish you wouldn't."

When I turn, she moves aside in the bed, making room. I curl up in an armchair. "Have it your way then," she sighs, and, with a blanket shawled around her as if suddenly ashamed of her nakedness, brings the comforter from her bed, tucking it about me. Looking down, an airline stewardess's smile. "Nothing to pull you out of your own troubles like someone else's."

I lie listening to the duet of breathing — mother and child — chilled by that deeper cold no blankets can relieve, wanting only to go back and be close to another human being, shivering a prayer. *Please, God, make me not queer.* Too messed up, hollowed out, scruffy-souled even to cry — like the "Me" at the core of Natalie Bach has become a stranger. An alien. I decide to leave, decide there isn't a more desperate certain place to find a prayer than three o'clock of a Bowery morning. Then, down inside, I am making that animal whine Jamilla had made — collapsing into nervous exhaustion.

And next I know morning is spilling the first of its bladder, a few listless rays through bead curtains. From the bed comes regular breathing, large and small. Without a glance, I tiptoe to the door. Outside, buildings lean together dangerously — a house of cards propped on hollowest dawn. A dawn with stink and groan and truckroar and menacing hunchbacked shadows but without a whimper of color.

*   *   *

The super's Doberman rattling its claws against the gate is nothing to my own image sliding past in the full-length bedroom mirror, where Claude spent blissful hours admiring himself. Marcelloshit pocks the room in dried mounds mixed with ragged chunks torn from the couch. It all seems quite natural. My little hungry, neglected puppy leaping up my leg, whining and wiggling his ass. I snatch him up, touched by the loyalty, kiss all over the wiggly grasshopper body and sit crying with him on my lap, licking tears from my cheeks. The door opens. Enter a pride of Claudes . . . clones! One needs a pack of cigarettes, another asks offhandedly for a few bucks, the smilingest of all unzips his pants, cock bulging in its nylon pocket. I refuse them all. Though too late, for they have stepped in dog shit by the door and are peevishly wiping elegant shoes on the rug — chide me for the filth, my dowdy outlook, that shitty little dog. They have grabbed Marcello by the scruff of the neck and I fear will drop him out the window, his little paws clipping the air. My eyes follow, haggard, impassive. I suffer their sniping glances, expect any moment for them to remind me that love is only vulva deep.

I walk to the bathroom slow as Quaaludes, stand at the cabinet mirror, eyes burning back at me from a ghostly face, luminescent in the soupy light; they are the red of Legionnaire's poppies, barns in summerstock Connecticut, little tumors of my tits, nipples (as Richard says) pink as baby tongues — nipples of a woman not meant to bear children. My eyes dig into themselves. I remember this same face in a breathing, undulant subway window long ago, Karl's dandruff and Carol's false eyelashes, Adam's piano and Mattie's smile and Agnes's fishgut breath . . . all of life, it's said, reviewed in a rush that may be regret. Or just farewell. I pick up a razor blade — one of his left-behinds — and cut my finger testing the edge, a little rust mixing with blood. Got to leave a note, but too much to say. Besides, the wrong impression: that I am doing it for their sake, not my own. Blood runnels, splays like a river delta over my wrist. I daub into it and begin:

DEAR PRICK

. . . sick to my stomach, smear it out with water — a spiraling mess on the glass — grab his discarded white towel and wipe the mirror. Spit laughter to imagine him finding it: ostrich eggs of his eyes. My own gaze steady beyond the chalky blood. I look into it — the floating, exquisite radials extending from pupils, yellow halos around the irises —

and feel nothing. Those eyes shockingly detached, ironical. You get nauseous, I've heard, as it spills, can easily panic, cop out at the last minute. Need something to concentrate upon. That note. *Mom/Dad, don't take this too hard, it really isn't your fault.* Must be kidding! Look fiercely into the mirror: I will do it, force myself to make letters while it gushes and finally drips. Enough food in Marcello's bowl. He will miss me, will cry and scratch at the door. Finally it will be his yapping that brings someone to find me. Otherwise it could be weeks. Or the smell, I guess. Not really something I want to think about. Can feel tears beginning; I stare hard, squeezing them off.

You're a queer. How do you feel about it, huh? Does it make you gay and want to dance happy about the room and smile just at being alive? A lesbian. Sleazy disgusting dyke cunt sucker finger fucker. Go ahead! Accept it, kiddo. There's not much time left.

Feel no pity for the staring eyes. I spit at them and they spit back — two gobs meeting at the plane between us.

DON'T BLAME YOURSELVES
THERE ARE THINGS I CAN'T ACCEPT

Deep breaths, bring blade to wrist, hand shaking pathetic . . . Maybe? . . . if I don't look . . . Blood splotching Claude's towel, a spurt. How can I be certain it will be him and not the super with her sniffing Doberman? Imagine him pushing the door into my limp resistance. All the virgins, the saints and archbishops of his pomposity outraged by blood that has sprayed a fleur-de-lis across ceiling, dried on green tiles, hangs suspended in toilet water, stiffens my clothes and clots my hair. And sends him reeling, puking, fainting — not from shock but merely disgust.

Incredibly, as blood drips onto my bare toes, I think of that time in Huntington Park when David dumped ketchup over my head and ran in to tell Daddy: "Nattie had an accident with the lawn mower." Dad got one look at the thick stuff oozing down around my ears and went over in a dead faint. I begin to laugh — howl gulp yowl. Marcello yipping at the door. I open up, kiss that damp, insistent nose. Kill myself for that asshole! Dumbest thing, Bach, you ever almost did.

Packing what remains in a plastic garbage bag: few drawings, some dirty laundry, that bloody towel. *Just let it go*, a voice advises, *forget him.* I ride the subway to Long Island City where he is ensconced in the loft of his gallery witch. Imagining as I go, torturing myself with carp flesh about the eager maws of her eyes, a calligraphy of fine lines and peach fuzz around mouth pit. *C'mere my little fingerling, pussy cat, fountain of youth, come help me out of my girdle.* A squatting concrete hulk amid litter strewn lots and gutted buildings, industrial desolation. *Artist in Residence* reads a sign on the roll-up steel door. I ring the bell of a smaller door beside it. A voice answers, directly inside — remarkably, his voice!

"Who is it?"

"A package —" I nasal.

Door opens a crack, I throw my shoulder into it, he flies back, a towel looping his waist. Fling the bag into his stomach and my knee up simultaneously. His shock! a spasm of breath as kneecap finds the soft stuff of his groin. Across an ocean of floor, a girl (perhaps sixteen) stands in flowered panties beside the bed, hand in stop-action near her mouth. She screams. I rush for his eyes, scratch, sock, tear out a chunk of scalp. He doubles up, revolves slowly, fingers clamped over genitals. I kick again: there is blood, but not enough. Grab the wooden slide bar from the door; hit once, the shoulder, know I am going to kill him, observing from that other place. While he has limped outside, stumbled down steps into gray morning screeching for mercy. Me just behind, bar raised — when I remember the little cunt beside his bed. Go for her.

"YOU WANNA GET FUCKED?"

She flees for the bathroom, deer frightened, locks the door. But I understand how this is to be done — Mother has taught me — ramming the two-by-four, splintering veneer, while the girl wails. A hole broken through. See her huddled, a ball of knees and elbows squeezed into the niche between wall and toilet. "Don't . . . please don't," she moans. "I don't want him."

I stare, heart sloshing blood around my eyes, focus. She's a child, a bird. For one horrid moment her glistening tears seem to be blood — everywhere! enough to fill a bucket, the stub of my two-by-four red-soaked. I drop it with a clatter that fills the huge room. "I don't either," I whisper.

Run out, through an assemblage of overalled workmen in front, black faces ringed about Claude, sitting against the wall on the towel that has slipped from his waist, gripping his shoulder. He watches me pass with the expression of a wounded child, fear that can't surrender its truculence. The men move aside to let me by, heads tilted back as if in respect, brows furrowed. "Man," says one of them, somberly shaking his head, "you playin' with too much woman. Too much woman."

Somewhere amid that wandering of mismatched tenements and warehouse streets ornamented in stripped cars I stumble upon a park. A tiny memory of spring: chirping birds and thousand-fingered green. Mothers side by side on benches, rocking baby carriages, staring after my wild hair and flaming cheeks. Children stop in play to watch me pass. Two old Jews, who share a bench and a primitive tongue, graybeards, look up at me as if on a single impulse. Their thoughts trail little patterns over the sidewalk and into the grass. They know it is spring but the world doesn't interest them. I stand frozen before them. An intruder. *But I am of you. In the quietest zone of my heart I speak Hebrew too. It spills like birdsong.*

The white haired one with the scraggly beard, eyes lost in milk behind glasses, leans to whisper in his companion's ear. The other looks directly up into my soul. He nods his head, his entire body rocking back and forth, and says "I see —" His eyes are gentle and wise. They leave me the eerie, quintessential certainty that this is the same man, Elijah, who appeared to brother Adam in King David's Park not so long ago.

CHAPTER FOURTEEN

ZION

ONE WATERMELON EVENING ANGEL FOLLOWED ME HOME. I UN-
zipped his fly, while he demurred that this was the man's job. "If I
wanted a man," I said, saddling his flat belly, "I'd seduce my thesis ad-
visor." The little prick insulted only so long as it took to send him
sprinting from base to base of my willingness, his cock polished smooth
as the water at Mayagüez. Later, he pulled skintight jeans up scrawny
legs, lit a cigarette and proposed marriage. "Maybe you think I'm too
young, but I get you everything you want, man." I laughed inadvertently, touching his chest in apology and assuring him that this was
probably the most generous offer I would receive, but I couldn't do it to
him. He would go mad trying to keep his promise.

On the way out, we met Jesse on his way to see me. He and I had
been carrying on an intermittent affair. It was easy, the best relationship

I'd ever had with a man. Not a lot of demands and expectations. The two men exchanged a sparring panther quick glance. Then Jesse turned to me, ignoring Angel completely. While Angel kneaded his shoulders and shifted weight from foot to foot, eyes stuck into his rival. He mock-sneezed, spraying us with spittle. Jesse merely swiveled his head, light flashing from glasses, hurling a menacing eye-corner glance. Hostility charged the dead air. "Okay, you two —" I said, hooking an elbow of each and walking on, "— macho displays don't impress me. If you want to fight, go fight the bastards who control things in this world."

At the corner, Angel remembered some business he had to attend to; he kissed me almost tenderly on the lips, turned and strutted away. Jesse dropped hands to his sides, exasperated. "You mean to tell me you're sleeping with that punk?"

"I haven't said a word."

"I got something to say —" shaking a lecturing finger in my face "— this man has too much self-respect to take seconds from that ass-wipe. It ain't happening, baby, you understand? Either he walks or I walk." Bringing fingers back with a thud against his chest.

"Now you listen! This is *my* body. And I make decisions for it. I don't like bullies, sexist or otherwise. I think they're cowards. They don't have the wisdom to be passing out advice."

Jesse stared at me, the anger in his eyes gradually supplanted by wry, appreciative laughter. "Too much," he barked at some passersby. "She's one heavy mama. I wouldn't want to mess with her."

He suggested we go to dinner. While we ate he talked, as always, about Vietnam. Not that the war was a tragedy, a national disgrace, but that it was an opportunity that couldn't be missed. "That's where it's all happening now for photojournalists. People over there are scoring big, like making reputations for themselves overnight. It's the real thing. None of this around-the-town dipshit."

"The Movement is dipshit?"

Shaking an impatient hand. "You aren't hearing what I am saying. Civil Rights was happening five years ago. You gotta keep on top of what's shaking if you want to make it."

"Go to Vietnam then. There are plenty body bags. The body bag in-dustry has thrived in this country since that war started."

"I'd just be taking pictures, baby. That's all!"

"You think the bullets really care what you're doing?"

Jesse looked at me a long time, his mouth pinching into a gradual frown. It was that same old incontrovertible story: Vietnam wasn't what he chose to do; the decision had been made for him.

My life, meanwhile, had its own futile logic. And dipshit. There was the new apartment off Delancey, furnished with leftovers (typewriter alone salvaged from Scotto's — and the novel, forming a reassuring, if untouched, pile on the floor). Lucy brought lamps, chairs, obvious orphans, and coached me in Canal Street bargains. "Bargains don't interest me," I told her. It's the direction I've been moving my entire life: casting off, stripping down to the essential core. Neighbors, watching me move in with no more furniture than a couple of boxes and a key, became alarmed (perhaps thinking my furnishings of a numinous, intangible sort) and advised that I pile the fire escape deep in beer bottles to discourage junkies and thieves. "They going to rattle and make lossa noise. Maybe even fall down on their head."

My typewriter sat idle. First there must be a desk, I comforted myself. An agreement with the room. A resolve greater than the inertia of everyday. Because that's what it was, of course. Though knowing well enough that art can make peace with the day-to-day — and thrive even against its banality. All right, then, it's this dervish of constant change and unsettlement that defeats creativity. *My life more compelling at the moment than my work. It demands everything I've got.* Then, woefully, I thought of D. H. Lawrence, Yeats, other proofs to the contrary. Even Natalie. Resolve cutting a clean, certain trail through the head over heels of her life. In spite of everything, she sits down and paints. Need, discipline, whatever it is, the woman has it.

I put the writing aside and took a job counseling young mothers from Haiti and the Dominican Republic (who had just learned it is sinful to bear a child at fifteen, when their bodies and heritage told them it's quite natural) at a community center in Brooklyn's Bushwick section. I walked each morning from the subway past Warsaw Ghetto blight: tiny bodegas and auto repair shops, lots that were merely wounds where the earth had opened and swallowed entire buildings; houses, brick or frame, standing like forlorn dollhouse dioramas with cutaway walls, their innards exposed to the world; fire-gutted stores wherein voodoo chickens scratched the rubble for roaches. Here and there, tiny garden plots of beet greens and collard: postage stamps of hope. A zone where temperate met tropic head-on, a dozen pasts could find little peace with the mongrel present. They coexisted like a tumultuous family. Barefoot children and idle men in clots on the corners followed me with sizzling eyes as I passed — here! where there wasn't another white face within thirty blocks. Muttering prayers to Hermes and all the deities of free passage as I walked. Hoping I'd come one morning and find this travesty of concrete and deadend days supplanted by tiny fishermen's huts thatched in palm leaves, repatriated sunshine and joy. Resisting, each afternoon as I returned home, the impulse to stoop and kiss my "safe" apartment floor. No, I wasn't going to cop to paranoia. It was a job. We work in order to possess; we possess in order that we must work. The dialectic of our age. Who am I to refute it?

One day, passing Sally Scotto's establishment, I saw a yellowed note hanging by a sinew of tape beneath my old bell. A faded message in Nat's free-flowing hand:

Hi,

It's been so long since I've seen you I forget what you look like. You haven't even met my little dog yet. I named him après tu: L'Étrangère. Why not call me sometime? My number's in the book, between Baal and Belch.

LOVE, NAT

I laughed, thinking, Yes, how long it has been. Fond memories, questions: Was she carving another duck? Had she thrown out her Christopher Street surfer yet? I put everything aside and walked at once to her place.

Rang and rang the bell. Finally noticed the name tag gone. I hesitated a moment (remembering the stories about Nat's crazy super and her dog) before ringing the woman's bell. An immediate yarooing outcry inside. The buzzer rang and, charily, I let myself in. Greeted by a ruddy face and a rag of hair poked from a doorway down the hall. A sleek, nervous snout at thigh level, twisting like an eel.

"Come in, come in. Don't be bashful. You come to see the apartment." She presumed.

My yelled response drowned out completely by the crazed barking that echoed off bare walls, filling both the hallway and my head. "Shuddup!" she bellowed, giving a fierce jerk to the collar. The dog yelped. I edged forward, readying a toe.

"Actually, I only wanted some information."

"We don't mind showing it none. It's just upstairs. A little exercise didn't never hurt anybody." Her beery grin.

"Well, you see, I don't —" Cutting off before her close inspection, dipping chin side to side and cinching her brow.

"Ain't I seen you somewheres? You look farmiliar. Aw, who remembers? I seen a million people if I seen one."

I eyed the dog, who eyed me, sniffing and pulling at his collar with a lusty whine. She had to brace her feet to hold him back. "C'mon," she snapped, limping to the stairs in the manner of one who is mostly sedentary, dragging the dog along behind like a shopping cart. "It ain't no trouble. It's a nice apartment. He could get more for it, but he don't listen to us. Just a little messy at the moment. We ain't had time to clean up."

I followed resignedly after ragged tails of her robe, unable to wedge a word into the prattle. At Nat's landing, she pulled a key ring from pocket. "If we was to say the truth, she was a pig, that one. Let the dog shit anywhere. Think she done it on purpose, we does." I stood astonished as she opened Nat's door, turning that wrecked face toward me, letting out the full leash of her animus. "A nigger lover, 'at's what she was. Same as all the rest of 'em." Screwing up an eye and surveying me head to foot. "We won't rent to that trash no more. We looked you over careful when you come in." She allowed me her bileish lopsided confidence, neither quite smile nor smirk. I felt implicated by my silence, ashamed at not declaring myself and coming to Nat's defense. But felt I must play out the game. Fascinated, too, by this unholy duo. First person plural.

Nat's apartment was a minor replica of my own St. Marks diggings after the guinea goons: holocaust of scrambled clothes, books, art materials. Things abandoned. I picked up a canvas board, deliberately folded in two: a honeymoon couple arm in arm; a crude Jacob Bach as a young man, with a bulging, misshapen forehead, smile alone giving him away; an accompanying smile had just begun on the bride's lips, then was lost to white canvas. I shuddered. The super admonished me to watch out for the dog pucky if I wanted to be poking about. The apartment darkened towards the rear; I had no desire to explore further.

"What happened to her?" I demanded, not even attempting to sound disinterested. She gave me that odd tangential smirk.

"We don't pay no attention."

Back in the hall, she asked me to go down first. "We don't like no one coming down behind us." I hurried, skin crawling up my spine. From beyond her open door a radio computed American GI deaths in Vietnam as opposed to dead Viet Cong. *Kill ratio* they called it. "Have a cup of coffee, dear?" she asked. I thanked her, No, I really had to run. She appeared honestly disappointed. She's human, too, I prompted myself to remember. Maybe it was curiosity, or the need in her voice as she said, "We don't get many visitors," or the slim hope of gaining some further clue about Nat. I followed her inside, sat at a tiny table cluttered with cloth scrap and yellowed newspapers; its clutter seemed to spill over and deposit in corners of the filthy kitchen, haunt of a stationary bag lady. As I sipped coffee from a chipped china cup, I struggled to keep from gagging on the pervasive stench — like the smell dogs carry home from the woods after rolling in the remains of dead animals.

"I'm a old Irishman," she bragged. "He's Irish, too!" She grinned at the dog, who was rubbing his snout against my knee and whining. "Oh, you c'n pet 'im," she said. "He don't bite." Smiling that grotesque nonsmile, colorless eyes moving back in their hollow places, coming to rest on the beads around my neck.

On pins and needles, I touched the greased eel's head, while the dog sniffed and poked, attempting to force his nose between my locked knees, lips pushed back in a hideous grin. Frustrated, he fell hard on his haunches and began chewing on my shoe, playful, but more and more intently as his mistress chatted, words sloughing off like an old skin.

"This ain't Jew York no more, it's Nigger York. We wouldn't rent to 'em but they get the N dubba A Cee Pee on you —"

"I really must go." The chewing had begun to hurt; I could feel teeth through the leather, the wet of lather. I started to rise, attempting a smile. "Thanks for coffee."

"No rush, dear. We was enjoying it." She touched my hand with liver brown fingers. Suddenly her face changed. She spoke more to the dog than to me — in a confiding tone. "Oh, she wasn't never late with the rent . . . not like some of 'em. That we could say for her. We Irish b'lieve in discharging our responsibilities, we do." She paused as though expecting me to speak. I tried to edge my foot away, but with each tug the dog tightened its jaws in warning. My heart thumping, loose-hinged, getting him more agitated, I knew, but couldn't control it. And her ophidian eyes, not unlike the dog's, seemed to sense and savor my predicament. I recalled that Nat had nicknamed her Bull Conners.

"We wasn't fooled none," she said in an almost intimate tone. "We knew right along you was a friend of hers. We don't forget. No, you couldn't 'a fooled us —" grinning at the dog. "We don't care, do we?"

My foot twisted in the shoe like raw steak, soapy with spittle, as I worked frantically to free it, staring at her, frightened now. "Would you make him stop?" I pleaded.

She laughed. "Now 'e's a bugger!"

I raised a hand, the dog snarled and chomped down. I cried out. It felt as if he'd broken the skin.

"Don't be getting 'im excited," she snapped. "The dog's had police training. Well now, she's a nice lady," she cooed. The Doberman ignored her. " 'E smells the Jew on you is what it is."

By some miracle, the dog eased up a moment and my foot slipped from shoe like a hand from a glove, leaving it in his teeth. I bolted for the door, grabbed the handle, but it didn't turn. Behind me the dog let go a startled yelp and lunged at my retreating back. I screamed. Bull Conners snagged his collar and kicked her dog in the stomach. His jaws snapped back for her wrist, and she brought the coffeepot down full on his skull. The dog sprawled dead-hard on the floor, and she dragged him like a potato sack, opening a door and flinging him into an adjacent room. She wiped hands on her robe and looked at me — those corpse gray eyes sprung suddenly to life. " 'E gets too excited. Oh, 'e'll be full of spit again in an hour."

I stared at her dumbly as she opened the door to let me out. "Young ones does that to 'im," she said. "Especially, they got their monthlies. 'E scare you, did he?" Her laughter chasing me down the hall and out into the open air.

I was truly shaken, needing to know what had become of Nat. Those myriad possibilities: this city devours people, chews them up, leaving nothing but old hair clips and painters' rags. After sitting a moment on a stoop, removing the ravaged shoe and massaging my foot, I went to a pay phone to call Zilla Bach. A chillingly weighted silence on the far end when I identified myself.

"You have a lot of gall calling here."

"Listen, I know that you've never liked me. That doesn't matter. I just want to know if Natalie is all right."

"You would? That's thoughtful of you, Maxine. I just want you to know that I hold you directly to blame for the loss of my daughter."

"What do you mean? Has something happened? I'd like to know —"
I stood on the street yelling into the receiver, aware that she'd hung up
the phone. *Loss of my daughter*, you silly bitch! What the fuck does
that mean?

I walked straight to Richard's.

"Pearlman!" he cried, swinging open that armored door without hes-
itation. "Fuckinay it's good to see you. It musta been six months —"

His eyes widened when I asked about Natalie. "Shit! I hoped you
could tell me. Last I knew she put her fag boyfriend in the hospital with
a fractured collarbone and gouged a respectable scar across her left
wrist." He shrugged. "Went through a militant stage. Israel seemed a
natural continuation."

"She went to Israel? Her mother made it sound terminal." I laughed
relief.

It's the custom in America, Richard explained as if I'd just stepped
off the boat, that parents should kill off their children in stages. For a
segment of assimilated American Jewry the penultimate stage is when
the kid goes to Israel. "*Finito!*" he said. "David and Absalom. The kid's
a traitor to the great cause of the Melting Pot. They'll send money but
not offspring. You look distraught, kid. It's not that heavy."

I told him that she hadn't even said good-bye. Richard nodded, firming lips together in a grim smile. "To me either. Look, maybe she's the
realist and we're the romantics. Face it, the whole fucking group's
breaking up: Paynor gone to Toronto and Lucy off to California. It's
the old cliché, you know: You got your needs, I got mine. Friendship is
for adolescence. They call it *maturity*. In five years we'll pass on the
street and pretend not to see each other." There were tears in his eyes.

Some weeks later I received a letter.

July 9 Nahariyya

SHALOM,

NOW THE LORD SAID UNTO
ABRAM, GET THEE OUT OF THY
COUNTRY, AND FROM THY KINDRED,
AND FROM THY FATHER'S HOUSE,
UNTO THE LAND THAT I WILL SHOW
THEE. . . .

GENESIS: 12

Except Genesis doesn't record Abraham's reaction when he looked out across the land of rocks and low places called Canaan, down through the haze into the shimmering shit-hole of the Dead Sea and close to it Jericho — oldest of all cities; so decrepit six thousand years ago that the walls collapsed when Joshua walked around them, you can imagine what a wreck it is today — and upon seeing this "Promised Land" turned his countenance to the Lord and sayeth:

"You gotta be kidding!"

Since coming here I have thought a lot about what you used to call our "outsider mentality." It seems like we do have an inclination, we Jews (now I see myself as totally, joyfully Jewish), to settle in hostile environments. Adam says for Jews every place is hostile; I disagree. It's our world, too; not just this tiny little scrap of it. I have decided that we Jews are either the starry-eyed van Goghs of the human race — in our mind's eye the desert is always just about to bloom, and maybe we can help make it happen — or it has become our instinct to settle for leftovers. Because we've learned by now they aren't about to let us stay in the suburbs.

What should I say next? I don't know how to begin. Seems like it's been soooo long. Forever! Here I am lying on my cot, pad propped against my knees, in a cabin shared with three other girls/women on a kibbutz . . . in Israel. Sounds almost exotic. But mostly it's a lot of hard work. I could begin by saying how much I miss you, how much I'd like to talk to you now. Very often I see women here who remind me of you. Sabras. But they're snooty, won't speak to us "holiday kibbutzniks." I gave up trying to see you before I left, but now I have your new address from Richard. I don't really even expect you to answer this letter. I'm not that naive anymore. And letters are satisfying by themselves. First you write them, then you read them. So, in a way, they answer themselves.

Adam. I'm not sure you would recognize him. Speaks English in a foreign accent, looks like a farmer kibbutznik. He's stuck back in the fifties — convinced the rebels still wear Jimmy Dean haircuts. Israel isn't a place where people grow. Full of American kids with chips on their shoulders who disdain their brothers and sisters who stayed home to work it out. Adam's philosophy is that one has to abandon the past completely and find life on his own. Each one of us has to be Adam/Eve all over again, not just wimpily accept our fate and ape our parents' ways. Total renunciation. He tears up Mom/Dad's letters without even opening them (except peeks inside to see if there is a check first). Once, feeling brave, I said that according to his philosophy his own children must rebel some day. Maybe even abandon Israel. The Pentateuch Patriarch looked at me like I'm loony. "Nonsense," he said, "Israel is the only secure and sensible place for a Jew to live. It has nothing to do with me. Nothing at all."

Secure, right! Under the guns of the Syrians.

He disrespects me for being raised more Christian than Jewish — like he came from some different family. So maybe Ma/Pa Bach made a mistake and maybe it's some wonderful dream to be part of something bigger — a People, a Nation — that I'm missing out on in life. But I'm not sure I believe it. Not even sure there's any difference between puffing out your chest and squawking, "I'm Jewish, I'm Jewish!" and potting out your belly, wearing a flag lapel button and fat American smile and shouting, "I'm American thru and thru and I hate all the rest of you." Why must everyone define themselves by who they hate in this world? (Seems like we Jews have been hated enough to be perfectly defined by now.) Yes, I'm proud to be Jewish. But the answer to this world's problems — our problems! — isn't more division, but more togetherness.

Young Americans are the worst. They come here and say, "Gee whiz, we've been missing out on all the fun." Like the two guys with dumpy Brooklyn vowels standing on a curb in Jerusalem watching Palestinians protest the jailing of an Arab mayor. They stood there screaming until veins bulged on their necks: "Kill the nigger bastards! Turn the dogs on 'em!"

"They aren't Jews," I told Adam. "They're fascists."

"Jews aren't perfect," he replied. "Not with our backs to the wall."

But if we haven't learned the evil of hatred is there any hope anyone ever will?

Sometimes Adam won't talk to me for days. The smallest thing can set him off — like me complaining about having to get up at 4:00 A.M. to work in the fields. The other day while I was working, tying up banana clusters, one of the big rats that live in the trees jumped on my head, then to the ground. I threw my machete at it, but missed. When I took the rat's nest down to burn it, I found cute, fuzzy baby rats inside. All of a sudden my creep brother came stomping over and literally smacked them out of my hands, so red-faced I thought his nose would

*blow off. "Just the smallest cut," he yelled, "urine gets in and you are
dead!" He mashed the babies into the dirt with his boot heel. I felt
something in common with those baby rats. I mean, I'm sick and tired
of his stomping.*

*Last night I told him to screw off with all his criticism and mental
censorship. I don't need Big Brother telling me how to perceive things.
I'm an artist, I see what I see. That's what an artist is first and foremost — one who can't stop seeing. Rachel, who is a real sweetheart, immediately backed me up. We stood together before that big bully, and
he was speechless at our rebellion. Women United! Watch out all you
big cowards.*

*Gotta get on 'cause a war might break out any minute. Everyone
tense, lotsa patrols at the kibbutz (we're right on the Lebanese border).
Two days ago, terrorists placed a bomb in a grocery store Coke bottle; it
blew up in a tourist's face. Civilization has regressed to Biblical times.
Israel. Land of love and hate.*

*I hear that famous Pearlman brain buzzing, trying to understand my
reasons for coming. Was it to join the Stern Gang? Or to meet Moshe
Dayan and ask how he lost his eye? I can assure you, Miss P., I didn't
come here to find my roots. I'm no tree. Maybe in a way I am like
Adam, looking for some better solution to life. Most people just live,
never try to find solutions. Maybe I don't feel that's enough. You used
to say that people can't live effective lives unless they live by a philosophy. I'm looking for my philosophy. Or maybe I just wanted something
bigger: skies spread from Crete to Alexandria, Hear, O Israel, the Lord
thy God, the Lord is One. Dr. Kaufman had something to do with it.
She taught me that I'm too volatile — must learn to think before I act.
Oh! so right. Maybe Israel won't teach me patience, but at least it stops
action. I really had to slow down.*

*Imagine me standing in the twilight before the bathroom cabinet
mirror holding a rusty razor blade to wrist: one corner is embedded in
flesh and blood mounds up around it, splotzes down over the white
sink. But suicide just wasn't my thing. I stopped the bleeding and went
off to settle some unfinished business with Claude.*

*When I returned home I was not in a normal state. All I could think
about was that rent was due and I hadn't enough money to pay it.
Maybe I'd just go — get out! Outside, I heard a radio: something about
San Francisco and flowers in your hair. I searched the apartment for
flowers, wishing I had some good smoke so I could spend the rest of the*

*day inside record albums where there's never any rent due. I was spaced
out on lovers who don't love and bosses who stink so bad of BO and
keep pinching my tits and the rest of the crapbaggage of my life, stuck
on St. Marks Place with a few scraggly paintbrushes. While the world
was being reborn. I stood looking out a window. New York sparkled like
broken glass atop the heap of rags and bones we call Civilization. I had
never felt lower.*

*And then life came to my rescue. A letter from Adam. Come over, he
wrote, work in the fields; mornings early enough to surprise your heart,
bright breakfasts grown right on the kibbutz — eggs, melons, oranges,
yogurt, figs, olives. Will you think I'm nuts if I tell you I got so excited I
danced around the room with Marcello? Felt so full, like I was mag-
ically pregnant with the whole world, expected it to come hatching out
of my mouth.*

*The most poignant thing was waving goodbye out the airplane win-
dow: Dad crying, of course, Mother's face refusing, frozen like a plate
glass window. Me jittery with anticipation, feeling I'd just stepped onto
a whole new self, thinking about an old friend of mine who I really
wished had been there to see me off.*

*Un-oh, lights out! gotta finish by flashlight under the covers, like
summer camp. Israel. Just another trip to summer camp. Growing up is
a big fraud. Nothing is ever resolved, just more added on.*

> *i will dream of*
> *picking bananas*
> *in the darkness*
> *under Syrian guns*

Shalom aleikhem. I miss you,

NAT

Only a few weeks had passed before I heard from her again. The
brightest possible Sunday morning. East Village alive with rock music,
Fred Neil's voice floating atop waves of street chatter: "I've been
searching for the dolphin in the seaaaa . . ." Nat parked beneath my
window bleating the horn of a spanking new VW bus Ma and Pa Bach
had just given her, waving hands as I leaned out my window. "It's a
bribe —" she shouted in her tell-the-world manner. "— They know I'm

not staying in New York. Now they're trying to keep me in North America."

The short ride up to Central Park was trip to California, march on Washington and voyage in a Yellow Submarine in one; FDR on-ramps attended by smiling long-haired couples, thumbs stuck out, holding up sign scrawls requesting Ann Arbor, Taos, San Francisco . . . *Pick us up, sisters. We'll float west on love, peace and sunshine.* Why not? I discovered myself asking. What keeps me here?

"There's grass in the glove compartment," Nat said, "if you want to roll a number."

"You mean here! in the car?"

"Sure." She laughed. "The whole world is stoned."

I studied her obliquely, this new Natalie, seeming as high and giddy as the time. "I was hurt that you didn't say good-bye before leaving for Israel," I said. She stared straight ahead over the wheel. For a moment it didn't seem she would answer.

"Y'r like Aunt Berty. Whenever I see her she spends the whole time bawling me out for never seeing her. Anyway, you don't have to feel so slighted. I didn't really say good-bye to anyone. I wanted to make a fresh start."

"You burn bridges with a vengeance, kiddo."

Her eyes reached for me quickly. "There were things I had to think about."

"What's the big mystery?"

"Look!" She pointed at hitchhikers. "Everyone's leaving. Life is impossible now in New York. People live by myths here. If you don't buy the Big Apple hype there's no reason to stay."

"I disagree."

She swerved suddenly to miss a pothole, nearly swiping a taxi next lane, sending my stomach caroming. "Careful," I said, "I'm underinsured. So you just get back and you're on your way again? One fast operator."

A sudden dour expression in marked contrast to the airy Israeli blouse. Though this was not the old volatile Natalie; this woman exercised studied self-control. "I'm not sure yet. Right now I'm building up confidence in my driving."

"So I noticed."

In the park we joined a game of softball. Nat slammed three homers

into the piling heat of afternoon, then lay stretched in the shade of a
canopying maple, a rosary of sweat beads across her upper lip, coils of
hair peeping from under sleeves of a T-shirt stretched sweat-tight. Nostalgia cut me like a blade: remembering Nat, the undecided girl; now a
woman deciding.

"You still play a mean game of ball," I said.

Suddenly she was exuberant, bouncing to knees on the overused
grass. "Let's drive to the country; I want to see green and blue sky." Almost flighty, stretching arms at the lovely day. I swatted grass litter
from her back, releasing chalky dust. She leaned forward and planted a
surprise kiss on my lips. "You're the best friend I ever had. A beautiful
person. A beautiful woman! All those kids just fell madly in love with
you, even the girls."

"Wowie! what inspired this? We're never seeing each other again or
what?"

"Who knows —?" she said, with something approaching enthusiasm. "Look at you —" gesturing at my dark legs "— looks like you have
been working in the banana fields all summer."

"Who's talking!"

"I mean it. You could pass for a sabra."

I winked, making muscles with both arms. "Runs in the family." Nat
threw a handful of grass at me; her kiss clinging to my lips like a light
coating of dust.

"Listen," I said, "let's drive up to my parents' house in Connecticut.
They're away for the weekend."

Instantly her face changed. All reluctance. She shook her head. "I
have to go home and pack now. I'm leaving for California in a few
days."

I laughed. "Wow, am I getting dizzy."

"But I didn't know I was going. I really didn't. Not until just a minute ago."

CHAPTER FIFTEEN

CALIFORNIA

I

I AM CUT OFF, A SHIP WITHOUT BEARINGS, FLOATING IN A TINY CABIN through perpetual fog on fringes of the redwood forest. The doleful moan of the buoy off headlands, steady drip-a-drop from branches. I jump each time stunted pines scratch fingers across windowpanes or wind rattles the door; sit straight up in bed in a blackness illumined only by the orange fireglow as footsteps creak across the underside of floorboards and Marcello creeps deeper under the covers. "Whole durned coast is haunted," Mr. Jakes tells me. "Murdered too many Indians." This city girl tries to adjust: learns to split kindling and use the outdoor shitter even in the stormy rain of a spookdark night, acclimates to damp that forms a moldy pellicle over everything, mouse droppings amid forks and spoons, develops an affection for a mournful foghorn keeping watch out in the darkness beyond a white lace of waves. Who could guess California would be like this?

I paint, stereo blasting — a New York remedy for all this silence. Art monopolizes consciousness until reality loses its edges and I plunge like a hermit thrush into the fog. Marcello whines at my feet. *It's what we came for,* I remind him, *work and solitude. Artists must learn to live alone. Who said it would be easy?* He whines. I set paintbrush aside in despair, stare out at pines seducing the fog. Begin a letter . . . but to whom? Everyone too far away. Think I hear the whine of the mail van at the end of the drive, but for once do not dash out to check the box, knowing there will be nothing. Later, I will take a walk along country roads, past lazy dogs and uneasy houses, will breathe the tart of apples on cool air. Here the trees are too stingy to change colors, cars pass but never stop, driven by ghosts.

I sit to dinner at a heavy wooden table that came with the cabin, mocked by its emptiness. Perhaps Mr. Jakes will drop by tonight to check the chimney draft, will stay for coffee. Tomorrow morning I will stand on icy bathroom tiles, find my eyes grown a little larger in the clouded mirror, like the gouges in Georgia O'Keeffe's skulls. I wonder if I am going mad. More and more of my day evaporates into fantasy. I read van Gogh's letters. Must tear myself from the cabin for walks to town, over headlands — slowly eroding continental wall against the waves. I know why it is called Pacific, because it takes its time. There are herb gardens atop the bluffs, Solomon's seal and wild ginger, blowholes through which the sea wheezes like Jacob Bach, whales far out, leaving misty tracks against the horizon, at times another stroller — one of the strange, aloof townspeople who come to the ocean as though it is a form of sustenance. Me standing above a clatter of waves, giving red cheeks to the wind, with its many voices, suffering a longing that is nearly joy. Then eyes falling hard into that black-green woebegone, kelptangles writhing like lusty snakes. I return, inspired, to my cabin, nature-filled, anxious to paint — but can do nothing. How to compete with all this splendor? Art and nature are enemies. The masterwork is completed.

There was the trip across. Nature expanding as I crossed the continent. Each river — Delaware, Allegheny, Ohio, Mississippi — seeming a truer gateway to the West, until I didn't think there could be any more. Through endless Iowa cornrustle, till came names like Bismarck

and Cheyenne, naive, broadshouldered. I understood then that
America is a country that has never shaken off restlessness, never settled
down. Then the continent arched its back, sky ruptured and WEST
came in the mouth like a parch — all around me but never reach-
able — and me unable to sort excitement from awe; with each sprawling horizon, wanting more. Shaking off narrow streets.

I'd intended to visit David in Chicago. After studying medicine
there, he'd stayed on, raising a family and a pediatric practice in the
suburbs. I imagined him, stethoscope dangling from pocket, torturing
his small patients with a cloven-hoofed grin and grisly sequels of the
Bellybutton Monster, while their unsuspecting mothers waited outside.
But could no longer imagine that we'd once been close. Intervening
years, our disparate paths, had driven a wedge between us, forcing us
further and further apart, until our childhood together seemed a surreal
realm of talking cornflakes and Headless Hallmen, something I'd only
read about. A favorite family photo from which, by some perverse
chemistry, images fade and become mere ghosts of themselves. Chicago
symbolized our separation. Even California always seemed closer than
Chicago — which I pictured as a sweating urban drive shaft, heaving in
its fetid jelly of slaughtered animal souls and yellow smelter smoke,
glistening steel in vast stockyard carnage. There, separated from New
York by corn flats of Indiana and Ohio, and from my topsy-turvy life by
his regular office hours and professional smile, David might have been
on the far side of space, dropped out of my life completely. Somewhere
near Gary, Indiana, while seeking the exit to the proper suburb, I passed
a rank pond between factory yards, next to the Interstate, covered in a
fluorescent metallic scum, or maybe grease, orange and slimy — upon
which a man was waterskiing. I pointed the car west and kept going.

One Montana night in a thunderstorm I saw lightning poke out a jagged finger and touch a barn. It sat a moment, placid, framed in ghostly
blue — before spitting a yellow cough straight up into blackness. I
drove up the long drive and banged on a farmhouse door. The whole
family, dinner still in their mouths, farmer saying "B'God . . . b'God!"
Neighbors appearing out of nowhere in pickups and something like a
fire engine. After a frantic hour of shouts and passing water buckets
along a brigade right out of the movies, the farmer said, "She'll burn
herself out." A collective shrug. All stood about talking in low tones
until walls of the barn peeled back and the roof groaned and dropped
like a jaunty sailor's cap onto the mass of molten hay, glowing forge-hot,

illuminating the stark white house a quarter mile off. Miniature burning barns afloat in the farmer's eyes. "That's all she wrote," he said with such tender sadness, and his wife invited everyone for coffee and dessert as though nothing had happened. But they touched her arm one by one and went home. Then she turned to me and said they'd be mighty pleased to put me up for the night.

These were the Americans I thought existed only in literature.

But I found another America, too (I had hoped existed only in pages of the *National Enquirer*), that made any woman's solo Odyssey across this land of psychos an act of extreme folly.

There was Mother's reaction when I first told her my plans. "Why west, honey?" she had asked — the incredulity of Eastern provincialism, which still regards *The West* as a highnoon frontier. Nature, I had explained, a slower, saner reality. "I don't look at New York as the only way to live." She reminded me that I had just returned from Israel. Anticipating argument, Dad leapt in, skittish as an Idaho rabbit crossing the road.

"It's a wonderful opportunity, Natalie. When I was your age I wanted to see the world in the worst way. But those were depression days . . . ," he sighed. "Life is long but youth is short."

Mother's eyes cut at him. "I never knew you felt that way, Jacob. I, for one, was already raising a family at Natalie's age."

"So what?" I demanded. "Do I have to do what you did? Don't you believe in progress?"

Mother sized me up. "You know, you're awfully naive, honey. It can be very dangerous for a woman traveling on her own. The world's full of some pretty nasty characters."

I kissed Dad's cheek, still flushed from Mother's rebuke. He chuckled a little. Mother's lips had stitched together into a frown. "I can't stop you," she said, a tone rich in self-pity.

"You will never think I'm ready to travel on my own. But Dr. Kaufman does. And I do, too."

Not doubting it until a truck stop near Boise, Idaho, where a rancher type, round-headed with a straw stubble of hair, leered at me from the counter, making lewd cracks about the breast pocket in my T-shirt, while his girlfriend threw back her apricot hair and laughed like a coyote. I asked if he was talking to me. He leaned forward over stumpy forearms. "Yeah, I'm talking to you. I got twelve inches for you any way you want it."

I got up to leave. Had driven barely a mile when a pickup — I recognized it from the diner — came squealing up behind, blinking headlights, honking its horn. It followed me for miles, while I gripped the wheel, whispering to Marcello, battling panic. Finally, he pulled off at a junction. I stopped and stepped into the fragrant night, knees quaking, clutching the door. Below in its canyon the Snake River hissed and thrashed. I squatted and diarrhea poured out over my bare legs and sandals.

I scarcely stopped or slept from then to San Francisco, crossing the lizard's hide of Nevada that night — thinking of Dad's paintings, often set in such moonscapes, feeling an affinity blood-deep and mystical. Fear had become anxiety, huge and incomprehensible, in a land where starlight glistened from mountains I never reached; I could enter desert or forest and not emerge for days. When I stopped for coffee, waitresses' faces blurred like surfaces Grunewald had never stopped erasing, peering at my hand doodling on place mats and demanding, "You an artist?" as if asking: You on welfare? or You a dirty Jew?

I picked up a hitchhiking couple on Highway 101 in northern California, hippies in long hair and leather. "There are heavy tensions out here," the guy told me. "It's polarized." Out of sheer exhaustion I let him drive and went to sleep in back. They woke me as we were coming down beside Mount Tamalpais, the lights of San Francisco glittering below, beyond the Golden Gate. One of the loveliest sights I had ever seen.

Spent two weeks in *the city*, sleeping in my VW bus on the street, waking each morning to a city scrubbed clean by ocean breezes. People smiled and traded peace signs; there were free concerts in the park: Joan Baez, the Jefferson Airplane and Grateful Dead, a woman named Janis Joplin with salt in her soul; Allen Ginsberg read in coffeehouses that might've been Village. A generation converging on this tiny peninsula, storming gates of tradition. Haight-Ashbury, Berkeley, Taos, Czechago — yet another version of America. New York resisted. On ground level revolt seemed imminent, but along vertical skyscraper sidewalks business still wore its polyester, and the underground was occupied by derelicts and thieves. Besides, New York had too many subcultures already to be impressed by another. "New York reaches out to the Old World; San Francisco reaches to the Orient," my new friends told me in solemn tones. "We have discovered something new here, something better." Pacific breezes took the burr off street voices, brought Buddhist chants up in the night from basement ashrams. I stayed stoned and was nearly convinced.

Though I wanted desperately to paint. Someone gave me a name, a seacoast town up north. I drove up-coast and fell under the spell of waves frothing white against headlands, primal forests and shakeroof houses. Here! at the continent's edge where restlessness could wander no further, so broke against the sea. Found Mr. Jakes with his piney drawl and a secluded cabin down a muddy drive. What did I care, as he told me, that the place was filling up with hippies who stole apples and swam naked in the river? I had come to paint.

I started a correspondence with Dad — his letters witty, lyrical, packed with a boldness and experience that came not from the father I knew but another, richer self. He wrote that Gauguin also foundered before all that Pacific splendor:

It seems human sensitivities find beauty a poor diet. Without tension we lose our edge. Where is the balance? It can take a lifetime to find it.

Is it presumptuous of me, here in the bosom of family and friend, to suggest that I too have some experience of isolation (albeit not life in the redwood wilds)? Mine is an isolation of weak lungs. One can feel horribly cut off from the breathy ones who jog up stairs. I believe every artist possesses a fine-tuned mechanism of isolation (or better "separateness") from whence spring the best of his creative energies. The "sincerity" and "originality" of which Tolstoy wrote. At the moment your solitude may seem a difficult burden. I assure you that it will finally seem an old friend, perhaps the best one can have.

His letters the one thing in my life going well. Finally I had a relationship with my father. With distance, an empathy grew between us that had always been foiled by fear, embarrassment — whatever it was — up close. I wrote one day that I loved him.

At night I threw the I Ching (not exactly conversation, but I asked questions and it answered them). I fantasized for hours on end: rapping with Max over coffee . . . imagined Richard dropping by. Sat reading Thomas Mann before the fire, until the book slipped from my lap and I was making love to Ron Sterges, my painting teacher those last weeks in New York, gorging on fantasy, fireflicker staining my bare legs blood red — until my clitoris was an electric bud and I had broken out in a sweat of orgasm. Realizing, mortified, that my thoughts had drifted again to Maxine.

I forced myself out for coffee or wine at the Inn in town, doodling, glancing shy as a virgin at those who passed. Wasn't there even one kind stranger or Samaritan who would sit with me? Remoteness a virtue here. People are outwardly cordial, inwardly building fences. They sense another's loneliness and quickly find something needs doing. In the East people stay lonely because they are so busy. In the West they stay busy because they are so lonely. Not much difference at all.

Then the rains come.

But no rain that I have ever known — doesn't fall but floods the air. Roofs leak, fires barely smolder, dogs stink. Nature has its way. I run out of firewood and am forced to inquire about more.

As I leave the cabin, the gray sky splits open; sunlight sparkles on wet leaves, turns moss the green of new grass. I walk the river estuary below town, past cattail kingdoms and pampas plumes, a sharp spice of bay laurel on the heavy warm air. Nature a frolic of giggling light and clashing vocals of crows and hang-gliding vultures, dash of a pileated woodpecker across river. In the shallows a great blue heron waits on one leg like a yogi. The river is in no rush, taking the long curves. A grebe floats, holding its white throat high, regal in its domain of solitude and self-sufficiency, trailing a white wake through brown water, where sunlight is cut neatly by the blue blade of a hill shadow.

I go to the Inn, feeling almost happy (later I can ask the butcher, who smiles and gives me scraps for Marcello, about firewood), sit watching the come and go of the country hip in long skirts and loggers' boots, who've come to liberate northern California in a campaign of hair and herpes. They kiss easily and float in the room like water flowers, drifting together in self-conscious conversation. I ignore them, distant as that grebe on the river, begin a letter to Dad. Startled when I look up and find the most flamboyant of them all staring at me, her elbows planted on my table. Her hair dances in cabalistic blonde ecstasies, Hare Krishna eyes goatleap, scamper on barrels and click heels in the air. She is a fortune teller in black cape and billowing bright skirt, pounds of jewelry and a tight vest, from which her breasts swell creamily. "Writing a letter?" she demands, decapitating her vowels. "I don't write letters, man. Letters are to friendship what reviews are to books. Hey, cheer up. Wha'sa trouble? This time around doesn't count." I stare. She laughs, cocking a finger. "New York!" she guesses. "Me, too.

Queens, the Village. Far out! I left, I'm like a receiver. The Center will
not hold and all that shit. A hard rain's gonna fall. My name's Gypsy."
Her teeth flash like castanets.

We talk. I feel nunnish — trying my voice after a long silence. When
she says that she sings, I mention I play guitar; Gypsy claps her hands
and says, "We gotta get it on!" I smile shyly and tell how hard it is to
meet people here. "Hard? Baby, it's easy. But you gotta try." She gestures at tables surrounding us. "I wanna introduce you to my friends." I
seize her arm.

"Not now . . . please."

"It's okay, relax. Whenever y'r ready. They're good people. I got an
idea. C'mon over. We'll put on the Chambers Brothers and get loaded,
maybe make some music together."

"Outtafuckinsight!" she exclaims over my Microbus, grabs Marcello
and rubs noses, while he squirms and tailwags and is instantly in love.
We drive to a cottage snugged in deep woods, make giddy conversation
while, outside, the eternal twilight gradually deepens, me strumming an
old Martin while she sings — a deep velvety voice, bust swelling like an
opera singer's — get wasted on Acapulco dynamite which she super-
charges straight down into me, munch granola and red apples, laughing
until my face is numb and we are drifting in black space, rain tiptoeing
on windows. I watch the orange elf of Gypsy's face in light leaking from
a woodstove: she smiles, sitting on the bed like a Shakti, unbuttons her
vest, releasing the cantaloupe flesh of breasts and rich carmine nipples,
lifts the skirt over her head and lies back on elbows, eyes tiny teasing
dybbuks, lips forming a whisper or a kiss; while I giggle at the henna
mound of her pussy and Marcello sniffs a foot. Curling up on a rug in
front of the stove, I fall blissfully asleep.

Next morning she is someone else: bronze skin gone sallow, hair lifeless. "Ignore me," she says. "I'm fucked up. I got teensy worms crawling around in my head." Before going I ask where I can buy firewood.
She has a friend; she promises to send him over.

I wait, try burning waterlogged twigs I have scavenged in the woods.
After three heatless days, with cold bolting deep into my bones, I drive
to the Inn to warm up. Gypsy jumps up from a tableful of people and
throws arms around me. "Everyone! Meet my friend, Nat," she announces. I get nods, shallow smiles before they turn back to each other.
I stand there, feeling color crawl in my cheeks. "We'll get together —"
Gypsy assures me. I realize she isn't going to invite me to sit down. I am

thoroughly humiliated, don't know what to do next. Then I remember the firewood.

Gypsy laughs. "Y'r in luck." She leads me to a bearded man sitting at a window table, reading. "Gene love," she cries, "Natalie needs firewood."

"Soft, hard or mixed?" he asks without looking up.

"Is there a difference?" I ask.

He glances up at Gypsy, his face relenting a little at mouth corners. A ruggedly handsome man — long brown hair brushed back, beard a thick nap, almost hiding ruddy cheeks, a precise nose and eyes that take direct hold of me. "Another city chick," he guesses.

Embarrassed, I ask what he is reading. He turns the book over in burled hands. "Robinson Jeffers. America's forgotten poet." He runs a palm back through his hair and asks Gypsy, "Full cord or face?" as if she is buying the wood. She glances at me.

"I don't even know what language he is speaking." She translates: "One pickup load or two?" I shrug; she laughs.

"You see —" he leans forward over the table bringing palms close together "— there's just exactly twice as much wood in two." I stick out my tongue. His eyes sparkle. But then have slitted, glaring past me at a group of tourists passing the table — suburban types led by a balding heavy-bellied man. "Parasites," Gene mutters. "Go the fuck back home." The bald man's cheek twitches but he moves on, perhaps abashed by Gene's broad shoulders. Gypsy pats his arm as she might a large angry dog. I decide "One load," remembering my dwindling cash. Gene throws me a sullen glance.

"I guess you're not a tourist, are you?"

"I'm from New York," I blurt.

He extends a hand. "I'm from Idaho. Maybe you've heard of it. Just north of Las Vegas."

"I know. I was practically raped there."

He studies me a moment, then snaps the book closed and stands up. "Ought to be tomorrow. Maybe day after." Gypsy shrugs as he goes out. "He's a freak but a responsible dude. Guess somebody's got to cut firewood."

Just getting out of bed when a dilapidated pickup clattered up the drive; barely got my robe on before his face appeared at the kitchen door. "I have to get dressed," I shouted. "You're early." He eyed my bare legs and nodded. When I came out he was stacking wood beside the porch. "Won't it get wet there?" I asked. He glanced up, forehead flushed.

"I only sell firewood. Don't handle the weather end."

I wondered if this was the man I had met at the Inn — the same checked logger's jacket, but hair unkempt, a silence about him that seemed impenetrable. Did everyone here change personalities in the morning? I started helping unload the truck. "That's all right," he said, "I can handle it."

"But I enjoy it. I need the exercise."

We stacked wood in pitchy silence. Nervously, I began to prattle about how I hadn't been dry in weeks, even my bed was damp. He leapt up into the pickup bed, slinging wood out in long-hinged movements, wrapped in his solitude. I picked up a dense chunk. "It's beautiful wood, especially the cut ends. Nature does everything so ... exquisitely." *Why couldn't I just shut up?* I brought the split to my nose: it smelled wet. "It's awfully heavy. Do you think it will burn?"

"Wood, isn't it?" he snapped. "A little kindling will dry it right out."

I nodded and dug at a sliver. He had gloves, I didn't.

He came inside when he had finished, glanced at coffee — a fog hanging over mugs in the cool air. I asked if he'd like a cup before going. His eyes did an antsy jog around cabin and porch studio, unfinished canvases — the latest primed but untouched upon the easel.

"You an artist?"

I sighed. "I'm trying. Coffee?" I repeated.

He stared at the mugs. "Seems unnecessary."

I flinched. "I just thought you'd like something warm —"

"It's already there, why repeat it? Photography's even worse."

I gaped. His eyes came to me, gray-blue, clear as tide pools. He averted them and quoted a price that took me by surprise. I paid him, stretching out each bill reluctantly. As he was leaving, he pulled a newsprint pamphlet from his pocket and handed it over. "That'll warm your heart," he said; was out the door before I could give it back. Titled *Dear Jesus: A Child's Letter to God.*

Later, I went down the road to ask Mr. Jakes if he could help me get a fire going. "Not with that wood —" he announced before we'd even reached the pile. "Be months before she's dry enough to burn."

"It smells okay."

"By golly!" old Mr. Jakes chuckled. "Only smell I ever knew gave any heat was wet manure. It ain't my business, but what'd the fella get for it?" When I told him he removed his cap and scratched his leathery scalp. I asked if the creep had ripped me off. "Well —" eyebrows pasted high up his long forehead "— you might'a had it cheaper."

Depression inhabited the dampness. The last few geese honked, doleful, as they passed south over the cabin, hidden in clouds, killdeer hopped in little gangs on beaches, bishop pine bent together in the same wind. I was a freak of nature. Alone. Running out of money. The choice was simple: either I found a job or split for the East — at once! before I hadn't enough to make it.

Instead, lay all day in my sleeping bag to stay warm, sunk down in feathery ennui in an acid pungency of damp ashes, comforting myself with nostalgia, fantasy run amok. Knowing it wasn't Richard but Max who sat beside me on the couch arm, caressing my hair, lips soft at my ear, but words nearly stern, short skirt far up brown thighs; she unbuttons her blouse and places my fingertips against a naked breast, pushing her tongue between my lips . . . hands lathering me beneath the shower jet, jagged nipples grazing my back; I tingle at the furtive brush of her mons across my ass, soapy fingers slipping up between buttocks into the waiting delight of my cunt. I buck with desire. Afterwards, feel such awful shame. "I'm so lonely . . ." My words balloon on the cold air. Why kid myself? *I have been doing it for years.*

It was days before his pickup returned, clattering up the drive. I was out of the cabin before it had lurched into a puddle and stopped. He climbed out, staring over my head as though some rare bird was perched on the roof, looking Rastafarian with his crazy hair. Marcello made little nipping lunges at this boots and he hopped about, trying an ameliorative smile.

"It doesn't burn at all!" I shouted.

Gene nodded. Placid bastard.

"I want my money back."

His eyes fixed on my feet. "I'm sorry about that."

"Sorry? You're like all the other Christians — hiding behind your little pieties."

He knelt on a knee, reaching for Marcello — who almost got his thumb. "Jeezus! You two make a real team." Rising, he tucked thumbs in his belt and nodded back at the laden pickup. "Brought you another load. Bone dry. I guarantee it. By the time you burn this load the other should be too."

I stared at him. He had the audacity of a New York landlord. "Are you nuts? I can't afford another load. I'm broke."

"This one's on the house." Taking out his wallet and offering me two tens and a shy smile. "Little refund." I took the bills — by reflex — but immediately let them go. He cocked his head, stooped quickly and snatched them out of the driveway muck. "Wish you'd take it. You'd be letting me off the hook. I haven't slept so well lately."

"I haven't even gotten out of bed."

His teeth cringed. "I'm sorry. What can I say? Once in a while I fuck up and get greedy." He rolled the bills, almost delicately, into a tube and pushed them gently into the breast pocket of my T-shirt under the Mexican sweater. Then nodded down at my feet, a quick grin. "See you've gone country funk, New York." I glanced down at bootless stockinged feet, mud squishing up between webbed toes. We exchanged a look, my chin bunching toward laughter.

Gene restacked the wood, old and new, in a shed behind the cabin, then built a roaring fire, rubbing hands on dirty jeans as he stood up. "You still offering that coffee?" We sat before the firecrackle. When I asked if he was really a Jesus freak, he stooped forward, repositioning a log on the fire.

"Who was it that said fireplaces pull cold air into a room, heat it up, then send it straight on out the chimney?"

"Do you always avoid answering questions?"

The flash of his teeth. "Depends on the question."

"I can't figure you out."

"We're off to an even start then." He smiled.

"You're meshugga."

"Mishu-what?"

"It's Yiddish for *crazy*."

"Nnnhh —" His lips opening, a hollow ellipse, nodding his head slightly. "You're *Jewish*. I might have guessed that."

"What's that supposed to mean?"

"Means you aren't anything like Miss Prish, my old Sunday school teacher."

"Miss Prish?"

Gene tapped my knee. "That's a compliment. Except —" lazy eyes brushing my boobs " — she had great tits. Straight out!" He pulled hands in two generous scoops away from his chest.

I frowned. "You don't have to rub it in."

Gene blushed. "All us boys competed for dumbest kid in class so she'd stick those Holy Ghosts in our faces and explain the opening of the Red Sea."

Giggling. "I thought that was against your religion."

"It's my whole religion."

"You're a pretty weird Christian."

Gene was insulted. "Who's Christian?"

"You left one of your stupid propaganda pamphlets —"

"I have hundreds. My ex-lady was a Jesus freak. Finally, she heard what I was saying about the sexism implicit in Christianity and left both me and Jesus, flat! Became feminist. I got the pamphlets." He shrugged. "She did have one sweet ass."

"You really are a nut."

Gene bent forward, using a stick of kindling to coax more heat from the blaze, tilting his head and looking straight into my eyes. "And you're a very pretty lady."

Then he lapsed into an abashed shyness, and only after hours of talk — his Rousseauian philosophy, mistrust of civilized man, love of things natural — dinner, finally a stuttering discussion of our affairs, like a stoking up of libido, did he finally find courage to ask if he could spend the night.

I painted Gene sitting naked on the porch step, coffee mug in hand, staring straight ahead into pygmy forest with a sober, nearly stern expression — beard did that. Hard to know what he was thinking: that he should find another commercial fishing gig, or return to school, or write a book, assassinate the President, tell this chick good-bye and be on his way. I had never known anyone like him. Woodsman simple but full of surprises, shy and arrogantly confident, brilliant and molasses slow. Absolutely alive.

Me hoping out loud that first morning together — a miracle of sunlight finding holes in the trees and splashing in the window — that he didn't have to work today. He looked at me sidelong, his head on the pillow, throwing a vague hand. "Work is for *them*. I survive." He was Adam without a cause, shifting mood to mood just as he pleased.

"You don't know what it means to me to be painting again," I said. Gene nodded. I wondered if he took my work seriously.

We went to the beach and made love on a blanket amid driftwood litter, Marcello dashing about, insanely jealous, nipping at Gene's ass

("Dog smart," as Max would say, sensing a serious rival), while laughter rolled in tears down my lover's cheeks, and I lay with pale October sun on my stomach, a gritty breeze slapping my breasts, telling him that Marcello was my oracle; I never ignored his advice about men. Sifting sand through my fingers, thinking I had always known this man.

Gene took me woodcutting into slash left by loggers. I was appalled by the twisted, splintered carcasses of trees ("culls" he called them), the rutted earth and foliage crushed into the mud, a few pathetic snags left standing as a kind of taunt. "They must hate trees," I said. "It's like those burned-out blocks in Bed-Stuy." Gene called it the Vietnam of the housing developers. "Then I come along and pick scraps off the bones of progress." Shrugging. "People need firewood."

One night he made venison stew. When I doubted I could eat it, he said, "Have some respect for the animal." I looked at him, astonished. "*Me* have some respect? *You* shot it!" Gene shook his head. "Doesn't work like that. Respect means getting right up there close. A hunter who doesn't respect, doesn't eat." I found myself wondering if I could ever understand this man. He proposed we take a honeymoon to Berkeley. "People's Park is happening down there," he said excitedly. "A homegrown Tet Offensive."

"To me it's just college kids playing games."

"It's bigger than that," he insisted.

It did seem bigger when we arrived next day in that Berkeley war zone: air thick with pepper gas and excitement, helicopters whirly-twirling overhead, police sirens and small bursts of demonstration. Police, it seemed, had gone berserk and were battling the entire populace. We walked along Telegraph Avenue over broken glass, past boarded store windows. Gene strolling with a huge smile. Suddenly a cop car leapt around a corner with a squeal of glee, shotguns bristling from windows. Before we could gather wits, there was a wink of flame, a blast; across the street a tear gas canister exploded at a stroller's feet. He leapt high into the air, then disappeared in dirty yellow smoke. A broad copface grinned at us along a gun barrel. I screamed, Gene threw me against a building, shielding with his body. Then we were running — everyone! half-blinded with gas and panic. Ahead, a student dormitory: broken windows, ruddy liquid faces shouting "Come up! Come up!" Fleeing up into corridors — doors torn from hinges like a Bronx tenement — full of refugees and tear gas hacking, hoarse shouts and birdshrill screams. A fat kid hanging like a flounder out a window — friends gripping his legs for fear he will fall — delirious with rage, his trowel mouth shoveling obscenities down at cops below, who were beating a man in a tweed sportsjacket, guilty of our same crime: being in the wrong place.

Later, we drove through blanketing gas that lay dense over the city, our eyes raw bleeding flowers, tears cutting red troughs down our cheeks. I clutched a damp handkerchief over my mouth and told Gene I'd had enough. Ahead, a mean-looking bunch had gathered in front of a Cadillac show window, while salesmen huddled behind a shiny car inside. They wore miscellaneous helmets, flak jackets, gas masks. Some carried stones. One stepped away from the others, cocked her arm and hurled a brick through the huge pane of glass. It turned liquid and came splashing down over sidewalk, salesmen, shiny car. The woman froze in follow-through, then straightened and turned to the street, tentative, as if uncertain what to do next.

It was Marty McCoy.

No mistaking those tits and dumpster mouth. I screeched over to the curb, waving my arms. "Marty! Over here!" The whole bunch of them stampeded, began shoving and jostling to get into the bus, becoming argumentative, finicking like theatregoers over seats, while a salesman goggled through glass fragments for our license number. "Just get the fuck in!" yelled Gene. And Marty rammed the last ones in from behind like a subway vet, throwing herself into the front seat and Gene's lap. Out of some nearby street leapt the yowl of a siren and I drove like a madwoman.

Marty, understated as ever, mumbled an address as if she had been expecting me — restless on my lover's lap, her sphinx eyes knifing back at him, offering a joint. "What are you doing in Berkeley?" I demanded. "What's a Jew doing driving a Volkswagen?" she replied.

Somehow we spent the night at her battle HQ amidst radio reports of next day's tandem anti-war demonstrations in New York and San Francisco, a litany of busted comrades' names passing lip to lip back through rooms of the house, machine gun chatter of Ché Mao Venceremos Huey Newton Power to the People off the motherfucksexistcapitalistpigs rhetoric and news of a man shotgunned off a roof on Telegraph Avenue. Someone singing Bob Dylan off key. "The nonviolent era is over; it's time to go underground," Marty insisted to a grad student — another Barney, his watery eyes debating a silkscreen fist with huge deformed knuckles across her chest (I could never understand why they fell so crazy in love with those fatty deposits, while she looked more and more like Mussolini — face puffy around her gaunt, sleepless eyes).

We slept atop sleeping bags in a stuffy hot room crowded with snores and lovemoans. Me whispering "No, not here —" when Gene ran fingers up my thigh. He sighed at my ear. "I'm about to burst, baby." Cursing softly as I turned away. I awoke early, missing him. Neither fully conscious nor aware I had gone looking, I made my way to the bathroom, stepping over breathers wounded with sleep. Gene just emerging from the tub as I entered — cock at half-mast, a princely smile — leaving Marty's circus tent thighs and padded shoulders, nipples standing like carnival barkers. A freak of oversized sex splayed over demolished shampoo tubes and soap dishes. He flinched, eyes flashing wide at me then narrowing into a sheepish grin, sweat beading his forehead, effusing her rut rankness. Marty's bloodshot eyes rolled, amused. And Gene disappeared completely. Her huge fuzzy mouth licking its chops, promising to regurgitate his expired driver's license and library card in a few days.

I tore the medicine cabinet from the wall and Frisbeed it through a window, pushing my way past gawkish half-naked sleepers, getting out of there. Out of Gene.

I ignored the truck still parked by my cabin. This wasn't New York; the city wouldn't haul it away. No tears, I promised myself each night, crawling between cold sheets. What was he anyway? Swindler. Asshole. "Marty! for shitsake —" I threw myself into work on a large canvas: a collage of images which I titled *Bachanalia*. At center, Mother naked-dancing to the delight of her button-eyed offspring, while Dad stood watching with a smile dapper as the crease in his trousers. In one corner he was at work painting nudes that extended back into infinity . . . so many nudes, as if afraid the world would run out. I had scrawled in a passage from his latest letter: *We are a faithless, hedonistic people who believe in nothing beyond the five senses. Sensation alone is important to us. We are doomed.*

One day I met Gypsy in town. We walked together on the headlands under sharp November sunlight, sat on a rock looking out over the ocean, and I gave her all the tears I had been hoarding. "He's a sweet dude," she said. "He'll be back. He knows where to find Mama." I squeezed her fingers, shaking my head.

Meanwhile, I was broke. Forced to call Mom/Dad to ask for help, knowing it a mistake, remembering Dr. Kaufman's warning when I had told her about the VW bus. "Don't take any more from your mother," she had said. "You have to establish your own independence." I called. Dad said, "Certainly!" Mother was cold.

"You know, we can't support you out there, Natalie."

"It's only temporary," I insisted. "I just need some time to work things out."

"You've needed a lot of time."

Furious when I hung up — at myself for asking, at that bitch for forcing me to grovel. Dr. Kaufman was right. I couldn't afford to take anything from her. Then, a few days later, I received a money order, with it a note in Mother's hand accusing me of being interested only in her money — my whole life! For hours I raged, considered sending it back. But I needed that money. When Max used to tell me that the Almighty Dollar destroys everyone's principles, I passionately disagreed. Now I wouldn't have. Along with that check I cashed in my idealism. I bought a bottle of Metaxa and went to visit Gypsy, but she wasn't home. So I drove back to my cabin, got blotto drunk all by myself and dreamed about the friends I had left behind.

Was splitting wood beside the shed next day when I sensed a presence and swung around — to find him watching, sleeping bag under arm. He stepped forward and took the maul from my hands. "You have to see that split and keep your eye on it, like hitting a baseball. Now watch." He snapped forward; the wood popped open. "Not strength. Will power. Like anything else." He smiled. "How you been?" I pointed on down the road.

"It leads to Comptche. You can't miss it. The women there are so horny they hang panties on their mailboxes."

Gene nodded. "I know all about Comptche women. I kinda had my heart set on a gal right here in Little River."

I turned and walked to the cabin. He strode toward the outhouse. After a minute came knocking on the bolted cabin door. "That's full up," he shouted. "Any more rain and she'll spill over."

"Just leave," I yelled back, "before I call the sheriff."

"I'd rather you didn't."

He went into the shed and emerged with a rusty shovel, then disappeared back into the woods. After what seemed hours of pacing and muttering, I went out to see. Gene worked bare-chested in the cool air, breaking concrete-hard soil ("podsol" he called it) with the ax and spooning it from the shallow trench onto a mound of corpse gray clay brindled with orange veins.

"What are you doing?" I demanded.

"I sure could use a pick," he answered.

"I wish you would just go."

His eyebrows froze upwards, half amused. "I come all this way to dig you a new shitter hole and this is the gratitude I get."

"Gawd! what happened to your eye?" Words leapt out. An ugly yellow bruise bloomed across his cheek and forehead.

"I thought you'd never ask. Why the hell do you think it took me so long to get back here?" He sat on a lip of the hole rolling a cigarette and told me his story:

That morning when everyone else had gone to the demonstration in San Francisco, Gene walked Berkeley streets, disgusted with himself, not at all in the mood for a cop car that screeched to the curb beside him. He called them pigs; they worked him over with their nightsticks. "They took me out to Santa Rita where there must've been three hundred of us lying buck-naked on our bellies, while they poked us with shotguns and dared us to move. I spent ten days in one crowded sonuvabitch nasty cell. Not even any toilet paper. Little things like constitutional rights they had no use for. That's what sprang most of us. A bald eagle judge released me on my own recognizance and some public defender assured me I had nothing to worry about. I told him he didn't see the way you tore that mirror off the wall. I had all kinds of worries."

I blinked my eyes. "What are you charged with?"

"Resisting arrest. A light felony. I should get off with six months digging outhouse holes." He grinned.

I went back to the cabin.

Later, he walked right in and stripped by the fire — me refusing even a glance at the firm fist of his ass as he washed at the sink. We sat to dinner and I explained, "This is because of the outhouse. That's all."

He nodded, kept saying how good it tasted, paraded about all night in jockey shorts, staring into fire castles between his feet propped on the hearth, telling how, lying belly-down on that cold asphalt, he'd realized that the momentum of the sixties wouldn't last. "We don't have the guts. They'll hang us by the hair, ram their billysticks up our assholes. There's too much to lose; we aren't Viet Cong. And now with Governor Reagan and his sort — they mean to crush us. We scare the living b'Jesus out of them. That dude's a second-rate John Wayne, loves to hear the creak of his own boot leather. Be thankful he's not as smart as Hitler." Gene's eyes gone flame red. "He doesn't have to be. We'll cop out — run back home to middle-classdom."

"I'm going to bed," I said.

Gene followed me, bare feet squeaking on the wooden floor.

"Forget it!" I turned on him. Marcello bared white teeth. Gene threw up his hands.

"Take it easy, you two. I wanted to bank your stove for the night."

"I don't even know what you're doing here. No one invited you to stay."

"I can sleep on the couch. It's fine, really."

I screamed, begged, reasoned, ordered, ignored him over those next days. Nothing worked. His snores fulminated unabashedly from the couch, he had coffee waiting when I groaned from bed, red-eyed resentful, irritated by his early morning get-up-and-go. Although I sneaked out at times to watch from behind trees: the ripple of his muscles as he worked, a sting of sweat on the air. Teenage infatuation, I scolded myself. The third day, helped him drag the unwieldy outhouse over its new pit. Tottering woozily as the yeasty breath of that full shitpit took the wind out of me, feeling my knees go, slumping toward that open sewer. Gene grabbed the handle of my shirt and pulled me to safety. "You going swimming?" he grinned. And I threw my arms around him.

That night my breast brushed his arm as I served dinner. He sat stiffly, stealing furtive glances in the lantern light. Followed me, as on every night, into the bedroom to check the stove. He crouched, firelight spilling over him in the dark room as he banked the embers, almost solemnly. "I guess you'll be going tomorrow —" My voice edgy, unconvincing. Gene crouched, the potbelly's vents painting orange slots down his face, nickering in the whites of his eyes. Tension in the room almost unbearable. I began undressing, defiant — unbuttoned sailor pants, straightened panty band, peeled off top layers till I stood in goosebumps, my body a pink minnow, licked by the tongue of the kerosene lamp. Gene's eyes beatific, woggling over my tits, playing monster with my bellybutton.

"Come get warm." His voice hoarse.

I did, as if it were a game of dare. Standing side by side, our autumn eyes holding. He reached to touch my face, I slapped him away. "But it's inevitable. Can't you see that?" Eyes rolling over on their backs.

"You can't seriously hold that Irish cooze against me. F'r crissake she followed me into the john and starting giving head —"

"SHUT UP GENE! Just shut up!"

His hand sliding up my belly, cupping a breast. "Look, I dug you a new shitter hole, what more do you want? I have to clean out the old one?"

I smiled, giving him all he needed.

Gene carried me to bed, lay beside me kissing place by place. While I touched the saffron welt around his eye, heard the whish of his zipper. Huge and throbbing, whispering he'd never hurt so long, never been so hungry baby I'll fuck your brains out make that sweet slit sing with my tongue eat you suck you love you fuck you . . . Please ohhh do me, my cock is an eagle trapped in a tiny bird that wants to soar and fly away on the wings of your lips . . . Ohhh Please. And me gripping him, gasping loving needing, shrieking out and beating his chest with my fists, sinking teeth into neck sinew, tasting surprised blood, taking as much of him as I can hold in my mouth — wanting it all, his ivory hugeness — nibbling, driving fingernails into that firm ass, clawing for blood and wailing RAAAAPE into the earless night. Fucking bastard! Marty McCoy of all people, stinking horse perspiring Marty cow udders who I still taste on you like grease, crying yowling letting it come. My friend Marty. Then my hands fall limp, there is nearly silence, a breathlike whimper. He enters me and I hold on for dear life.

II

Months came together into years, meshed of winter rain and summer fog, one much the same as another. Gene and I growing upon one another like moss in the endless damp. A honeymoon of planting gardens, working bare-chested amid corn and tomatoes while the sun made big promises, firewood cutting, gathering wild mushrooms, milking goats, skinny-dipping in summerrivers — a generation of nakedness on the beach like the coming of a New Eden. Work for money when we couldn't avoid it. Dirt poor and good at it. It was a lark, a trapeze act above all those gaping mouths below in potbellied America: *To be poor, my God! how scary.* Not knowing what a huge net life has spread under us. For quite a time I was charmed, almost happy with the life. I continued painting, making progress.

Then, gradually, I began to feel closed in — those claustrophobic studios in cabin corners where every movement of an elbow threatened catastrophe, lit by the meager arc of a kerosene lamp — felt I was missing something "out there." I asked Gene, "Why bother to paint if it's only to stick canvases in a back room?" He had no patience with such feelings. "We create for ourselves, no one else matters," he said. "Artists must remain separate, isolated from others or else they lose the critical eye." Francis Bacon isn't cut off, I told him, or Siqueiros. He would shrug and say he hated to see me go "commercial" in a patronizing tone that infuriated me. Cheap words coming from one who merely wrote an occasional poem. Everyone in northern California wrote poetry. Life itself was a sort of poetry — a rarefied sleep.

Once, I tried hawking my paintings on a Mendocino street corner, propped against our mud-spattered pickup. Citrus fresh California smiles passed on their way to a craft fair, regarding me no less than paintings and truck as part of the same aesthetic package. "How lovely," they whispered of us — and hurried on. Art in California! It smiles, its teeth are clean, it wears deodorant and is devotedly democratic. Later, depressed, I told Gene, "This is no place for a serious artist. I'll never get anywhere here." He brushed hair from my face. "Isn't anywhere to go," he said. "You can paint here just as well as anyplace else. The coast is full of painters."

"Hobbyists!" I cried. "Artists aren't concerned with filling our leisure time; we're trying to *say* something."

"Look, maybe you've got to smile a little for those customers. Be cheerful. Make 'em think their living room isn't complete without a Bach-Hjalstead painting."

"I thought you were against commercial hypes."

"This isn't commercial, baby. This is small town."

Gene had begun to change, fulfilling his own prophecy about everyone dropping sixties radicalism and running home to middle-classdom. He trimmed the hair that had once puffed off his head in a mushroom cloud, began working long hours and soon was calling himself "contractor" instead of "carpenter." Like he had blown his nose and forgotten that huge collective sneeze of the sixties, or it had only been a costume party. Losing his zest for life by the minute, becoming as staid and humorless as an old house. Once he'd been a crazy idealist with the courage to be arrested for what he believed in; now he argued with his helper over a quarter's raise in wages. "I'm not going to apologize for becoming more security conscious," he said. "As you approach your thirties you begin to realize that this ride doesn't last forever. There are things I want to accomplish in life — like raising a family." I was shocked. The first I'd heard about *family*.

"With whom?" I asked.

Two vertical lines puzzled his brow. "You, baby."

"And I have nothing to say about it?"

The argument over children became continuous. I would tell him, "I'm an artist, I don't want to piss my life away on kids. It won't work. I learned that much from Mother anyway. If a woman tries to have both children and a career, they both get cheated." Gene would become red-faced, anger coiling quietly out of him.

"Why do you think women were put on this planet?"

"I can't even respect that question enough to answer."

"Love ripens with children, can't you see that? Even a woman's breasts ripen, her nipples turn brown."

"So do her hands, from changing diapers."

He had all the arguments down pat, as though he'd done research: increased odds of breast cancer for childless women, clotting during menstruation, psychological crisis in the late thirties, dissatisfaction . . . panic! You'll want kids then when it has become dangerous to have them. He was becoming an obstetrical fanatic. Our relationship stuck on that groove in the record. Why can't you see that kids give so much and take so little? *Yes, for the man. It's a lark. Mama raises the brats. Look, I'm a developing artist — a swimmer just learning the strokes with miles to go — and you want to put these huge weights around my neck.* A silence hung in the room. I could hear the crackle of corn in the garden, flies dashing their hopes against the screen door. An irony in the nod of his head. That's one fucking negative outlook.

Lovemaking became a battle of wills. First, he tried hiding my birth control pills. When recurrent headaches forced me to give up the pill, he would grab me, try to get it in before I could insert diaphragm and foam, or maneuver me into odd positions hoping to penetrate my protection. To him it was a game. I wasn't amused. I started avoiding him. Once grabbed his balls and squeezed so hard he cried out, "Are you trying to castrate me?" Cupping hands there, shielding himself.

"You're wrecking our sex life with your babymaking fascism," I shouted. "It's getting so I hate balling. You're a selfish bastard. You can't force me to want a child. You can't rape my mind." I began crying. Gene seemed at last to understand. For a time he was gentle, solicitous. But he hadn't given up hope.

I painted Maxine from memory and hung her portrait in my studio — crude, but the lips and eyes right, the cautious opening of her smile. Gene thought it fantastic, the first of my work he'd really liked. "I miss her," I told him.

At first I had attempted to deny it. Just a vagrant thought, I'd tell myself, like seeing a mouse out of the corner of an eye, knowing it isn't really there. Then it had become a daily thing and there was no denying it. I would lie in the morning and wonder what she was doing, or if she had found someone — feeling incipiently jealous of whomever she had found. Taking a nap in the afternoon, would find myself fantasizing: remembering her thick eyebrows and strong tan thighs, touching myself. I was tormented. How was it possible? I had a man; I was happy. How could I still be haunted by what Dr. Kaufman had assured me was only a passing fancy, nothing unnatural?

Desperate, I approached Gene. "You have to help me," I begged, speaking in a whisper just audible over the tapdance of rain on the roof, feeling a chill seep into the cabin. "It's when I'm feeling down or insecure. Sometimes I think it's something unresolved in my life. Like maybe we should've done it."

He stared at me, that stern paterfamilias expression, his eyes tightened into hard little kernels, voice splintering: "You fantasize fucking her?"

"It's not like that —"

"When? When we're making love?" Anger brewing in him.

I shook my head.

A slow, hard-breathing silence of accommodation. When I finally looked at him, those broken-dish eyes were coming and going about the room in desperation. I hadn't imagined he would take it this badly. "Do you hate me?" He didn't answer. "Please, honey . . . don't be like this."

But I spoke into that Hjalsteadhardness. That fear.

"I'm not attracted to other women," I whispered, "just Maxine. She's a hero to me. The mother I never had."

Gene's eyes glazed. "Y'r too old for heroes."

"I'm still *your woman*." I touched him.

He threw my hand off and went for the door, shouting, "I can't make you a woman. Having children makes a woman." He started out, but turned, his arm arrowed at her portrait. "That's down when I get back here or it's finished. You understand? You can pack your shit and cart your ass out."

Hours later he returned, nearly contrite, apologizing for the little redneck number. "Nothing to freak out about, right?" He was half-drunk. Gallantly, he returned Max's portrait to its place, giving her a firm smack on the lips, a smile. "I like Nat, too," he said. And took me to bed.

Then Gene got his wish. I became pregnant. I knew it at once. Not the easy warm feeling I'd heard women talk about but almost creepy — like something alien was taking over my body. I didn't dare tell him, but immediately took a job waitressing at the Inn. Gene was baffled and a little hurt. "You don't need to work, babe," he assured me. "I'm earning enough bread." I made up excuses. It gives me a sense of independence, I said. "Everyone should have money of their own, to spend any way they want."

That was the spring neighbor children brought us a fledgling swallow that had fallen from its nest. It perched on the rim of a cardboard box, spike-feathered, fluffy, while I played mama, catching grasshoppers in the meadow and poking their wiggly bodies down its gaping maw. Its insatiable squawk discordant with the "Woodland Bird Songs" record we played over and over to keep it company. Each time the pure, fluted voice of a hermit thrush came around, our little swallow opened its songbox in revelation and peeped accompaniment. Gene fingerstroked the tiny head. "Brother, y'r headed for a heavy identity crisis," he said. Our friend chirped cheerfully and gobbled another grasshopper. After a few days of this, Gene decided it was time for a flying lesson; he carried the bird outside perched on a finger. I followed him, protesting that my baby couldn't survive yet on its own. "Are you going to spend the whole year catching grasshoppers?" he asked. A point.

Our swallow made four frantic winglopes across the yard before colliding with a chicken-wire fence, where it hung by one spindly leg. I thought of Gypsy, who had worked her wings with that same desperate esprit before being caught at last in a mental hospital. All of the sixties! a flash of exuberant wings. That's all. Hanging upside down in the flight of history. But Gene rescued our little bird: took him out to the big meadow, tossing with a slow-motion underhand pitch that sent him tumbling topsy-turvy in airborne somersaults, then finding wings and swallowing to a line of distant trees in graceful strokes that made our hearts sing. Gene threw an arm around my shoulders and we cheered. "Good-bye little bird." We, too, were just learning to fly. Some of us, like Gypsy, would never find wings to emerge from that epoch, would remain fluttering like "Lucy in the Sky with Diamonds" long after anyone bothered looking up.

That swallow's flight symbolized a change to me. I had finished going back to the land. To me it was a dead end. "Retirement is wonderful," Gene himself had once said, "but you kind of feel like you should have earned it."

CHAPTER SIXTEEN

DUET

MY HEAD ACHES LIKE AN UNDER-JUICED COMPUTER TERMINAL. *Liberating the couch (a Babylon of coffee cups, American Journals of Psychiatry, of Gerontology, New England of Medicine . . .) I lie back and wonder what in christ's name this paper is about. Hospices maybe? (Last week's was hospices.) The treatment of autism in the Soviet Union? Or perhaps the chatter in the frontal lobe of Ezra Pound's poetry? Wondering how dear Murray talked me into a research job with his old friend Davidoff. Oy! what charm in the dismissive shrug of his hands:* Twenty hours a week maybe it takes you. . . . *(Is it snowing out? The heat is too high. Maybe it's summer, with all these windows open.)* True, the pay is not so good, but is good training. *My eyes are tumors. If I were smart, I would call Davidoff, tell him they never heard of autism in the Soviet Union, the* Journal of

Medical Education *has no listing for Ezra Pound . . . how crazy horny
I get with my eyes schlonging six inches over my cheeks. See! I'm not
wearing underwear. You'll get your Pound of statistics, synaptic
poetry, hospices. Maybe. Do your own fucking research! I got a novel
to write.*

*I laugh aloud. Murray, is that why you pushed this job on me? Sly
bastard. Shvindl! In the mirror, my breasts are milk and honey as I strip
for a much needed shower. I can imagine Murray's Old World eyes
prostrate before them as he opens my bra, a balding Moses before the
Promised Land. Yes, Pearlman, you still have good tits.*

*The phone rings. I regard it, speculating on a catechism of bad news:
Davidoff with another fucking assignment, Mom calling from the hospital, Uncle Sam dunning for back taxes, perhaps just Murray to heckle
with his affections:*

How are you this morning, my dear?

Frazzlehausted . . . as usual.

You are too hard, working.

*Yes, I am too hard, working. Your friend Davidoff has a curious no-
tion of part-time work. Germans are all the same.*

*He laughs. I ask if you marry me and you tell me, "I must have my
freedom." But, you see, you are in a slavery. I would never keep you
half the night working.*

You certainly try —

*Uproarious laughter. No . . . oh no! I must do the working. Suddenly
serious. If you marry me you will have to work again never. You are
thinking maybe, "He is too old." But Europeans are not like American
husbands. If you wish, you will keep a lover.*

I wish it were so simple.

He sighs.

*The phone rings, fanatical. Okay, I'll answer if you shut up. A
woman's voice, oddly familiar. I am cautious. "Natalie —?" I repeat
like a word from a forgotten language. Then realize! "My God, Natalie!" She is in New York. She has left her husband . . . well, maybe she
hasn't left him. I laugh. "It has to be Nat. No one else could be in so
many places at once."*

*"You stopped answering my letters," she complains. I tell her I've
written many letters; they just never get to paper. A letter for me is
harder than a short story: I can't trick myself into believing it has beginning or end. Her tinkling laugh. She tells me I haven't changed.*

"Plenty, kiddo. It's been some ride. I am now seriously considering be-trothal to a man merely two years younger than my father. It's true. An Old World gentleman who chuckles at me in my underwear and turns his back so I may take them off. I find him charming. Besides, he's rich."

She asks about Dad. "He's dying. I'm furiously trying to finish a sort of Daughter's Last Testament. I wake up every morning with a nose full of cedar dust — I'm not sure, from the pencil or cutting coffin boards. Listen! tell me what's new with Natalie . . . what is it now? Hjalstead! Sounds very legitimate. What are you doing in Nueva York, Hjalstead?"

She wants me to come over; she's at her parents' apartment. "Love to . . . I really would. Not sure I have the time. No! I am not one of those New Yorkers —" looking about with resentment at my quarters, trashed with industry "— Maybe I am. What sort of day is it out?" She asks if I'm locked in a cell or something. "Nearly. Why bother opening the drapes when I'm at the desk day and night? Yes, I'm still writing . . . in a manner of speaking. Research papers for second-rate minds who wish to be thought first-rate — and will pay the price. Don't be so heartbroken. It's what a master's in Psych is good for nowadays. I could be a social worker. Or selling cunt on the corner."

"You're still a nut anyway." Nat's voice alive at my ear.

"And you still have a gift for making people feel they are cheating themselves." Feeding out cord, I make my way across sublunar spaces, tug up the blinds. Stunned by inflooding light. "I am cheating myself. What a lovely day. You're right! It's a shit job. I have considered it temporary. The real story of my life is that I'm working on my doctor-ate."

"Woowie, Doctor Pearlman!"

"Sounds like an authority on athlete's foot, doesn't it?"

She gives me her full delight. "You have to come over. I came three thousand miles to see you."

"You're giving me cold feet. Listen, is your mother home?"

"What does it matter? She'd love to see you, too."

"Would she? There was a time when she thought I was about to de-vour her daughter and spit out the bones on some Aegean island."

"Mother doesn't trust people who have Rasputin eyebrows."

I laugh with her, cupping my forehead in a palm, beyond exhaustion but suddenly very clear: I know what I am going to do. "Dear Nat, you

*do have a talent for showing up at the right moment. I'm on my way.
But first I must call Davidoff and quit this fucking job."*

Peeking past me as I opened the door. "Is she home?" Ducking her
head, then beaming broad, embracing me, squeezing tight. Max
stepped back. "Look at you! California agrees." She held my hands,
eyes sparkling.
   "Natalie's blushing — "
   "You're embarrassing me." I broke away. Max laughed.
   "How long is it . . . six years? So tell me —" making a sweeping ges-
ture down her body "— any changes? Signs of decrepitude?"
   "Your hair is shorter," I stumbled. "Frizzy."
   "That's safe."
   "Makes you look like a go-gettum lawyer."
   "Not a brilliant psychologist?"
   "Really," I laughed, "you look fantastic."
She followed me gingerly down-hall to my old bedroom. "What
schmutz! Are you sorting things for the Salvation Army? You haven't
changed either, kiddo."
   "No, I really have. I'm just packing. Remember Carol? I'm moving
to her place. Being here drives me nuts; it's like reverting back. When I
am around Mother too long I start projecting her view of me onto my-
self. Ugh! I hate it."
   "What is that view?" Max's manner suddenly professional.
   "Very ambivalent. Half the time I'm a genius, the other half a
fuckup, like I'm four years old and she can't decide. People in her generation can't separate their children from themselves. They'll never see
us as solid adult people."
   "Nnnnh —" Max sat edgily on the bed, flinching when I closed the
door.
   "Relax. She isn't home. I think you have bigger problems with
Mother than I do."
   "I'm leading a ragged life now. What you out in California would
call 'intense, man.' " We laughed, that old electric attraction between
us still sparking.
   On first impression, it seemed time hadn't touched her, but looking
closely I saw a kind of shadow: lips chapped, eyes bruised with fatigue,
cheekbones more pronounced, Navajoish. "You do look worn out," I
said. "Did you really quit your job?"

"Next gig something mindlessly undemanding." She sighed dubiously. "There's the doctoral work . . . and my novel —"

"Tell me about your novel."

"I'd rather hear about your husband, Hjalstead. I picture a lanky blond Scandinavian with big white teeth, hung like a mule."

"All but the blond." I brought out the photo album from the living room: Gene laughing, an arm around Dad's shoulder, Gene mugging over a beer, Gene showing Dad how to grip an ax. Max hunched eyebrows and shot me a look, while I warred with a headful of wing-flapping demons.

"Mmm-hmmm. Good going, Bach-Hjalstead. I wouldn't kick him out of bed for eating soda crackers. Mama/Papa Bach like him, too." She studied celluloid documents of affection as if hoping to see more, not trusting the camera's fickle understanding.

"Dad loves Gene. They went fishing and stayed up late drinking Scotch when my parents came out to visit. He's improved Mother's perception of me; like she's thinking, 'My daughter couldn't really be a schlepp to have landed such a good catch.' But now that I've left him she thinks I'm a fuckup again."

Max continued browsing through pictures of our cabin, the beach, Gene atop a load of firewood. "Looks idyllic," she said.

"It is . . . in some ways."

Her brow dickered. "Y'r a rebel angel, you got no use for paradise?"

"I'm a serious painter now. Out there art is considered a form of low cost therapy, like knitting. California has a way of reducing things to the lowest common denominator. Everything is 'arty' — even their bathrooms."

"This drives you to dump a beautiful man and good life to come to New York where artists are throwing themselves on the third rail?"

I sighed. "I'm not sure I've left him. I just needed to get away. Gene is obsessed with having six kids and a cakebaking wife. I can't do that for him. I'm an artist. I don't even like kids. Aunty Berty used to say if you don't go slushy over babies you got no business having any. I think Gene feels if he doesn't have children he's failing somehow as a man. There's something he's not living up to."

"Time works wonders. One of you may change your mind."

"Not me. I've just had an abortion."

"Oy!" Giving me her dark eyes.

"Gene doesn't know. He would've tried to prevent it —" whispering as though he were next door, placing hands on my stomach. "I knew even before I'd missed a period. I felt it in there. My body was going through all these changes. It didn't seem like a baby, but an intruder growing inside me, threatening to take over my life. I wanted it out. Had to get the money myself, so I took a waitressing job. Gene felt very threatened, took it as a blow to his masculinity; because in Idaho, where he comes from, the only women who work are women who don't have a man to support them. I think he was afraid that once I became financially independent he would lose me.

"I made an appointment at a clinic in San Francisco and drove down by myself, told Gene I was going to look at galleries. It was the suction kind — local anesthetic — but they wanted to keep me in overnight. I refused; somehow drove back home. Gene never knew. Except, it was weird . . . I got into bed the moment I got home, told him I was sick. He sat on the edge of the bed next to me holding his hand on my stomach, like he had some kind of father's sixth sense. Do you think he could have —"

Max shook her head slowly, eyes brimming with compassion or sadness. She said nothing.

"It isn't the abortion I feel bad about, really. I don't buy the right-to-life garbage. What kind of life will a kid have if his mother doesn't want him around? There are already so many uncared-for kids in this world; to make such a fuss about those not born yet is insane. What about the born? Still, I felt confused afterwards, felt I was cheating Gene — making a decision I had only half a right to make."

Max shaking her head in earnest now. "It is your right," she insisted; "the woman's right to choose. Hers alone. If men want that right they will have to produce babies in test tubes. Nature didn't give them the choice."

I hugged her. "Thanks. I needed to hear that. But I do love Gene . . . I really do." Falling back on the bed, hand to my forehead. "He keeps calling, says if I don't come home soon he's coming to get me. Each time he sounds a bit more betrayed and lovelorn."

"Maybe you should go. You seem a bit lovelorn yourself."

I propped up on an elbow. "I thought you were against relationships."

"Me? Against relationships?"

"You used to say you choose your men the way men choose women — just to enjoy. A lay."

"Nu —" Max's self-mocking chuckle "— my every idle utterance returns to haunt me."

The juxtaposition of her quattrocento face, even leaner now, to jaunty decolleté blouse of polished cotton and flaring sleeves is ironic. She is trim and lovely: that flawless complexion and the perennial apples of her cheeks, scalded with good health and intensity. Crossing legs beneath her, she attempts to be cheery over the photo album as I flip through, pursuing less troubled times. Adam and the inevitable uniforms, teeth posed in a clipped regiment above the sullen lower lip. She tells me he "disinherited" her after she rejected Zionism, disinherited the entire family. "Were you having an affair with him?" she wants to know. I flip hair into her eyes. "Matchmaker. What's this?" A page from twenty years in the past: Zilla Bach in see-through negligée twining arms in the air, surrounded by her nickel-eyed offspring.
　　"Christ, was that woman a seductress."
　　Nat studies the photo, chin at a tilt. "I never thought of her as a seductress." *Her eyes prowl the room, going to the door.* "What ever happened to your friend," *she asks,* "the black guy you had a thing with on St. Marks Place? Remember?"
　　"I remember you nearly assaulted him one night. Jesse! Yes, I remember. One day he knocked on my door with his lousy camera. 'Vietnam calls,' he said, 'that's where the best shots are.' So right. Jesse was hit in the spine; he lived a few weeks, brain severed from his body, then was lucky enough to die. He always insisted that any brother stupid enough to take part in that war deserved to die." *A mound of clothes — hunched, headless torso — on the dresser drops a sleeve and I start, looking quickly away from my expression in the mirror.* "Yes, Natalie, I believe in relationships."
　　"I'm really sorry." *Her eyes go again to the door.*
　　"Maybe it's time for me to go, huh?"
　　"You just got here."
　　"You're so antsy I find it hard to relax."
　　She stretches, breasts outlined against hard fabric; her expression perched like a cat on a twig. "I feel like I'm in high school again," *she says.* "Nineteen-sixty-three!" *Seizing a pillow, she whumps me. I smack blindly back with the other, giggling like a kid. The air fills with fluff, dry and gentle snow, catching in our hair, bringing sneezes of laughter. Through a sleeve I find the mouse of an armpit and tickle till she curls*

up, bug-like; quick! have her shoulders pinned. But somehow she has me in a scissors hold — sinewy as a twelve-year-old, windfly hair and snowball-throwing face. "Uncle," I breathe. Nat punch-drunk, frilly underpants pulled over her head like a battle helmet.

I catch my breath, feeling reinvigorated. She has always been able to do that for me. "You're strong, kiddo. I'm impressed." She tells me it's from cutting firewood. I pluck feathers from her hair — monkey grooming — remember lying side by side in Central Park before she'd left for California. That time coming back like an old wound. "Why did you avoid me those last weeks before going west?" I ask.

She stares glassily upward, pleasure slowly draining from her features. At last, turns to me almost coyly. "You still haven't told me about your novel. I'd like to hear about it. Really!"

"Would you? It's historical, a romance about Boston marriages."

"What's a Boston marriage?"

"In the last century, before the current rash of homophobia, enduring affairs between women were admired as an advanced form of human relationship: lifelong companionships, often platonic, and if sexual, not carnal anyway. The book combines two romans à clef. One based on an affair of George Sand; the other . . . well, contemporary."

"You mean homosexuals?"

"Homosexuals, lesbians . . . people!"

She shrugs. "Sounds like it'll make you rich and famous."

"Doubtful. Anglo-Saxon males are terribly threatened by same-sex friendships. Any suggestion that women might prefer a relationship based on equality and trust gets them panicky."

"Women can have that with a man, too, you know."

"I didn't say they couldn't."

She pulls away, sitting up. "How can you write sex scenes between women?"

"With plenty moans, groans and flashing teeth."

Nat broods over cigarette smoke, nostrils dilated. "All this gay stuff that's become the big rage doesn't interest me. Just another decadence of a culture that stuffs its face while two-thirds of the world starves." Her eyes touching me, askance.

The front door slams, Zilla Bach's voice sing-songing. I hesitate a moment, baffled, time-lost — seems just yesterday I last heard that voice. Then I'm up. "Where can I go?" Falling to my knees, peeking under the bed: hopeless. Zilla calling again nearly outside the door.

"Where?" I demand, sotto voce. Nat regards me, face puckered, pick-
led in amusement. "Damn you, Nat." I lunge for the closet, crushing
boxes, suffocating in a subway crush of fur, manage to close the door
just as her mother's voice enters the room.

"Golly, were you talking to yourself?" she asks.

Through the door crack she appears no older, hair maybe blonder.
She gapes at panties capped over her daughter's ears and giggles. "Is
that what you use them for?" Nat sputters. "Y'r giddy," her mother re-
bukes, eyes sweeping the room — over clothes piles and furniture
dusted in a light snow of feathers. She finds the gutted pillow, holds its
split carcass away from her like a dead animal. "Jeepers!" Looking at
Nat in bewilderment. "Did you bang it?"

Nat, damn her! glances at the closet and squawks, "I had a hard
night last night." I barely suppress a burp of laughter. Zilla's eyes flash.
"You popped it all over," she says, puzzling whether it's possible.
"Can't you pack up? You need a suitcase." Her glacial blue geist and
stolid chin are instantly inches away through the door crack; I panic
back into the crowd of coats. Zilla's face replaced by a dark head; Nat
insisting the suitcase isn't there; scuffling sounds, giggles. Nat bargains:
"You go get the vacuum, I'll pack up." Her mother sits on the bed,
catching her breath. She nods at my closet. "D'you have a fella in
there?"

Tempted to tell her the truth, but I nodded "yes." Mother's face
tight as she went out, turning at the door. "Doesn't it bother you to entertain in such a rumpus?"

"Just go, Mother."

Max emerged, candle-white, gesturing at a dark blotch forming moth
wings around her crotch. "I peed —" she spluttered. We made huge
gulpy laughter like actors in a silent film while she changed into a pair
of my jeans and a sweatshirt, tucked hair up into a cap I'd found and
swaggered down the hall — not looking back to see if Mother was
watching.

Next day I moved to Carol's.

Crazy iconoclastic Carol had been replaced by a Park Avenue prima
donna who had abandoned painting, married a corporate type, and
lived in a sprawling apartment furnished with spoils of European an-
tique safaris. She had a daughter and a heavy social schedule. Of Al,
whom she had married soon after leaving New Art, she said, "He was

wearing more money on his feet than I paid in six months rent. I was in
love." As we talked in a snobbish room that could have been Paris, an
au pair girl in a mod pantsuit led a pouty miniCarol in to see
"Mummy," who pecked angel's forehead and tousled blonde braids, till
the little girl shrugged her off and returned to Nanny's hem, slitting
eyes at me as if I were a rival sibling. Carol chatted French with the *au
pair*, finally dismissed them with a caramel smile, blowing a kiss at her
precious, saying, "Now maybe you see why I find life so fulfilling." I
wondered what movie she thought she was in. It had been charming
when she was younger.

She wanted to take me to the Four Seasons. I suggested the Figaro in
the Village. "Always the *déclassé*," she said, giving me a ceramic smile.

"It isn't *déclassé*. It's my *life*."

Her husband Al regarded me in unconcealed amusement, but attracted, too — the attraction men of his type feel for the woman who
won't play along — with his blue sloop jaw and songbird eyes. He spoke
as if delivering an endless news release. Oddly, I found myself becoming
aroused. Maybe I just wanted to knock the complacency from his eyes?
Maybe I'd been away from Gene too long?

One morning Carol lectured: "I can dig the *Lady Chatterley's Lover*
thing, but you can't seriously expect to make a life with your Montana
mountain man. Y'r a sophisticated New Yorker. Find yourself a reliable
dude who can pay for the groceries."

"Someone like Al, you mean?"

She shrugged. "Al's a sweetheart. A wonderful daddy."

"I don't want a sugardaddy, Carol. I'm my own person."

She laughed, a fragile, glazed sort of laugh and quickly changed sub-
jects. But she had touched a nerve.

Maybe Carol was right: I had little in common with Gene and his
woodsplitting life. Maybe I'd come east for good. Those last weeks in
California, after the abortion, our relationship had been more that of
uneasy roommates than of man and wife. Though I couldn't disagree
when Mother said, "I believe you still love him, honey. You shouldn't
throw that away; it's the most precious thing in the world." Mom/Dad,
heartbroken when I told them I was thinking of leaving Gene for good,
begged me to call at once and assure him I would be back soon. I had
backed out of the apartment, apprehended by their eager, flushed faces,
promising: "It'll work out . . . don't worry." Wondering how I had ever
imagined I could make mature decisions while staying with my parents.

Carol's crinoline guestroom was the perfect incubator of nightmares. Babies pouting blue lips, umbilicals tangled around their tiny necks. Gene pursuing me through endless subway cars; just as he reached out for me, I would wake up. Lying in dark polluted with milky light, hearing the citychatter outside, I thought I'd returned to an earlier time — California no more than a dream. Then, remembering, would begin to tremble, missing Gene's warm body. I tortured myself rehashing the evening I'd told him I was going to New York. Sitting on the bed dressing for work, pulling on nylons, the words I'd painstakingly rehearsed jumbling out. "What's the big rush?" Gene had said lightly. "We can go next spring — both of us."

"I'm going now," I said quietly.

"What's now?" Gene was puzzled.

"My career is now. I'm tired of waiting. The isolation is driving me nuts."

Sitting beside me, his carpenter's hand made a slow rasp to my breast. "I yam a Noo Yawker . . . I yam too good f'r dose boonie San Francisco galleries —"

I pushed him off. "I'm serious about this."

"And I'm seriously telling you there's no money for New York."

"I have the money."

He watched as I wiggled into tights, eyes smoke blue against the wood of his face. "That's why you've been working?" he asked, watching as I dropped a skirt over my head. "That the only reason you got to run off to New York City, damned art galleries?"

"That's the only reason —" rotating skirt on my hips, offering him a Fifth Avenue smile "— I'm sure I'll see my friends, too."

Gene studied me in his inimitable manner — half hangdog, half intimidation — motionless; eyes alone moving like slow suns across the arcs of sockets. "Which friends you planning to see?"

I turned on him. "Look, I just need a little time to myself. I need to think things over." Feeling all that tension in my face, just wanting to get out.

Gene came behind as I was brushing my hair, clamped arms around my waist, nuzzling in between brush strokes. "My little meshugga —" he cooed, a reek of stale sweat and sawdust, a smell I have liked, charging the dull air, his hands making moves. I tried to slide away, but he held me tight.

"I have to go to work."

"Screw it tonight, baby," he pleaded.

I sensed my resolve losing its gristle before his vulnerability. "Gene!" I had snapped. "You're messing up my clothes." Sighing hard, he dropped his arms — eyes sliding across room to the door that seemed to open out to almost anywhere.

"Sometimes I don't think I know you anymore."

I turned and fumbled with his collar, touched the creases in his cheeks. "It's not forever, honey, just a few weeks." Couldn't stand it, everything gone artificial, writing myself these crappy stage directions. His eyes damp, devoid of all the hope and playfulness of the Gene I had married. Taking his hand, I placed it on my stomach — almost as if I wanted to tell him the truth. I heard his sharp curse as I went out. Something crashed against the door.

Now Carol gave me continuous phone messages from California. And I despised the part of him that skulked about like a jackal through my conscience. I prowled former haunts hoping to regain some of my old independence; Gene was always there first — through the turbojet roar of motorcycles, last dregs of Hells Angels and hippies on St. Marks Place, blacklight spilling from adult novelty shops, girls with blooming acne faces sitting open-legged on stoops, sullen pink eyes watching as I slipped past. On Second Avenue derelicts thrust filthy palms in my face. Pay up! they demanded. My eyes dodging over to find Gene watching me from a newsstand across the street. Life offers no escape. I touched the flatland of my belly. Maybe motherhood is the apple of our eye; I would return and have a baby in a living room full of cheery friends, pattycake and applecan . . . now and then paint a watercolor rose.

Passing the Studio School one day, I was struck with a startlingly limpid memory of Ron Sterges, my painting teacher in those long-ago days — his handsome, subtly effete features — and how his eyes kept coming to me as he lectured. Some electricity had worked between us. One night I had fallen asleep in class, was awakened by Ron tapping my shoulder. "Go home," he had whispered, as if those two words promised everything. Terribly embarrassed, I had thrown my things together and hurried out. Ron abandoned his class and caught up with me. We went for a drink. After that we had gone out together several times to bars and coffeehouses. But, though he'd made fervid love to me with his eyes, nothing really happened. I was living with pig Marty so couldn't comfortably invite him home. For some reason he didn't invite me.

Now whenever Gene entered my thoughts I called up Ron, recalling how touched I had been by his shy, gentlemanly style, about him an existential sadness I have always associated with good lovers. As days passed and I sensed Gene's long-distance uneasiness, my walks often led me past the Studio School. One afternoon I entered; for nostalgia's sake, I convinced myself, but then was studying a class schedule. Ron was still teaching. Once they've found a job or apartment, New Yorkers don't let go.

I hesitated in an agony of doubt and anticipation just outside the classroom door, freezing when I heard his gentle voice coaxing a student just inside. Peeking slowly around, I saw the hips of the nude model on her mat, Ron's tangled brown hair. I leapt away, paced fast down the hall. Reaching the front door, I looked out at determined pedestrians along Eighth Street, thought of Max striding into the café where we'd met for coffee the day before. She too had that New Yorker's furious gait — as if throwing herself in the path of fate. Her dark eyes nearly cynical as I tried to explain why I'd left Gene and come east, uptilting her chin as if to ask, *What do you want from me?* Dubious as he had been. So that I ended blabbering about the closeness of our marriage, making no sense even to myself, was left feeling rejected, stung by her remoteness. The same old husk of our relationship.

I turned and tiptoed back to his room, sick with anticipation. Ron had called a break and was just emerging with the model, now in her robe, for a smoke. He excused himself and came directly over to me. "How are you?" he asked, as if it had been only weeks since we last met.

"You remember me?"

"You're kidding —" gallantly taking my hand. I giggled and asked about his work. "I'm seeking a gallery now," he said. "Same old obsession. I recently had an offer in L.A." His lips puckered.

"I'm looking for a gallery, too," I admitted, agreeing with him about California. Art with sand in its hair. His eyes had hooked me again. "You're making me nervous," I said.

Ron touched my arm and said he had to get back to class. "I want you to come to dinner Friday. I'd like to show you my work." I told him I'd love to see it. We embraced, locking lips with a hunger that astonished us both.

Friday night a cab deposited me amid warehouses in the squalor of Tribeca. I was admitted to a loft building: a dim, filthy stairwell off of which Ron's door opened in a lightscream. He kissed prissily Frenchish on both cheeks, welcoming me to a gun-barrel room pinned in place by the reverberant glare of highly glazed canvases along the walls. It was entry to a sideshow of carnal heat: skin-varnished nudes spread-eagled, pink genital lips smiling between double moustaches, each hair meticulously painted; breasts held an auto fender sheen and bellies caved under the weight of light. A foreshortened man sprawled on a grainy beach, his vein-bulging cock like a carrot before outstretched lips of a deformed woman perched on his shoulders, her bulbous ass leering out at the viewer, lit by nylon jewels of her panties. Ron studied my reaction. Then, very quietly, said, "I don't believe you've met my wife."

I turned, startled. For a second couldn't find her; she was hidden behind a tablelamp. A sparrowish woman in a wheelchair, arms, legs and torso shriveled, like a flimsy toy wearing a woman's head, lips a bright carmine swipe. I shot a hand at her in awkward greeting. She touched it limply, giving me a fleeting sad smile. Then stared — not so much hostilely as with unapologetic dissection. Deep mauve eye hollows gave her a sagelike, nearly Eastern aura. I was greatly relieved when she turned finally to her husband and said, "She's young." I released a coiled laugh, insisting, "Not as young as people think."

I suffered through a meal, while Ron talked, unable to shake fascination with his wife — her birdquick movements, spindly froggish arms, head canted painfully to one side. Noticing this, he said, "Belva is a marvelous cook, don't you think?" She smiled at him; I nodded a vigorous "yes" and guzzled wine. When he gestured at his paintings, my eyes followed, then leapt immediately away. No escape in that Guernica of flesh. Even the goulashy stuff on my plate seemed part of a conspiracy to some bizarre consummation; conversation a mere social form, I understood, having nothing to do with the real reason for my visit. I became quickly soused, almost laughed when he began discussing his work with two-thumbed art critic's adjectives, bristled when he said he hoped I had moved away from that neo-expressionism kick I'd been on.

"Why should I move away?"

"It isn't what artists are doing now," he said smugly.

"It's what I am doing and I'm an artist."

His wife's eyes flashed at me, he laughed. I couldn't understand what I had found attractive in him. Here in his nest, with that deformed bird of a wife, his shyness was supplanted by breezy self-importance. When he started cleaning up, I carried dishes to the sink. A tiny painting peeped from among teas and spices: Belva, a Yorkshire terrier on her knees, a lusty smile, not a trace of deformity. "A beautiful woman, isn't she?" His voice a surprise at my ear. "Good days. California days."

I looked into the full need of his smile, thick muff of blond hair spilling from the open shirt collar. "What happened?" I whispered.

"Muscular dystrophy," he answered absently, his eyes basking on the beach of my lips. "You're lovely . . . beautiful." I wasn't able to break the current between us. Behind me dishes clattered; I slid away. Wife Belva gazing down at her plate. Ron bustled, washing up, wheeling his wife beneath a floor lamp beside a stack of dogeared magazines. She began thumbing through. "Will you be all right?" he asked. She nodded. Businesslike, he pulled a screen across the room, bisecting it, and summoned me to his side. I followed in a sort of trance, a suspension of belief, as he closed the screen on the crow movements of her arms, isolating us in what was ostensibly a bedroom — a low leopard spread bed appearing by inspiration, as did everything in this quixotic realm. "A bit makeshift," he shrugged. "I hope you won't mind." Studiedly fingering a stray curl off my forehead. "Would you like to make love?"

"Your wife is right in there!" I protested.

He made no attempt to lower his voice. "It gives her pleasure." Stepping close, he fingered the top button of my blouse. My hand moved reflexively: the slap of skin on skin hanging in the room.

"What kind of person do you think I am?"

"Please don't be upset —" rubbing his cheek. " — Please! I thought you understood . . . " It seemed he might cry.

I retreated through the partition. The tiny woman glanced up at me, cloying sadness in her eyes. "Please!" she echoed. Only then did I realize that a nude directly above her, lounging on an air mattress, wore her features, though a body too voluptuous for even her healthiest days. To my horror so did every other figure across that Tenderloin of eroticism — her face again and again in black, California brown and Russian white . . . the Everywoman of their common tragedy in all those glossy smiles shooing me out the door.

Into New York . . . the sleep in Mother's eye corners as she answers the bell. "Natalie!" Dad coming down hall, looking very Semitic at this hour of surprise, like a guard sniffing for danger at a border post. "Are you all right, honey?" Eliot was wrong, I answer, August is the cruelest month. New York, the rasp in Dad's throat . . . the queer who winks haughty as a princess on the corner of Canal Street as I flee that couple's abjection, feeling somehow morally inadequate — even ashamed.

(How often was that tableau enacted? Students he met at coffeehouses, black ones, white ones. Did she smile up from her magazine as his lover emerged buttoning her blouse? Point the way to the bathroom? Offer tea?) I consider returning. Kindness has many faces. A black prostitute laughs silkenly — not at me exactly but at my vulnerability, that a woman should be walking these streets alone at night without she have to . . . at my womanhood. New York! Feeling at that instant a compassion big enough to wrap its arms around this whole impossible dream of a city. I hurry on.

What time is it? Perhaps what year? And is it maybe her Forty-second Street beach bum she is fleeing middle of the night instead of a husband? Probably on his way to New York right now. I don't want his child . . . any child! *"Let me break in one second, do you want a brandy? If we're going to be up all night —"* "You're the only person I can talk to. Not Mother and her platitudes or Carol and her sugar-daddy. Maybe I should go back to California. Don't you see how they always force their trips on us? We're their fucks and freaks. Don't you see how humiliated she must be, crippled up helpless as a bean? They never really care; the final solver is the little Nazi between their legs. Self-satisfied bastard! telling me my work is passé. Right, art is passé. Nothing left but businessmen. Christos and Warhols. Promoters. It's what America deserves. But not me." *(Hand thrust to chest)* "I'm no ad agency." *"Right! Let's get some sleep. I'd like to go to Connecticut tomorrow. Mom has driven Dad up to Boston, Harvard Medical School. We'd have the run of the place."*

Her face a moody, waning half-moon in the aureole thrown by a desk lamp. "You can have the couch," *I tell her.* "Believe me, it's the first time it's been cleared off in months."

"I'm horny," *Nat says grumpily, pitching eyes as though it's my fault.*

Morning cacophony of traffic, pink Dolly Varden hat yanked down Janis Joplin style over her eyes, brim flopping in the breeze as I drive my invalid wagon up the Major Deegan, along that urban girdle of huge despair — shattered windows, smoke curdled against a smutty blue sky, and the sweet, incongruous aroma of Stella d'Oro cookies — before the Taconic uncoils its green tongue, and Nat shouting over the blare of a rock station that friend Carol is obsessively pushing her to have a kid. "She takes it as a personal affront that I'm committed to painting instead of homehood. I tell her it's a choice I've made. But no one trusts artists willing to make sacrifices for their work anymore. That's why today's art is so uninspired. Gutless."

"That can be debated —"

"America can't produce great art anymore. Everything has become hype. Money/Success. Artists don't have time to develop; they remain in permanent adolescence. And if you do hit you have to stay right where you are, repeating yourself ad nauseam. It's all just gimmicks now. One trend after another, like pop music."

"And artists have nothing to say about it?"

"If you don't follow along — or you lack the current certified point of view — you won't show at all," *she says, perhaps ignoring my question, perhaps in brooding reply.* "Sometimes I think Americans despise true individuality. It makes them nervous. Even the artists! We complain so much about the Russians that we've stopped looking at ourselves. Maybe what we see in Russia is really just our own reflection."

"Consider it a compliment to be left out then. Sounds to me like a moral choice."

Onto the Taconic now, trees crouched sullen and heavy along shoulders, as if anticipating the approaching heat and humidity. Nat stares ahead, defying the green tunnel boring its way north, her tone muggy in resentment. "I want to show my work. Every artist does."

"Show then, by all means. On the street if you must —"

"I mean really show!"

"Nu, you want to be radical, just don't want to pay the radical's price."

Her forehead tautens. "You're the one who doesn't want to pay the price," *she mutters.* "Isn't that why you're getting your doctorate, to be able to publish? You know, I used to have really high hopes in you. Every time I went into a bookstore I'd find myself drifting towards the P's in the novel racks. But I never saw your book —"

I swerve just in time to miss the huge American deathship embezzling my lane, license plate "TONY 3," a pair of teeth grinning back from the suicide seat, reach for a cigarette from her pack on the dashboard but gag on the smoke and crush it out. "Sorry to have disappointed you, Natalie."

We ride on a while, tires clomp. Her eyes flicker at me, like the highway center line. "I didn't mean it like that," *she says.* "I still think you can write a masterpiece."

I build her a smile. "I'm glad you have faith in me."

White lines blink beneath us — an ellipsis, flick flick flick; Nat offers a joint, sinsemilla she calls it, from the coast. "A friend in California says I'm down on women," *she tells me.* "That's because for years I've been comparing other women to you and they always disappoint me."

Wheeling onto a side road where maples wait, a breeze stirs corn tassels, cicadas fiddle their hearts out in woodlots — a great big God Bless America chorus, enough to make any city dweller giddy. "I don't want to spoil your rapport with other women," *I tell her. Her eyes dig imperative into my territory — blimp barns, cow caucuses, sweet-sour of manure . . . nothing distracts them.*

"*I wish we could just relax.*"

Nat takes a lungful of smoke, closing her eyes. "I'm relaxed."

"*I'd love to go swimming later.*"

Her eyes open. "I thought we were going for a drive."

"*We'll drive. We can stop in Danbury on the way back. Don't you want we should go skinny-dipping?*"

Nat works the landscape. "I'm starving," *she moans.*

JIM'S LUNCH. Flyspecks, copulative initials cut into a wooden table, sunlight splashing her uplifted face as she watches pickups pass. Air thickened by the unnerving thrum of flies. She says I look good today, "getting back that old Pearlman luster." *Dollops of mustard like small flowers at corners of her mouth.*

"Thanks, Nat. I needed that."

Max smiled and swatted at a plump fly, studied a family just emerging from a car displaying Midwestern plates. "Gene would drool over you," I said. "Dark Jewish women with big tits are his weakness. All women are Gene's weakness." Max's a cappella laughter on the limp air bringing the suspicious eyes of the family from Peoria.

"Remember," I said, "how everyone at Whitman fell in love with you? Allie and Ellie and all the other twits buzzing around Miss P.; while you sat back and laughed at us."

"*All right, kiddo, you've made up for any ego damage —*" touching the knuckles of my hand "*— I'm enjoying this. Finally getting some sun.*" She rolled the peasant blouse off her shoulders, exposing bleached skin at the bell of breasts, beneath a chocolate dark collarbone, cinnamon freckles sprinkled profligately down her cleavage.

"Woo-wooo, cheesecake!" I cried, tickling her with a straw. Max giggled, glancing aslant at the Midwestern family — taut Pat Nixon smiles, cartons of soggy fries and wilted burgers.

"*Hey, kiddo, it's muggyhot. I'd like to get in the water. Oy, these artists: talktalktalk.*"

"I wanted to ask you something —"

Her eyebrows arched, expectant, chin hammocked on linked fingers over the ruins of lunch. Midwestern faces chewed and stared.

"Were you and Lucy having an affair? I'm just curious. Richard said you were."

Her eyes juggled me; she made a sighing sound in her throat. "*Is it an obsession with you to scratch in all the scrappy corners of my life? Listen, Richard had a rich fantasy life.*"

"I think you were, too."

Predictable as cows plodding across road on shit-stained haunches, turning earthen eyes on us, lowing sweet breath, feathered wings of sumac along ditches crackling in afternoon heat; Nat's eyes fixed ahead on a road traipsed with baked mud where tractors have crossed, not a word spoken since the snack bar. She lolls smoke in her cheeks before expelling it in a spout at the windshield. A woman now, womanly imperative. I sigh.

"*If you must know, Natalie, I had a bleak affair in college. A psychology teaching assistant. I was in love; she was adding notches to her belt —*" *glancing at the outback handsome farmer who shoos cows from the road and motions us on with country graciousness* "*— Later it was the same affair, but another lover. The basis for the contemporary portion of my novel. Nothing to do with your fads. A rich, wonderful relationship. But if it satisfies some prurient fascination in you . . . I suppose, yes, it qualifies me as homosexual.*"

"You mean bisexual."

"*Does that redeem it?*"

Her brow a troubled mosaic. She smokes, eyes ponder the scenery. "Sometimes," *she says,* "I used to think you were coming on to me. I wasn't ever sure . . . like the time you asked me to take a shower —"

"*I don't recall any shower.*"

She is agitated, nipping at a cigarette, voice just nudging resentment. "You were a paragon to me. Brainy and beautiful and really knew what you wanted. You had strong moral convictions. Compared to you everyone else seemed wishywashy. You cared about other people; that impressed me. I thought: this is what a woman should be. Hoped some of your qualities would rub off on me."

"*Jesus, I don't know if I'm up to this.*"

"It isn't funny to me, Max."

"*It was an adolescent crush, for shitsake —*" *wheeling hard around a tractor pulling a wagon load of pulvered green, a teenage boy waving his cap from the high seat* "*— d'you think I wasn't aware of it?*"

"You sure were. You teased and played hard to get."

"*I can't keep up. First I'm a saint, now fairy teacher out to seduce teenage student.*" *Snatching a look at her. Sullen eyes fixed on the broken center stripe, like a tear line extending back through memory. I speak gently.* "Your affection had an impact on me, Natalie. What could you expect?"

"I didn't expect anything. I never knew what you wanted, had to get away from your influence to find out who I am."

"*Have you found out?*"

Driving on in tense silence through that pacific landscape of centenary barns and old women tying up tomatoes.

"I'd like to go back," *she mutters.*

"*Hey listen, I'm enjoying this: rustling corn stalks, air full of green grass. Maybe y'r jaded with all that California?*"

She shrugs, averting her face into the brunt of leafy wind, hair shotgunned, settling again into the solace of movement. Something works in her. "You weren't the only reason I went to Israel —" *Wanting me to press it.*

"*I'm a real believer in secrets,*" *I assure her.*

"I had an affair with my friend Barbara, the sculptor. I was all fucked up . . . all that garbage Mother laid on me. Almost killed myself. Dr. Kaufman thought I should get away." *She peeks from behind a lattice of fingers, perspiration forming a tiara of glistening opals across her scalp.* "I couldn't even say good-bye to you." *Wind snatches her words.*

Through fingercracks, Max sits tensed above the wheel, hair limp and curl-swollen, *Semitisch* eyebrows fusing at the pout of her brow. Why had I exaggerated the Barbara thing? Like a teenage kid wanting to be hip. Maxine insisting that close friendships always include sexual feelings. "*It's nothing shameful.*"

"I felt ashamed. A lot of people would. Gene freaked out when I told him my feelings. Later he kept pushing a thing with Gypsy, *ménage d trois.* He said it might help me figure this thing out. One night she came over; we were all stoned and took off our clothes, just messing around. At first it was kind of exciting, but then she was touching me and kissing and Gene kept insisting, 'Go ahead, I want to watch.' I realized it was his trip, not mine at all. Really sleazy. Told them to leave me alone. Later Gene said I was aroused, I just couldn't relax. But it isn't true. I have to feel something for the person to be aroused." Max's fingers tapped the steering wheel — trapped, impatient energy. "I think I could've been aroused —"

The car swerved onto a shoulder, gravel screaming like her anger. *"You can't agonize so much over these things. The libido doesn't share our compunctions. That's facts! I don't give a damn what husband Gene or Mother Bach says."* Sitting sidesaddle, a prim, captured posture, bare knees pinned under the wheel. I escaped her eyes to a wriggly white scar crawling up a tan thigh.

"Maybe I am queer."

"That's an ugly word. Nobody's queer."

"What do you call it then, lovemaking?"

"I call it fucking."

Holding her eyes a moment before turning away. "That's sick."

"Why did you tell me you'd had an affair with Barbara?"

I turned my head to the window. "Leave me alone."

"What is it you want from me, Natalie?"

Turning on her. "I want you to stay out of my dreams. You call Mother a seductress . . . you're the seductress. You manipulate people, you have a kind of power. Even now you're using it."

"I am?" Hands folded like wings to her chest. *"Believe me, I want nothing to do with your dreams. I think y'r projecting a whole lot, kiddo."*

"Don't call me a kid. I'm not taking that patronizing crap from you anymore."

A fury of swollen red eyes and puffy cheeks, she sulks, palming away loose tears, half growling, "Mother always said you were a witch."

"The feeling is mutual." I turn onto Highway Eighty-four, east, towards Danbury, still the upside of afternoon. "It's been a losing day —" muttering perhaps to myself "— first a failed writer, then fairy child molester, now a witch!" We ride for miles without a word. Finally I speak (at her back, not certain she is listening). "All right, imagine I did

have an affair with Lucy. Why must it be the seamy debauch that you apparently envision? Neither of us is that kind of person. Sure, there's sex — maybe wonderful crazy erotic . . . I would hope. But there's love, too. We might conceivably grow as close as you and Gene have grown."

She turns slowly, the cool judgment of Dresden blue eyes, heavy lids fanning. "Am I s'posed to be impressed or something?"

Her light tone an immense relief; like a swallow I find myself gliding down the slope of my malaise, then sprinting upward with a cautious laugh. "Wha'd'you think? Swim time? We could use a cooling out."

"I was only a kid, you know," *she says defensively.* "Maybe I was infatuated. How could I have known what the consequences would be?"

"Do you think anyone knows? I was infatuated too, Natalie, mostly with your infatuation." I sigh. "All this sludge raking. Ugh! I thought we came for some fun. Do you remember last time I invited you to Connecticut? You refused to come."

"I'm still not going to come."

"I'm only teasing, dummy."

"I don't like that kind of teasing."

Pushing eyes at her. "Listen, dear, if I had wanted you I could have had you long ago. We both know that."

She studies me a long moment, brow dented, then curls into a shoulder of the seat, into herself. After a time, her breath comes in a soft rattle. Though when we swing off the highway onto Connecticut back roads, she sits straight up, pigeon-eyed. "I have to get back to the city," *she insists, her groggy innocence almost touching.*

"It will be marvelous: the pool and barbecued sirloins —"

"I didn't bring my suit."

"Don't be silly."

Suburban glitz: picture windows spoiling lines of a Tudor manor, statuette of a black boy in jockey garb — with antebellum white teeth and an arm stuck out in permanent erection. Out back, the pool a Hollywood turquoise. Max carries dewy cold beer out to the patio; we spread towels on warm terracotta in sunlight softened by the green of grass and maples and share a joint in quick little sips. *"You've been trying to get me stoned all day,"* she mumbles, lying back, eyes closed, smoke a mischievous djinni leaking from her nostrils. "Gene's the beer drinker," I say, sipping, while Max downs hers in two glugs. Unbuttons blouse, rises and unsnaps shorts, letting them slither down tan legs, stands hands-a-hip, sunlight glazing planes of her body. *"Did we come to swim?"* I nod at a house just visible through the hedge.

"I'm not wearing any underwear."

Max's tinkly laugh. *"Sounds very California."* Gesturing at her sheer bra and panties — blur of nipples and dark pubic smudge. *"What does this hide? Listen, Mr. Jarboe doesn't see that well, even with binoculars. You may fool him completely. On Monday, he'll ask Dad who was the fellow swimming with Maxie Saturday."*

"Just for that I'm not going in at all."

"Chicken!" Prodding me with a toe. She grabs suddenly at the hem of my shirt; I scream and hold on tight. Then she's doing a Las Vegas shimmy along the pool rim, wiggling her ass, reaching back to unhook bra and burlesquing it slowly for the mysterious Mr. Jarboe. She is sexual hyperbole, epitomizing the song Gene used to sing: *"My gal's a corker, she's a New Yorker ..."* Hips too hippy, udder tits, eagle's nest cunt. I begin to giggle. For an instant panties form a puddle at her feet, then she steps away almost daintily, giving me the apartment white wink of her ass as she knifes smoothly into green water — bra abandoned over pool rim, one strap a snake, buoyant on shivering ripples.

I slip off my shirt and lie back. Sun groggy hot, mixing with smoke and beer, a bird chirps, Max's hands slap water ... me drifting down river through frogbelch and dragonfly rattle, rowboat gently rocking ... Waves clatter like broken pottery about our waists — Marty Carol Juli Max leaping high, tits bouncing, shrieking surprise as Poseidon tackles them, the Aegean! Fishermen cheering from rocks ... *Down!* she barks, *Natalie, your ass is a frosted lightbulb. Get down! Sweethard*, they cry, *My sweethard*, olive brown faces; all of us tumbling giddy in a meringue of foam ... Whir of a lawnmower, Huntington Park. Though it's not Mother but Maxine standing naked at pool edge, smoothing black coils of hair, her body seemingly oiled, Bathsheba brown and prosperous in womanhood — a bit thicker-waisted than when Dad painted his "Maxine Series" from imagination: manstrong thighs, black swirl at the crotch of an arm, bright bloom of nipples. A woman to seduce Psalms from his soul. Eyelids closed in a tiny smile against the sun, she slides a slow hand, herding water beads down across tummy towards a glistening pubic fleece. It's as if she wears a transparent bikini — pale breasts and bottom against darker ambient skin — and I wonder why she has fibbed, claiming she gets no sun. She is watching me, sun dots shimmying across her face, coalescing in sluggish rivers, infinity of liquid light. I turn queasily onto my stomach (I shouldn't drink beer) and drowse. Awakening to a cold tickle down my spine, a tiny damp tongue.

Sneak thief! filling her curiosity with my belly, breasts, swell of thighs. Hey listen, you with the peacock feather, we're no longer kids in a tent behind the house. Fidgety, your mouth O'd, a dried pool in the sun, jeans a blue puddle around calves. I chuckle when you flip onto your belly and those jeans flip with you. I have given up on laps, not so much out of shape as intent. Sit rubbing lotion into your pinkening flesh — while you toss and mutter, burning up, kiddo, that delicate Ashkenazi hide guzzling lotion. Such a lovely back, Natalie. I squeeze a lazy bead down your spine, knead the warm white dimpled hemispheres — fingers shying from between your thighs, peek-a-boo of pubic fluff. The sun on my shoulders: Helios reining horses fiercely before his red plunge to the west. I whisper you over. The dreamer moans, turns with a protesting exhalation onto her back, eyes blinking wide a moment. "Y'r burning up," I whisper. Fingertips trace the flaming V of collarbone, bump down the washboard between recumbent breasts, crush blonde fuzz in the sink of your belly; bubbles pucking from lotion bottle lips as I daub breasttips — pink baby mouths, the slightest pout. You squint, neither acceptance nor surrender, mouth drawn either in pleasure or feeble pain. Beneath my fingers your nipples tauten to copper cones. Your lips quiver.

Trying to say no . . . but time moves too slowly, her breasts pendulum like watch fobs, dark-eyed with milk white bellies, Scotch whiskey whisper of fingertips, voicedrone mesmeric as Dad and Mr. Cherry — warmly gently motherly sisterly spreading slow numbness up my spine. What are you doing? I lick papery lips but can't lift my head, heat-drunk, eyelids stupefied under the white weight of sunlight . . . and cool wonderful lotion at my thighs, fingertips wedging discreet, just touching me there. A jolt that gallops up the Saratoga of nerves. But now she is sitting erect in a cocoa butter shimmer, half-smiles at a job well done, cross-legged, skin shining warmgolden, nipple shafts like twin sundials throwing identical shadows. I touch her knee.

"Don't stop . . ."

Eyes wavering unsure over my body, coming with soft hope to my face. "Please —" I whisper; courage quick-going, leaving me limp as I

think of Gene . . . husband. A shock! like the thick nap of her quim —
so close. On her knees, one sure finger compassing a breast. *"The little
hairs are sexy,"* Max whispers, bending close, frizzy hair tickling my
neck. And I gasp as she kisses me there.

*Salt-sweet, sweat and lotion. But something has happened. She
tenses, sits straight, eyes frightened rabbits, blinking accusal. "Your
turn." I motion the suntan bottle, but she shoves it away, works jeans
up over her ass and is up, weaving unsteady, plunging into the pool.
Nat surfaces: an otter, magician of mood changes, startled by the cold
water. She wears an expression borrowed from her mother, relegating
me to the smallest pocket of concern. Little cunt. Takes a few brisk
strokes but falters, flails. The jeans, I realize; the nut has gone swimming in her jeans. Her head ducks under. I am about to go in after her
when jeans come out over the side with a hard slap.*

The smell water has on summer afternoons — I remember since a
kid at camp. Max emerges from the house, wearing panties which ride
high up one buttock, forming crinkles as she walks. *"I put the steaks out
to defrost,"* she says, eyes bumping at me. Shadows have begun to
stretch across the yard. I roll onto my back, water slipping across my
stomach. She sits on the pool rim, immodest as St. Marks stoopgirls, lazily kicking her feet and sipping a beer, back arched in a cover girl pose,
breasts pushed high, russet coronas troubling me with forbidden fascination — like summercamp sun that can scar your retinas if you stare,
so you can't help staring. She licks a moustache of lotion from her
upper lip and smiles.

"Don't look at me like that," I protest. "The way Mother used to
look at me when I was in the bathtub."

"Natalie's shy —"

"She said I'd always have little boobs, like she was putting a life-long
hex on them."

"You have lovely breasts."

I swat a lapful of water at her. Max frowns and stands up, wipes peevishly at water beads. Walks over to inspect the grill.

"Just forget it, all right? I don't like being pushed."

"Pushed!" Her eyes flash under ringlets tumbling down forehead.
"I'm pushing something?" She thrusts arms into a robe and snaps the
band of panties which cling obscenely, stained now with the wet dark of
her pubis. I look away.

"What do you want, Natalie?" Her voice taut, straining.

"Nothing. I don't want anything. Could we just forget it?"

Little tease, lolling from stomach to back, coy as a seal flirting for food, water laking at navel, pooling about breast cones, cunt hair whorled in a glazed peak. You aren't a kid anymore; I don't trust the sham of innocence — with your hair splayed wantonly over the water. I return to the house. When I emerge Nat sits on a pool step, arms hugged tight around her.

"Are you planning to stay in there all night? For chrissake, Nat, you're shivering."

"Something's happened," *she mumbles, staring across water.* "I sense it." *Looks up at me.* "I really have to get back."

"What, no barbecue? You should see them: thick red sirloins."

"Something's happened!" *she insists.* "I think maybe Gene is in New York."

"You're becoming hysterical. Relax." *(She stares through me, eyes glassy, feverish.)* "Listen, I'd like to lie down a while, then we can decide whether to barbecue or go back. But I think you should get out of the water."

Obediently, she climbs the stairs, arms clasped over her girl's breasts, hair pasted to shoulders. Neither quite child nor woman — even in nakedness. "Can I use the phone?" *she asks.*

Shadows fill the house, cavish relief from the sultry onslaught of dusk and whirring insects. I move through strange rooms, a malted chiaroscuro of light and darkness, vague smell of familiar medicines, feel my way along a dark hallway, groggy still, my face burning. From a room ahead comes the rise and fall of even breathing. I stand in the doorway letting my eyes adjust to what light remains suspended in the room, milky at windows, varnishing book shelves, dresser, and van Gogh in his straw hat — where she has grown up — vegetable smells spill in from outside, suburban chitter of crickets. Sheet thrown back, phosphorescent; light glazing her features, swashing breasts, stingy at belly. Max stirs as though sensing my presence. I move forward, feet sucking parquet floor, blood a horserace in my ears, hover hawkish above her, peering down into the half-smile on her lips, ghost of irony even in sleep, eyebrows nearly joining, hair tangled on pillowcase. I bend closer, seized with shivering excitement that swells blood vessels to bursting — impressions gone liquid, wooziness threatening my knees. Imp thoughts. Desires cavorting like happy, shameless devils. She shifts slightly and I realize, as if for the first time, she is naked, fascinated by the thick, glossy pussymuff matching her black brows. Watch as my psyche splits and an elfchild steps away from me, feel the trembling of fingers as it pulls off the sheet and slips in beside her. Max opens her eyes, smiles, teeth animal-gleaming, raises a knee and throws the sheet aside.

Why do you stand, dear, shivering in the muggy evening? Waiting perhaps for me to say, Come here beside me. Eyes fervid sparks, breasts rising falling, canescent eggs beneath the white T-shirt. "I called Mother —" *telling me hoarsely* "— she asked, 'Where have you been? Your husband is on his way to New York.' I hung up on her, didn't say where I was." *You sit at bed edge, bare knees clenched like a child's, saying you don't know what to do.* "You're a big girl now, you must decide for yourself." *Fireflies flicker in calycanthus outside the window.* She combs fingers through my hair, I find her face aslant on the pillow, softsmiling. "You don't understand, I love Gene. I told him —" whispering "— how sometimes I fantasize about you. I only wish someone could tell me what to do." "*Yes, don't we all?*" "Fuck off, Max. Don't mock me." Silence, but the nightsounds: insect chirr filling the room. Her fingers touching first lips, my eyes. Me breathing raggedly. "Once I thought you were that person. . ." *You say so very quietly as if to protect us both from your secret; take my hand, placing it under the shirt on your fevered belly. I swallow, dear, as you lay your gentle head on my stomach.* "Tell me what I should do, Maxine." *Such longing in your voice.* I hear your heartbeat — lips opening, opening — slide my cheek up between the butter of your breasts, cocoa sweet, a nipple stiff against my chin; I stroke it gingerly, uncertain, sweat bites my nostrils; shivering as your fingers slip down. "I'm so scared." "*Yes, love, I know.*" *Teasing those first wiry coils of your cunt, your belly tautens.* "Just relax now —" *holding you to breast, rocking as you mutter:* "I do love him. I love you, too, Maxine." "Yes, now let it go, relax." *So I must poke under your ribs, tickle an armpit (whispering, I am world champion, Daddy taught me), while you writhe and giggle, throw a leg and mount me.* Your muscles so hard, like Gene's, and the damp stiff fur at your armpits — sexy! you told me long ago. We wrestle like kids, lie at last side by side, catching breath. "I do love you, I really do," incantation echoing while you kneel above me, dark silhouette, kissing my hot tummy and pelvic peaks, sensations shivering as your lips move upward kiss by kiss. "*Arch your back,*" you whisper, sliding the shirt over my tits, finding first one nipple then the other, babysucking — Ohhh please — pulling almost cruelly, and I seize the flounce of your hair in fingers, bringing your face close, kissing those thatchy brows. And your hand, OhsweetGod! plunging reckless as my Greek sailor, raking through pubic tangle, opening thighs, a single finger parting lips of my new virginity. *You whimper, eyelids fluttering, brow troubled, and I must guide your fingers, love, like moth wings about a light, fragile with wonder, coaching the soft of your palm to caress nipples, discovering small erections; my shoulders spasming when you pinch a teat between thumb and finger like an adolescent boy. Then groan, sing out as my knee replaces fingers at the moist velvet mouth of your cunt, you buck, grinding your sex against my thigh, chirping bird.* Kissing her hair neck shoulders breasts which are heavy oblong fruit my tongue a proboscis tasting secrets of those swollen flowers, on to the wire of an armpit — I nibble there, tasting acid . . . exploring musky shag of pussyhair, puppypetting, fingers slipping between her legs — dewy flower, swollen petals. Show me how, lover. *Touching that stiff little nob that makes you moan, slipping into you.* I want to bury my face in your silky muff, nibble lick fuck to love you taste that perfume, as you do now. "Yes, love." *Hissing promises to your clitoris, I lick and tease, plunge my tongue deep down inside.* And when I have come and come and calmed, take me in your arms, nipple teasing nipple, *your cunt warm wet against my hip, white prowl of your eyes.* Terrible joy as your lips take mine.

Hunger that wakes me, or the slam of a car door on the street. In light from the window, just the suggestion of Nat's eyes, staring into darkness. She sits up and begins to shiver. "Do you think it's Gene?"

"Gene?" I laugh. "How would it be Gene?"

The heave of springs; I sense her moving in the darkness, searching for clothes. Then close again, the warmth of her breath on my cheek. "Don't tell him I'm here."

I sit up and hug her. "You're being irrational, dear. He couldn't know you are here." *She huddles close, intermittently shuddering. I kiss her forehead: hot, sunburn feverish.* "That was very lovely, Natalie."

A match flares across her vagrant eyes as she lights a cigarette.

I get up and turn on the overhead. *Feeling your gaze, lover — a cat leaping away the moment I turn. You smoke, troubled, studying your feet. How overrated sex must be that we cannot lie together now side*

*by side, laughing softly in the warm evening. You, dear, with the sheet
wrapped round, still flushed from our love.*

"I'm famished. Why don't I start the fire and make a salad?"
Abashed at the defeat in my voice.

Your eyes come up, clouded. "I have to get back."

"I thought we'd stay the night."

Nat shakes her head. "I really need to be alone right now."

I watch her smoking. "All right. I'll start the barbecue."

"Could we just go? I'm too anxious to eat." *Her eyes imploring, a
little bloodshot in the yellow light.*

"Natalie, I'm famished! How can you be so brazen when we've just
made love? Didn't anyone ever teach you about love? It isn't all take
and take and discovering what it is you want. Love is taking only what's
left over."

*She studies me, golden coronas warming the snow-shadow blue of
her eyes; for a moment the young, impressionable Natalie. She releases
a jagged breath.* "I'm sorry —" *her face collapsing as she begins to cry*
"— I really am."

Those ceremonial baths Adam talked about — baths bubbling, selt-
zering about calves and bellies of Singer's Jews in dark Polish shtetls or
the seedy Upper West Side of Saul Bellow's imagination. Bathing —
washing clean. Moving into the unwashed world to begin again. She
appears, carrying a tray into buggy haze cast by patio lights, cheery
again in white shorts and halter top, like a stewardess in the flight of
another Natalie Bach. "I've made sandwiches and coffee," she says, sitting in a canvas chair, wearing her affection like a new blouse. Gazing
up then into a star-blessed night. "Perfect temperature," she decides,
fortune teller's eyes glazed in Delphic sadness. That Maxine smile —
lip clenched and knowing — which lectures about love and says I must
remain where I have wished to grow beyond.

I turn away, wary of emotions that fester in me like eels, rubbing
across one another — love and rage and fear and dissatisfaction. I feel
strangely cheated . . . and ashamed. Can't even think of Gene without
another fit of trembling. What is love? An overcoat, always with someone else's name monogrammed inside? A bouquet of dead flowers? Yet
somehow holding emotions far off as if hoarding them for later. I feel
poignantly aloof.

"Dear Natalie . . ." She regards me vaguely as I come up steps, that old distraction. One minute close as two people can be, the next you are a stranger. Like Mother. And isn't our friendship just another notch in your belt? What could I have been thinking to leave Gene and come here? Suddenly I know. It knocks the breath out of me. It is memory's Maxine I love. True, inviolable. Perhaps she never really existed — that Maxine of mine.

Yet when you throw a towel around my shoulders, rubbing vigorously, and I turn, clutching it to my nakedness, quick-looking into your hazel eyes, certainty abandons my knees. Woozy still with unreachable longing.

You offer to drive me back when I tell you I'm too tired, wondering aloud whether you should return to Carol's. "I can't go to my parents', Gene will be there now. I don't think I could take that."

"You are welcome to stay with me until you've decided."

Slowly shaking your head. "Don't push me, okay? You want me to make a choice. I just can't do that now."

"No choices. I'm offering a couch, that's all. No strings attached."

"There are always strings. . . . I'm finally learning." Your voice just audible above the tire thump. "You used to tell me we have to make choices, remember?" Your eyes come to me, jinxed with dashlight. "But I'll always value your friendship."

"I'm glad you have decided." My words seeming to whist — as Shakespeare might say — into the brooding night, firefly flicker, heavy listless breath of summer.

She touches my knee. "I'm not sure what I want but it really isn't that. I'm sorry, Max."

After a time I speak. "So you failed with us both, the painting teacher and me. Neither of us could banish your husband. And now I should graciously fuck off."

Eyes straight ahead down the parkway. "It's something that began a long time ago. All these years you've wanted to seduce me. Finally I let you succeed."

I turn in the seat. "Maybe there's some perversity in me that wants to keep the record straight. You knew as well as I, Natalie, what would happen if we came out here. Tell me, what is it you want me to be? Lover? Friend? Mother? I can't be kept in suspense forever."

"I want to go back to Carol's to think things over. I feel pretty awful."

"That's just perfect. The kind of reply that would make your mother proud of you."

She drives on with steady intent towards where New York makes its nuclear glow, eyes tiny white cones, poking ahead, too fiercely proud to glance aside. When at last I ask if she will return now to California, she doesn't answer. Though at times her fingers appear to tremble on the wheel. I study her in sweet sadness — beloved silhouette. Friendship a spot frozen in time, a neighborhood that despises intrusion, a provincialism fine and French and spiteful of change. Every movement onward is a movement away. If only . . . if I possessed her boldness I would explain this. No, dear Natalie, it is you who have seduced me. First into friendship and now, any moment, into tears.

PART THREE

DEPARTURES

CHAPTER SEVENTEEN

NEW YORK

Gene entered the café in a checked flannel shirt, head cocked forward like the tourist he was — from Idaho. I rushed to embrace him. Him cooing at my ear and me a fool with tears, before those tablesful of lovecynics. We sat holding hands in a window corner, alternately giddy and dampeyed, lines riven deep in his cheeks. "Jesus, baby," he mumbled, "I didn't think you were ever coming home to me. It about drove me crazy . . . your smell on the pillows. Every day I found another one of your hairs. I couldn't work, couldn't get you off my mind." Sunlight broke on a water glass and splashed across his face, country eyes sparkling in a way city eyes never do.

"I couldn't get you off mine either," I said, caressing the back of his hand, groping for some way to soften what I had to say. "Things have changed, honey. I don't think I can go back to California." Gene's mouth opened, eyes flew on panicked wings about the room. "Please try to understand," I pleaded.

He nodded. "I'm trying." That Hjalsteadfastness.

"Please, love . . ."

"That's what you want then, you want to leave me?" Hard plains of his face like the rough work of a carpenter. I touched his cheeks, feeling vertigo at the brink of that neediness, but sat up straight with the resolve I had promised myself.

"Not you, Gene. California! I wanted to leave years ago. I suffocated in that environment, hated it. It's time for me to stop fulfilling other people's wishes and go after my own." My voice unsure of itself. "I'd like to spend some time in New York again."

He turned a spoon round and round in his fingers as I had often seen him turn a nail, nodding his head — not so much agreement as resignation. "I half expected that." Lips set in a grim smile. "Problem is I live in California."

I gripped his thick arm. "I want you to stay here with me, honey . . . in New York. I know we can work it out."

Gene said nothing, all that worry deviling his eyes.

I showed him around town: tourist Times Square Fifth Avenue Rockefeller Central Park Village winding streets — like a tour promoter trying to sell him the package, while he wore a look of reserved astonishment. *You want to trade the redwoods for this!* He gripped my ass in the jam-packed elevator at the World Trade Center that plummeted like a rocket sled one hundred stories, describing in my ear the erotic wonders he could work with his tongue. I wanted him something terribly. But became furious as Mom/Dad conspired with him over dinner, as if settling a bride price — patronizing me with their avaricious benediction. Snapping as he dog-fawned up close while I undressed for bed: "Quit pushing me!" Gene backed off, hands raised along with his cock.

"Take your time . . . really. It's up to you."

Decision is always a kill, licking its chops over uncertainty. Teeth, fingernails, knees locked behind necks, heaving hips, sodomizing tongues, swallowed balls cock and nipples. Afterwards I lay in the crook of his arm and shared a cigarette. "I feel like I've failed already; I promised myself not to be bulldozed." Gene found his full-throated laugh, that old Hjalstead confidence. Beside him, I found the deepest sleep in weeks.

Next morning he suggested we go camping. He had always wanted to see New England.

"You just arrived in New York!"

"Guess I'm not much of a city boy."

We borrowed Dad's car and drove north, camped the first night near Bellows Falls, Vermont. Gene had built a fire, night air already nippy in August, sat elbows on knees in a red flannel shirt, the Big Dipper off his left shoulder, staring into the flames, a liquid glow pooling in cheek hollows above his beard. Might have been years earlier — that first night in my cabin on the Redwood Coast, though lines more incised, eye sockets deeper. His words leapt at somber trees, gathered about us like eavesdropping ghosts. "I wish I could convince you to come home with me."

"You can't," I said at last. "It might be possible if California was only a place, not a state of mind. Accomplishment is very important to me; it's time to stop denying that. I felt suspect out there, like people thought I was a snob — calling myself an artist. 'My daughter's an artist, too,' they'd always say; 'she makes the crêpes at Connie's Deli.'"

"You painted dozens of paintings out there."

"Listen, I'm sick of the WASP West. New York may be sleazo, may be a shitheap, but it's still the melting pot. Everything hasn't been boiled down to beige yet."

Gene's face struggled; orange firelight stained his teeth.

"We have different outlooks," I said quietly. "I didn't just come east to check out galleries, you know. I was thinking of leaving you."

His eyes coming up like flaming pools. "Why in hell do you think I came back here after you?"

"I love you, honey . . . I really do. But I can't go back there." Staring as if melting into his face, while the fire let go an occasional melancholy hiss.

"Well, if you're that certain about being where you want to be I don't know why you'd have to leave," he grumbled.

"What does that mean?"

"Means I likely have less sense than my ancestors since I'll be moving east when they all busted ass to get out west."

I just gawked at him a moment. "Really!" Went to him — hugging, kissing, knocking him off the log into dust and pine needles. "Jee-zus . . ." He sat up, brushing off shoulders, blushing at my delight. I had squirmed into his lap. Impetuously, was whispering about having had an affair "with someone back here." The silence of the night pressed on us, disturbed only by the homey cracking of the fire. Gene's hand a red claw on my knee. "It's over now?" he asked. I nodded. A sigh came up from him and he smiled. "I've had a try or two of my own."

Together, we leaned forward, the amber horizons of his eyes harboring a longing sadness, as if this were the last campfire he would ever see. "So frowzy back here — old, decaying, conservative," he said. "Everyone like us went west."

"You can have them. They aren't what you think they are. For a while it was fashionable to have a social conscience. Now that the fashion has passed our generation is just as disappointing as all the others."

Gene's eyes didn't stir from the fire — staring as if he saw things there that I couldn't see.

For Gene, New York was a war with taxi drivers and Latino hotheads in battered lowrider sedans. Twice he came home bloodied. "This is New York, honey," I pleaded. "People are crazy here." He would rage: "New Yorkers aren't men. They're rodents. Sewer rats." We moved to Brooklyn, near Prospect Park, because he said he'd never make it without a little green around. He found a carpentry partner, soon was going to Yankee games and had buddies with pancake vowels who spoke as though language came from the belly not the brain, making a big hit in his checked shirts, Idaho style. I suspected he took many maiden voyages in the loft beds he designed for women customers in Manhattan studios. "You just paint," he told me; "I'll get rich here building shelves." "No, thanks," I replied. "It would be bad enough if I were kept, intolerable if my paintings were kept, too." Besides, it didn't work out. He was continuously beset with troubles — checks bouncing, his tools stolen, and some days he simply could not face the city.

But finding work for myself was far more difficult than I had anticipated. Everything was already taken, competition fierce; you needed an advanced degree just to answer the telephone. A person with gaps in her résumé was particularly suspect, considered immature and unreliable, if not outright irresponsible and perhaps emotionally unstable. Once you've dropped out it's nearly impossible to get back in. Another of society's methods for making us toe the line. I settled for an art store job — having come full circle, right back to where I was before leaving New York.

Gene and I right back where we had left off in California. The city itself a source of friction between us. Gene restless, malcontent, endlessly harping on filth crime crazies crowded subways . . . as though I were to blame. While I threw myself into workaholic New York, ignored the mundane day-to-day of shopping/cooking and painted. In the evenings, rushed around kitchen throwing hurryfood together, Gene following me with his seaport eyes. "You have to stay positive here," I lectured; "then New York opens its heart to you." "Now and again," he said, "I wish we could get together." When I crawled late into bed beside him — thoughts still in the studio — and his fingers began explorations, I would ease his hand away, whispering, "Not tonight, honey, I'm exhausted." Until at last he threw legs over the side of the bed, sat red-eyed, staring ahead like a shock victim.

"What is this? We fuck once a month like old people. I could maybe handle another guy, but it's hard being outclassed by a paintbrush."

"You've always been hostile to my work."

He threw me a smoldering look. "Damn it! you're obsessed. I come east, resign myself to a life without kids. Now and again you got to throw me a bone."

It wasn't long before other anxieties, successfully repressed for months, began to surface — subliminally at first. A malaise each time we went to our favorite Ukrainian restaurant in the East Village, extending soon to Village cafés and movie theatres. Just the thought of lower Manhattan made me antsy. It's SoHo, I told myself, though knew it wasn't only galleries. From the moment I stepped off the subway at West Fourth Street, I walked very erect, face rigid, like a deer ready to bolt. One evening at the Kiev on Second Avenue Gene and I had taken a table, and there, staring me in the face from the cover of a ditsy art magazine someone had left behind, was a photo of Barbara standing beside one of her pieces — a hollow, pendent breast, emptied of all human kindness — smiling as if she had long harbored a grudge against happiness. The article said she had founded a feminist co-op gallery and was prominent in the Women's Movement. "Oh Gawd," I moaned, "she's gotten into that stuff."

"Who is she?" Gene asked.

"An old friend. She was the first person who really encouraged me to become an artist." Musing: Barbara at work in the basement studio, hard jazz, dust rising above spasming biceps and soft curses. "I guess she was always kind of a feminist."

Gene threw sullen glances at her picture while we ate. Later he lay in bed, mulling as I undressed, seeming to find uncertainty in my nakedness. "Do you still have those fantasies?" he asked. I lit a cigarette, goosebumps crawling up my arms.

"Could we just forget it? I'm finished with all that."

Gene spread his hands. "Just a question, that's all."

After this, I realized my Manhattan nervousness formed precise coordinates with my old neighborhood — old friends! The thought of encountering one of them on the street filled me with shame and confusion. There is a description by Konrad Lorenz of the meeting of two estranged geese, former mates. They avert their heads, walk clumsily, sneaking canny glances at one another, displaying all the signs of acute embarrassment. If it were possible for geese to do so, they would certainly blush. That image stuck with me. Whenever I envisioned an accidental meeting with Maxine on the street, I imagined the two of us snorkeling wordless, eyebulging, turning and cackling off, throwing hot backwards glances. Two blushing geese.

I had despaired of placing my work. New York was world capital, empyrean of art gimmick and cheaptrick. In the minds of both art public and critic, originality had become confused with outrageousness and showmanship. My own work seemed to scoff at the entire notion of gallery success. I couldn't control it. Cockeyed generals popped out of cityscapes, death-headed, gripping ICBM's in clenched fists, landlords with baboon grins threw babies out of tenement windows — all of it witnessed by hundreds of gaping Last Judgement faces. "Who's going to buy this?" I asked Dad one day when he'd come to visit my studio, sat watching as I posted pins in floor planks, devising horizon lines for a large painting cartoon. "I don't seem to have anything to say about it: I pick up pencil or brush and that's what comes out, like Georgia O'Keeffe when she first started painting her flowers."

He chuckled. "Of course there is no controlling it. Not if it's honest. Artists are primitives, can't take anything on faith. We must learn it all over again — for ourselves. It's risky business."

"Very risky. The dealers just love my work."

His face reddened. "What do they know about painting?" he demanded. "I was a businessman, too. But I kept business away from my painting."

"You were . . . you *are* a very talented painter."

Dad shook his head, lips pressed together in surprising bitterness.

"Talent is cheap. Persistence is what counts. 'Constancy of effort,' as Disraeli said. I didn't have the stamina to be a painter." He sulked, his eyes clouded and distant. But suddenly focusing, bright and sharp. "Stick to your guns, Natalie. It may take a bit longer to get what you want, but it's worth it."

Now he had retired, but instead of painting pined back and forth between Florida and Long Island, brooded and scooped leaves from the swimming pool, suffered emphysema attacks. Now and again he bought another of my paintings, and I would kiss his cheek, very touched. Damp-eyed, he would assure me that some day lots of people would be buying my paintings. He had begun appearing regularly in my work — just a small face, like an old-fashioned daguerreotype, peeping out a window or lost in a crowd. A document.

Stirring a spoon endlessly in coffee one bright May morning when birds had taken over a moment from barking dogs and off-to-work bustle, Gene gave me a sheepish look and said he'd figured it out. He had jobs all spring; if I were willing to give up painting a few months and work full time we could put together enough for a down payment on his Vermont dream by July. "Likely we'd have to give up the apartment," he said, peering down into dirty brown coffee as though its eye was softer than mine. "No way we could make both rent and house payments. I'm not saying it's permanent. Just till we got our feet on the ground up there. Then we could find something here in the city again." Glancing up with those dented gray eyes, giving the impression he had been working up to this for a long time.

"So all you're asking me to do is give up my painting and New York?"

"Just for a while."

I left the table without another word and went to work.

That evening, while I dawdled along Eighth Street, depressed and not much wanting to go home, the past continued to perfect its conspiracy against me. I stood looking in the window of the pet shop where I'd found Marcello, nose squashed to glass — though these were Scotty puppies leaping and yipping — overcome with nostalgia for my little friend who had disappeared one California night without a trace. I glanced up, startled, directly into a face looming towards me, squinty-eyed behind glasses taped together at the bridge — blue-shadowed cheeks and sarcastic mouth, hair tousled, forever cynical features focusing slowly in memory. His face split open like a melon, grinning ear to ear.

"It can't be . . . ," he said.

"Richard!" I cried, embracing him.

"Watch it! Careful . . . careful! My back —"

"Are you okay? What happened?"

"Life happened." Ducking his head to display a bald spot. "Fuckinay! I thought you joined the Manson gang out there. You look psychologically intact." Turning to his friend — a slender man in tight nylon T-shirt and close-cropped beard. "Nat's an old friend from way back in the sixties."

His friend offered a tepid smile. "Ancient history."

"I knew you'd still be in New York," I laughed.

Richard shrugged. "Someone's got to preserve the vowels. Besides, what's happening in this world you can't find between Canal and Forty-second Street?"

Richard's friend laughed too ardently, while I was experiencing shock at what time had given him: cheeks hollow and pocked, balding, not pudgy so much as loosefleshed, as if the tone had gone from his skin. Not older so much as demoralized. In my confusion, I blurted that I was a painter now. Richard's cynical eyes leapt from me to his friend, whose own orbs dissected me, glazed and ungenerous.

"I could never keep up. Sculpture, theatre, music and wasn't there a horticultural stint in Israel? But overall I considered Natalie a closet goodwill ambassador: she slept with every race, creed and national origin." The friend simpered. Richard snapped at me. "Would you relax. I haven't felt so scrutinized since I was bar mitzvahed."

I looked reflexively away, mumbling that I was married now.

"So I hear. I bumped into Maxine maybe six months back. A bit dumpy, still a nice pair of jugs. Dennis doesn't like to hear these things." Tweaking his friend's cheek.

"You saw her?"

Throwing hands to chest. "I only saw her, I didn't molest the woman!"

"She's still in New York?"

He shrugged. "New York, Israel, Switzerland. Always on the move. She married a financier — whatever he is — I think a functionary for the Israeli arms industry. They live 'ah-broad.' But she gets here. The old boy keeps a loose leash."

"She married him?"

"Her father died, next thing she'd married a sexagenarian. You figure it out."

"That old geezer?"

"Don't blame me —" hands back to chest "— I don't favor old men." His friend found that quite funny.

"What about her book?"

Richard frowned. "There isn't any book. She writes articles for psychology journals." He regarded me steely-eyed; it seemed bitterness had routed the old irreverent sarcasm. "Hey, the world needs psychologists too, you know. What's all the fucking disappointment? Everyone let you down. No one could live up to Bach's adolescent ideals. Aach, life! What a banquet of leftovers. Jee-zus!" He whirled on his friend. "What are you smirking about? You never had an adolescence; life buggered you in grammar school."

The friend's smile stuck between hurt and humor. I just wanted to extract myself, feeling almost physically repulsed by Richard's wagging chin, dry spittle at lip corners. This wasn't the Richard I had loved but a sardonic caricature. He touched my shoulder.

"Forget the disappointment. I doubt you really knew Maxine."

"I knew her. Look, I gotta run, really." I closed my eyes and pecked the sunlight splotched tracks on his cheek.

"I've despaired of understanding the female mind, but I suppose you expected something else —" gesturing at himself, his eyes blinking almost painfully behind glasses.

"What could I have expected?" Touching his sleeve, afraid my lips might split open with the tension of a smile. "We'll have to get together sometime. I want you to meet my husband."

Richard pooled his shoulders. "I don't like husbands."

I retreated. Turning at the corner, saw the two walking on, Richard's arm around his friend's waist. I shuddered inside.

Gene's expression, when I entered the apartment, was undecided between contrition and anger, still stuck on the morning. I showered and returned to the kitchen where he sat over the *Times*. "I'm going to cook the best dinner you've had in six months," I said, "but first I want you to take out your fat prick and fuck me." I threw off my robe. Gene's mouth gaped surprise.

Afterwards, I volunteered that the affair I'd had two summers ago had really been a one-night-stand with Max.

"Where did you meet this Max?" he asked.

"Maxine," I managed. The word like a Salvador Dali clock dripping down shadowed walls.

Gene released a breath, glass splintering in his throat. Finally he said, "I kind of suspected that."

Me hiding in the hollow of his shoulder, squeaking that I hoped . . . please, he didn't hate me. *Hate you? I wish I'd been there!* I felt him hardening against my thigh. *It's over now. It wasn't what I wanted.* Just a tiny voicecreak. Stroking him, whispering in his ear: *I wish . . . just once! you could be her . . . both of you. Will you please? So I can take her inside me and keep her there.* Gene, frothy excited, entered me a second time. Me thrusting, grinding hard into him, growling whimpering seeking what cannot be found. Until he lay hunched, animal groaning, and I had found some catharsis. Revelation! "You have to live beyond yourself," I whispered (how strange, the way we learn these things). "You have to live for others —" But Gene had fallen asleep.

Things came apart. Beginning with the awful night Gene was mugged on a late walk, thoroughly shaken. "Just a fucking kid," he yelled. "I always thought if a kid tried it I'd break his neck, but the little fucker had a knife; I could see in his eyes he would use it." From then on he had nothing but complaint for New York; bought a pistol and carried it illegally, plastered his van with warnings to thieves. Becoming a redneck. I could no longer mention an old friend without rage peeking up like an evil moon in his eyes. At times I found him studying me, gone cold and speculative: a biologist dissecting some oddity. When I said I had been thinking about calling Barbara (who else did I know in the art world? you have to start somewhere), he brooded and said nothing.

I waited until he'd gone to work one morning before calling. "This is some surprise," she answered in a voice nearly as flat and jaded as her face had been in the newspaper photo. Confronted by her dense passivity, I began talking, almost frantic: I'm married in Brooklyn I paint quasi-realistic still don't like unemotive abstract stuff or the *avant-cafard* SoHo shit or how artists are no longer bohemian, gone slick! and the art world fragmented into cliques and "isms" like the Italian parliament. "Sure, I'm a woman artist," I said, piqued by her brooding silence, "but I'm tired of all the angry stuff. I've probably seen ten thousand scowling vaginas —"

She cut me off. "I don't think we have much in common, Natalie. I'm a real fan of those scowling vaginas."

"I'm not attacking you."

"Don't patronize me, Natalie."

"All right, forget it." I hung up. What could we understand of one another's lives . . . old friends? Is this what life is all about —slow alienation from our commonality?

It was about then that a pimple appeared on Gene's penis. I refused to sleep with him. What is it? I demanded. Had he picked up herpes on one of his escapades? He said, "I was about to ask you the same thing."

"Me?"

"It's been known to happen."

Next morning he woke up bleary-eyed and bad-tempered, asked if I'd seen any more of Maxine. I could feel color mounting in my cheeks, thought at once of the clandestine phone conversation with Barbara and was angry at myself. What did she have to do with it? "Don't be ridiculous," I told him.

"She lives in New York, doesn't she?"

"I don't know where she lives."

He was examining the pimple with an apish troubled brow, said he'd had a dream about me last night.

"Must've been bad."

"The worst!"

It took time to coax it out of him: "Started with a pimple," he said. "I'm not sure it was on my cock, but it was a weird, hard little thing. I squeezed it. What popped into my hand wasn't a blackhead but a tiny steel cylinder like a morel mushroom. I pulled it apart with my fingernails; a second cylinder was fitted inside, a bit smaller, another inside that, and so on, like the wooden dolls Russian peasants make. I mean tiny. I had to use tweezers finally to get them apart. At the core — so small I could only see it with a magnifying glass — was a figurine, looked like Annie Oakley with a hand on her hip." Gene looked at me as though expecting I could explain the significance of this.

"Then we were at a sort of nightclub, definitely exotic. Soldiers were coming in with naked, creamy-assed girls over their shoulders; there were reggae bands and brown women in slit dresses, hippies and playboys in white chinos — sort of a magic theatre affair. A pair of short-cropped Marin County feminist types came in, exuding remoteness and disdain for the rest of us. Your mouth fell wide open, you half-stood, gaping after them as they passed by the tables towards another magic theatre beyond, like you couldn't make up your mind. Then you screamed out a name and ran after them. At that moment I felt like I'd dropped through a trapdoor out of your life. Like I had passed from my dream into yours and was only just visiting.

"You were touching each other and smiling and she introducing her buddy — who didn't seem all that happy about it. And I thought: That's Maxine! Couldn't believe it. I mean, wasn't even a good looker: mousy gray hair clipped close, cheeks too pudgy, hardbodied. The other one at least had nice hair and tits. But I thought, Well, maybe there is something to it. Kind of bullish assertiveness. Macho. Anyway, who can account for a woman's tastes? You were giddy, giggling and swashbuckling your eyes at her, ready to lick grease from her fingers. It disgusted me. I was desperately trying to figure out how to make her disappear, like you can sometimes in dreams. I heard you say, 'You must come meet Gene.' And they parroted, 'Oh, we just absolutely must meet Gene.' Frowned at me. So when you came over I could barely squawk a 'How d'you do,' the rage was that big in me. When I offered my hand your friend just looked at it. You were already discussing some project. Seems she and her buddy were artists, too, but consummate artists. They had created all of this, they said. Even my dreamscape! You followed after them like a disciple as they opened a gate into a huge plowed field. A painting was beginning to take shape, floating mysteriously above it. Enormous. A mockup, your friend said, for a better world.

"I felt desperate. Knew I was about to lose you for good, because I could never equal the promises they were making. Actually, you were making them to yourself and they nodded. Maxine seemed so remote and heartless I couldn't understand her power over you. Her eyes were like the capsules I'd dug out of my skin, licking right at the crotch of your soul. I took you aside, could barely talk my teeth were chattering so hard, but managed to say I was leaving. You could come with me now or we could say good-bye. You just laughed and said I was acting like a jealous kid. I held your hands and told you how bad I was hurting, how much I loved you and how crazy it was to throw away all these hard-earned years in a few flighty minutes. Didn't loyalty mean anything to you? But I saw it was hopeless. Your friends were impatient, muttering about husbands. You threw me off and shouted that I couldn't stop you from having friends. 'This is it then,' I warned you;

'I'm leaving.' You just shrugged. And I saw that your eyes had become capsules, too."

Gene stared at me, eyes sweltering.

"God!" I cried, "what a creepy awful dream. Don't worry, honey —" massaging the back of his neck "— I love you, Gene. I could never hurt you like that." But he was very troubled, beyond soothing.

"That's not all," he grumbled. "It went on. We were still together, but you were rushing out morning and night — right in the middle of meals — to help her with mysterious projects. We would be fucking and the phone would ring; right in the middle of an orgasm you'd leap up to get it. And I could hear you laughing from the living room. That hurt so bad I kept replaying it to try and make it better. Then realized her face was grinning from the pillow beside me and you had crawled down under the covers. She sat beside the bed in her gym trunks like a coach while we balled, kept blowing her whistle and coaching me to do better. I knew there was only one thing to do.

"I jumped up and went to the bathroom for the scissors. You two had gotten there ahead of me. You sat naked between her hairy legs, resting your head back on her twat, dreamy-eyed, and she was clipping your hair short, like hers. I shouted and wrested the scissors out of her hand. Began stabbing, everywhere — back, head, breasts, groin — chopped her up in little pieces while you screamed and screamed. I tried to tell you that you were free now, but you kept screaming. Then I saw your eyes were little metallic bubbles and rage came up in me like red vomit. I raised the gory scissors and clenched my teeth. And at that instant I looked up and saw your blue eyes, and it was *you* telling me coffee was ready. Jesus Christ Awmighty . . ." Shaking as if he'd caught a chill.

"Baby —" I held him "— it isn't true; it's only a dream."

"Christ, I hope so —"

"What do you mean, hope so?" I stared at him, feeling quite shaken myself. His suffering eyes brushed past and on to the floor. "You could never hurt me, could you, honey?"

He shook his head, a spasm.

After this, I was aware of a fury in him I hadn't seen before. An instability. Like that night he sat watching TV, cleaning his pistol — actually leering like a wacko kid down the barrel at the picture tube. "It's not loaded," he said, noticing my uneasiness.

"If you don't put it away I'm getting out of here," I warned.

"An unloaded weapon is as harmless as a baby bottle. See!" He aimed at the newscaster and squeezed the trigger. A blast. His eyes nearly sprang from their sockets. The set exploded in a fireworks shower of light and glass.

A few days later we sat on a park bench along Central Park West. Nearby, some teenagers (maybe Whitman students) played baseball in the swale where Maxine had dragged me into the field hockey game long ago. Gene leaned forward, watching low-browed as rush hour refugees sprang up out of the subway. "What's the rush?" he muttered, his eyes stumbling on me, then past with a half-smile at towers fronting the park. "There are better ways to live. You gotta admit the Green Mountains sound mighty good right now."

"Okay! We've been over this a million times." Part of me wanting so badly to say I'd go — to Alaska, Maine, the outback of his choice. Instead, I rested a cheek on his shoulder and commiserated that New York must be tough for someone who didn't have good reason to be here.

"There are no good reasons," he snapped, bucking me off his shoulder. "All right, don't just think of yourself, think of our children. This is no place to raise kids."

I was incredulous. "What kids, Gene? We don't have kids."

"But I want them and I'm damned tired of apologizing for it. It's only by having kids that people fully mature."

"Have them then . . . mature! I have a lifetime of maturing ahead. I'm in no rush."

"It really comes down to this thing about kids between us, doesn't it? It's wrecking our marriage."

"How —" struggling to keep my voice steady "— can two people who love each other consider splitting up over children who don't even exist?"

Gene continued, a nearly gentle tone, gazing off at monoliths along Central Park West. "I can imagine that place in Vermont . . . kids making a rope swing in the barn — gotta be a barn — snowball fights on the front lawn. Jeezus, I can see it." Eyes tearbright, reflecting the calamity of passing traffic.

My voice emerging very small. "Maybe you should go. I'd come visit."

"Sure! why not?" His eyes focused. "Give you a chance to look up your old kissing buddy again."

"I didn't choose that, love. I chose you."

"You did it, didn't you?"

"Maybe it was something I had to do to leave behind." I could barely look at him; he'd changed, an alien, hostile presence within the man I loved. "If I had known it was going to destroy our marriage, I wouldn't have told you. I thought you had more faith in me."

"A man harbors illusions he might be satisfying his woman."

"That had nothing to do with it."

"You were confused, right? That's fucking pathetic. You're more of a woman than you realize."

"It isn't being a woman; it's needing a woman's love. I saw Maxine couldn't give me that, even if she'd wanted to."

"So I have you till some mama comes along who's willing to give you a permanent side of her bed? That's real fine."

I practiced breathing (plenty experience watching Dad all those years). "Before I slept with her that would have sent me into a tailspin. Now it doesn't. I love her, but the rest was too disturbing to me. I've learned since then that wounds close, even if they don't always heal completely. Maybe that's all you can hope for. And I've learned that my choice is to have a man. I thought it was you." I attempted a smile.

As we walked back to Rockefeller Center and the F train, Gene saw a car with Vermont plates. "I'm getting out of here," he said huskily. "You can come or stay. It's your choice —"

It was like a dream: me telling him I'd stick it out here, a histrionic bravado that got me through the evening, diarrhea after dinner, shaky-fingered helping him pack, while he fussed and patted at neat shirts as if every tuck and fold were vital to his release. I lay awake as he tossed and muttered, trying to convince myself it would be best this way. Free of his complaints, I might make peace with a city where there isn't any.

Next morning he packed the car — a kind of bleak resignation — while I pulled a light-hearted act, full of cheery I'll-visit-you-and-you'll-visit-me embraces. Then, to my bewilderment, Gene was kissing me good-bye. Just like that. "I don't know if it'll work," he said with a pa-thetic smile. *Of course not. You can't leave me. We love each other.* But I said nothing, unwilling to beg. Knowing he could stay, knowing he couldn't. Yes, you must have good reason to put up with New York. I wasn't reason enough.

* * *

The alarm wakened me. Feeling out with a hand to the other side of the bed, I whispered, "Honey —" But no one was there. Of course! He would be up making coffee.

"Gene —?" I called.

Books answered, a thousand bare-toothed grins up the wall. I shut my eyes against them, slipped down again into unconsciousness. Didn't get up till noon, limping about on my grief, staring blankly into the sink, weeping over coffee grounds. A pilgrimage room to room, touching artifacts — so much of him left behind, the bed itself fashioned by his sure hands. My life, it seemed, built on that solidity.

Days passed. I ate the last egg, last oatmeal leavings, unable to face the scrutiny of the grocer. My boss called each morning to warn I couldn't stand him up forever. I wondered if I would end up like Liz: abandoned, bitter in defeat. Looked through canvases racked in the studio. What good had they done me? No gallery, no success, no husband. They demanded everything and gave nothing. Taking sharp scissors, I began slashing them from stretcher bars. But art has its own will to survive; after a few, I stood on bright canvas strips and began to cry.

Later I called Mother. She wasn't surprised — as if she had been expecting some day just such a call. Her daughter would reach out to her — must! In the end there is no one else. She came at once and, late into the night, I told all of it. "He'll be back, honey," she assured me. Though I'd begun to doubt it. "It's not just children," I told her. "It's Maxine, too. I hurt his pride."

"You're no lesbian, honey. You just needed a friend who could pinch-hit as a mother."

"I never really believed a woman could care for me. I've always been hung up about it, even when I was with Gene. Guess I'm still the little girl whose mother abandoned her. It's a deep wound. Max seemed to care, but I didn't trust her either. After all, you seemed to care too . . . sometimes."

Mother's eyes clouded, that old milk of defensiveness, then she nodded. "But I always cared nonetheless. I do now." She squeezed my hand, mouth crumpling, eyes small frightened sparrows, a wetness crawling down cheeks over the first wrinkles, catching lamplight that spun and glistened in perpetually blonde hair. "She used you, honey. I knew she was capable of that."

"No, I used her. I seduced her. And when I knew what I had to know I threw her away."

Mother frowned; it was something she couldn't accept.

She held me, nestling chin into my hair and moaning as I sobbed. Near dawn we went to bed in that huge berth Gene had built, first light bone-cold across features as she tucked covers beneath her chin, snuggling warm beside me — those fragrances carried up from childhood. I felt nearly secure. When I turned out the light her voice tinkled like purest crystal on the air: "There's been enough pain, now it's time to go on living. Sweet dreams, honey."

She got me up in the mornings — to museums, long lunches, Village strolls (an expression of admixed horror and fascination at the Haight-Ashbury of downbeats-punkers-pushers-pinheads-Fellini rollerskaters that Washington Square Park had become). Before she left, I told her without any irony at all that it was good to have a mother. For days afterward, signs of her visit lingered in strategic places — gefilte fish in the fridge, a new blouse in the closet — her earnest mouth, crowsfeet at eye corners like badges time had given, fist popping (hope's piston) haunting the rooms, reminders of our marathon shmoozing. *You don't need me anymore. Y'r a strong woman who can get whatever she wants in this world. Hope works. And belief in yourself. Believe me, I know.* I had laughed at her Pollyanna insistence and said I thought courage is like the aroma of fresh coffee — doesn't last long after brewing. She hugged me. "It's good to hear you laugh. If sometimes you need me just a little, that's okay, too."

Within weeks I had accepted the empty side of the bed, actually enjoyed not having to cook on those warm September evenings, and if I became morose over a memory, chided myself: *Don't be foolish, he'll be back.* But started living as though he wouldn't. I rented a studio on the Lower East Side, happy to leave the Brooklyn outback, finding at once a renewed vigor I had left here years back. I schlepped slides around to galleries — whitewashed caverns, acres of wall and paintings in standard sizes, copying one another with tedious technique. I approached the quick mealy smiles of indifferent dealers, who poked viewers before their noses and ladled words: "Juicy . . . nice juicy work." Returning my slides without further comment — the mode of rejection among lovers who care nothing for love. Ushered out by my own humiliation, those licking eyes and mocking wallfuls of success, and the impression they had made up their minds before I stepped in the door.

I lost my job, but said "no thanks" when Dad offered to help with rent. Soon found teaching work at senior centers, instructing old bats who squabbled like kids and smeared paint behind their ears. When the weather turned, my hopes were one-eyed crows pecking in the snow. Maybe there is a Chinese proverb: *Life is not eaten with one chopstick*. For years love was enough. Then in its insinuating way career presumed; being more bellicose, it dominated. Now, alone, it clicketed garish as a cricket on a November night. *Love*, how I ached for its quiet knowing. A hurt that made those ego wants of Nat the needy artist seem trivial.

I visited Gene in Vermont, already a frozen tomb in October, helped him cut firewood — his red-cheeked heartiness seeming another element of rejection — and tear out walls of that dismal house he was renovating, hair filling with mouse turds and plaster dust. "It's gonna be a beauty," he kept saying, wanting to convince me. We slept together . . . cordially. Hadn't yet reached the stage of Lorenz's geese; still finches hopping about the entwined branches of our loyalty. Though seasons had passed between us.

An awful odor permeated the place. Gene couldn't smell it, nor hear the slow creaking of the house in first winter winds heralding that endless season of despair. I would return to New York, relieved to be back.

On one of those returns a letter awaited me: a clutter of Israeli stamps and familiar handwriting. My heart skipped. It was from Rachel. She wrote that Adam had been wounded in a border skirmish near the Golan Heights. An artillery shell had exploded near him and a piece of shrapnel had just missed his spine. He would walk with a slight limp, nothing more. He had received leave to come to the States and visit his family. They would be arriving with their children in a month.

A family reunion was planned: David flying out with his family from Chicago. Dad was agitated. When I went out to the Island to visit, he talked of nothing but Adam — how he still disliked his oldest son. They were opposites, he said, Adam a militarist — bully, really! — while he himself had always been a pacifist. He was certain there would be trouble. Mother scolded, "There's bound to be trouble if you take that attitude."

I told them about a recurrent dream I had been having. We were in the backyard at Huntington Park: Dad playing football with Adam and David, and me, little Nattie, holding onto his pants leg. Except the lawn was really a beach and waves rolled onto the grass and Mother sat far away in a beach chair waving a hand; I could just hear her crying, "Bye bye, Jake. I love you . . ." Dad said he couldn't remember ever playing football. He had never been much of an athlete, with his asthma.

A week before Adam and family were due to arrive, Gene called and said he would be down, he'd always wanted to meet my brother. "Wonderful," I said. "You'll come for my brother but not for me."

"I've been planning to come. There's something I have to tell you."

"Tell me now, I'm listening."

"It isn't something for the telephone," he muttered.

When I got off the phone I began a large canvas. *Family Reunion.* All of us swimming in Mom/Dad's pool, the scene midwinter and the water frozen, locking each of us in our separate antics.

On impulse I called Barbara again. Fuck pride. How else do you get anywhere in this world? Told her bluntly, "I'm trying to break in with my work. I need your advice."

There was a long pause, then she started to laugh — a hint of my old friend Barbara. "You are really something," she gasped. "I don't hear from you in maybe eight years. One day I get this off the wall phone call: Nonobjective art sucks, feminism sucks, SoHo sucks. I live in SoHo, I'm a Movement activist, I sculpt nonobjective! Do you always insult people before finessing them?"

"Do we have to agree on everything?"

I thought she would croak laughing. In the background a dog yowled. "Okay —" she managed "— you win. There's a party Friday night if you want to meet people."

I was delighted. Friday was the night of Adam's arrival. As the one sibling who had failed at the art of family, I had been dreading it.

I rode down to SoHo from work on a jammed Friday evening subway, gagging on the urine stench of a filthy wino, limply hinged to a hand hanger. Completely out of it, eyes rolled back in his head, whumping into fellow passengers with each jolt of the train. People eyed him savagely. To many of them even his skin color was offensive. I felt a strange mixture of sympathy and disgust.

At Broadway-Lafayette, he managed to stumble off the train, just in front of me. His knees crumpled and he collapsed, falling face down on the filthy platform. He lay there, eyelids fluttering and tongue lolling out. His thin coat had split up the back like a beetle shell. Quickly, a crowd gathered around; but though several people bent close to inspect him, no one offered any help. Transit cops arrived. But they, too, simply stood about, officiously watching him. I took off my sweater and stooped beside him, the wino's eyes crinkling a little as I slipped it under his head. A pasty-faced subway cop immediately retrieved it. "Y'r sweatah's gonna get dirty. The platforms is dirty," he admonished, lowering his voice confidentially. "He's just a pisshead. Don't worry about it, lady."

"He's a human being," I snapped. "As much as you or me."

The cop's eyes flared menacingly. And I got out of there, walked the ten blocks to Barbara's.

She came down in a freight elevator accompanied by a snarling German shepherd, yanking at the dog's collar each time it lunged and warning, "Don't try to hug me. I can't take chances here." I hugged a corner, eyeing the dog, told her she looked great — very strong. She made a dismissive gesture, and the elevator door opened directly into a loft cramfull of track lighting and potted green. "I did it all myself," she explained, "years ago after I kicked Rafael out." Her dog had instantly transformed — all wet tongue and friendly tail.

She asked if I had brought slides of my work, and while I wandered amidst sculpture — Sabine women, hunkered over the floor, not raped but napalmed — she slipped my slides into a viewer, snapping them back on the table like playing cards. "To be frank, it won't be easy in this town," she said without looking up. "It's never easy in New York." I shrugged and asked why she had abandoned realism. A blue vein winced at her temple. "This *is* my realism. Reality is in the eye of the beholder."

I wasn't in the mood to dicker. "Your work reminds me a little of Arp's." I could think of nothing else to say.

Barbara put the viewer down. "Did you come here to pan me? I don't have male influences, friend. Not many women artists I know do. We are developing our own aesthetic. The men have nothing to teach us."

I glanced over feminist publications and mailings covering the coffee table. "I guess you're really into this stuff?"

"We're all really into *this stuff*. Though some of us aren't aware of it."

"Gawd! Can't I say anything? All right, let me tell you what I think. There are too many divisions between people in this world already without men and women going at each others' throats."

Her gaze level, mirthless, a soreness about her eyes as if they'd lost the blessing of sleep. "Still the romantic," she grumbled. I felt a sudden compassion for her — for all those lives that had betrayed their idealism.

"Don't you ever smile anymore?" I asked.

She smiled at that, a mere swelling of the upper lip. Leaning forward, I placed a kiss on her cheek. The dog snarled; I jumped away. "God! what happens when you make love?"

"It's pretty crazy. C'mon, let's go to our party."

SoHo cheek by jowl of loftelegance and cardboard moldering underfoot. We entered a plosion of voices, faces checking us out, women in leather jumpsuits and men who looked more like stock brokers than artists. Barbara quickly found friends — grim-visaged women who huddled close in conversation as if plotting sedition — leaving me on my own. All over the room strangers touched and smiled. It was that kind of age — fickle, ready-made. I realized I wasn't much in the mood for this, downed two quick brandies before a roosterish open-shirted man asked me to dance.

He was lithe, inventive, bending at knees, nearly touching his back on the floor, and I began to cheer up. Our pelvises flirted, my breasts brushing him; I felt free and confident. It was healing to be courted, troubling as he held my gaze, wiping me off the lips of his complacency.

Nearby, a heavy-set, scruffy man with a monk's beard and pitted oversized nose argued with a younger man, dark and muscular. "We're nothing but whores," he roared. "A lot of parrots painting shit that can be safely hung in executive lunchrooms."

"Executives pay their bills," said the younger man. He wore an army shirt, the name "Appinelli" stitched across its pocket.

"Jesus, I can't talk to you. Americans are the most brainwashed fucking people on the planet. That includes Russians! Give 'em shit, tell 'em it's caviar, they dig right in." Appinelli slugged down a beer, eyes focused menacingly on the heavy man, who turned to me and growled. "Am I right? Look at 'em —" sweeping a big hand to encompass the room "— gloating over their goddamned Cinzano and scouting pussy while the world goes to hell around them. They call themselves artists!" he bellowed. "Hasn't been an artist in this country since Robert Frost died."

Startled, I realized I knew this drunk monk with the oversized head. He raised his glass in salutation as he had on our first meeting. My loverboy puckered lips and mumbled, "Artists have to get beyond politics."

"Amen!" said a woman in a low-cut gown, a gold chai dangling between her breasts. "Afraid it's hopeless. Jud is the Qaddafi of nonobjective painting."

"Do your own thing well, the rest of it takes care of itself," loverboy advised me, totally self-impressed. I was suddenly annoyed.

"Goebbels and his gang did their *own thing* very well."

" 'Attagirl!" cried Jud Biggs.

"Fact is," said Appinelli, "the planet spins out of control till it smashes into doomsday. Nothing we got to say about it."

"It's our job to say something about it," I insisted. "Not just mope about Hilton Kramer ignoring us in his reviews. Artists have lost their balls."

"Maybe you have." Appinelli curled a lip.

The amen woman let go a crinkly laugh.

I said I thought nonobjective art was largely responsible for the current state of affairs, looking directly at Jud Biggs, whose little satyr eyes leapt from place to place on my body. "No comment art. America's great contribution to art history." By now, others had gathered, faces regarding me with stilted, uneasy smiles.

"Oh rat piss!" said the amen woman.

I turned to her. "It's a tragedy so many of us Jews got into it. Now they're going to accuse us not only of killing Christ but killing art, too."

Jud Biggs belly-laughed, loverboy shrieked, "Pisser! what a kvetsh. Did your mother get run over by a Jewish cabby or what?"

"Oh no, we're not still into this," groaned our hostess as she glided past, a few frazzles come loose from her beehive of hair. And me — with chutzpah that astonished me — proposing a contest. We would all take paper and crayons and draw something abstract, including Biggs and any nonobjective artists who wanted to join us, to see if we could differentiate between experts' and novices' work. There was an uproar. Jud Biggs thought it a great idea; the amen woman and loverboy walked away in a huff; an effete man in a dainty moustache, who I later learned was Arnold Rothstein, reluctantly agreed to participate; Barbara evileyed me from across the room. The hostess ran off to find paper and craypas. Then she and the two others who were to be judges left the room, and we spread out across the floor to draw.

Barbara appeared, leaning on one knee above the quick hatchwork of lines on my paper. "What is it with you," she grumbled, "some kind of imperative to fuck up?"

I smiled at her. "I'm creating a scene. I mean, aren't we here to be noticed?"

She scuttled back to her friends. I never saw her again.

A dentist's work was unanimously attributed to Arnold Rothstein, the abstract expressionist (whose own sketch was considered "too unevolved"). "That's 'cause I plagiarized Rothstein," said the gleeful dentist. Biggs' work was selected too — to shouts of "unfair," since it included his scrawled signature. "Arnie should be ashamed of himself," he said. "He knows nothing is finished without signing it; upon that calligraphic foundation rests the entire edifice of modern painting." He shrugged and turned out his lips like a bluegill. "What can I say?" winking at me. "Jews don't understand art." Rothstein chuckled. Someone growled:

"Hey y' fuckin anti-Semite, I ain't gonna listen to no more shit from y'r Nazi mouth."

We turned to Appinelli, sprawled bulldoggish against the wall. Biggs' eyes widened. "Who's anti-Semitic? I'm anti-everything. Anti-black, anti-white, anti-chink, anti-spick, anti-Yid, anti-Arab . . . I even hate wop bastards like you who think their macho-man hard-on gives 'em the right to blow the whistle on old farts like me 'cause I think hebes who make a profession of it are as obnoxious as Lutheran bigots who keep them out of their country clubs."

Appinelli rose languidly up the wall, shaking out his legs and approaching Biggs. "The *wop bastard* you eat."

Biggs rooted in a scrag of hair, one eye squinting. "Aren't you a wop bastard? An outside chance you could be a bleached Gree —" gurgling his last words, for Appinelli had seized his shirt collar, bringing Biggs' crimson face close to his own. The hostess tapped Appinelli's swollen biceps.

"Please don't spoil my party, Tony."

Appinelli's eyes flared; he let go and Biggs dropped back into his apathetic posture as if nothing had happened. "Or you might be a high-yellow nigger," he wheezed. Appinelli stared, incredulous. The hostess patted his T-shirt muscled arm, making gentle noises.

"Y'r fuckin sick, you know that," Appinelli hissed.

"I'm an artist. I simply reflect my environment."

Later, the hostess took Appinelli and me aside, her hand a soft wing fluttering against my arm. "We get used to Judson," she said, a vaguely southern lilt. "It doesn't mean anything. A remarkable thing happened to him as a boy growin' up in New Or-leans. Some white boys were beating up a colored boy and Judson intervened. The boys turned on him and beat him very severely. For six months he lost his vision altogether. Then, miraculously, it returned. Ah don't b'lieve he evah quite got over that."

I have found many reasons for going home with Jud Biggs that night. Sympathy. His huge need and my own to defy that news I expected Gene to deliver the next day; or an uncanny capacity for marking important transitions in my life with some ill-starred debauch. Only later would I perceive it as a premonition — this sudden compassion for a man nearly my father's age through those fateful hours.

But nothing calculated — as eyes around the room hinted while we stood talking and drinking. I told him frankly about my career: gallery honchos who rejected your work before even seeing it. He nodded his huge head. "New York is no longer the place for artists," he said. "Corporations have it all now. Throw a few coins to the constituencies through arts councils to keep them quiet, hand out an occasional prize in the name of Free Expression to some Polack or Argentine. American prophets they don't need. American kvetshers! We're s'posed to be mainstreamed, programmed for complacency, s'posed to play footsies with the academic fucks." Leaning close, shaggy and growling, exuding tobacco and turpentine, poking an emphatic finger into the dent between my breasts, his bleary eyes unbudging on the knobs they made beneath my shirt.

I told him about the incident on the subway platform. "I know that putting my sweater under his head was merely a gesture, but I had to do something. I believe in involvement, as a person and an artist. If we artists don't care about humanity, who will? This current fad disgusts me — artists standing aside, looking down on others' suffering from our aesthetic heights, saying it's really not our concern. Our only concern is style."

"You're right," he mumbled, staring at my cleavage.

"There's no spirit of protest in America now. It's becoming a Ray Bradbury nightmare."

"I'm not saying I disagree. I simply doubt you'll find any better on this planet," he said. Then asked if I would come home with him.

Bull chested, penis so huge I feared it would tear me open, lumbering on thick arms that could've broken Appinelli like a twig; the intimacy of his foul breath, gasping Mars of a face that hurt and hurt, finally shouting and me hoping to God it was over, but he was a kid feeling the train in rails long before it arrives, screaming out again and again as it nears, face flinching in paroxysms of need, bed lamp flickering like a star on his baldness; me accompanying with moans, tweets, chortles — not false exactly 'cause it was goodness I was doing — grinding for what sensation I could salvage, praying he wouldn't drop down dead of a heart attack . . . till that final shriek like a freight hooting around the bend, reechoing, pistoning the scalding chug-chug-chug of his virility deep down inside. My orgasm like a drop of moisture carried past at the bull's nostril. And he collapsed, moaning. Somehow I extracted myself, disgusted nearly by the thick nap over his shoulders — his manstink.

Waking to the chafings of frightened voices. Only a dream. Ashes on the pillow, shit stains on sheets, sour smell of unwashed laundry and unemptied ashtrays, his huge iconoclasm breathing beside me, staring up into muffled light from a filthy skylight. I couldn't imagine what I was doing here. Up quickly and dressing, his eyes following, wordless. At last he said, almost wistful, "You have the body of a young girl." Hoisted himself up on an elbow. "Coffee?" he asked. No, I was in a hurry. He proposed I might model for him. No, I wasn't interested in modeling. He sighed and mentioned my work. "I could ask my dealer. . . . No promises!" No, smiling at him, I can't do it like that.

"Good for you," he bellowed, heaving himself upright. "Y'r all right, kid." Watching as I brushed my hair, unable to delete an irony from my smile.

"Thanks." I meant it.

"Get outta this town . . . the whole fuckin country!" he growled. "Take your talent and go. This is no place for honest artists. It chews 'em up."

I kissed his forehead. Maybe I'd call sometime, I said.

"No you won't. Go on before I start blubbering."

Outside in the derelict morning kids trash an abandoned car, their lingo of choppy delight hanging on damp air. The crump of metal and tinkle of glass. A tearing shriek, like fingernails across a blackboard, takes me to the window. A Puerto Rican boy with anthracite eyes gives a slick two-fingered whistle as a woman passes. He leaps up and down, using cartop for trampoline; manhood too big on him, like his trousers. His buddies grin up from fractured windshield and fenderdent, pursuing the woman with gestures pink and pointy-tongued.

My eyes traipse the gray cityscape: fire escapes clinging like cat burglars to eyeless tenements, near where Holland Tunnel lets gas each morning. That shattered car, all the aimless antipathy troubles me. I have the dead weight of last night's wine on the back of my eyes. I turn away from the window to fluorescent brightness, clean walls, workbench bustling with energy — brushes in tin cans, colored pencils, gum turpentine and gum erasers, stand oil and oil paints in dawdled tubes, bent at waist, rags dappled with color . . . all that cheery clutter of intent. Along the walls my paintings present a canny history, beginning with Gene on a cabin porch in California . . . ending with Dad standing by his new Long Island swimming pool, water ripples shimmering across his face, ear cocked as if listening to bird calls. The bed has nothing to hide, unmade and not even used last night — a body-shaped depression and yesterday's dirty socks.

I urge myself to work, sigh at a canvas — nearly blocked in now — a woman peeking from a brownstone window, face a shaded half-moon, half-Hopper-sun, eyes pursuing a dark figure just disappearing around the corner, leaving her his shadow. I find it nearly impossible to continue. Think of Dad's pink-cheeked clowns breathing up whales, fishes, cities on the plain, juggling cigarette packs in candied tempera, wizards who could breathe up the world — while he hacked and sputtered. I glance at the phone machine. Undoubtedly a message there from the family. The reunion on Long Island: David's booming baritone wanting to know why I haven't joined them for brunch. "C'mon, Nat. We miss ya!" Or Adam wishing hello in English thick with Israel. Wonder how it's going. Dad nervous for weeks anticipating Adam's visit, first in nine years. "It's going to be a disaster," he kept saying, even more intimidated by his son the Israeli army captain than he'd been by his son the football fullback. Mother told him to take it easy. "The visit can be whatever you make it. No reason for a ruckus."

Or perhaps Gene has called. Would that be good news? No news is best news. I turn from the machine back to my work.

Outside the kids shout; they are the city's locusts, devouring everything in their path. New York has changed. It is like the moment before God struck down the Tower of Babel. Gene calls it "Civilization's last curtain call." Some days there is agreement, people laugh on porch stoops; other days growl at one another like dogs. In the end no one really cares. So much for Western Civilization. It didn't work.

Outside, a shriek of metal as something else is torn from the car. A bird takes flight under my fingers as if by magic, sprinting across canvas, downscooping wings and lofting body. "My work is all that matters now —" I whisper aloud "— it won't slip away from me." Perhaps this is what it means to be an artist: when the rest of your life is in shambles, you can still create.

Life is a marathon, a long piece of bad news. For some there may be a few certainties: children, family life, Chanukah arriving each year like clockwork. But for artists only the chaos singlemindedness creates. A solid core with utter Pandemonium all around. We choose New York . . . other absurdities! It makes no difference which. Wonder is our refuge. Pipe dreams. We are humankind's adolescents, never maturing past the experimental stage. We know nothing for certain — except that nothing lasts. We float like those red and white bobbers I fished with off summercamp docks, never knowing when a bluegill will strike and we will duck under water.

The phone rings. I stare at its lidless eye, experiencing inexplicable dread. Then, of course, I answer.

David's frightened, watery voice barely holds on. "Afraid I've got some pretty sad news, Nat," he says — delivering me Dad's death in a croaky whisper.

CHAPTER EIGHTEEN

THE FUNERAL

SOMETHING HAD AWAKENED ME. I PUSHED UP ONTO AN ELBOW, feeling out with the other hand — surprised, nearly, to touch the warm hollow of Gene's back. The clock on the rug beside the mattress read six. A soft morning glow poured through glass doors of the cottage, bringing up toxic-smelling chemical newness. The room furnitureless, bare walls plastered but unpainted — a project Dad had been promising himself. Wincing under the quick blade of grief, wanting to slide back into forgetful sleep. But the noise again, almost at my ear, raucous and insistent as a brawling baby. Then I saw it, beyond glass doors: a raven pacing back and forth, swiveling its small head and scrutinizing me one eye at a time. It flurried a quick iridescence of wings, folding them back neatly.

"Dad —?" I whispered.

The bird tilted a wary eye.

I sat up, pulling the sheet along to cover my nakedness. "Please don't go," I pleaded. The raven made low comforting sounds, retreated a few paces as I slipped legs out from under covers and knelt naked before the glass, peering into its dark soul. "You were always afraid, weren't you? I don't know what she's going to do now. I can't take care of her; I'm barely managing my own life."

The bird flapped wings in protest, jiggling dice back in its throat. Hoarse, inhuman utterances.

"Remember how, when I was little, you told me artists' souls become blackbirds when they die? Every morning you threw out bread crumbs on the patio and said, 'I'm feeding my Gauguins.' "

Behind me Gene sat up in bed and asked, "Who you talking to?"

"To my father — There he goes! — Wait!" I cried as the raven dove off like a swimmer into the breeze, skimmed the blue belly of the pool and was gone in a quick sprint over a neighbor's roof, his rattling cries echoing off the morning.

"Quick, catch him. He's getting away!"

Gene had me then, though I squirmed and protested, insisting we must stop him. "You're a lousy chicken," I shouted after the bird, my voice squawking off into tears. Gene licking up my grief with fingertips, while I clung tight to his arms — love husband of mine — fearing they, too, would become wings.

Maybe it's true, as Adam said, that Dad chose the occasion of the family reunion to die as a politician chooses the moment to declare his candidacy. A terrible, macabre idea, but when I pieced together details of his death (from Berty and Rachel and Mother when she was ready to talk) it looked that way.

I can picture Mother's arms spread wide to the Israeli Bachs, approaching gingerly along a corridor at Kennedy Airport, tan and unmistakably foreign. Grandparents giddy over grandchildren they scarcely knew, who spoke not a word of English, lavishing presents while the kids squealed delight — running to show their soft-voiced mother and father with his lip-clenched smile. Later, David offered his older brother an arm, but Adam ignored it, limping stoically up restaurant steps. Nervous spurts of conversation through dinner, David's booming laugh and the background chafing of Dad's emphysematous breath, his eyes near frantic as they fished for cordial topics. They arrived at Mom/Dad's

new house near the Sound just as fireflies announced dusk. The Israeli
kids sang out in ancient accents over the pool; answered in English by
their American cousins. Adam commented there were no houses fine as
this in Israel: "We Israeli Jews live humbly." Dad chuckled, then had a
wheezing fit over his Scotch. "Lay off!" Mother snapped. "We worked
hard for this house." She brought Dad's respirator and fretted over him,
while his lungs crinkled like paper bags.

Later, in the bedroom, Dad muttered over his personal pharmacy
(Thorazine, tetracycline, Elavil) that it had been a mistake to bring that
bastard over. Mother assured him everything would work out. Hey! take
it easy on the Miltown. "Self-righteous bum. Schnorrer!" Dad grumbled. "He can keep his lousy mitts off our house." Mother coaxed him
to bed, where his eyes kept closing through a Second World War movie
on TV. Just before falling off to sleep, Dad jabbed a finger at the stock
German officer. "That's him! General Taunt. The Nazi son of a bitch!"

Near dawn, Mother awoke and panicked at his empty side of the bed.
She ran down the hall for David — in her distress, completely forgetting Adam in the room next door, with his medic's training. Together
they searched the house, before discovering Dad wedged like a huge insect between bed and wall, his white ass sticking in the air. The Fleet
enema he had been trying to administer himself when the emphysema
attack came — I imagine him kneeling on the bed, gasping, too groggy
to save himself — still death-gripped in his fingers. Awakened by their
squeals and shrieks, Adam arrived in jockey shorts to find them
cramped into that space between bed and wall, trying to ram the respirator mouthpiece between Dad's stiff purple lips.

Shoving the bed aside, Adam pronounced his father dead. Mother's
eyes bulged; she pounded his chest with her fists and begged him to
take it back. While the children, filled with white horror, gathered in
the doorway, staring at their naked grandpa who wouldn't move, kneeling in frozen prayer, his unblinking eyes staring at the rug. Death could
come and harden a man upright like Lot's wife. A pillar of salt.

I waited for Gene to arrive from Vermont, resting my head on his
shoulder as he drove out the Long Island Expressway, silent, respecting
my grief. We parked amid other quickly gathered cars. Adam running
across the lawn, lifting me in strong arms, moaning as I moaned. "Your
back!" I cried, remembering the wound. "I have bigger pains," he said
in a thick accent. Jaunty open shirt collar spilling a shock of sun-

bleached hair that contrasted touchingly to his dark face — willful, beyond reach of pain, deep-furrowed. He shook hands with Gene, taking the suitcase from him and limping off over the lawn.

Back through sprawling, many-windowed rooms, hushed now, friends and relatives — some no more than strangers — kissed, consoled, hung liverish wet faces before me. I pushed past to Mother, walled into the innermost tabernacle, her cornflower blue eyes askew, clouded over in bewilderment. "Nattie dear," she cried, half rising, but sinking at once, as if grief had taken the gristle from her knees. I sat on the couch holding her while she sobbed, aware of many presences, like vague crows gathered around us in a dismal chorus. Her tears wet my shoulder, went right through to my heart. "I miss him," she squealed, "I miss my Jacob. . . ."

The morning we were to give Dad's ashes to the sea came in warm and hazy. Low gliding gulls passed over in long-voiced processions, wings wet-glistening from the Sound, mowers whirred like a low flight of suburban bombers, air green with grass-scent. We limousined out to the pier where a fishing trawler waited. The entire lost tribe of my family come together at last; Dad in his tiny ornate coffin riding on Mother's lap. Me cramped between Gene and the blimp stomach Aunt Berty had developed since moving to Florida. He kept a token arm around me — tribute to a family that didn't know how to interpret our relationship, a mini-funeral on its own. "How is it with you kids?" Berty had asked that first night in a voice that had never left Coney Island Avenue. "You still carrying on the long distance love affair? You know, that's some great invitation for some other fella to get into her pants." Gene had merely smiled and touched her arm. Later, he tried making love to me on the guest cottage mattress. A sweaty, miserable failure. Something that had never happened before. Grief, I consoled him. Though we both knew it wasn't grief.

Berty rested her chin on my shoulder, bringing raw red cheeks very close, reeking of onions. "G'wan and cry, honey. It's okay." In that frogcroak belly her voice had found a natural habitat missing all those years of slim, high-breasted New York Berty. Across the backseat, Mother's puffy eyes above flushed hard apple cheeks seemed to scream "Help! Help me —" at fleeting lawns houses maples quick clumps of oak, which might have been suburban New Jersey where the Bachs bought their first house in those happy years when business kicked up its heels and flung them into prosperity. Mothers visored hands over

eyes from porches, children anchored bikes to watch us pass, a man
emerged from an outbuilding (I imagined it a studio), solemnly watching this funeral caravan move towards the Sound. Me stung with nostalgia. A ten-year-old girl again, standing mesmerized in the doorway of
Dad's studio, where an alchemy of smells and the sound of the brush
ringing in cleaning jar filled me with a secret, wordless excitement. Remembering how, when I was sick and he came to arrange covers around
my chin, a faint turpentinic incense clung to his manicured fingers.
Now, if he could have seen her crumpled mouth, doorcracks of
Mother's eyes, lost in but unseeing the landscape . . . Jerseyscape, he
might have painted her like that — epilogue to an oeuvre peopled by
her image: Mother surrounded by Hebrew village, Rousseauian jungle,
Tooker New York.

I leaned forward and touched her knee. She tried a smile, which
tightened her face to tears, falling in little pit-a-pats on Dad in his
wooden box. "I love you, Mom," I mouthed, moving my lips. She
swallowed, craning her neck forward in that eager expression, mouth
ajar, eyes frightened, white fingers seizing Dad's tiny casket to her stomach as if she would not be able to let him go.

But did. All of us. Crowded onto the chartered boat. Adam read a
Hebrew prayer, voice wavering through conflicting emotions, while we
hung our heads as if ashamed at not understanding the words. Then everyone sang the theme from *Midnight Cowboy* that Dad had loved,
dipping our fingers into the box Mother offered around like chocolates,
scooping up sparkling white ash and bone chip, while waves slapped the
boat in a kind of dirge and tatters of fog purled around us. Mother letting him go with fervent little girl tosses, crying "Good-bye Jacob . . ."
A breeze lifting him back into our faces. Me, crazed with grief, rubbing
those death jewels over my face, singing in a frenzy. David and Berty,
too, daubing cheeks and foreheads with his scintillant remains. While
crew members watched spellbound from the flying bridge.

Gene sits at a table in back, where we had passed many hours over
cappuccino before he left New York, stares off with a stern, troubled
expression, woodcutter's frown he'd worn the day we met in a California café. We exchange an awkward kiss, like the kisses of beginners.
Odd, the embarrassment with which love begins — and ends. I recall
how he'd gripped my hand on the fishing boat, lamented in a voice that
was itself a midnight cowboy, beard ash-smudged. His eyes hardly left

me then, full, it seemed, of other bad news. The night before we left, Berty had raised her wine glass to toast the "backtogetherniks," David cheered, Mother smiled, I thought Gene's face would crack open like a dead animal at the side of the road.

"Your call surprised me; I thought you had gone home," I say, banning any need or possession from my voice.

After a moment he glances up, a lean smile. "We were together out on the Island. I thought you'd want time alone."

"My father just died," I snap, nearly losing it. "Oh fuck! What am I doing?"

"It's all right."

"It's not all right. I don't want your sympathy."

"It's free." He pats my hand. "Been a tough time, huh?"

"Would you get rid of that phony Buddha smile? You look like God glazed you and left you in the kiln too long."

Gene — the old California Gene — throws his head back and laughs. I look straight into him. "Where have you been staying?" He opens his hands — saved by the waitress with iced cappuccinos. His eyes flirt, first to her chest then dark Italian eyes: a cleareyed, appreciatory gaze. I stir white milk at bottom of parfait up in Rorschach suspension through darker liquid atop, hanging like the tension between us — the undertalk plotted over these months of separation. What am I jealous of exactly? His love affair with nature? The woman's panties I had discovered one visit at bottom of his wash?

"So how you doing? How's your mother?" he asks.

"She threw everyone out, said she wanted to be alone now with her memories."

"She'll make it. She's a strong woman. Like her daughter."

"Poor Adam," I mutter, ignoring what might be sarcasm — or resentment? "You don't see your father in nine years, then on the night you arrive home he dies. He was really shaken up. He told me Dad didn't die of heart failure. 'He died to spite me,' he said. I empathize with his feelings. Dad's death did seem like one final rejection."

Gene squinches lips in protest. "Everyone feels like that when a parent dies."

"Only parents who were too self-involved, like my father. Dad took it as a personal affront when Adam went to Israel: like his son had joined forces with his own father, who disinherited him because he wasn't religious. It's stupid: generations disdaining each other. Seems like we could find something bigger to live for than competition with our parents."

"Why is parenting always some kind of criminal act with you? Our parents knew what they wanted. Their only mistake was expecting we'd want it, too. Maybe they're right; we just haven't gotten there yet."

I study him — former generation gap agitator gone middle-aged, soon paunchy. We started in the sixties with a big shout; by thirty we've all lost our voices.

"No, Dad never knew what he wanted. He could've been a fine painter but didn't have the guts to devote himself to it. 'Wait till I retire,' he'd say. Look what he got."

"Not you, babe. Career first, above everything, right?"

I hold his eyes. "Artists can't afford to wait. I learned that much from my father."

I glance out at a couple wilted on a bench in the mini-park on Sixth Avenue. They argue: the woman's blonde hair gathered severely back from a round Nordic face, fingers playing the air like a harpist's; her Mediterranean opposite interrupting with staccato jabs of a hand. The heat wave frames them in a Vesuvian moment. Gene stares at me, love husband of mine. He lips a smile. All at once, I desire him, flirt with his knees under the table, while he peers into his glass, clutched in bone white knuckles. "Ooops! —" glancing at his watch "— I have to go —"

"That drives me nuts. Maxine used to do that all the time. You haven't even told me what you came here to tell me."

"How is Maxine?" His bonhomie isn't convincing.

"I haven't seen her, Gene."

An awkward silence. He nods. "Probably better that way."

"Let's drop it, all right?"

"I only meant . . . That kind of friendship doesn't survive well into adulthood. That's all I'm saying."

"I know what you're saying, Gene."

He dismembers a napkin. "I can't relate to friendships like that."

"Maybe you've missed something."

His eyes jump up, alarmed. I watch as his fingers shred the napkin in quiet, pointless violence along invisible veins.

"You still hold that against me, don't you?"

"I know how much you loved her," he murmurs.

"I love you more, honey."

"You aren't obsessed with me."

Taking his hand. "I've been obsessed with you all summer."

Gene eyes me askance. "I could live with the rest, but I'll never forgive the woman for planting the crap in your head about children being taboo for the liberated woman — whatever it is. What kind of woman is she? What kind of a Jew?"

"You have no right to decide what kind of Jew anyone is. Woman either for that matter. No kids was my idea. *Mine!* Natalie Bach Hjalstead . . . minus the Hjalstead."

He frowns. "You have a case of lemmingitis, you know that. You're one of those lunatics who wants to shove the human race overboard. Starting with me."

"*You* left *me*, Gene. Remember?"

His eyes sidle to a woman in a Perrier T-shirt sitting on the terrace — straight blonde hair and pointy tits, laughing as if she has the world on a leash. "I just couldn't live with the chauvinist asshole role, my woman enslaved by my needs — all that crap."

"I never felt enslaved. If anything has enslaved women it's shitty diapers and sore nipples. Though I began to doubt I could live with a man as fanatical about children as a born-again Christian."

"It's fanatical to want to be a father?"

I laugh, feeling sudden tenderness. "I wish you'd tell me what it is you've come to say, honey. I really can take it, you know. This seems to be my summer for rejections."

"Calling your father's death a rejection is bullshit."

"I'm talking about us."

"Okay, who did the rejecting? Seems like a relationship that can't agree on geography. The obsession now is Noo Yawk and Big League success —"

"Or Vermont and Little League misery." I touch his sleeve, appeasingly. "I don't want fame, honey. Don't want feminism. Or to be gay. Don't want to be some man's incubator either. I just want to be me. To live, be a decent person. A painter. That means figuring things out for myself. No shortcuts, no basic recipes. That may be scary, isolating, but in the end I don't think there's any choice. And I had hoped to be with you. It's a pretty sick irony that two people who love each other can't be together — for whatever silly reasons." I sigh long, wishing to expel all my despair in one breath. "But maybe you've joined our generation of love haters."

Gene gazes off at the Perrier blonde — talking as if through glibness she may discover substance where there isn't any. A type I suspect he finds attractive. "Children, careers, are they so silly?" he grumbles. I wonder if I know this man, if I ever did. It's nearly a relief to be free of him . . . a desolation.

"Maybe it's better this way," he says. "Otherwise, some day, you'd face what your mother is facing now."

"You've been spending too much time in singles bars. Please tell me what's on your mind, Gene. I'm imagining the worst stuff." Blowing into a wind of evasion, his troubled eyes simply watching. How I wish I could hate him now. Feel instead biting nostalgia for better days: the Inn on the Redwood Coast where he charmed me with his poetry and plaid shirt style. California his natural habitat, too bad I ever coaxed him away.

"You couldn't expect me to stay celibate up there," he mumbles. "I'm not your monkish type."

"Just tell me. Don't pussyfoot around."

A brassy voice shatters conversation in the room as a woman opens the door, looking back over a shoulder at her companion as if not fully decided upon entering. Hair grips her skull in a flapper's cap. "Brrrr! it's a refrigerator in here. They got the air conditioning too high," she yowls as her companion steps past her into the café.

I nearly cry out.

Freeze as those dark eyes inquire about the room — goggle at her, battling panic, drop my face towards the table as her gaze slides by without recognition. I hear brassy voice saying, "Coffeehouses bore me, actually. I'd love a drink." Sweat itches at my collar, pastes shirt to my back, blood burns my cheeks. I peek — snorkeling like a Lorenz goose — seeing her make that chin wrinkled so-let's-do-it expression I know so well. They turn to leave; I half rise, her name stumbling on my lips, while Gene's eyes dart back and forth. And the two women are gone, just like that — as if they hadn't come in at all.

Me slumping back into the chair, convinced it wasn't an illusion only because Gene persists: "Who was it? What's happening?" His lips as tight as on the night Berty proposed her toast. I wonder, sitting with a hand over my face, why I don't tell him . . . or he admit he knows.

"You can still catch her," he insists. "Really, run! She probably isn't to the corner yet. Go ahead." He prods my elbow.

I shake my head like a kid, trying to gain control of a runaway heartbeat, shivers that come all in a rush. "I don't want to catch her. Just want to catch my breath."

"Go on. You could do it!" His brow furled. He seems almost desperate, grabbing at a straw, an improbable comfort.

"No —" I say, astonished at his insistence and my own resistance, as if we've got it backwards, "— that's your fantasy." Collecting myself; though inside I am sick, doubts and anxieties feeding upon each other like sharks. "There's no going back. Some bridges burn by themselves."

CHAPTER NINETEEN

EPILOGUE

"MAXINE?" HE ASKS.

"She saw me, I'm sure. She pretended not to."

"That makes two of you."

I hyperventilate a minute, watching Gene push napkin shreds about like chess pieces. Hadn't she herself told me that every road can't be taken? At the coffee bar, steam from the espresso machine gurgles into a cup. Gene mutters, "She's a beautiful woman; wouldn't be hard at all going to bed with her."

I pin down those evasive eyes, wait for my stomach to stop churning. "I've made my choices, Gene. And apparently you've made yours."

There is silence between us, built anomalously of clinking glasses and spoonfuls of conversation. Gene says he hopes I never turn my head away and pretend I don't know him. I feel suddenly almost serene. Self certain.

"You're a lot like Dad, you know: a coward when it comes to hard things that have to be said."

He glances about, nuzzling shoulders in what is becoming a tic, giving me pointless half-smiles.

"Don't you realize I already know? I just need to hear you say it." Feeling compassion — and impatience — for the part of him that doesn't like to hurt, I touch his hand. "I can handle it."

His eyes take quick bites of me, giving the impression he may bolt for the door. "Sorry about the timing —" he splutters, then explodes, "— Look, I can't stand this bachelor crap. I sit listening to frost creep around the windows, catch a whiff of woodsmoke from the place down the road and feel miserable lonely. I've missed you something awful up there, but I can't convince you to stay. Nat, there's someone I met up there. We have a lot in common. I mean, it's real. We care for each other."

"You don't have to convince me."

He leans intently forward, eyes full of anguish. "I didn't think this could happen, babe. Honest I didn't. Ginny wants kids. She has a five-year-old daughter of her own. She wants to go back to California with me."

"Ginny —?" Mimicking Mother's lipcurl.

"She's a fantastic person. You'd like her."

"I don't like her already. I really don't want to know about your Ginny — even if she has three heads and four dozen kids. You still love me. You'll always love me. It's pathetic that love can't be enough between two people."

A long moment of suffering between us. Gene's calloused hand chafing his forehead, bovine eyes chewing the cud of his guilt. On the patio, the woman in the Perrier T-shirt rises to leave. *Ginny!* I grind the name back in my molars. "So now what?" I ask. "We hire separate lawyers and file for divorce?"

Gene winces. "Now wait a minute —"

"Are you planning to have a wife on each coast? I'm not much into the bigamy shtick, love. Don't worry, I don't want anything from you. I just like clean endings."

He nods unhappily.

While I am trying, frantic, to convince myself it's better than the current limbo: that I prefer living alone, and he'll be happier with his *Ginny*. Some putti — Kitty at the kitchen table — coaxing me to go for his heart: *You can win him back, girl.*

"I'm glad you've found someone who can give you what you want, Gene. I'm happy for you, really," I manage. "I just don't understand why all at once I feel like bawling."

Gene's hand comes across table for mine, eyes gone damp.

"What a shitty time. Everyone getting abandoned. Mother and me losing our men —" letting him take my hand "— I offered to stay with her for a while out there. But she said she has to learn to live on her own."

Gene, fixing me with that mournful hound expression, mumbles platitudes about time healing wounds.

"I'm too down to give her much anyway." I sip at breath, tears taking me in huge yolky gulps, breaking through the background tinkle of spoons and laughter.

When, at last, the table is full of damp napkinwads and I have reined myself in — sensing the delicate acknowledgement of waitresses and others, pressing close, nourishing — Gene asks what I will do, his neck fever red. "What I've been doing, I guess. I could chase you out to California and win you back from this Ginny. But it wouldn't be fair. You want kids, I can't do that for you." He nods, attempting a smile. Neither of us worth a shit at good-byes. "I won't ever forget you," he manages. I caress the stubble on the back of his hand. So familiar, so foreign.

New York has a way of bringing you in — reaching out a scabbed, filthy hand like an old woman on a street corner, begging help to cross the street, muttering obscenities in your ear. Sits on a bench in Central Park like John Lennon, waiting to discuss life with a stranger . . . or sits with the mumbling lips of subway *yeshiva bukhers*, throwing hot glances at Muslim four-percenters come aboard to give their save-the-babies spiel. Laughs explosively from bodegas, exchanges good-natured curses across the street, skips rope on numberless Brooklyn blocks and makes graffiti of every passing face, ignores the tears making red claw-marks down your cheeks . . . in its indifference. Its overworked humanity.

New York, you are Mother's girlish bewilderment at daybreak as she opens the door of Berty's Fifth Avenue apartment (to which B. left her the keys before returning to Florida), the years sagging in the loose flesh of her face. You are the cars starting out already from commuter outposts on Long Island, the milky halflight, the Wall Street haze and first wakeful blinkings at the World Trade Center, the Forty-second Street moan, the shriek at Kew Gardens . . . and that watery gaze of the waiter in a Chino-Rican dive on Seventh Avenue, stinking of *frijoles negros* and *plátanos fritos*, the chitter of Spanish and inquisitiveness of a chunky red-haired woman, peeking from beyond her friend's shoulder as I compose upon a napkin:

> *Dreams are only dreams*
>   *nothing more*
> *All those young dreams*
>   *great expectations*
>   *entertainments*
> *Old dreams —*
>   *maimed*
>   *club-footed*
>
> *Life, the dream crusher*
> *Disappointer and wild duck*
> *A banquet of leftovers*
> *Why should we expect so much*
>   *of it?*
> *We are only beggars*
> *Millions have come with their bowls*
>   *before us*
> *They will keep coming*

I have begun, quietly, to weep. The red-haired woman frowns concern; her dark-haired friend turns, alarmed, sharing with her black eyes my grief, our commonality, the jangle of her charm bracelet. Near the door a boy shouts, his head closely shaven, eyes imbecilic, choked with menace.

"These fellas are always leaving us high and dry," Mother says, after she has kissed me and taken my coat, quickly made up her face in a smile. Says she will spend a few weeks here at Berty's apartment. "They wanted me to go down with them, but I couldn't stand all that drinking-sitting-around-the-pool stuff now. Oy! they think life is one big party down there." Her voice dipping: "I just had to get away from the house . . . all those artifacts —" crossing her arms in the crisp blue robe as if suddenly chilled "— they aren't really Jacob. They are dead but he isn't. He's spread out across the ocean; he's still alive there. Currents are spreading him all over the world. . . ." Looking at me with that insistent, open-eyed expression. "I'm going to sell the house, then I want to go out and be with him." Me blinking back sleeplessness, probing her face for meaning. "I want to get on to the future. And you should, too, honey. You know, I love Gene, but frankly he was a stone around your neck. Besides, he is a *yentzer*. You know what a *yentzer* is? It means he has an itchy pecker!" She giggles.

My footsteps slap the pavement, echoing back from buildings. On my own stage again — Raskolnikov and Lizzie Borden and Elizabeth Proctor in one kiting through every emotion this city has offered — reliving my life with the clairvoyance that supposedly precedes death . . . the secrets of lights burning in unexpected places, scuffle of movement in a doorway, long eyes of passing police . . . and I am not sure! Were they the ones shooting tear gas? And just around the corner — if we can make it — the dormitory with its broken windows and students hanging out, beckoning, their mouths gaping wounds. For at certain special moments, as when the mind slumps with grief or sleeplessness, we walk through the tenses of our lives, unimpeded by chronological one-ways or the present's tyranny, using time as a hang glider. There is the drag queen who winks regally on the corner of Canal Street as I flee from Ron Sterges and his wifetoad in the wheelchair, the black prostitute laughing at me — a woman! walking these streets alone at this hour without she have a knife in her boot and know how to use it — an open window spilling a preacher's voice. New York, you are the Tree of Knowledge, Eden sold off by real estate developers, the Angel Gabriel hustling three-card monte on street corners. God is at times seen strolling in Central Park, where they say the Tree of Life survives, but has stopped bearing fruit.

"I walked," I tell Mother. "I drank coffee in all-night cafés, thinking about the rest of my life. And about you, too. Walked through warehouse districts on the West Side, over those filthy streets, and got very depressed. New York is like a phonograph playing the same old worn-out record over and over. Nobody thinks of changing it, 'cause every time it's played again they are convinced it's a new tune.

"On Seventh Avenue every couple I saw was gay, along Eighth everyone was nuts. I sat on my old stoop on St. Marks and an old bag lady I used to see years ago came along and sat below me on the bottom step. Neither of us said a word. Finally, she looked up at me with a tooth-missing grin and said, 'You think I'm crazy too, don't you, dear?' She asked how she could be crazy when she was closely related to the Prince of Wales and Winston Churchill himself had once dated her. 'Oh, I was something to look at then,' she said. Besides, she had often been to dine with the Roosevelts at the White House. 'But these presidents here lately don't have no class. Why, I wouldn't go if they did invite me.'"

Mother laughs gaily.

"I felt sorry for her. Maybe she's not so nutty. Maybe she's just realized there aren't any easy answers. Life keeps throwing curves. Opportunities for disaster. Maybe once you've realized that it makes no sense to hold on to any pretense of success or control. You can carry your wishes around with you in old shopping bags and laugh at the preppy junior exec. types who stagger out of bars singing old college songs."

Mother regards me with concern. She clenches a fist for me at fate. "You'll make it, honey. Whatever you want to do. You are a strong woman. Golly! were you some tough kid. You used to scare the hell out of me sometimes."

"You scared me, too. I couldn't live in the same house with you, remember? You picked on me so much I had to get out."

"Yeah . . . ?" She is skeptical, convinced I am talking about someone else. "I want to bury the past now," she says. "I did bury it. I took an old handbag Jacob gave me years ago and filled it full of costume jewelry and things; then I dug a hole in the backyard and buried it."

I laugh and hug her. "You nut."

"I buried it for you too, you know. And it's a big relief to be rid of it. Now we can move on — into the future!" She pronounces the "r" like a small girl regressed to Coney Island Avenue, staring out the huge windows — the park a dark empire beaded by a few pale strands of light, West Side a great ocean liner against the pellucid dawn, buildings salmon gleaming. I hold her hand; we watch the born-again day. "In many ways Jacob was a burden," she whispers. "Life frightened him. Still, I loved him. Who can understand love?" She squeezes my hand. "I'm scared, too." Sunrise makes orange pools of her eyes, spreads in a

slow glaze down her cheeks. And I wish only to protect her, shield her
in a way even daughters are not given to do. "We're going to make it!"
she insists, suddenly defiant, shaking a white fist at fate.

I stroll somewhere near Houston Street, another warehouse district of
human poverty stacked floor by floor, Federal project of despair. I paint
it daub by daub: a few lit windows, bumps of yellow on black, a desolate
openness, concrete hulks rising from squalor to squalor, monuments to
their own hopelessness. As the sky loses its density, softens to depthless
lavender, the first orange juice spray of dawn adds a hint of gold to cold
concrete. Streetlights cast forlorn penumbras, tawdry with gutter trash.
I wouldn't chance walking here a few hours earlier, but even street
punks must sleep . . . in these purgatory hours. Out on the river a tug
gives a plaintive horn blast. I have the city to myself, sniffing about its
nastiest corners. A cop car stops. They ask if I need a lift somewheres,
trading glances back and forth. I'm going too far, I answer. I could get
you there, baby, says the young wop one. Naw, says his partner, she's a
crazy. Get outta the neighborhood, young lady. We don't want another
statistic.

Garbage seized mid-flight at the foot of park benches, a flotsam in
puddles. A window creaks like our cabin door in California: a woman in
a red bathrobe and hair to match gazes out from the junkyard of dreams
. . . seeing, perhaps, Puerto Rico . . . perhaps nothing. Like Gene on
West Coast mornings, sun splashing a huge bucketful of promise; he
notes the progress of tomatoes, lettuce stippled with dew. . . . Today I
will hunt mushrooms: calfskin of *Boletus edulis* beneath scrappy pines;
down canyonsides in the twilight hush of redwood forest will discover
chanterelles, like eggs hidden in the primordial litter, like the small surprises of childhood. Later, will fill drying racks above the woodstove,
catch a splinter of reflection in that mirror above the sink — scarf like
the babushkas old Ukrainian women in the East Village wear, a sadness
that was never in my cityeyes . . . not then! Dream-seizer California.

Yet New York offers no solutions. Scumheap. I make a promise to a
bum asleep in a doorway that I will move on. He responds in ragged
snores. *Adiós Nueva York, adieu,* been nice knowing you. An ironic
chuckle, for I have lost my simple faith in movement. That earlier
creed: when things didn't work out, when life bogged down, I moved on
like Sherman to the sea, burning every bridge behind me. Finding my
same old self at the next address. But hope works like that; it must sus-
pend disbelief.

To my right, a vacant lot, rubble of bricks and broken bottles. At the curb, a station wagon with a young woman slumped behind the wheel. In the meager light, her eyes are small white fish, flashing quickly; I sense them following as I continue down the derelict street. Abruptly, I turn and go back to the car. She appears frightened, waving me away while I make hand signals, ask with exaggerated lip movements if she needs help. She lowers the window a crack, demanding "What do you want?" in a hoarse voice. "Are you all right?" my own gritty with sleeplessness.

"Do I look all right?" Ratsnest hair and harrowed cheeks, a red welt on her neck, nylons slumped down one leg.

I speak softly. "I just wanted to see if you needed help."

"Yeah . . . I need help." Staring ahead at a building chopped in two, spilling rooms, her features aligning in a puffy, ironic smile. Then relaxing. "I'm sorry. It's very kind of you to ask. There's nothing you can do."

"If you need a place to stay, I'm moving out of my apartment. You can stay there until I leave . . . maybe longer."

"You're really very kind." She gazes up the desolate street, sighing. "People don't bother much with kindness anymore. Thanks, whoever you are. I'll have to work it out. . . ." She smiles.

I place my palm against the glass; hers rises to meet it a moment inside. Then I go on, flag down the first of a fleet of taxis announcing another day is on . . . New York.

Uptown. Mother announces her plans for a long cruise — Japan and Australia. "Your father always wanted to go to the far Pacific," she says. "Now I'll go for both of us. He's out there and I want to be close to him. I have my own cabin, like Jacob and I always did. Why not? I'm going to treat myself. And I'd like you to come with me, honey. I think you would enjoy yourself. It would do you lotsa good to get your mind off y'r troubles."

I tell her it's tempting but I can't. I have a journey of my own to take. Off to conquer the world.

"Very frankly," she says, "I'd like you to come for me. I could use some companionship. I'm excited, but a little scared too. I've never been on such a big trip . . . without Jacob. Will you do it, honey?"

"I have to say no, Mother. I really can't fill that gap for you. It won't work. I'm your daughter; I can't be your companion."

For a moment there is the old bitterness and betrayal in those deep-water eyes — for the daughter who has once again let her down. Then she smiles, just barely, and whispers "Y'r right."

Raw excitement as we pull out *Britannica* maps, spinning the globe, plotting routes. Mother announces that she may take along a sketchpad. And I stand at the window telling her, the awakening city at my feet, "I know now what it means to be an artist. You have to despair of husbands, friends . . . even mothers! and find your own road. It's lonely, since you are the first and the last ever to travel that particular route. But artists have no choice. Discovery is our calling. Artists are nomadic, like the Jews. Diaspora isn't any temporary dislocation; it's our understanding of things. We appreciate that life is a venture into uncertainty."

"None of us has a choice," Mother says, pouring more coffee. Either side of her mouth pinched severely in small crow's feet — but there is a kind of movement in her expression, flapping of the spirit's wings across that seaworthy smile, moving beyond the practical side of her which asks, "How do you think you will support yourself, honey? Will you teach?"

I do not answer. My thoughts focusing already far ahead . . . past a sign announcing "Albuquerque 33 miles" as the highway makes a slow swagger up into mountains, or "Mexico City," or "Paris 80 kilometres" or "fame" or "failure" (with dignity as Maxine would say) or LIFE DEAD AHEAD.